hand-me-down

hand-me-down

LEE NICHOLS

**RED
DRESS
INK**
™

First edition June 2005

HAND-ME-DOWN

A Red Dress Ink novel

ISBN 0-373-89523-2

www.RedDressInk.com

Printed in U.S.A.

Thanks are long overdue to Nancy Coffey, Farrin Jacobs, Lynn Nichols, Jessica Alvarez, Helen Ross, Paula Ross and Constance Wall.

CHAPTER

01

The second time Ian Dunne came into my life, I was trapped under a pile of bodies, behind a sheet of plate glass.

I'd just graduated from UC Santa Barbara, my hometown school. I'd finished at the top of the middle of my class—which is the story of my life—and a week later had grabbed the bottom rung of corporate America.

I was folding men's charcoal woolens at Banana Republic when my manager materialized at my shoulder.

"You've almost got it!" Jenny chirped. "First the sleeve, then over, over…" Showing me, yet again, how to fold a sweater.

I gritted my teeth, and gestured to my pile. "Mine are fine."

"Good enough for the Gap." Jenny smiled encouragingly. "Maybe."

"Maybe I should do the windows instead."

"You can't do the windows."

"But I want to do the windows."

"Sorry," she said, and scurried into the back office.

My problem was that I was assertive enough to annoy, but not enough to succeed. That's always been my problem: I'm the uneasy medium. Pretty enough, but not beautiful. Smart enough, but not brilliant. If I were a college, I'd be a safety school. If I were a skirt, I'd be basic black.

Wren finished ringing up a sale and drifted over. We'd started work the same day, and she'd been promoted to the register by the end of the morning. I liked her despite her obnoxious competence and her glossy dark hair and clear olive skin. She smiled and neatened my sweater stack. "Jenny's teaching you to fold again?"

"Folding's not really my strength." I glanced toward the front of the store. "What I should be doing is—"

"Oh, Anne, not again. She'll never let you do the windows."

"But I'm pretty sure that window design is my thing." I stacked the last sweater. "I'm sort of arty."

"You were a business major."

"Well, arty-businessy. Anyway, I have the soul of an artist." Since graduating, I'd been doing some thinking. It was clear I wasn't going to make it on looks alone. Not like my oldest sister Charlotte. Nor was I anyone's idea of a girl-genius, like my other sister, Emily. So I figured I'd be the next Paloma Picasso. Artist/designer. Of course, my dad was no Pablo, but still.

"How many art classes did you take?" Wren asked.

"Does pottery count?"

"Only if you got an A."

"Oh. Anyway—" I lowered my voice. "Aren't you a little embarrassed to be working here?" Wren had just graduated from Pomona.

She shook her head. "I love clothes."

"Yeah," I said, unconvinced. I liked clothes, too. New ones, at least. "Still. Shouldn't we aspire to greater things than our fifty-percent discount?"

"Like a sixty-percent discount?"

"Exactly! Or, for instance…"

"The windows," Wren finished.

I smiled. And ten minutes later, when Jenny was on the phone to the head office and Wren—in a fit of self-preservation—disappeared for an early lunch, I crammed myself into the front window with six mannequins.

An assortment of mall-walkers noticed me, and paused and pointed. Enjoying the celebrity, I gave them a queen's wave and got to work. How hard could it be? Easy as stacking wood, I told myself—ignoring for the moment that I'd never actually stacked wood.

The official theme for the Fall windows was the stunningly original "Back to School." I decided to stay on topic and create the Banana Republic Cheerleading Squad. Given Jenny's level of pep, she'd have to approve.

I wrestled the first mannequin, dressed in denims and suede jacket, into a crouching position. It took some doing, as she was not at all limber, but I finally grappled her onto all fours. The second mannequin was easier, but the third required that I kneel on her stomach and roughly yank her legs. The fourth and fifth, wearing light gray sweaters and khaki cords, were male. I twisted them onto their hands and knees and turned to the sixth mannequin, a recalcitrant squad leader in a plaid mini. By the time I finished tangling with her, I was sweaty and exhausted…and had attracted a crowd.

I loftily ignored them, and arranged the first three mannequins. Easy enough. Side by side, on hands and knees— the two males on the outside, a female in the middle. I manhandled the next one on top, balanced another next to her, and stepped back to admire my handiwork. Looking good. Jenny was going to be amazed.

They say a pyramid is a totally stable structure, but I challenge anyone to prove it with cheerleading mannequins. I lifted Plaid Mini, the recalcitrant squad leader, over my head and stepped forward. Neatly avoiding the sprawled limbs of the other mannequins, I rose onto tiptoes and gently flipped Plaid Mini onto the very apex of the pyramid.

She teetered. She tottered. The crowd hushed…and the sixth mannequin settled perfectly into place!

I beamed.

The crowd applauded.

And as I curtsied, there was a knock at the window. My sister Emily. I almost didn't recognize her. She's sort of severe and intellectual-looking, not exactly a mall rat. Standing next to her, smiling, was a tall, blond, handsome man.

"I did it!" I told Emily triumphantly through the glass.

"What?" she yelled.

"I did it!" I gestured behind me at the pyramid. "My first window!"

"What?" she shouted again.

She turned to the blond man, and I saw him say: *she says she does windows.*

Emily frowned as she answered. I couldn't hear the words, but from her expression I could tell they were pretty ripe. She'd just had her first book published—an indecipherable academic feminist treatise which for some reason had been getting press in *Cosmo* and *Newsweek*—and she wanted to be this classy, cool philosopher-queen. Not someone whose sister wrestles cheerleading mannequins in mall windows.

"Back to school!" I mouthed, as if that were an explanation.

This didn't soothe Emily. The man turned to calm her, and I suddenly recognized him.

I said, "Ian?"

He saw the word. He nodded.

I startled backward, almost tripping on a splayed plastic hand—I grabbed an errant elbow to steady myself. The elbow joggled the barest inch and the mannequin under-neath twisted slightly. I lunged to steady him—and slipped. My knee whacked Suede Jacket square in the face and she squirted out of the pyramid like a wet watermelon seed. Then Plaid Mini leapt at me from above and grabbed me in an obscene scissors-hold between her thighs. I struggled for air and popped one of her legs off—I twirled and spun as the pyramid collapsed around me in a hail of cheerlead-ers, and finally ended on my back, with Khaki Cords splayed on top.

The applause was louder, this time.

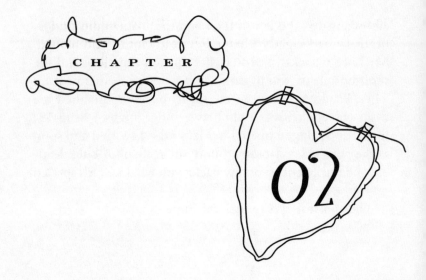

CHAPTER

02

Emily slammed her bag onto the table at the Coffee Bean and scowled. After the collapse of the Great Pyramid, Jenny decided it was my turn to take lunch—preferably in another state. I didn't argue, even though Emily was lurking outside the store with smoke issuing from her nostrils. Emily is the middle sister, so she's supposed to be mild and quiet and timid, but nobody's ever been foolish enough to mention that to her.

"Well?" she said.

"I'll have a mocha blended?"

Her eyebrows became an angry V. "You know exactly what I mean, Anne."

"Oh, *that,*" I said with an airy laugh, gesturing back toward Banana. "That was just, y'know. So, what're you doing at the mall?"

"Great show, Anne," Ian said, returning with our coffees to the table. "I wanted to put out a little cup for you."

I smiled sweetly at Emily. "And where'd you find *him?*"

Ian Dunne was six feet tall with blond hair and blue eyes.

He was wearing green shorts, a navy T-shirt and flip-flops, and had a Santa Barbara tan—the deep bronze of the pre-skin-cancer era. He looked even more surfer-delicious than when he'd dated Charlotte in high school.

"Anne," Emily said, as calm as the eye of a storm. "You graduated with a low B average with a degree you don't value. You're living with Dad. You're barely employed at Banana Republic. You don't have the slightest inkling of a career, a future, a—"

"I'm going back to school," I said, cringing inwardly at the phrase.

She brightened. "To get your master's?"

"Art school," I said. "So Ian, how've you been?"

"Art?" Emily said. "You can't draw a straight line with a ruler."

"I most certainly can!"

"And you know nothing about art theory. If I asked you to choose between appropriationist and cultural predialectic in the structural paradigm of visual art, which would you defend?"

"Um, the first one?"

She sighed. "Who's your favorite artist?"

"Paloma Picasso?" I said, in a small voice.

"She makes perfume."

"And handbags!"

"Anne, you need to focus on your future—"

"I'm fine," Ian cut in. "How have you been?"

I winced, waiting for the explosion. Emily would reduce him to paste with a handful of words. But, oddly, no explosion came. Maybe micro-celebrity was calming her.

"I've been good," I said, after a short silence. "So where did you two—?"

"We ran into each other in the mall," Emily said. "Watching you make a spectacle of yourself."

"A spectacle? It's not like I was strutting around in a bikini."

"How *is* Charlotte?" Ian casually asked, and those three words told me everything: he was still in love with her. After all the years—her marriage, her celebrity, and her pregnancy—he was still in love.

It explained why he'd finagled an invitation to coffee with us. Emily usually wasn't so welcoming, but she'd responded eagerly to his hints. Of course, her book was out, the early reviews were disgustingly positive, and the publication party was tonight. So she had an ulterior motive: to brag.

"Charlotte's fine," she said shortly, and turned to me. "I told Ian about my book."

"Porn Is Film," Ian said, as if reciting the title of her book proved something.

"What does that even mean?" I said. "Is *Penthouse* film? It's porn. If porn is film, does that mean film is porn? Is *The Bicycle Thief* porn?"

Usually I can get Emily worked up and defensive about the title. It's like bullfighting, you have to know exactly how far you can go before you get gored. As long as she sputters angrily, I'm okay. The minute she says something like "the postmodern praxis of potentiality," I run.

This time, she simply asked, "You're coming to the reading tonight?"

"I never miss a party."

"Party?" Ian said.

"It's a reading," Emily said.

"With booze," I said. "So it's a party."

"Are you bringing a date?" Emily asked.

"Of course." I hadn't planned to, but I sure as hell was going to now. There was plenty of time to dig up a date. It was positively…six hours away.

"Not Matthew," Emily said.

I rolled my eyes. "He wasn't that bad." He was also out of town, or he'd be the first I called.

"He was worse. Good thing he didn't even make par."

"What's par?" Ian asked.

"Anne never dates anyone more than three months."

"That is so not true!" I said. "What about Kyle?"

"Four months," she said. "And that was high school."

"It still counts," I said—and noticed Ian's expression.

There was something wistful in his deep blue eyes. He was thinking about Charlotte. About tragic, doomed high school love. He knew Charlotte would be at the party, and he longed to see her. He knew she was famous, he knew she was married. He only wanted to watch her from across the room, his heart silently breaking. And, well, I know I shouldn't have done it. You'd think I'd have learned my lesson last time: *never invite Ian anywhere.* But I'd learned nothing.

So I looked at his injured-puppy eyes and said, "Would you like to come?"

"To the reading?"

"If you're free tonight?"

He smiled. "I'd love to."

Emily fiddled with her water glass, and I thought, *uh-oh.* Not good, inviting Charlotte's ex-boyfriend to Emily's party. "That'd be...nice," she said.

"If you're sure," he asked her politely.

"Of course," she said.

"I wouldn't want to intrude," he said.

"Come or don't come," she snapped. "I could care less."

"Then I'll definitely come."

"And I'll definitely go," I said. "Lunch break's over. If I give Jenny a reason to fire me—"

"*Another* reason," Emily said, as I left.

Okay, it was a mistake to invite Ian. But it wasn't a disaster. It had been ten years since *it* happened, and he clearly didn't remember.

Which was almost as galling as if he had.

Wren was fixing the window when I returned.

"Very avant-garde," she said.

"I don't want to talk about it."

She laughed and turned back to the mannequins, sorting them out with efficient, professional motions.

"It was a popular triumph," I told her. "The people loved me."

"But *not* critically acclaimed. Jenny isn't happy." She straightened the plaid mini. "Who's the guy?"

"That's Khaki Cords." I kicked the mannequin. "I hate him."

"The guy at the Coffee Bean."

"Oh, him. Ian. My sister's ex."

"They're back together?"

"Not Emily's—Charlotte's."

"Ah. That explains it."

"What?"

"He's gorgeous."

I wrinkled my nose. "I guess, if you like the blond, blue-eyed…gorgeous type. Oh! Speaking of which—I need a date for tonight."

"Your sister's book thing?"

"Yeah. I was gonna go stag, but…"

"Uh-huh." She nodded knowingly. "Ian's going?"

"Well, I sort of accidentally invited him."

"You have a crush on Charlotte's ex."

"I don't! Not a crush. But I, um…"

"You what?"

"Let's just say I did something really stupid, once. I

wouldn't want him to think it ruined me for guys ever since."

"What'd you do?"

"I invited him to a party," I said.

"I mean last time," she said.

"That's what I did last time, too. I don't know what it is. I see him, I invite him somewhere inappropriate. It's Pavlovian."

"Because he makes you salivate."

I ignored her. "Anyway, I need a presentable date, fast."

"My brother would do it for ten bucks."

Her brother is thirteen. "I'm looking for clean-shaven, not pre-shaven."

Jenny suddenly loomed. She edged between me and the nearest mannequin, as if afraid I'd go for its throat. "You're back," she said.

"With bells on!" I told her, smiling gaily as if nothing had happened.

"We have to talk," Jenny told me.

"Anne needs a date tonight," Wren said. "She's got nobody to take to her sister's party."

For a moment, I was pissed at Wren. How could she tell Jenny I needed a date? Then I realized it was a perfect distraction. Jenny was a little starstruck by Charlotte, so there was no need to mention the party was for my other sister.

"Your sister?" Jenny considered. "Well, there's always Billy."

Billy was one of the Banana boys. Wren and I both had crushes on him—he was a young Brad Pitt—but Wren was the absolute worst flirt you've ever seen. As a rule, she was competent and pretty and perfect—but when flirting she flipped a switch, and a stuttering Elmer Fudd took over her body.

"He'll go out with anyone," Jenny said.

"Even Anne?" Wren asked.

"Oh, thanks," I said.

Jenny shrugged. "Why not? I'll get him to teach you how to use the register. Then you can ask."

"The register!" I said. That was even better than Billy.

"There's got to be something you can do around here."

It turns out she was right. I was a cash register genius. Born to ring. After an hour behind the counter, hitting Sale, No Sale, Taxable and Return while trying to be fascinating, I turned to Billy with a smile. "You have plans tonight?"

He grinned and shrugged. His expression said, make me an offer.

"There's a party," I said. "My sister wrote a book. It's sort of a publication thing."

"A book party?" He sounded dubious.

"There'll be booze. Well, wine…"

"Wine?" More dubious.

"Um, yeah." Time to swallow my pride. "And it's at Charlotte Olsen's house in Montecito."

He straightened slightly, in awe. "You know Charlotte Olsen?"

"A little."

"The swimsuit model?"

"Is there another Charlotte Olsen?"

"Not in my life," he said.

Mine either.

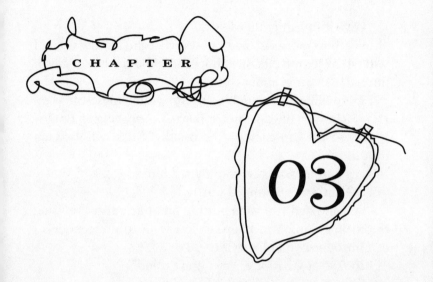

CHAPTER

03

Early evening. I sprawled across the bed and painted my fingernails with Charlotte's blue polish.

"Not that," Charlotte said, from her palatial walk-in closet. "It's so last season."

"It's Hard Candy. I like it."

She shook her head, but didn't push me. Charlotte never did. "Well, on you, it still works." She rummaged in the closet and held up a satin blouse and velvet jeans in a gorgeous powder blue. "Here, these'll match."

"I don't think so, Charlotte…."

"They're Gucci."

My jaw tightened. I loved Gucci. She knew I loved Gucci. But I had my principles. Or at least I had my single solitary principle: not to wear my sisters' hand-me-downs. "Why don't you wear it?" I said, with a straight face.

She was eight months pregnant, and a honker. She was wearing a black tank top, a long knit skirt and a belly like an overinflated beach ball. "Because it's not a size seventy-two."

"Give it to Emily then."

Charlotte snorted. "God knows what she'll show up in. I wish she'd let me take her shopping." She held up a cream linen dress. "How about this?"

I ignored her. I was sticking to the white blouse and jeans I'd bought with my discount at Banana. "Speaking of Emily." I screwed the cap back on the polish. "Guess who we ran into today?"

"Ian Dunne. She said you invited him."

"Well, it sort of popped out...."

"She also said you were putting on quite a show dressing the mannequins. You know, if you want to dress models I can introduce you to a stylist."

I looked at Charlotte. "You don't mind?"

"Of course not, Annie." Her natural pregnancy-glow doubled in wattage. "And I know just the woman. She dressed me for my calendar."

"I meant, you don't mind that I invited Ian. And it's exaggerating to say you were *dressed* for your calendar." Charlotte was America's favorite swimsuit model. She'd won the cover of *Sports Illustrated*'s swimsuit issue two years in a row. Her calendar sold a zillion copies and I've seen her naked looking more modest than she did in some of those swimsuits.

"Why would I mind about Ian?" Charlotte smiled. "Do you remember how you asked him—"

"I remember."

"It'll be fun to see him. I can't wait for David to meet him."

David was Charlotte's husband. She'd always dated gorgeous men, because they were the only ones with the egos to think they deserved Charlotte Olsen. Then she'd met David. A shy, unassuming anesthesiologist who looked like a young Billy Crystal. It was love at first sight.

"When's he get home?" I asked.

Charlotte glanced at the clock. "An hour. And *InStyle* should be here soon."

"I still don't know how you convinced them to shoot Emily's book party."

"It wasn't that hard—*The Nation* did name Emily one of the ten most dangerous young minds in America."

"Yeah, number seven," I said dismissively, because having *two* famous older sisters was more than I could bear. I'd thought Emily was safely obscure, but as a new Ph.D. at twenty-seven, she'd rocked the feminist world with her dissonant thoughts on pornography. Wonderful. "Somehow I don't see *InStyle* caring about dangerous minds."

Charlotte became suddenly fascinated by the shoes she was holding. "I can't even wear normal shoes. I have hippo feet."

"What did you do?" I asked.

"Nothing."

"Something with *InStyle?*"

She lowered her bulk into a velvet boudoir chair. "I had to promise *People,* which is owned by the same parent company, exclusive pictures of me and the baby after the birth."

"Charlotte!" She always tried to keep her personal life out of the spotlight.

"Well, you know. For Emily. David said it would be okay."

"For that, they should put her in the '50 Most Beautiful' issue."

She inspected the shoes more closely.

"You asked and they said no?" I said.

"Don't tell Emily."

"Believe me, I won't."

When a model breaks out like Charlotte had, agents start looking at her sisters—same genes, right? Her agency offered to test shoot me when I turned fourteen. I was tempted, despite them wanting me to lose fifteen pounds, but Charlotte and Dad said no. I sulked, but was secretly pleased. I do look vaguely—very vaguely—like Charlotte. Except in front of a camera, her light hair shines, her tawny skin glows, and her smile blinds unprepared passersby. In front of a camera, I just look like me. Plus, I like to eat.

Nobody ever offered to test shoot Emily.

Dad showed up before David or *InStyle,* and immediately headed for the buffet.

I knocked a taquito from his fingers. "Wait till the guests arrive."

"I'm starving. I held off lunch for this."

"And if Emily catches you?"

He stepped away from the buffet, almost knocking over a vase of flowers. Dad was always nervous at Charlotte's. The reek of wealth was disconcerting—the mansion in Montecito, the garden, the pool. Actually I was a little nervous myself, as Billy would arrive in an hour and I had no idea what I was supposed to do with him. At least I looked all right. Charlotte hadn't convinced me to wear her clothes, but she'd done my hair and makeup. She was a cosmetics genius—with me spackled and shellacked, it was obvious we were sisters.

Then she waddled into the living room on David's arm, and I sighed. She'd made herself up, too, so we were back to looking like strangers. Even pregnant, she was gorgeous. It was rare for me to see her fully made-up, and I'd forgotten how stunning she was. Perfect bone structure, large blue eyes, and lustrous hair that was meant to be long.

"Dad's hungry," I said.

"I skipped lunch," Dad explained.

David's admiring gaze broke from Charlotte. "I'll get a plate from the buffet."

"Emily," Charlotte and I said.

"Right," David said. "There's chips in the kitchen. Back in a second."

"Get me a slice of cheese," Charlotte said.

David headed off and I eyed Charlotte's enormous stomach, realizing I hadn't capitalized on her condition as much as I should have. She'd grown positively huge. "Sit by me," I said, and patted the couch. If I were lucky, the *InStyle* photographer would get a shot of this. The caption: *A grotesquely pregnant Charlotte Olsen, and her svelte, much younger sister, Anne.*

Charlotte sat beside me and the cushions seesawed me into the air. "You two sick of each other yet?" she asked. Meaning me and Dad, living together.

Dad and I looked at each other. Why get sick? We got along great. Plus, I didn't have to pay rent, so I could spend my little all on necessities like clothes, mochas, and alcohol.

"Because the guest house is empty," Charlotte said. "With the baby coming, I thought it'd be nice to have Anne close."

Sure. I'd already had a lifetime of Charlotte's secondhand goods, the last thing I wanted was to take care of her second generation. Then reason lifted its shaggy head. The guest house was a cozy cottage with one bedroom, a kitchen with a Wolf stove and Sub-Zero fridge, and a living room out of *Metropolitan Home.*

"How much for rent?" Dad asked, a shade too eagerly.

"Well, if she'd baby-sit every now and then…"

"No." Dad shook his head. "Anne needs to pay rent. It'll be good for her."

"Dad."

"How about three hundred?" Charlotte said. "Including utilities."

Three hundred I could swing.

"Not enough," Dad said.

"But if she takes the baby a couple times a week."

"Wait one infantile second," I said. "I never said I'd help with the baby."

"Of course not," Charlotte said. "Only if you had time." She and Dad looked a little nervous. There's a bit of Emily in me.

"What do you think?" I asked Dad.

"I'd miss you…" he said, gloomily.

And I realized I couldn't leave him. It wasn't like he still had Mom to take care of him. Maybe it's a youngest daughter thing, but I felt I had a responsibility. And he did like having me around, even if he grumbled about it occasionally.

"…but I'll help you move next week," he finished.

When Emily arrived, the photographers positioned her in front of a huge poster for a film called *Spanking School-girls.* She'd been posed to hide the naughty bits, and hadn't budged since. I guess she had a little of the model in her after all. Her publisher, Jamie Lombard—early thirties, an ink-stained cowboy, with rugged good looks and a receding hairline—stood proudly beside her. He was a local publisher, and few of his books had ever sold more than five hundred copies. The unexpected success of Emily's book had left him slightly shell-shocked.

Emily, on the other hand, looked utterly comfortable chatting with a reporter about the dichotomizing of sub-textual prurience or something. As far as I could understand, her point was this: women like to fuck. Not exactly an earth-shattering insight, but apparently if you dress it up in postmodern theory, you get famous for your dangerous mind.

It did make me eye Emily speculatively. She'd been secretly dating someone all summer, and my bet was that he was someone in the "film" trade who she was too embarrassed to introduce to her family. A porn star like Johnny Deep, maybe, or Roger More.

I looked for Charlotte, to expand upon this theory—why had none of us met this mystery man?—and my Aunt Regina drifted into range. She eyed me and said, "I'm glad you're finally out of mourning."

This was her joke. Her only joke. My mom—her sister—had died when I was ten, and though I sometimes missed her, I hadn't been in mourning for twelve years. But Aunt Regina had an arrested image of me from what she called my "Goth Phase" in high school. Every time she saw me since, she was amazed anew that I wasn't wearing black lipstick.

I gave a courtesy laugh, and starting heaping food on my plate.

"Now you've stopped coloring your hair black," she said, "you look much more like Charlotte."

"We're often taken for twins," I lied.

"Surely not identical," she said. "Now if only you were a success, like your sisters. How proud your mother would be."

Before I could kill Aunt Regina and stuff her body in the crawlspace, Billy and Ian arrived—at the same time, like they'd shared a ride. This worried me for some reason, so I raced over to introduce them and be sure the introduction was necessary.

"Ian, this is Billy," I said, taking Billy's hand in a loverlike fashion. "Billy, Ian."

They said hello.

"So this is your boyfriend," Ian said.

"Yep," I said—giving Billy's hand a warning squeeze.

"What?" Billy said. "Me?"

I laughed and dragged him to a corner where I hissingly instructed him that, for the duration of the evening, he *was* my boyfriend. He claimed he wasn't. I told him he was. He became stubborn. So I offered an introduction to Charlotte, and he said he'd be my boyfriend for a whole week if he could shake her hand. A month if he could lick it.

We threaded through the crowd as I internally debated the merits of allowing the lick, but Billy dug in his heels when he spotted Charlotte.

"That really *is* Charlotte Olsen!" he said.

"Yeah."

"No way. She's totally—"

"Pregnant," I explained.

"—hot. She's totally hot."

"She's a water buffalo."

"She's a fox."

"But she's five hundred pounds!" I pointed out.

"I need a cold shower just looking at her," he said. "Oh, man."

"Her feet are bloated." I thought he should know. "She's a bloated hippo with clown feet."

"She's even hotter than her calendar."

"And bigger than her car."

"You know," he told me, man to man, "I jerked off to that calendar three times a day for like two months."

Fifteen minutes later, I slipped onto the patio. There was a couple sitting on the Adirondacks overlooking the pool, and chatting in low tones. I was going to sneak past, but it was only Ian and Emily.

"Why aren't you inside with your adoring fans?" I asked.

"I needed some air," Emily said. "The photographers…"

Ian shot a longing glance back at the house. "A little peace and quiet."

It was disgusting. Even in herd-of-buffalo form, Charlotte was breaking his heart. "She's enormous," I mumbled. "She's a one-woman stampede."

"What?" Ian gestured toward the party. "Is that what that crash was?"

"Oh. Um. That was me. I broke up with Billy."

Ian opened his mouth like he was going to say something, then closed it again.

"A long way from par," Emily said. "He didn't even make it to the first hole."

"Emily!" I said.

She blushed bright red. "I meant golf hole—like in golf."

"You've been watching too much porn," Ian told her.

"Porn is film," I observed.

"Why'd you break up?" Ian asked me.

"We'd grown apart." I turned to Emily. "So where's *your* invisible boyfriend?"

"We broke up, too."

"Really? When? Why?" The relationship may have been clandestine, but she'd seemed happy.

"It was only sex," Emily said.

"Well, what did you expect from a porn star? Intellectual fulfillment? I don't know what—"

"A porn star?" she said.

Ian laughed. "Hung like a moose, I bet."

Emily shot him a stern look, then finally copped to her blue-movie adventure. "The sex *was* great," she admitted, "although his idea of a good film was *The Sperminator*. He just wasn't right for me. We didn't have anything—" Her face lit up as Jamie Lombard stepped out of the house with two margaritas. "Jamie! Over here."

He headed our way and she sprang at him like a hungry lioness and dragged him to the corner of the deck, where they could talk privately. Did she have her eye on Jamie? They'd make a perfect pair.

I looked at Ian. "Did I imagine that?"

"Maybe she had *two* secret boyfriends."

"The porn star and the publisher. Sounds like a sitcom."

"On the Spice Channel."

I laughed more than that deserved, because I liked Ian. And he looked good. And apparently *had* forgotten what I did last time we met. "So...you saw Charlotte," I said.

"More beautiful than ever."

"She makes a very attractive Mack truck. Meet my sisters: dangerous mind and dangerous curves."

"Not feeling dangerous, yourself?"

I held up the plate of food that hadn't left my side all evening. "Only to the buffet."

"Oh, I'm sure there's a little wickedness in you."

Okay, he was Charlotte's ex, so this was marginally incestuous and repulsively secondhand. But he was handsome, single, funny, smart...and nobody had ever called me potentially wicked before. I gave him my lower-wattage version of Charlotte's smile and said, "A lot of wickedness."

He laughed. "Remember last time we met? You invited me to your school dance."

My smile dimmed.

"You were what?" he said. "In seventh grade? I was a senior in high school. It was so sweet. What was the theme again?"

Hawaiian luau. "No idea."

"Hula or something. You were cute in your little grass skirt."

Actually, I was. I'd wanted to wear a coconut bra, too, but Dad wouldn't let me.

Ian smiled at the memory. "You marched up to me with a flower necklace and asked if I wanted to get laid."

"Lei-ed," I said faintly, remembering the mortification. I was trying on my outfit and had gone to Charlotte's room to show her. A half-dozen other kids had been there, Charlotte's friends, and they'd howled with laughter. Not Ian, though. He'd said, very kindly, no, and on the night of the dance had actually sent me a corsage.

We were silent a moment, listening to the party sounds from the house. Then I turned to him and—God help me— I said, "The offer's still good."

Ian took my hand. He told me how flattered he was. He said I was beautiful, wonderful, perfect in every way—but he'd rather staple his earlobes to the deck than sleep with me. Well, I don't know exactly what he said, because I was busy trying to transform my utter mortification into the ability to sink unnoticed into the ground, leaving behind only a thin film of humiliation.

Okay. So he hadn't forgotten.

The next morning Dad and I met in the living room for coffee. We usually chatted for about twenty minutes before I left for Banana and he headed to his office at UCSB.

"You looked pretty last night," he said.

"Nice that someone thought so," I muttered into my coffee.

"Hmm?"

"Nothing." I put my cup on the coffee table and held out my arms to show off my new red T-shirt and black mini. "And what do we think of today's ensemble?"

"Not the book!" he said.

I grabbed my cup from the book I'd used as a coaster. It was *Porn Is Film*. Emily had placed it there, and we didn't dare move it. She'd come on a surprise inspection last Tuesday and found it buried at the bottom of the bookcase. The echoes were still fading.

Dad inspected the cover for stains and declared us safe when he found none. He smiled at the book, from fondness for Emily. "Mom would be so proud. Little did she know when she named you after the Brontë sisters, one of you'd become an author."

"Mom published stuff. So did you," I said sulkily. "All professors get published."

"In journals. Not like this."

"Well, Charlotte helped."

His smile wavered. "Your mom never would have expected her daughter to become a swimsuit model, though. I *think* she'd have supported it…." This was an old conflict with Dad.

"Dad, she's still Charlotte. Fame, fortune, and public nudity haven't done a single bad thing to her. Look what she's made of herself."

"Speaking of which…" he said, and I realized I'd been deftly maneuvered into this conversation.

"I like Banana."

"Anne—"

"Yes, *Anne,*" I said. "The Brontë sister no one's ever heard of. So lay off!"

"That doesn't mean—"

"Dad."

"I'm only saying—"

"Dad."

"Okay, okay. I'm saying nothing."

"And I've heard it all before."

At the end of that summer, Emily and Jamie were married. Charlotte had a baby girl. And I got a job working for a dot-com. I was destined to make millions—in an artsy-businessy way, of course.

I heard Ian moved to New York.

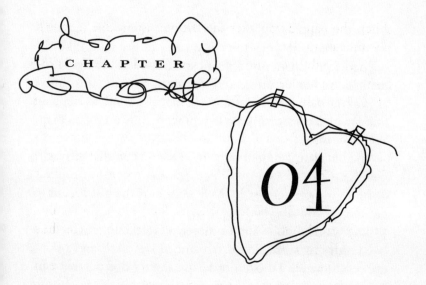

CHAPTER

04

The third time Ian Dunne came into my life was eight years later.

I was twenty-nine, with a steady job and a steady boyfriend and a steady life. And I *still* managed to invite my sister's ex-boyfriend to an inappropriate party. There's a word for that: Fate.

Or maybe it's: Stupid.

It started when Emily and I were having lunch at the Sojourner, a natural foods restaurant downtown. We were arguing over a gift for Charlotte's birthday. Emily and I always joined forces to buy presents for Charlotte. Even though Charlotte insisted she loved everything we got her, together we could afford something unembarrassing.

"You know what she gave me last year?" I asked.

"A mahogany tilt-top occasional table."

I nodded. "Used furniture."

"It's an antique. Must've cost thousands. And it's in perfect condition—it looks brand-new."

"But it isn't."

"I'll take it, if you don't want it," Emily said. Like she needed secondhand used furniture. Between her book and her articles, her lectures and TV appearances, she was almost as stinking rich as Charlotte. Well, maybe a tenth as rich, but that was still pretty stinking if you were only an office manager, like me.

"I didn't say I didn't want it," I said. "Just that it wasn't new."

Emily shook her head. "Well, neither is the gift I want to get her, so you're even."

The waitress came and I ordered a Gorilla Fizz, which I'd been ordering at the Sojourner since I was a kid, and a Popeye Salad, which I'd been ordering since I had trouble zipping my Levi's last week. Emily quizzed the waitress about what exactly was in the vegetable timbale, then ordered the pumpkin ravioli with a totally different sauce than was on the menu. Then called the waitress back and changed to the stew. When she finished, she turned to me. "Charlotte and I found a new antiques place in El Paseo a couple weeks ago."

"Antiques," I said, disgusted, "are the world's biggest scam. First something is *new*. Pristine. Unsullied. Then it's *gently used*. Crusty. Questionable. Then *used*. Old. Nasty. And finally, if nobody's thrown it away, it becomes *antique*. Repulsive, rancid, swirling with layers of greasy body oil. And more expensive than when it was new."

"It amazes me you can eat in a restaurant," Emily said. "You know other people have used that fork."

I paused midbite, trying not to think about it. Hundreds of mouths sliding wet tongues over the prongs. It was deeply off-putting—but fortunately, my fondness for all things new and unused was (mostly) limited to what I owned. Besides, I liked to eat. I put the forkful of salad in my mouth and smiled triumphantly at Emily. "See! Not crazy."

"Good," she said. "Prove it by picking up Charlotte's gift at the antiques store."

"What is it?" I asked.

"A lacquer box. She loved it when she saw it in the window."

"Why can't you get it?"

"Because I have a *real* job, Anne." Emily thought I wasn't living up to my potential, answering phones at a real estate company. She didn't understand that that *was* my potential.

"Oh, yeah," I said. "Academia. Nothing more real than that."

"At least I enjoy what I'm doing," she said.

"So do I. Putting people in real homes, with roofs and doors—things they can use. Not theories about how porn queens articulate their genitalia." Emily had actually said that once, *articulate her genitalia,* on *Crossfire* or *Politically Incorrect* or somewhere. She hated to be teased about it. "Don't tell me how important your work is compared to mine."

"I didn't say it was important. I said I enjoyed it." She looked down at her plate. "At least I used to."

I immediately felt awful for snapping at her. She'd been having a terrible time with her second book, struggling with it for years. "Problems with the book again?"

"No, it's—well, it's finished. The first draft."

"But…" I prompted.

"But nothing."

"What does Jamie think?"

"He *says* he likes it." She dipped a hunk of bread in her stew. "My agent wants to shop it elsewhere."

"You mean—elsewhere?"

"She says I should get a big-name publisher."

"Instead of Jamie?"

She nodded.

It would kill Jamie. Emily was his lead author as well as

his wife. The reason he'd been able to attract other good writers was because of *Porn Is Film*. And Emily relied on him more than she knew, and not only because he stayed in Santa Barbara with their son, Zach, while she commuted three days a week to UCLA.

"You can't do that," I said.

"No," she said. "I know."

"Do you want to?"

"I don't know. Not really. Remember when my first book came out? How excited I was? Everything seemed possible. I just want to feel that way again."

I felt for Emily—and still wanted to stab her in the eye with my fork. She had a career she loved. She was famous enough to get mentioned on NPR—though, I'm pleased to say, not on *SNL*. She had Jamie, who doted on her, and Zach, who was a great kid. Yeah, she wasn't a dangerous young mind anymore, but she had the perfect life. Well, *Charlotte* had the perfect life. But Emily's was first runner-up.

Still, because I'm a good sister, I made sympathetic noises and kept my fork to myself. I even paid for lunch—treating Emily as a reward for finishing her book.

She gave me a quick hug outside the restaurant. "You won't forget Charlotte's gift? The place is called Tazza."

I wrinkled my nose.

"Just buy it, Anne."

"Okay, okay. But if I come down with medieval squirrel-pox, it's your fault."

"What are the symptoms?" Emily asked. "Irritability, lack of ambition, fear of commitment—Annie, you've already got a terminal case."

After the EMTs arrived to remove my fork from Emily's forehead, I rushed back to my job at Parsons Realty. I tried not to take long lunches, even though I'd been dating the owner, Rip Parsons, for six months. Knowing where the boss sleeps at night (the right side of the bed) is pretty good job security.

I'd been working there for eight months, and considered the longevity of both relationship and job fairly impressive. The longest I'd worked anywhere was at the dot-com, a little-used search engine called The Ask It Basket. A name even lamer than "Rip," but the company had been started back in the days when all you had to say was, "It's a company on the World Wide Web. Which is on the Internet. Which is a global network of computers," and millions dropped into your lap.

I'd worked three years at The Ask It Basket. My job title was Coordinator of Technology, but my business card said Geek Wrangler. I basically translated requests from management into geek-speak and back again. If a manager asked: "Why are the coders three weeks behind deadline?" I'd ask the geeks: "Would you stop downloading porn and get to work?" Or if the coders said, "Seagate's got a brand-new campus, with a video-game room and everything," I'd tell my boss: "They want free Mountain Dew and fruit leather."

Then I'd sold my stock. But you weren't supposed to sell stock, you were supposed to spend hours online every day, watching it go up and up and up and up. Selling stock was a betrayal worse than corporate espionage or claiming that Bill Gates wasn't actually Rosemary's Baby. I became persona not-entirely grata, and quit shortly thereafter, clutching the meager proceeds of my stock sale close to my heart.

Then I spent a depressing year watching the stock go up and up and up and up.

Then down. Wheeeee!

Everyone had thought I was crazy to sell, but after the dot-com crash I felt like Warren Buffet's love child with Suze Orman, despite having sold a year early and spending nearly

everything. Still, Dad was so impressed he said I should become a stockbroker. Instead I convinced Wren to hire me
at Element—the clothing boutique she managed. We'd been
best friends since working together at Banana, so she sort of
had to hire me. Sadly, I was so bad at selling clothes that she
sort of had to fire me three months later. But at least she wept
while giving me the pink slip, so I forgave her.

After Wren fired me, I starting doing temp work—which
I loved. Every job was a new job. I worked for an interior
designer, the community college, a sheet music business, and
World of Goods, a nonprofit. A local title company hired
me permanently, and I stayed six months before I realized
I'd paper-cut my throat if I had to type one more set of title
instructions.

Right on cue, Rip Parsons had wandered into the office.
A little flirting, an extra-long lunch, and I had a new job. He
wanted an assistant, but I insisted on "office manager," because it sounded almost reputable. Plus, I figured it was a
good way to explore the possibility of becoming a Realtor
(who basically mints money in Santa Barbara) without actually taking the courses and test.

A couple months later—a little more flirting, a few din-
ners added to the lunches—and I had a boyfriend. Rip had
short brown hair and green eyes and I liked his arms, mus-
cular from tennis, with the hair bleached blond from the sun.
He looked faintly like Peter Gallagher, and on paper seemed
like a jerk—a too-handsome young Realtor, a smarmy salesman. But he was lovely, super kind and always caring.

So, sure, I was twenty-nine and working behind the front
desk of a real estate company—my career peak apparently
long past—but at least I had a wonderful boyfriend.

Actually, *getting* boyfriends had never been a problem for
me. I have a system. *Wanting* them after a few months was
tougher.

There was Matthew. I broke up with him when he said, "Because I'm Matthew, that's why," once too often. There was Billy from Banana. My "dumping" him at Emily's party had somehow ignited his interest, but I dumped him for real after he admitted he fantasized about Charlotte when we had sex. I didn't mind him doing it, but couldn't forgive him admitting it. Then Doug, the creative genius behind The Ask It Basket. I broke up with him when he started a porn-only search engine, called The Beaver Basket. There had been Mason, the public defender who was great fun when drunk, incredibly tedious when sober. Nick, the portrait artist with the trust fund who I had to leave because he wore Mary Janes. Arthur, the world's sexiest plumber who liked laying pipe a bit too much. Alex, the wannabe screenwriter who asked me to give him "notes" about his lovemaking.

And Rip. Who had just buzzed me from his office. I hated that buzzer—sounded like I'd said the wrong thing on *Family Feud*—and had warned Rip not to touch it. Now he only buzzed to annoy me.

I opened the door to his office. "What?"

He grinned.

"I'm on a deadline, Rip. The ads are due."

"Guess who just sold Knox Tower."

I looked at him. "No!"

"Yes!"

"Oh, my God! That's fantastic. Who? When?"

The Knox Tower wasn't a tower. It was an old lodge in the Santa Barbara mountains, with 360-degree views of the valleys below and the distant crystal blue of Lake Cachuma. A rich socialite of the Great Gatsby type—though named Knox, I presume—had hosted lavish parties there until it burned down into ruins, many decades ago. It was never rebuilt, and the land and rubble had been on the market since. For millions.

"Just now," Rip said. "That was the buyer on the phone."

"Who is he?"

"Super rich L.A. contractor. CEO of Keebler, Inc."

"Keebler? Like the elves?"

"If you meet him," Rip said, "that's the first thing you *shouldn't* ask. Anyway, he's big into low-impact, green construction. Fell in love with the place."

"I thought you couldn't build up there."

"Green construction, Annie. He's gonna put up tents. Or yurts or something, a cistern, solar energy, the whole deal."

I shook my head. "Will it actually close?"

"I spoke to the lender. It's a go." A gleam came into his eyes. "I'm thinking I deserve a reward."

"Oh, is that what you think?"

"Mmm-hmm." He put his hands on my hips and pulled me close. "That was a good movie last night."

We'd watched *Secretary* on video. "You want me to play your secretary?"

"You *are* my secretary."

I nipped his ear. "Office manager."

"Even better." He nuzzled me. "Besides, you told me you liked spanking."

"When? I never!"

"You're always begging for it."

I started to giggle. "I am not."

"I can't get into bed without you shouting, 'Smack me, baby.'"

"I have never in my life said, 'Smack me, baby.'"

"And 'tan my naughty ass!'"

I shoved him, laughing. "'Tan my naughty ass?'"

"See! There you go again!" He ran his palms down my hips, took both my hands in one of his and rubbed my bottom with the other. "Just one?"

I bit my lip. "Okay. One."

He gave my ass a wallop and his eyes lit up—meaning he was ready for business.

"Later," I said. Because we'd agreed: never in the office. But I could still tease. I kissed his neck and wriggled as he ran his hands over me.

"You'll play secretary tonight?" he asked, a bit breathlessly.

"Office manager."

"Office manager it is," he said, and spanked me again.

Rip was out all afternoon, so I had time to finish the ads before they were due. It was a near thing though, and I was halfway home before I realized I hadn't stopped at Tazza Antiques. I wasn't exactly bothered—if I forgot to buy the desiccated old pot, maybe Emily would agree to get something else. Something better. Like a magazine subscription.

I picked up my dog, Ny—a ridiculously red chow mix—and took him to the beach before going to my dad's house. I stopped at Dad's two or three times a week, to check in and mooch dinner. Actually, checking and mooching were one and the same. Because if he knew I was coming, he'd buy food. Otherwise, he'd eat cold cereal three times a day. He was a bit of an absentminded professor.

Ny romped with his dog buddies and chased seabirds through the waves until he was exhausted. I toweled him dry and helped him scramble into the cab of the pickup—he was getting chubby and needed an extra boost.

My truck was a silver Ford Ranger pickup, the Splash model with chrome wheels. I'd bought it with my Ask It Basket money—the only new vehicle I'd ever owned. If I closed my eyes and sniffed deeply, I could still smell the new-car perfume. Plus, it was half of the patented Anne Olsen System for Being Semi-Successful with Men. Step One: don't care about long-term relationships. Men love this. They swarm. Step Two: drive a pickup. Women driving pickups are to men what men driving Armani suits are to women. Don't ask me why.

Dad lived in the same old Victorian on the upper east side where I'd grown up. It was a mixed neighborhood, filled with old houses like my dad's that locals had owned for thirty years, and the updated versions that wealthy L.A. people had recently bought and renovated.

Dad glanced up from his newspaper when I let myself in. "What's hanging?"

"'What's hanging?'" I let Ny track his sandy paws inside and closed the door. "Where'd you hear that?"

"I like to keep up with you young people," he said.

"I don't know, Dad. I don't feel so young anymore."

"Of course." He shook his newspaper derisively. "You're bent with age at twenty-six."

"Nine," I said. "Twenty-nine."

"Really?" he said. "That *is* old."

"What?"

He laughed. You'd think after twenty-nine years, I'd know when he was teasing.

"Still gullible as a teenager," he said. "Have you eaten?"

"Of course not." I headed for the kitchen. "What's for dinner?"

"Stuffed pork chops. You're staying?"

"I am for pork chops."

He followed me into the kitchen and checked the oven. Two pork chops and two potatoes were already baking.

"Why two?" I asked. "Am I stealing one of yours?"

"No," he said, "I was making leftovers for tomorrow."

I glanced upstairs. "You haven't got a woman hiding in your bedroom, waiting for me to leave?"

"Of course not," he said. "She's in the bathroom."

"Oh! Sorry! I should've called—" I saw his expression. "Ha-ha. Very funny." I opened the fridge and grabbed a soda.

"But the way you play the field, I keep expecting to hear you eloped."

He shook his head. "Three girls is enough."

"Why *haven't* you remarried?" I wasn't sure if I liked the idea, but my dad wasn't really meant to live alone. "It's been almost twenty years."

"You're one to talk, with all your boyfriends." He grabbed lettuce and carrots for a salad. "You're a female Lothario."

"I am not."

"You're Lotharia."

"I'm *not* Lotharia."

"You break up with every man you date. I can't imagine Rip'll last much longer, poor guy."

"You like him?" Every time Rip met my father, he tried to sell him a new house.

"The question is, do you?"

"He's funny and smart and wonderful—what's not to like?"

"You're not getting VD?" Dad asked.

No, he didn't mean *VD* VD. He meant Vague Dissatisfaction. I'd stupidly confessed to him once that I had an acute case of Vague Dissatisfaction. Nothing in particular was wrong, but nothing felt right. It was why I never stuck with things very long. Dad considered it a low-level social disease, which would flare up periodically into unsightly outbreaks: VD. Dad thought he was pretty funny.

I glared. "Everything's fine. I don't want to talk about it."

"Then give me an onion."

I gave him an onion, and we let the subject drop. He told university stories over dinner, and when we'd finished, he offered me Oreos for dessert.

"Is it a new package?" I asked.

"Anne, you've got to stop this."

"My diet starts tomorrow."

"You know what I mean. Your obsession with newness."

Easy for him to say. With two older sisters, hand-me-downs had been the primary fact of my young life.

Charlotte had a Malibu Barbie with a full wardrobe. Emily had a slightly used Malibu Barbie with two outfits. I had a one-armed, bald Barbie who enjoyed nudist colonies.

Charlotte wore Jordache when it was popular. Emily wore Jordache when it was passable. I wore Jordache when it was passé.

Charlotte learned to drive on a six-year-old VW Rabbit. Emily learned on a seven-year-old VW Rabbit. I learned on a twelve-year-old, rusted-out junker with suspicious stains on the seats and the faint odor of Gruyère.

But all I said to Dad was, "I don't like stale Oreos is all."

He lifted his pipe from the ashtray on the kitchen table and packed it with tobacco. "They're fresh from the factory."

"Where are they?" I asked, heading toward the pantry.

"Bottom shelf."

I pulled the half-eaten package from the shelf and forced myself to take one. From the back. The very back. "Not bad."

Dad looked pleased as he lit up his pipe, and I surreptitiously pulled a brand-new carton of milk from the fridge—ignoring the one which was already open—and poured myself a glass. I'd let him discover that little treat tomorrow.

When I got home, I found a message from Rip. The nights we weren't together we usually talked before sleep, and lately we'd been discussing moving in together. I'd lived with other men—Doug and Alex, for about twenty minutes each—but always returned to Charlotte's guest house when things went awry. I wasn't sure if living with Rip was a good idea. We already worked in the same office, and spending more time together seemed a great way to kill a nice relationship.

I picked up the phone to call him back, but didn't feel like talking. I was itchy and restless. I switched on the TV. I'd see Rip at work tomorrow.

CHAPTER

05

By ten-thirty the next morning, I knew that Dad's words had ruined me. I'd been perfectly content and happy—or at least acceptably content and happy—until he'd mentioned my VD. Now I was in the grips of an enormous amorphous ennui.

The job was fine. Rip was great. I didn't care.

I sulked through the morning, and slipped out for an early liquid lunch. I sipped my peanut-butter-banana-chocolate smoothie and worried. Was I Lotharia? It wasn't like I cut a huge swath through the male population. I just hadn't found the right man, and couldn't quite bring myself to care. Could Rip be the one? Well, his name was Rip, but that's no worse than Ralph as in Fiennes, even if it is pronounced Rafe.

At least Rip was pronounced Rip. And his personality was as solid as his elocution. Perfect husband material…if only I were looking for a husband. I wasn't. It's far easier to have a relationship when you aren't. The pressure cooker is off. I've watched friends with their cookers clamped down tight, the steamer diddly whirling round and round. Every date, every conversation and sexual experience, every misunderstanding, deviant desire, ambition, frustration and inadequacy is added to the pot until the whole thing blows.

I prefer the omelet approach to relationships. You use what few ingredients you have at hand, scramble them in a hot pan, and enjoy. Quick and simple.

Then why was I feeling such discontent?

Back in the office, I did what I always did when sideswiped by dissatisfaction: a little personal research. I'd collected a file of real estate deals I was interested in—my Recent Developments file. From big money resorts to condo conversions to commercial buildings, all the deals I was sure would make me rich, if I actually pursued them. Well, and could afford them. And knew how to be a developer and all.

My file of dreams. I flipped through it, and decided to call about The Hole, one of my recurring dream deals. A block off downtown Santa Barbara, there used to be a residential hotel for old people. But it was on prime real estate, and the old people were considered well past their prime, so some developer kicked everyone out and tore the place down, with assurances that they'd find the seniors new homes and bring prosperity and joy to downtown. Five years later, all they'd brought was The Hole—the great gaping basement of the hotel they'd demolished.

Well, I had some plans for that gaping basement. I dialed.

"I'm calling about the property on the corner of Carrillo and Chapala," I told the man on the other end. "I'm representing—"

"You're not representing anyone," he said. "I recognize your voice."

So maybe I'd called once too often. But thank God he didn't know who I was. I'd never given a name.

"Well, if you'd just fax me the information—" I said.

"Are you a broker?"

"Not exactly."

"You still think it'd be a great place for an indoor driving range?"

"I never said that!" I said. "That was just my way of getting you to talk to me."

"And this is just my way of talking." He hung up.

I growled into the phone and flipped through the Recent Developments. Nothing else caught my eye. Maybe it wasn't a deal I needed. Maybe it was a new job. Rip walked in as I was glowering at the wall. He looked at my face, looked at the Recent Developments file open on my desk, and slipped into his office, closing his door for protection against the gathering clouds.

I guess I really am like Emily sometimes. But sometimes I'm like Charlotte, too. And I wasn't going to let myself ruin everything. So I opened the door softly and gave him a smile. It was the job I was VDed with, not the man.

He eyed me suspiciously. "What?"

"I was just thinking how much I like your arms."

"You want your desk moved again? It's not getting the afternoon sun?"

"My desk is perfect. So is my boss."

His suspicion grew into wariness. "How did your call go?"

"I'm *this* close to closing a big downtown deal."

"Hung up on you again, huh?"

"Yeah. But I've got a plan."

"Let me guess. It involves taking two-hour lunches?"

I waved an airy hand. "Oh, that—my boss is a pushover."

"That's not what I heard. I heard he wants to take it out of your hide."

"He has to catch me first."

★ ★ ★

Wren and I had a standing date Wednesday nights. We'd walk Ny at Hendry's beach, then head up to the Mesa for a burrito before class. I considered stopping at the antiques store before meeting her, but I wasn't going to be late to pick up some crusty old chamberpot.

"I'm thinking of quitting." I put the tray of food on our table outside the burrito place: veggie tacos for me, chicken burrito for Wren, and cheese quesadilla for Ny. "Salsa?"

Wren gave me a look as she unwrapped her burrito. "Why?"

"For spice," I said, tossing Ny's quesadilla to the ground. He engulfed it.

She gave me another look. "I mean, why quit?"

"Yeah, I know. For spice."

"Ha-ha."

"I dunno…I just think it's time."

"What would you do instead?"

"You know I never have trouble getting a job."

"Just keeping one."

"I'd still be working at Element, if you hadn't fired me."

"If I hadn't fired you," she said, biting into her burrito. "There wouldn't *be* an Element anymore."

I made a face at her. "I wasn't that bad."

"You were worse. You haven't broken up with Rip, have you?"

"No."

"Not yet," she said.

"You sound like my dad."

"I like your father."

"Yeah, a little *too* much. You want to get it on with my dad, don't you?"

"I'm serious. Rip is great. You don't deserve him."

"Thanks," I said.

"Give him a chance, Anne. I know you're approaching the sell-by date, but—"

"I'm *not,*" I insisted. "That's why I want a new job. To preserve the relationship."

"I thought you got along great at work."

"Well, aside from the buzzer." I toyed with my taco, before pushing it away. "God, Wren, I'm just so…*bored.* With me, with my job. Everything."

"Here." She dumped salsa verde on my taco. "A little more spice."

For some reason, this made me feel better. Maybe because she seemed to be agreeing with me, even if it was only about the taco. We finished our meals and Wren sat back in her chair, replete from her burrito. "Now all I need is a naked woman and fifty pounds of warm mud, and I'll be good."

Twenty minutes later, she got more than she asked for. We were in the main room, the drapes pulled tight over the windows, with spotlights on a beautiful naked *man,* and Wren was up to her elbows in clay. She rolled her sculpture stand closer to mine and dug a big hunk from a bag of terra-cotta.

We'd been attending the Adult Ed clay sculpture class for the past three years. Originally, we'd started because Wren thought it would be a good place to meet sensitive men, and I thought I'd like mucking around with mud. She'd never found a sensitive man—or an insensitive one, for that matter—but we kept coming.

Our patience had finally been rewarded. In three years, we'd only had a handful of male models, and none of them had looked like Mr. Nude America here. There were a dozen students in the class, held at the Schott Center on the upper west side. The sessions usually started with around twenty-five students, but it was fairly late in the season, and we'd dwindled down to the regulars.

I glanced briefly at the model, clinically observing his

broad shoulders and washboard stomach, and when I looked away I noticed that Wren had already roughed out his torso. In clay, that is.

"That was fast," I said.

She glanced at the clock. "You've been staring at the poor guy for twenty minutes."

"I was examining the subject."

"And drooling."

"I'm an artist, Wren. He might as well be a bowl of fruit."

She sighed. "It *is* a pity."

"What is?"

"That he's gay."

I glanced at the model again. "He's straight as a yardstick, Grasshopper," I said. Because Wren was a novice when it came to men.

"With that body?"

"From tip to toe."

Wren just shook her head sadly, so I sliced off a hunk of clay with my wire tool and started pushing it around. Making his feet. I thought I'd start low and move up. Let the anticipation build.

I was on his ankles when Claire, our teacher, drifted behind us.

"Excellent work, Wren," she said. "You might want to caliper his chest, though. It looks a bit off scale. Remember there's a rib cage under there."

We had big metal calipers to measure distances on the models and then convert them into 1/3 scale. But to measure you had to approach within nibbling distance, in the middle of the room, and share the spotlight with the gloriously defined and shamelessly undraped model. Wren was usually extremely businesslike about measuring models. This time, however…

She blushed. "Oh, I see—you're right." She fiddled with her clay. "I think I can eye it, though…."

Claire nodded and checked my work. "Feet," she said.

"I'm afraid to look any higher," I told her.

She didn't smile. She was very professional about the models. "At least give his feet arches, then. And his toes should not look like sausages."

"Yeah, you're right. Well—" I grabbed the calipers. "Only one way to fix that."

I strode into the limelight, offering up the calipers at the altar of this sex god. I measured the distance between his feet, the distance from heel to toe. I leaned forward a bit and smiled up at him. "Bored yet?"

He smiled down. "It's not as bad as my day job."

"What's that?"

"I'm a librarian."

"Get out of town." I leaned forward a bit more. "At the university?"

"No, the law school. It's not the boredom that bothers me, so much as the larval lawyers."

I laughed brightly and scurried back to Wren. I whispered: "Gay."

"What?"

"He didn't look at my cleavage."

"Well, it would've been pretty obvious if he had."

"He's got every right to look—it's not like *he's* hiding anything. But there wasn't even an eye-drift."

"Maybe he likes the flat-chested type," she said, meaning herself.

"Yeah. Men. He's totally gay."

She shook her head. "Now, I'm not sure."

"Wren, I'm telling you, not even a flicker."

"Maybe he's not gay," she said. "Maybe he just has good taste."

I made a face at her. "And a really fine pack—"

"Break time!" Claire called.

We squirted our sculptures with water, covered them in plastic to keep them moist, and headed outside. Ny was sitting contentedly in the back of the pickup. He loved break time, because a couple of the regulars always brought him treats.

"Hey, fatboy," I said, scratching his head.

He gave me a little love, then wagged hopefully as he was plied with cookies. When the snack-vending students left, Wren and I sat on the open tailgate and drank our waters.

"Ugg boots," I said. "I don't care that the stars are wearing them."

"Sleeve ruffles on men," Wren said.

"Unless they're on a mariachi outfit."

She shook her head. "I don't want to hear your mariachi fantasy again."

"I just liked the movie is all. How about black jeans after 1992?"

"Forget '92. Black jeans anytime after the Michael Penn song."

"What if I were Ro-me-o in black jeans?" we sang.

"Snap-on ties," I said.

"Too easy. Denim shorts."

I shuddered. "Denim shorts."

A male voice said, "Nice dog. Boy or girl?"

It was the male model, wearing a robe and flip-flops. I looked at his face for the first time. Boyishly handsome, with a lopsided smile. If I didn't have Rip, I'd have tossed my hair and got down to business. The thought made me turn cold, as I realized: Wren was going to flirt.

"A boy. He's a chow chow mutt," I said, before she could say anything. "Mixed with I don't know what. Chows have a bad reputation, but he's totally friendly."

"Hey there, boy." The model put his hand out, and Ny perked up.

"He's hoping for a treat," I said. "He's a bit spoiled—"

"I'm Wren!" She hopped off the truck and giggled nervously, looking up at him. "You're tall. What's your name?"

Oh, God.

"Kevin," he said, and offered his hand.

She took it in a sort of death grip. "Hi! Glad to meet you. I saw you in class."

"Yes, well—I'm the model," he said, and looked toward me.

"I'm Anne. Wren and I were just saying how nice it is to have a male model."

"We haven't had a man in a long time," Wren said, tilting her head. "I mean, not a man! A model. A male model. Not that a model's not a man. I mean—"

Wren had just cut her hair. It was short and pixielike, bringing out the brightness of her eyes, the daintiness of her features, and the dippiness of her flirting. Still, her smile was sweet and inviting, even after I slid off the tailgate and stomped on her foot to shut her up.

"Have you done a lot of modeling?" I asked.

"No, this is my first time. Claire's a friend, she asked as a favor?"

"That's asking a lot from a friend," I said. "How long will you model for?"

"A month. Then we'll see. I hear the drawing class wants a male model. I guess it's mostly women."

"Actually, it's mostly men who take figure drawing," Wren blurted.

"He meant the models, Wren."

"Oh, right! I did drawing for a while, but I like clay better. You shouldn't be embarrassed, though. You're a model. So your clothes are off. So you're nude. Buck naked." She offered a tinkly little laugh that ended in a snort. "Undraped, I mean. Not that I—I mean, you might as well be a fruit."

"Bowl of fruit," I said, grinding into her foot. "Wren loves doing still life."

"I'll try to remain motionless, then."

"Oh, no!" Wren said, clutching his arm. "Move around all you want. Well, not *all* you want. I mean—no dancing. Unless you like dancing. But I mean—"

"Was that Claire?" I asked, glancing toward the classroom.

"I didn't hear anything," Kevin said.

Wren giggled horribly. "Neither did I."

"And I *do* like dancing," he told her.

"Me, too! Anne and I took ballroom dancing for a while—she dropped out, though, because she kept forgetting to let the man lead."

"And you?"

She simpered. "I never forgot."

"Wren—" I started. And, seeing her expression, words failed me. A full-throttle simper is not an expression which encourages conversation.

"Wren?" he said, smiling. "As in Ren and Stimpy?"

"Wren with a 'W,'" she said. "Like the bird. The drab, brown bird."

"But you're not drab."

Fortunately, before Wren gave herself a hernia from simpering, we were called back into the classroom.

"Not gay!" I said.

"Gay," she said.

"He was flirting with you."

"Pity flirting. He couldn't believe what a dork I am. Why did you let me talk to him? I snorted. Did you hear me snort? I snorted. Like Miss Piggy."

"And Kevin's your Kermit."

"Gay," she said.

"Not gay. He likes you."

"He doesn't. He *couldn't*."

"He thinks you're cute. Not drab, not brown, but cute."

"He's gay," she hissed.

So I accidentally spilled the contents of my water bottle onto her white shirt. And you know what? I was right. He *wasn't* gay.

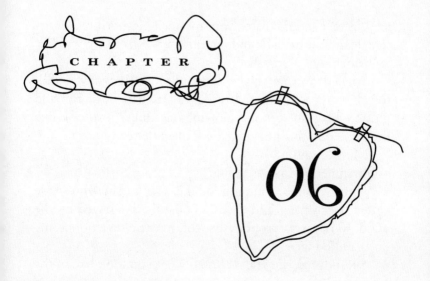

CHAPTER

06

I woke with a splash from a dream of falling and wrestled with the blanket. We were evenly matched, but I finally prevailed and shoved it away. I lay back, flush with triumph, and for a moment thought I was still asleep and the sound of running water was leftover dream.

Then I realized: Rip was in the shower.

I groaned, wishing Rip hadn't spent the night. He's unforgivably perky in the morning. Whatever happened to strong, silent men who grunt over the paper? Plus, he always woke up looking like the same guy he was the night before. I woke up looking tangled, puffy and ten years older.

And to top it off, there was only enough hot water for one shower. Judging from the steam billowing through the bathroom door, I was in for a cold shock.

I stumbled out of bed and parted the curtains. Another day in paradise—warm and clear, with a light breeze that floated in and kissed me good morning. It made me crankier. Weather should match your mood. This morning, for instance, should be dark and gloomy.

"Morning!" Rip called.

I turned, and he was in the bathroom doorway with a towel wrapped around his waist. His hair was wet and mussed, his skin wet and glowing. He didn't just look like the same guy this morning, he looked better.

"Muh," I said.

He smiled. "Coffee's going."

"Guh," I said, meaning good. I'd take a man who made coffee over strong-and-silent any day. Still, I stayed by the window. If I was properly backlit, he wouldn't notice my sleep-puffed face.

"Six months," he said. "I know what you look like in the morning."

I finally managed to croak out a real word. "Godzilla."

"More like Cameron."

"Cameron?" As in Diaz? Maybe not entirely true, but if that's how he wanted to see me—

"No. *Gamera*. Remember the Godzilla movie? Gamera's the big puffy turtle he fights."

Forget the lighting, I shot across the room and ripped his towel from him. He raced, laughing, to the safety of the bed before I could whip him with it. I fell in next to him and started smacking his bare skin. He caught my hands and kissed me. "You're beautiful in the morning."

I stopped struggling and pressed my face against his chest. My mood was beginning to match the sunshine.

He absently ran his fingers along my back. "What time is Charlotte's thing tonight?"

Charlotte's birthday party. Dark clouds gathered—I didn't want to talk about it. "You used all the hot water."

"Uh-huh. What time is it?"

I checked the clock. "Almost seven."

"I mean Charlotte's party," he said.

I stood and shrugged into my robe. "Six or something. I don't know."

"What's wrong?"

"Nothing."

"*Anne.*" He grabbed me by the sash. "What's wrong?"

"You sleep over, and you—you use all the hot water, and there's none left for me and I'm—what am I supposed to do? You never think. What about me? I'm stuck with a cold shower, that's what."

He mumbled something that sounded like, "You *need* a cold shower."

"Oh, *I'm* not the one who needs a cold shower!" I tightened my robe in a meaningful manner.

Rip pulled his boxers and pants on. He reached for his shirt and I considered slamming the bathroom door, but decided against it. I put my head on his shoulder instead.

"I hate Charlotte's birthday," I sniffled.

"We don't have to go," he said.

Of course we did. "So now you don't *want* to go?"

"Baby…"

"It's just—she's all perfect, and her kids are perfect and her husband's perfect and her life is perfect, and everyone loves her."

"And nobody loves you," he said, straight-faced.

"They don't. Not like—"

I realized where this conversation was going and sobered fast, suddenly terrified he'd think I wanted *him* to say he loved me. We'd never said "I love you," and I saw no reason to start now. Especially not if he thought this was a desperate bid for commitment, when it was clearly just a desperate bid for attention.

"I mean she's, um, loved by one and all," I said, flailing

around for dry ground and sinking deeper. "And I, on the other hand, am, um…"

"Anne," he said. "I—"

Was he going to say it? I willed him to say anything else: to tell me he was secretly married, or a post-operative transsexual, or moving to Arkansas. I tilted my head back to reveal the full horror of my morning face. No man could say "I love you" to that face.

He must've seen the naked terror in my eyes, because he smoothed my hair with his hand instead of finishing the sentence.

"I still haven't got Charlotte a gift," I blurted, to change the subject.

He smiled to tell me he knew what I was doing, but didn't mind. "Take the morning off to shop."

"Really?"

"Sure."

"But that's favoritism," I said.

"So? You're my favorite."

Couldn't argue with that. "Are we talking a *paid* morning off?"

He managed to sigh and smile at the same time. "Just be in before noon."

"Don't worry. Everything's all caught up."

"No more personal calls?"

"That was serious business," I said, with dignity. "We'll see who's laughing when I get the retirement village built."

"Uh-huh." He grabbed his wallet and extracted two twenties. "Speaking of business…"

"Forty bucks?" I shrugged out of my bathrobe and pressed my naked self against him. "You know I've raised my prices."

"That's not all you've raised, Polliwog." He called me that sometimes—his special love name for me, for reasons I refuse to divulge. He nuzzled my neck and put the money on my dresser. "Let me buy a gift with you. You know what Charlotte likes."

I decided not to tell him I was already splitting a gift with Emily and that going three ways wouldn't work, Emily being Emily. "I know what she likes," I said. "And she has all of it."

"Yeah?" he said, touching me. "Well, I wouldn't mind a little something, myself."

Rip left for work thirty minutes later, leaving me drowsing in post-coital contentment. I lay there a while, then went to open the kitchen door and release Ny. He followed me back to the bedroom, his claws clicking across the wood floor. I collapsed into bed and he eyed me dolefully.

"Don't blame me," I told him.

He stares when I have sex, intent and focused as a canine Kasparov trying to outthink Big Blue. I don't mind—he's just a dog, for God's sake—but men seem to find it unnerving. I think they think he's judging. Of course, Ny's hardly in a position to judge, as the only action he gets is with the hassock in Charlotte's family room, but I still lock him in the kitchen when things heat up.

"It's your own fault," I said. "Pervert."

He hopped onto the bed and licked my face.

The day was still bright and warm, and the next time I got out of bed, I smiled. No reason to live in paradise and not enjoy it. I had the morning off and plenty of time to walk Ny before shopping for Charlotte—for both the gifts I was splitting.

I showered and dressed and gulped two stale cups of the coffee Rip had brewed. He'd put the dinner dishes away, too, and probably would've made my bed if I hadn't still been in it. He's sort of terrific. But six months was scary—had it really been *six months*? We were closing in on my record.

"I dunno, fatboy," I told Ny. "Maybe me and Rip are meant for each other. What do you say?"

Ny eyed me for a long moment, then farted. He craned his neck around, peering dubiously towards his tail, like, *what was that?*

"That was you," I said. "Thanks for your input."

We got in the truck and drove through the upper village in Montecito. We passed the Pharmacy, and I considered stopping for some scrambled eggs—it's not just a pharmacy, it's also a celebrity-magnet coffee shop. The story goes that one morning Michael Keaton looked up from his paper at the corner table, and caught Dennis Miller's eye—he was at the counter—and the bell at the door jangled and in walks Michael Douglas. They all looked at each other and started laughing. They were the only three people in the store.

But if that's true, who told the story? If celebrities meet in a forest, do they make a sound? Plus, there must've been someone working behind the counter. I guess he doesn't count. Nothing like celebrity to render the non-famous invisible.

Ask me, I know.

So I didn't stop. I drove up to Cypress Road and parked by the wooden fence. Beyond the fence, there's a patch of woods and hill known only to dog-walkers, set behind and above the houses. It's an unofficial off-leash trail, a one-mile loop. At the top there's a view of the ocean, and although it's a bit of a climb, the property is stunning. It would be a phenomenal place to build a house—or a whole neighborhood—and I figured the only reason it hadn't been developed was because it was the forgotten edge of someone's sprawling estate, or county land of some sort.

I opened the door and Ny leapt from the truck and anointed the wooden fence and the manzanita tree beyond. There was a rocky gully to the right, with olive-green live oaks, a few blooming yucca, and a halfhearted blanket of magenta ice plant.

Ny startled a scrub jay, and barked happily as it flew away. An answering bark sounded from up the trail, and he cocked his head for a moment before bolting out of sight.

I followed the path around the hill and saw him playing with a yellow Lab named Tag. I knew the dog—and her owner. But I didn't know Tag's owner's name, even though we met at least once a week and knew intimate details of each other's dog's lives. He was a middle-aged man with a long, patrician face who always seemed slightly surprised.

"Mornin'," I said.

He glanced at the sky. "Beautiful day."

"Sure is."

We watched the dogs play for a minute. "Did you see the sign?" he asked.

"What sign?"

"Down at the bottom. For Sale. They're selling the land."

"This? Here? They can't be!"

"Already on the market." He seemed to take gloomy satisfaction in the bad news. "Lot for sale. Nine acres."

"I didn't even know it was private property."

"A shame to see it go."

"Are you sure?"

"It's what the sign said. Villa Real Estate."

I knew the name—a Montecito-based company we hadn't worked with much. They were a small office, just a broker and two agents, who mostly did commercial stuff.

I glowered. There weren't many places in Santa Barbara for off-leash dogs. It was a pretty anti-dog town, which made me gnash my teeth. I mean, all the Santa Barbara dog owners I knew were religious about poop-scooping. There were even two guys who went around with extra bags to pick up strange dog-poop, which I believe in many countries is illegal.

"There's always Butterfly Beach," he said sadly.

"Not at high tide."

Tag and her owner said goodbye, and Ny and I continued through the purple and white wildflowers lining the trail. The colors were often muted from dust, but it rained last night, leaving the world fresh and clean. At the top of the trail was a messy meadow with wild lavender and a riot of California poppies, and it was vibrant this morning. A hawk was circling above and bees were busily feeding, and Ny was adorable romping among the flowers and tall grass. I loved spring in Santa Barbara—way better than summer. I walked to the edge of a small overhang. The ocean sparkled in the distance, like it was winking at me.

Ny flopped at my feet, his spotted tongue hanging three feet from his mouth, like a cartoon wolf ogling a woman. I said, "Cool down, sailor," and fed him some water and caught myself gibbering baby-talk at him. I glanced furtively toward the meadow, but I was alone. Thank God. Nothing's more embarrassing than being overheard declaring your undying love to your dog. And was it normal that the only males to whom I've ever said "I love you" were my father and my dog?

Was it normal that I could neither commit to a man or a career?

I used to think I was missing the ambition gene, but actually it's the success gene. Specifically the "fame and fortune at a young age" gene which my sisters got in such abundance. One famous for her beauty, the other for her brains. I wasn't as beautiful as Charlotte or as clever as Emily—though I was prettier than Emily and smarter than Charlotte. So what was left for me—to be famous for my spirituality? Sports? My personality?

Great. My idea of spirituality is a chocolate éclair, my only sport is dog-walking, and my personality is composed of one part sibling rivalry and two parts vague dissatisfaction.

Ny barked and startled me from my self-indulgent gloominess. I was standing on a California mountain overlooking the ocean on a beautiful morning. I had a good man, a steady job and a loving family. It was time to stop whining about Charlotte and Emily.

Well, except I had to pick up Charlotte's gifts and be back to work by noon. Maybe I'd stop whining tomorrow.

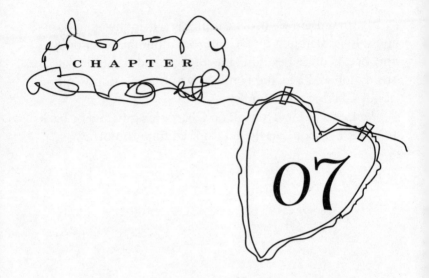

07

Tazza Antiques, scourge of all things new and improved, was located in El Paseo, a slightly old-world marketplace downtown. Traditional Spanish architecture and winding adobe hallways led to quaint gift shops and jewelry stores. It was old-world meets tourist trap. There were a few good restaurants, though—the always-delicious Wine Cask, the cheesy-but-fun Mexican restaurant—and a couple gift stores worth the visit, plus a scattering of offices on the second floor. Natives rarely entered the place, but Emily and Charlotte had stopped at the Wine Cask to buy a few bottles of wine, and had window-shopped the antiques store as they passed.

Tazza was my worst nightmare. Well, actually a thrift store was my greatest horror. I'd spent a decade and a half trapped in "vintage clothing," so the last thing I wanted was to see it displayed on a rack, advertised as if it were a *good* thing. Antiques were supposed to be better than Goodwill leftovers—valuable, chic, possibly elegant—but when you got right down to it, they were just thrift-store gunge from a previous era. Maybe there were no *recent* stains and fluids, but that's about all you could say.

Still, I mustered my familial loyalty, took a deep breath, and pushed my way inside.

The shop was cool, with stone floors, pale peach walls and a wide wooden staircase leading to a loft. A bell over the door jingled pleasantly, and despite the invisible clouds of noxious *old,* the shop smelled clean, of lemon and lavender. There were flowers in a pretty blue-and-white vase on a rich mahogany hall table which I pretended was new and perfectly hygienic. There was a set of Asian-looking chairs and a glass-front cupboard with jugs and spoons and things, and a couple rugs on the floor that were fairly gorgeous—just so long as you didn't start wondering how many generations of sweaty feet had tread upon them.

I stood awkwardly, afraid to venture too far into the sheer agedness of the place. "Hello?"

Movement in the loft. "Be with you in a second," a man's voice floated down. "Feel free to poke around."

The last thing I wanted was to poke. But hovering in the doorway wasn't polite, so I crept inside. I'd come straight from the walk with Ny, and was fairly repulsive and sweaty. I was wearing a gray T-shirt, black shorts, and last-gasp sneakers which were shedding mud from the wet trail onto the expensive aged rugs.

I was scuffing at the dirt, trying to conceal it among the ornate blue and gold pattern of one of the rugs, when the man cleared his throat on the stairs behind me.

I swiveled. My sweaty hair spun. My shoes flaked. I said, "Hi."

He was familiar but I couldn't place him. His hair was dirty-blond, his eyes dirty-blue—and they held a glint of mischief. He stood on the stairs, hand on the railing, looking self-confident and regal—the master of this ancient decrepit domain. He wore gray flannel trousers and a soft blue dress shirt, a thick cotton oxford that looked like it had been worn and washed into perfect comfort. He looked hot. I looked overripe. If I'd been between boyfriends, I would have felt self-conscious. Good thing I had Rip.

"See anything you like?" he asked, walking down the stairs toward me.

Oh, yeah. One thing I wouldn't mind taking home. "I, um—my sister saw an old pot—I mean, an old box. A lacquer box—"

He smiled at my words, and I realized who he was. Ian.

Oh, my God. Not in my loose gray tee and baggy soccer shorts. I crammed my hair behind my ears in a desperate attempt to tidy myself, and toed the ground. Knocking more mud to the floor, of course.

"Anne Olsen!" he said. "How are you? I haven't seen you in years."

"Oh, um—years," I said, thinking: *don't invite him anywhere, don't invite him anywhere.*

Ian hugged me, manfully unafraid of my pig-sweatiness. "You look great," he said, fudging the facts.

"Oh, um," I said. He smelled good, too.

"You don't remember me, do you?"

"Of course I do." What I didn't know—after all this time— was why he'd rejected me when I'd propositioned him eight years ago. I may not be Charlotte, but I'm not repulsive. And he was a man—he wasn't supposed to have standards. Especially not so high that I didn't meet them. "How are you?"

"You don't," he said. "You have no idea who I am."

"I know exactly who you are."

"What's my name, then?"

He looked so pleased with my faulty memory that I couldn't help saying, "Does it start with a D?"

"Sort of," he said. "I can't believe you don't remember."

"Oh, c'mon. How could I forget?" I smiled vaguely. "We had such…great times together."

"Sure did," he said, growing thoughtful. "Remember that time we went skinny-dipping at the reservoir?"

"When we *what?*"

"What a crazy summer that was."

We had never gone skinny-dipping, and he knew it. I tilted my head and said, "How could I forget?"

He nodded, eyes twinkling dangerously. "We'd been downtown for Fiesta, dancing to one of the bands. Back when the lambada was big, remember?" He curled his hands around an imaginary dance partner and rocked his hips—his leg between her imaginary thighs, his hand on her imaginary waist. "Dancing until dark. Midnight in August, one of those hot, steamy nights…"

I steadied myself against a worm-eaten coatrack.

"That's right," he said. "The full moon and the clear sky. We were hanging out on the hood of my car, edge of the water, and you suddenly said, 'That's it! I'm going in.'"

Well, two can play that game. I smiled wistfully, as if remembering. "We were high on Tecate and churro sugar. All sweaty from dancing. The air was sticky and warm and I needed to cool down."

"You took off your shirt…."

"I never! I mean, I never take my top off first. Bottoms up, for me. I took off my skirt, then my panties—"

His eyebrow twitched at *panties*. Men. "That's right," he said. "Bottoms up."

"Then you started stripping down…." Because I refused to be the only imaginary naked person in the game.

"Top down," he said. "Unbuttoned my shirt and tossed it on the hood. Then my jeans and underwear."

"Boxer briefs," I said, in a reverie. "You remember how I prefer boxer briefs."

"The breeze picked up and we walked toward the water and—"

The bell jingled and a middle-aged woman with her teen-age daughter entered. Ian and I sprang apart—I was surprised to discover that I didn't need to straighten my clothes or search for an errant bra. I halfheartedly smoothed my T-shirt anyway and remembered I looked like shit. Hair in pony-tail, no makeup, and soccer shorts. Is there anything de-signed to make a woman's ass look bigger than a pair of soccer shorts? Yeah: an inner tube.

I resolved to keep my front to Ian. Not that I cared. And I mean, who has this kind of conversation with a relative stranger? I hadn't seen the guy in eight years. I couldn't even blame it on alcohol. Must be Wren's influence, awkward flirt-ing. Except it hadn't felt awkward…

"Let me know if there's anything I can help you with," Ian said, looking at the customers but definitely talking to me.

The woman said she was looking for creamwear pitch-ers. Ian murmured something about Wedgwood Queen's Ware, and escorted the woman to a rubbish heap in the cor-ner. I didn't tell the poor woman that there was a Macy's down the block, if she was looking for a pitcher.

The teenage daughter and I rolled our eyes at each other, and I looked around for the lacquer pot Emily said Char-lotte liked. There were a lot of pots. None were new. Be-yond that, I had no idea.

I glanced at Ian. He'd grown. I mean, he wasn't taller or anything, but he'd grown—he was a *man*. Nothing boyish about him, except for the glint in his eye. And his voice, talk-ing about skinny-dipping. God, that was embarrassing. How could I have let this happen? With *Ian!* He was undoubt-edly still in love with Charlotte, too. He was just…used goods. Definitely incestuous. Disgusting. I can't believe I—

Okay, calm down. It was only words. No fluids were exchanged.

Still. Can't believe I had virtual fake memory sex with my sister's ex-boyfriend.

Evidently the woman found what she was looking for, because Ian quickly rang up the sale and came back to me.

"Still don't remember me?" he asked.

"You're starting to ring a distant bell," I said.

"I'll give you a hint. You asked me to your school—"

"I know who you are, Ian! Last I heard, you'd moved to New York."

"Small-town boy lost in the big city. And did you know—" he tried to look horrified "—they have no beach there?"

"Get out!"

"Yeah, and all their malls are *inside*. It's no Santa Barbara, I'll tell you that."

"But it's the place to be if you want to learn—" I waved a hand at the moldering goods he had on display "—all this?"

"Took a couple years, but I finally wandered into Sotheby's training. What've you been up to? What has it been—six years?"

"Eight," I said, then was sorry I'd let him know I'd been counting. "This and that."

"Married?" he asked.

"Divorced."

He eyed me. "Liar."

"Well, I *could've* married. I had offers. How did you know?" He was probably still following Charlotte's career, like a cyber-stalker or something. Probably knew her birthstone and exactly how many centimeters she dilated when she had her kids.

"You're not the marrying type," he said.

"I am too. I just never—"

"Met the right man?"

"Found the right dress. How about you?"

"I don't wear dresses."

"So not married?"

"Nope. I'm engaged, though."

"Engaged? Now? Currently?"

He nodded. "All of the above."

"You can't be flirting like that when you're engaged! Where is she? *Who* is she? What are you thinking? *Skinny-dipping at the reservoir.* You oughta be ashamed, flirting like that."

He laughed. "It's harmless. I dated your sister, so we're like siblings."

That stopped me. "Yuck."

"Well, I wouldn't flirt with my actual sister, Anne."

"Uh-huh. Anyway, Charlotte's why I'm here. I'm supposed to buy some old pot for her birthday."

"Some old pot?"

"Yeah, and if I don't get it Emily will kill me."

"So Emily hasn't changed?"

"No, she's mellowed. These days, she'd kill me painlessly."

"We can't have that. When's Charlotte's birthday? Wait, I should know this—must be this weekend."

I nodded. He still knew her birthday. Pathetic.

"How is she?"

"Good. Three kids. Happily married." I looked at him. "Very happily."

"Mmm. Pity I missed her. She came into the store? My assistant must've been here—I'm surprised she didn't mention seeing Charlotte Olsen."

"Maybe she was wearing a scarf and sunglasses. It's some kind of lacquer pot. Asian or something."

"The Japanese Three Friends teapot?" He moved toward

a display of Zen-looking kitchenware in a bright nook under the stairs. "The bamboo, pine, and plum design represents the Confucian virtue of integrity under—"

"No, no," I said. "Not a teapot. No virtues. It's a box, I think."

"Oh! The lacquerware cosmetic box?" He moved the teapot aside. "An interesting piece. Made from bamboo which is coated with layers of lacquer—twenty-five, thirty layers. The lacquer's a resin secreted by a plant at points of injuries—so they cut channels in the bark of the *Rhus verniciflua,* the sumac trees which…" He babbled on as he searched for the box—then suddenly stopped. "Oh, I forgot—it's gone."

"You sold it?!" I said. "I'm dead. I was supposed to come in two days ago."

"It's not sold. It's on loan to a decorator. When do you need it?"

"Tonight."

"Yikes. Well, I'll give him a call. What time?"

"Dinner's at six." Charlotte insisted on an early dinner, for the kids. And I'd promised her I'd bathe the little monsters before the party. I didn't have time to swing back here after work. "Do you think…it's asking a lot, but could you drop it by Charlotte's?"

"You want your antique delivered? Like it's a pizza?"

"Think of it more as a house call—like a doctor." It certainly wasn't an invitation. I'd meet him, grab the gift, and disappear. This was a delivery only.

He shook his head. "You're impossible."

"To resist?" I asked.

He made a noncommittal noise. "Okay, I'll deliver it."

"Thank you!" I said. "You saved my life."

I paid the extortionate sum for the old relic, sight unseen. Gave Ian Charlotte's address, pretending that I didn't know he'd memorized it from his cyber-stalking, and thanked him profusely.

He told me he'd see me a little before six. "Oh, and don't worry about the rug," he said, eyeing the mud.

I glanced down. "I won't."

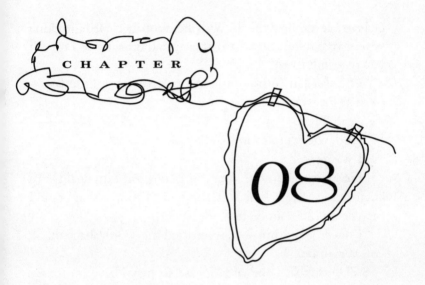

CHAPTER

08

I jogged muddily uptown a few blocks to Element and I slipped into Wren's office before the sleek and nonsweaty salesgirls could bar the door. Wren hit Enter a few times, pretending she hadn't been playing solitaire, and looked up at me. "You're a walking *Fashion Don't*."

"Oh yeah? Well, you're a—" She was impeccable. Wearing a deep V-neck black cashmere sweater, knee-length black skirt, a jade necklace and red heels. "You're a—okay, I'm a disaster. I need a new everything."

"Why?"

Because I just had false-memory sex with a man who thinks this is what I look like. "Charlotte's birthday's tonight."

"I thought it was just family."

"It is, mostly."

"Then why...?"

"You remember Ian?"

"With the overbite?" she asked.

"That's Liam, and it wasn't an overbite. It was a gap. A

chasm. He could whistle with his mouth closed. Anyone would've broken up with him. That wasn't my fault. If you're going to—"

"Oh, *that* Ian. Who you asked to give you a little *ba-da-boom* at Emily's book party."

"Yeah. Him."

"God, you were so in love."

"I wasn't—"

"He's back in town? Are you gonna ask him again?" In an atrocious English accent, she said, "Fancy a shag, Ian? I may be an old slapper, but—"

"I never asked him—I never used the word 'shag,' thank you very much."

Still Dickensian, she said, "Please, sir, may I have another?"

"Would you stop it?"

She giggled. "Well, you did ask if he wanted to get laid, right?"

"Lei-ed! Like a lei, a Hawaiian—" I said, and Wren snorted. "Hey, at least I *do* get laid. Don't make me talk about naked Kevin."

That sobered her right up. "I still can't believe you did that." She meant squirt her with water.

"Has he called yet?"

"If I get pneumonia, it's your fault."

"He'll call," I reassured her. "You'll see him Wednesday, anyway. Wet T-shirt night."

"This, from the girl who wants to use my discount?"

But Wren never could resist dressing me up. I wanted the green Ana Sui dress with red chrysanthemums—because it had the same color combination as Wren's necklace and shoes—but she insisted on more practical items. Although she did encourage me to splurge on a gorgeous pair of Blumarine shoes guaranteed to make my legs look like

Nicole Kidman's, and my feet feel like victims of Chinese foot-binding.

Still. When we finished shopping, I looked positively almost kinda Charlotte-esque. If you squinted.

Barely made it to work by one o'clock, wearing one of my new outfits. I'd bought three, but only spent $700, which sounds like a lot—sounds like more than my weekly after-tax pay, actually—but is in fact a bargain, as I got maybe $1000 worth of clothes. I could return one or two items, but these were the kind of prices—I mean, *pieces*—that made me look both curvy and skinny. I was definitely ten pounds lighter than I'd been in the soccer shorts. Maybe fifteen.

"Morning, Polliwog," Rip said when I knocked on his open door. "Or should I say afternoon? Hey, you know where I can find the Wilkenson file?"

I posed in the doorway instead of answering. He had to have noticed I'd dropped ten pounds.

"Oh, um—how'd the shopping go?" he asked. "What did you get Charlotte?"

I turned sideways to show off my new curves.

"Was forty bucks enough?"

I gave up and tromped into his office. "I got her a plant." I'd picked up something at Honeysuckle, Charlotte's favorite florist, after leaving Element. "Forty was fine."

"A plant?"

"She loves plants. It'll be great. Oh, and Emily insisted I go in with her on some antique thing, for Charlotte."

"So you got two gifts? She's the rich one, you know."

"Rich, beautiful, perfect. How could I forget?"

"How could *anyone* forget? You bring it up every ten minutes." He looked suddenly concerned "Um, listen. I'm showing the Brenners a couple houses at five o' clock—not sure when we'll be done…."

"You're going to miss the party."

"No, no. I'll be there."

"How late?"

He shook his head. "She's the mildew-sniffer, it's like showing a house to a bloodhound. I don't know if we'll be done by six. Probably not. Probably seven. You want me to cancel? I can put them off a few days."

"You'd put off clients, for me?" He'd built his company one client at a time, with word-of-mouth and customer service. He babied his clients terribly—and it was nice to hear he'd baby me even more. "What if you lose the sale?"

"You're worth it."

I gazed adoringly. "Wren says I don't deserve you."

"That's ridiculous," he said. "Of course you don't."

I laughed, hoping he was joking. "I promised Charlotte I'd bathe the kids before dinner, so I have to go early. Just come when you're finished. But thanks."

"It'll all be over tomorrow. At least for another year."

"Yeah."

Except it wouldn't. Sure, I hated Charlotte's birthday. And maybe I was overreacting to Ian's sudden reappearance. But what really troubled me was the VD. I didn't dislike my job, but it was going exactly nowhere. Rip was wonderful, but that made things even worse—why wasn't I head-over-heels?

I had no plan and no passion. I was cast in the shade of my sisters, and though I secretly longed for the sun I was like a…I was a, um…yeesh. I couldn't even think of a good metaphor. What I was, was a loser.

So I brought Rip the Wilkenson project. I updated the Web site with new listings, and returned a few phone calls. Then I fired up my properties database and stared at the wall. Ten minutes later, I grabbed my Recent Developments file. I had a new entry: The Cypress Property, where I walked

Ny. I called Villa Realty, and the receptionist put me through to the listing agent, a woman named Melissa Kent.

"Hi, I'm calling about the property for sale on Cypress Road."

"Have you driven by?" Melissa Kent said warmly. "It's a beautiful piece of land."

"Oh, I walk my dog there all the time," I blurted. "I love it. I was wondering who the owner is."

Her voice grew twenty degrees colder. "I'm not at liberty to say."

"Well…what?"

"I'm not at lib—"

"No. I mean why?"

"The owner would like to remain anonymous."

"How's he gonna sell it if he's hiding behind— What is he, the Wizard of Oz? I'm interested in information. Lot size, asking price, zoning and easements. I promise not to bother him. Or her. Them. Whatever."

"You walk your dog there?" she asked.

"That's how I saw the sign."

"I'm sorry, I wish I could help."

"Well, you *could*—by telling me what I want to know."

"The thing is, the issue is that the owner got some unpleasant phone calls from dog-walkers who felt he shouldn't sell 'their' land."

"Oh, this isn't like that. I'm in the business. I'm calling for an agent. All I need is a little information."

She said nothing, and her silence managed to convey deep suspicion.

"Honest," I said, and started lying. "The broker actually has a client already." More silence, so I got desperate. "A very eager client. Very wealthy. A sheik. From Kuwait."

"I see. And what was your name again?"

I lost my nerve, blurted "Paloma," and hung up. Dammit.

I tried to focus on work, but couldn't. Finally gave up and barged into Rip's office. "Would you call that sea hag at Villa Realty?"

Rip looked startled. "Um, Anne…"

One of the other agents sat across from him at the desk. Mike Malley. Mike was a straight-shooting, foul-mouthed man of about forty. Santa Barbara born and bred, his father had been a fisherman and Mike looked like that's where he belonged: on some boat slippery with fish guts, drinking beer with other burly men. He mostly sold commercial space and had one great advantage as a salesman—nothing ever entered his brain that didn't escape through his mouth, so you had to trust him.

"Sorry, Mike," I said. "Didn't see you there."

"Not a problem," Mike said, standing. "Sea hags wait for no man. I know, I married and divorced one."

"No, no—stay. I didn't mean to interrupt."

"We're done." Mike motioned closing the door behind him. "You want privacy?"

"Please," I said.

"You two keep it up," he said. "And we'll have to get a new cleaning company."

He closed the door, and Rip and I looked at each other— then, by common consent, decided to let Mike's last statement go unanswered.

"Which sea hag?" Rip said. "You really shouldn't barge in when I've got—"

"Melissa Kent," I said. "At Villa. She won't tell me who owns the property on Cypress—where Ny and I walk." I picked up his phone and started dialing.

"Wait," he said. "Anne. No."

"What?"

"I don't want to get between you and—I don't care if you—I think it's great that you have your ideas for development. You could get your license and really make them happen. I know you could. But—"

"It's ringing," I said, and handed him the phone. "Ask for Melissa."

He glared at me, but asked the receptionist for Melissa. They chattered happily for a minute—apparently they'd done some business together. Then they chattered happily for another minute. For a third. A fourth.

I poked Rip and whispered. "Ask her!"

He said, "Listen, Melissa, I've got a question for you." But before he could ask, she apparently started spilling the goods. He said, "Uh-huh? Interesting. Great. When?"

I handed him a pen and mimed that he should be writing this down. So he wrote. I flopped down in the other chair and waited. What I needed was a vision for the property. Maybe a long, winding drive which followed the existing trail, with just a few houses, Montecito cottages really—at two million a pop—hidden among the trees and meadows. Or possibly just one hilltop mansion, a sprawling property with an Olympic pool and more lawn than Versailles.

"Uh-huh," Rip said. "Right." More from Melissa. "Okay. Great, thanks." He made a final notation. "See you then. Bye."

"So?" I said, as he hung up. "What? What did she say?"

"She asked me to lunch." He showed me the paper. It said *Tuesday, 1:30, Village Grill.* "Wants some advice about a house in Summerland I sold a couple years ago."

"What about the Cypress property?"

"I didn't ask."

"Rip!"

"Polliwog, I'm not getting involved in your…whatever. Especially not after Melissa tells me this funny story about a crazy woman who just called, raving about sheiks."

"You could have pretended you had clients," I said. "All I wanted was the information."

"That's so unprofessional, I can't even tell you. Did you check MLS?" The multiple listing service.

"It's not in MLS yet."

"So wait." He stood and kissed me on the cheek. "I'm off to pick up the Brenners. See you tonight?"

"Maybe I should call the city clerk's office," I said. "The tax assessor. Get in touch with the owner directly."

"Why?"

"I don't know. Just because."

"You're bored. You don't like the job."

I didn't say anything.

"We can change your title," he offered. "VP of Administration."

"It's not that."

"Princess of Post-it Notes?"

"I'm fine, Rip. I just want—I dunno. I'm ready for a change."

"Take the course, get your license. You'd be a great Realtor. You know you should."

"Yeah, yeah. I'm not living up to my potential."

He shook his head. "Do I need to bring anything to Charlotte's?"

"Just the plant from the back of my truck when you get there. It's too heavy for me to lift."

"Sure. And Anne? Keep away from the tax assessor's office."

I worked until 5:15, and didn't place any calls Rip would disapprove of. Double-checked the weekend's open houses, and tidied some loose ends. It was Friday, and the weather was gearing up for the weekend. I stepped out of the office into a bright and balmy afternoon, with a hot sun and a cool breeze. One of those days that even the locals go to Longboards on the wharf to sip margaritas and eat calamari.

In even better news, my pale lilac top and linen skirt still looked good when I got home—the true test of new clothes. The linen didn't even wrinkle in the truck. See? It pays to spend more. Not to mention all the time I saved, not having to stare at my desolate closet, wondering what to wear.

Hair and makeup were another story. I was nearing the end of my haircut cycle, so everything was a bit shaggy and my roots were showing. A bad sign, considering my hair wasn't colored. I tended to be a makeup minimalist—lipstick, blush and mascara, all done in two minutes. If I wanted to go glossy I usually relied on Charlotte to fix me up, but I couldn't ask on her birthday. Besides, she'd wonder why, and I didn't want to explain about Ian. Not only that we'd had counterfeit imaginary sex, but that he was stopping by with her gift.

I honestly didn't know why I always skipped a beat with Ian. Kevin the nude model was just as handsome, and a whole lot nakeder. Rip was wonderful, and he was all mine— not engaged to some mysterious woman and a purveyor of aged yuck. Ian was an awkward childhood humiliation who kept reappearing, like an uncomfortable suspicion. At least I hadn't invited him anywhere. Sure he was going to stop by the party, but a delivery didn't count as an invitation.

So I did my hair and makeup myself, adding lip gloss and foundation in an attempt to appear polished, and avoided seeing Charlotte altogether.

I snuck in from the patio and up to the kids' bedrooms, where I found Hannah doing handstands against the wall in the hallway. She was seven, and from birth had been the prima donna her mother had never become. Hannah ruled the house with an iron—though diminutive—fist. The only person she'd consistently obey was David, who she physically resembled and completely adored. Charlotte was too gentle to impress her, and she listened to me about half the time. I'd gone Emily on her tiny pink butt once or twice, and it had apparently made an impression. Her little brothers—Kyle, five, and Tyler, four—were her minions, and did her evil bidding with hyperactive glee.

"I'm doing gymnastics," Hannah said, and shook her head to get the hair out of her face.

"You're getting dirt on the wall, banana," I told her. Like I was one to complain about making messes with sneakers. I grabbed her ankles and spun her around. She squealed—she loved roughhousing—and I carried her into her bedroom and tossed her on the bed.

She bounced on her mattress. "Do it again!"

But I sent her to round up the imps, instead. Fortunately, because this involved bossing them around, she was easy to convince.

Still, it was a quarter of six by the time I got the bath running. I offered a prayer to the God of Ritalin that the little nerve-wrackers would leap quickly in and out of the tub. Sadly, the God of Ritalin had apparently been replaced by the God of Cocoa Puffs.

I'd finally corralled the boys in the bathroom when Hannah discovered she couldn't find Bath Barbie.

"It's not a *bath* without Bath Barbie," she wailed.

"Check your room, quick, while the boys get in," I told her. "She's probably hiding under the bed."

"Bath Barbie doesn't hide."

"Then she's napping—go!"

"She doesn't nap, either," she said. "She's Bath Barbie. She *bathes.*"

I herded her into her room. "Check in the pile—" the mountain of toys in the corner. "And the closet."

"She's not in the closet," she whined. "I can't take a bath without Bath Barbie."

"You might have to make do with—" I glanced around the room "—Bath Bunny. Or I'll just toss you in the tub with your Bath Brothers."

That got her attention. She started digging through the heap of toys and I went back to the bathroom and was greeted by the sound of splashing. The little angels were bathing themselves!

"What great guys you are—" Then I stepped inside. They'd poured a gallon of shampoo into the tub, and were sitting amid heaps of bubbles, fully dressed. Playing Tidal Wave. "Out! Out!"

They collapsed in giggle fits. Usually they were easier than Hannah, because they were used to bowing under the lash of her tyranny. But, of course, not tonight. I grabbed a couple of soggy shirts and dragged them from the tub.

"You little monsters. You know better than that."

"Tyler had an accident," Kyle explained, as I yanked them out of their clothes.

"I had an accident," Tyler said.

"He was cleaning up."

"What kind of accident?" I asked, sniffing the air like a nervous antelope.

"She's not under the bed!" came Hannah's voice, from her room.

"Look in the closet!" I yelled. "Is she in the dollhouse?"

"A wee-wee accident," Tyler said.

Thank God. "So why'd *you* get in?" I asked Kyle, tugging his socks off as he sat with his bare bottom on the floor.

He started giggling again. Clearly it had just looked like a good time. "We used soap," he told me.

"You used shampoo." I sluiced off the top of the bubble-mountain with my arm, remembering a moment too late that I was still wearing my $200 pale lilac ensemble. "Dam-arnit!" I said. "Now you two—back in there and wash."

"She's not in the dollhouse!" came the Bath Barbie update. "Aunt Anne, the doorbell's ringing!"

"Look under the bed," I yelled. "Would someone get the door?" And, to the boys: "Back in the bath! Or you can forget about birthday cake."

"But we decorated it," Tyler said, tears imminent.

Like a good mother, I immediately backtracked. "You can have cake! Just take your bath fast, and I'll give you extra. You'll be fat as Ny in no time."

In their world, fat as Ny was a wonderful goal. They both did the hot-pepper-excited hop before splashing tubward. I'd have to sneak them extra bites, when Charlotte wasn't looking.

"It's still ringing!" Hannah yelled. "Somebody should get the door—oh!"

"Hannah?" I called from the hall. "Pick someone else if you can't find Bath Barbie."

"Help!" she cried, in a muffled voice. "Help me!"

Uh-oh. I raced into her room. She was gone. "Hannah?"

"I'm stuck." A little voice, from behind the bed. "Back here."

Only her calves were showing, sticking up between the bed and the wall. "You fell down the bunny hole," I said, laughing.

She kicked her feet. "Bath Barbie's down here, but I can't reach her."

"Hold on…" Her bed was a heavy wood four-poster, painted white with green vines on the posts. I heaved it away from the wall as the doorbell rang again—and Hannah fell sideways to the floor and disappeared with a clunk.

A second later, she poked her head up, dust bunnies tangled in her hair. Which now needed washing. "I can almost reach her!"

"Doesn't Mommy ever clean?" I crawled under the bed,

hooked a finger around Bath Barbie's neck and dragged her out. "Ta da!"

Hannah grabbed her triumphantly. I made her say thank you, and the doorbell was still ringing as we entered the hall on our way to the bathroom.

"Will somebody get that?" I yelled down the stairs.

"I'll get it," Hannah said.

"Someone other than you." I marched her into the bathroom and Kyle and Tyler were gone. All that remained was a pile of sodden clothes and a trail of wet footprints on the terra-cotta floor.

"Get in," I told Hannah.

"It's dirty." She wrinkled her nose.

"Run a new one. I'll be up in a minute to help wash your hair. I have to find your brothers."

I turned and caught sight of myself in the mirror. The steam from the bathroom and exertion from the kids had caused my face to sweat and my hair to frizz. One of my sleeves was frothed with bubbles and there were dust bunnies clinging to my skirt. I opened the bathroom door and Tyler launched himself at me like a greased piglet.

"Here we are!" he said. Wet, naked, and clinging to my new clothes.

"We answered the door." Kyle swaggered in, naked and dripping.

"Thanks," I said. "Who was it?"

A man stepped in from the hall. "Me."

I brushed a cobweb from my face. "Ian! Hi! How are you? Stay for dinner?"

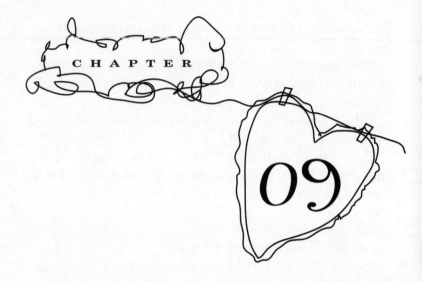

CHAPTER

09

Okay, so I invited him. So what? Anyone would have done it. It was a reflex. An impulse. It doesn't mean anything. I'd actually intended to invite him. It was planned. Premeditated. It was only polite. He'd delivered the gift, I couldn't *not* invite him. He was being kind of pushy, when you thought about it. What kind of person arrives to a party with a gift? The kind who expects to be invited. He basically invited himself. It was boorish. Rude. I really expected better....

Actually he'd been wonderful. He brought the age-encrusted relic, beautifully gift-wrapped. He didn't cringe at my dust-bunny meets bubble-thing appearance. And he'd even shepherded the naked boys into clothes while I finished with Hannah. I really had no other choice but to invite him.

I only hoped Charlotte wouldn't be mad. Emily certainly was. I was downstairs in the living room enjoying aperitifs and appetizers, when Emily culled me from the herd of crostini-eaters and backed me against the French doors. "It's her *birthday,*" she snapped. "Nobody wants the high school boyfriend at her thirty-fifth birthday."

"So I invited him," I said. "So what? Anyone would have done it. It wasn't planned or premeditated. There were dust bunnies on my ass—"

"How could you be so selfish? How do you think Charlotte feels?"

Before I could answer, Charlotte's silvery laugh floated from across the room where she was chatting with Ian. They were standing by the mantel, candlelight illuminating their faces. Charlotte was stunning in a short, burgundy velvet dress with a mandarin collar. She laughed again and touched Ian's arm. They were glowing so brightly, it took me a moment to realize that David, for some reason wearing a green Hawaiian shirt, was with them.

"Oh, she's weeping," I said, wondering why I'd chosen pale lilac instead of burgundy velvet.

"She always *looks* happy," Emily said. "That doesn't mean she is."

"What does Charlotte Olsen have to be unhappy about?"

"You'd be surprised," she said.

"Name one thing."

Emily opened her mouth, then closed it again. Even her oversized brain had trouble with that one. Finally, she said, "Her bratty younger sister."

"Oh, Emily, you're not that bad," I told her, and slipped back toward the safety of the herd.

There were about twenty people. The immediate family and a number of Charlotte's and David's closest friends, mostly from David's hospital. We milled around, sipping wine and talking about medicine: this crowd could really get in a lather about HMOs and payment plans. They were the unsexy friends that Charlotte and David preferred. There was a B-list of friends, too, made up of people on, well, the actual A-list, from Charlotte's modeling days. But most of her real friends were of the unglamorous sort.

I avoided Ian, doing an invisible contra dance with him across the room. Every time he approached, I withdrew. He went left, I went right. I almost got trapped between a blond sofa and a brunette neurologist during one do-se-do, but slipped nimbly out to the deck and back in through the kitchen to save myself. My theory was that if we weren't seen together, I could pretend it hadn't been me who'd invited him.

As I closed the door to the kitchen behind me, a heavy hand landed on my shoulder. I froze. It would be Emily hopping after me with her hatchet. I turned slowly, resolved to meet my doom, and saw that the heavy hand belonged to the caterer. A harried-looking woman in her late forties with no body fat and an inordinate number of freckles.

I beamed in relief and babbled, "Oh! I was just outside. On the deck. Then I came in. Here. To the kitchen."

"We're ready to serve dinner," she told me, wiping a strand of hair from her face.

"Right. Right! Should I let everyone know?"

She thought that was a fine idea, so I slunk into the other room and told Emily, the idea being that she'd spring into action and shove everyone into their chairs. She glared at me, instead. "He's flirting with her!"

Oh, here we go. I peeked over her shoulder. Ian was chatting with David. Charlotte was nowhere in sight. "What, telepathically?"

Her glare hardened. "Don't be stupid."

"Calm down, Em."

"I won't calm down. It's disgusting."

"It's harmless flirtation. They dated, they're like siblings." I shuddered, unable to believe I'd just said that. "I mean, not like sibling-siblings. More like cousins. Kissing cousins. No. That's wrong, too. Anyway, it's harmless."

"They *dated?*" she asked. "Who dated?"

I glanced at her wineglass. "How much have you had?"

"Anne, focus." She nodded across the room. "She's half his age."

I followed her nod. Dad was talking with the caterer at the kitchen door. Looking a little more animated than usual, but nothing sinister. Well, he was intensely focused on her face. Probably trying to see if he could identify freckle constellations. I expected him to rear back any moment and say: "There! I found Cassiopeia!"

But he didn't rear. He drained his wineglass and chuckled as the caterer refilled. He gestured, offering her a sip, and when she refused he made serious inroads into that glass, too. Hmm. He wasn't much of a drinker, normally.

"Ah-ha!" Emily said.

"So he's flirting a little…."

"She's half his age." Emily lived in fear that Dad would marry a woman who was younger than his daughters. "She's twelve!"

"She's pushing fifty," I said. "And he doesn't have a chance, anyway. Coming on to a caterer is no cakewalk."

"It's not funny."

"What is up with you? She's just asking if he wants tabouleh."

"You'll see," Emily said. "She's already got him drinking. She'll be bringing him waffles in bed, next."

"Better than cold cereal."

"Fine," she snapped. "Forget it."

She stalked into the thick of the party and herded everyone toward the dining room, like a bad-tempered sheepdog. I watched her and sighed. A bad-tempered sheepdog who was feeling out of control of her own life. Her book, her family: Emily always lashed out when she was worried.

I trailed behind as I worried about her being worried. Her

book must really be a problem. Maybe she'd told Jamie she wanted another publisher. I glanced at him, settling down between a househusband and a dermatologist. He was extracting his napkin from the napkin-ring, and he smiled when he saw me looking—totally unconcerned.

Maybe it was only my overactive imagination. I took a calming guzzle of wine and surveyed the room. The party had a Moroccan theme and the dining room had been decorated in casual Casbah. The room was lit by candles in the hanging silver candelabra, with other white candles placed among the fuchsia and violet silks lining the table. More silk had been artfully twined around the chair backs and gold-embroidered white pillows had been placed on the seats.

As I walked around the table, I saw that the children had made place cards, with Magic Markers on card stock. Mine had a picture of what I assumed was Ny, but might've been Hamtaro. The card next to mine was blank, and ripped in half. Hannah's work: she loved "Rip." Thought nothing was better than a verb for a first name. She spent three weeks after meeting Rip trying to convince her parents to call her "Crash."

But Rip himself wasn't there. He'd called to say the Brenners were making an offer on one of the houses, he'd be here as soon as he could, and we shouldn't wait. So we weren't—though we were keeping his seat warm. *We* being Ian.

I paused by my chair and looked down at him. There was no dance-step to get me out of *this.*

He glanced at my place card. "The resemblance is striking."

I thought of a hundred cutting responses, then said, "Ha, ha."

"No appreciation of primitive art? I thought you were an artist—weren't you going to art school?"

I plopped into my seat. "Sort of." Actually, I'd forgotten all about art school.

"Sort of?" His smile widened.

"I can't believe you remember that."

"I have the memory of an elephant."

I nodded solemnly. "And the huge gray ears."

"Fortunately the thick skin, too."

"So, you have any hobbies?"

"Hobbies?"

I shrugged. "It's a topic. I've got others, if you'd like to switch."

"Hobbies is fine," he said. "Just antiques."

"That's your job, not your hobby."

"That's the thing with antiques, they're more than a job. The more you learn, the more you realize you don't know— with history and greed and art all wrapped up together— until they become a consuming passion."

I smiled politely. "That's nice."

"What was *that?*" he asked.

"That what?"

"On your face. That sneer."

"It wasn't a sneer. It's a smile." I forced my face into a wide Charlotte beam. "See?"

"*That* is rictus."

"Hey! That's my Charlotte smile."

"When Charlotte smiles, she means it." He glanced down the table at Charlotte. "Nothing fake about her."

"Except her tits," I lied.

"What?"

"Implants."

"Oh, they are not."

"How would you know?"

A smug expression settled on his face, and I remembered: ex-boyfriend. Ick. Why was I even chatting with this second-hand man? He should've been tossed in the Goodwill bin years ago. Okay, maybe I found him attractive—but I found

Charlotte's cast-off clothing attractive, too, and I didn't go rummaging in her dirty laundry, did I?

"Well, gross," I said.

"Ah," he nodded, faux apologetically. "My mistake. I shouldn't have mentioned fake tits. Sometimes my mouth runs away from me."

I said, "Ha, ha."

Across the table, Charlotte was talking about an upcoming photo shoot for *Organic Style.*

"What sort of pictures are organic?" one of the anesthesiologists asked.

"The focus is on style, really," Charlotte said.

"Hemp bikinis," David teased.

Charlotte blushed. How could she still blush after appearing on newsstands for years wearing two square inches of Saran Wrap? Of course, she never really blushed. Not like I do, flushing and blotchy. She glowed. Her tawny skin deepened and her eyelashes lowered and the tinkling of silverware went silent as everyone stared. Sometimes her unearthly alien beauty was too much, like all of a sudden you realized you were having dinner with one of the elf women in *Lord of the Rings.*

I almost asked David to check if her ears were pointy. Instead, I caught Ian grinning down at his plate in a clearly meaningful manner.

"I don't want to hear it," I said.

"I was just thinking—you and your sisters."

"What about us?"

"That's it," he said, shaking his head. "You and your sisters."

"What's that supposed to mean? It's not English. There's no verb there. You need a verb. Me and my sisters *what?* Didn't you ever diagram sentences? Subject verb object. Like, 'You eat funny.' You can't just say, 'You.' There's no *there,* there."

"I eat funny?"

"There you go! Now *that* is a sentence!"

"'Funny' isn't a direct object, Anne."

"It is from where I'm sitting," I said. I didn't know exactly what that meant, but it made him laugh.

He started to reply but David caught his eye and said, "So, Ian—I hear you're engaged?"

"Yep." Ian nodded. "For three months, now."

"Have you set a date?" one of the women asked.

"Well, we have a date by which we intend to have a date. We're taking things slow. Actually, she'd have married me already, but she can't find the right dress." He smiled at Charlotte, across the table, and there was just a bit too much warmth. "Which brings back memories."

"Oh, God," Charlotte said. "I can't believe you remember that."

"Elephant," I muttered.

"Ian and I went out in high school," Charlotte explained to the table. "There was a prom dress fiasco."

"I bought the wrong corsage," Ian said.

"It clashed," Charlotte said. "So I broke up with him! Well, for ten minutes. My first true love."

She squeezed David's hand as she spoke, making it clear who her *final* true love was. Still, there was a fluttering of interest in Ian at these words, and the gastroenterologist said, "You must've been the luckiest boy in school."

"This was during Charlotte's looming, gawky phase," Ian said. "It was like dating Lurch from the Addams Family."

Everyone laughed, and Charlotte's color deepened. The truth was, despite what supermodels always say in interviews, Charlotte didn't have an awkward stage. She was a beautiful child. Then a beautiful teen, then a beautiful adult. She'd undoubtedly be a beautiful crone and leave a beautiful corpse.

"What does your fiancée do?" Emily asked, changing the subject in her subtle way. Because Emily was still in her awkward phase.

"She's a vice president at Mott & Kensig," Ian said. "Financial services. Far as I can tell, all she does is fire people. It seems like there should be more to it, but Helene says not."

I stabbed at my couscous moodily. *I* wanted to be a vice president at a place with an ampersand. The only person I could fire was the guy who took care of the office aquarium, and even that was questionable.

"How did you meet her?" Charlotte asked.

"She collects seals. Antique wax seals. I had an 18th-century French Rococo silver seal which…"

Everyone perked with interest when they realized Ian was an antiques dealer. You lower your vigilance for one second, and a birthday dinner turns into the fucking Antiques Roadshow.

"I have a family quilt," one of the women was saying. "Someone said it was an appliqué, and I've never understood what that is."

Ian said blah blah blah: "—most popular from about the 1770s to the 1850s, or thereabouts, and—"

The woman beamed as he spoke. She was thrilled to be using a quilt handed down by unwashed ancestors who'd undoubtedly died of the prehistoric crotch-pox.

I'd rather be skinny-dipping.

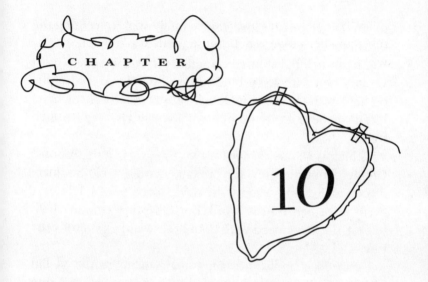

CHAPTER

10

Charlotte had always been a tedious gift opener. She unties the bows instead of yanking them off, and carefully unlatches each individual piece of tape instead of ripping the paper. Like she has to reuse the wrapping paper, because Charlotte Olsen can't afford to buy the whole factory.

Plus, she discusses the merits of each card before even beginning this quasi-surgical unwrapping procedure. And when I say merits, I mean merits. Discussing the flaws would be too much fun. Instead, she carefully removes the card—think a slow game of Operation—and reads it aloud, with real pleasure, before beginning her gift-wrap vivisection.

It's always driven me nuts. I'm a ripper and a shredder. I glance at the card to see who to thank—or blame—and fall on my presents like a hungry lion on a limping antelope. So I usually made a point of fleeing at the first sign of Charlotte's tape-lifting and bow-untying—to the bathroom, the kitchen, a root canal, *anything*—but tonight I was pinned next to my father on the love seat, with Emily's son Zach and Charlotte's boys sprawled on top of us.

Charlotte lifted a slim rectangular present, wrapped in silver and tied with a sky-blue ribbon. She placed it carefully on her lap and beamed at David. "Wasn't that lovely of Wes? I can't believe he remembered! I've always loved bonsai trees."

Which was fine, except for two things. First, she was still talking about the previous present, a coffee-table book on Zen gardens. And second, she never loved bonsai. I'd never even heard her use the word. But Charlotte couldn't help herself, she was cursed with both beauty and a generous nature.

I glanced at Emily, and caught her glancing at me. We did simultaneous eye rolls. Nothing like shared misery to bring us together.

"Who's that from?" I said, nodding toward the new present. If I didn't hurry things along, we'd be here till Wednesday.

"Remember that trip to Japan?" Charlotte said, still going on about the bonsai book. "I loved Kyoto."

I groaned.

Twenty minutes later, she'd untied the bow around the silver gift. She'd already admired the sentiments of the card, and it only took five more minutes to remove the wrapping without a single rip.

"It's beautiful paper," she said. "I love the pattern…"

And on it went. She gushed over a hideous malachite letter opener, a half-dozen salad forks to replace some missing from her pattern (which I considered a pretty good gift actually—they were new and cost a fortune) and a gift box of Kiehls cleansers and creams. You'd never guess the bathroom closet was already crammed with the same products.

Approximately three years later, she got to my gift. Well,

the first of my gifts—the antique *objet* I'd bought with Emily. Ian had wrapped it in glossy lavender paper with creamy French ribbon and a white rose which Emily eyed approvingly. I wasn't so sure. Was it really honest to camouflage an old, *old,* extremely used gift with expensive paper and a new ribbon? I'm thinking he should have rolled it up in last week's funny pages.

But I should count my blessings. At least it was actually here.

Charlotte painstakingly opened. Halfway through, she paused to ask Hannah to find a bud vase for the rose. We waited. The vase was found and rose admired. Finally, the unwrapping continued. And at tortuous length, she withdrew the antique box from the saved paper.

"It's a Chinese cosmetics box," Emily said. "From the Han Dynasty."

"When was that?" my father asked Ian.

"About 200 BC to 220 AD," he said. "This piece is late Western Han, definitely AD."

I suppressed a shudder. Can you even imagine how many people owned it over the past two thousand years, how many saved their germ-ridden cosmetics and greasy keepsakes inside? How many people had handled it, sneezed on it? We're talking a lot of personal oils and fluids. Back in 823 it was probably someone's chamber pot. Then was shipped to England just in time for the Black Plague. You wouldn't install a toilet from a public bathroom in your house, but you pay through the nose to put this thing on your mantel.

"Is it porcelain?" someone asked.

"It's lacquer," Emily said.

"Lacquerware," Ian said. "The structure is actually shaped from bamboo, then coated with lacquer for the finish."

I telepathically instructed him not to give his whole lacquerware lecture, with the *Rhus verniciflua* and secreted resin.

He apparently heard, because he subsided without saying more than, "Could be as many as thirty coats."

"It's beautiful." Charlotte smiled at Emily. "And almost exactly like the one we saw in Ian's shop." She turned the brilliant Charlotte Olsen smile on Ian, and I was surprised that his heart didn't burst from his chest. "I still can't believe you own that wonderful—"

"It's not *like* the one in his shop, Charlotte," Emily said.

"But it has the—"

"It *is* the one."

"Well, not exactly," Charlotte said.

"Chinese red and black lacquer cosmetics box." Emily stalked over to get a better look. "This is the one you liked."

"I love this one! I really do. It's lovely." Charlotte blushed, embarrassed that we'd think she didn't like our gift. "It's even better. But it's a little different. The pattern isn't the same. See?"

Emily inspected, and the room held its breath, sensing the perfect setup for an Emily explosion. She finally nodded and handed the box gently back to Charlotte and slowly swiveled until she had me in her sights. "This isn't the box," she said.

"It is!" I said, doomed.

"It's not. Ian?"

He lifted his hands to express neutrality. "It's a Chinese lacquer box. A very fine one."

"I told you to get the one in the window," Emily snapped at me.

The *window?* "She likes this one better," I said.

"She does not."

"She does." I turned to Charlotte. "Don't you?"

"Much better. I love it. It's wonderful. It's the best—"

"You hate it," Emily said.

"I don't!"

"Anne, I told you—"

"Emily," Ian interrupted, and Emily, uncharacteristically, let him continue. "The other box is in my shop. It's my fault. I was a little…distracted when Anne came in. We can exchange them, okay?"

"I like this one better," Charlotte insisted.

"You don't," Emily said. "We'll exchange it. And Anne," she said pointedly, "will be happy to pick it up."

"I'm not distracting," I said to no one in particular.

During the post-present lull, I happened to notice Ian standing by himself on the deck. He looked natural, standing there. At home in Montecito, sort of wealthy-casual. He fit the house, and the deck, and even Charlotte, better than her husband did. Not that David wasn't wonderful, but Ian looked more the part.

And since I'd sort of invited him—or whatever—I thought it'd only be polite if I did the hostess thing. He turned when he heard the French doors open, and smiled when he saw me. Possibly a trifle seductively. So maybe we flirted a bit at his shop—maybe more than a bit—but he was still Charlotte's ex-boyfriend. Which means first, it's quasi-incestuous for him to be smiling at me in a sexy fashion. And second, he's used goods. He's as bad as the Chinese box, though possibly without the Black Death. Plus, he's engaged and therefore shouldn't be smiling at me at all. So I'd have to let him down—politely, of course, and in a hostess-type fashion.

"It's great to see Charlotte again," he said. "Thanks for inviting me."

"Oh." The smile had been for Charlotte. "You're welcome."

He watched her through the doors. She was scolding the boys, and looked maternal and rather old, and I felt a warm rush of pleasure—for once, I outshone Charlotte.

"She's gotten even more beautiful," he said. "She has the sort of beauty that grows as she ages. Like a patina."

Wonderful. And worse, he was right. Despite no longer being swimsuit-ready, the years and a little extra weight had softened her. She may not have been model-skinny, but she glowed.

"Of course, she has an awful personality," I said.

"A real shrew."

I glanced at Emily, who was involved in a lively debate inside. "Which sister are we talking about?"

He laughed. "It's good to see Emily, too."

"Sorry about that mix-up with the gift."

"No problem. I'm actually sort of perversely pleased."

Because he'd get to see me again, when I picked up the correct box?

"Because Emily on the warpath is quite a sight." His tone was warm and admiring, so I figured he'd never *really* seen her on the warpath. "She kinda sparks when she gets going."

"Sparky Olsen, we call her."

He smiled softly into the living room. "I can't believe she married her publisher."

"Oh, that's right. You were here the summer they were secretly dating. She married him like a month later."

"They seem happy together."

I nodded.

"And you, Anne—you haven't changed much, have you?"

Didn't he notice I'd lost ten pounds since he saw me that morning? And my curves were curvier? And I wasn't wearing soccer shorts? "That's right, I'm still twenty-two," I said. "On the inside."

"Tell me about your boyfriend," he said, instead of telling me I was twenty-two on the outside, too. "What's he like?"

"Nothing special," I said. "Handsome, successful, charming. Smart and funny. Likes dogs and sunsets and water-skiing and long walks in the rain."

He laughed. "Sounds great."

"He is." I wanted to make Rip sound as glamorous and wonderful as Ian's fiancée. But, somehow, this slipped out: "He really rings my bell."

Rings my bell?

As I cast about for a way to extricate myself from my embarrassment, I saw the man himself enter the living room. Rip, bearing gifts. And even through the French doors I could see that his entrance was creating quite a stir.

He was carrying the plant I'd bought for Charlotte at Honeysuckle. It was a cactus with a large green spiky stem, and grafted on top was another cactus of bulbous proportions and a rosy hue. Among the other cacti at the flower shop, it had appeared festive and innocent. Clasped at Rip's waist, wiggling at Charlotte, it resembled nothing so much as an enormous spiny erection. Adding to this little tableau was Charlotte making her usual big-eyed pleasure at such a wonderful gift.

"That your boyfriend?" Ian asked.

I nodded.

"Rings your bell, huh?"

I looked from the cactus to Ian. "Don't be a prick."

Later, as I was sitting on the couch waiting for cake, Hannah plopped down next to me. She leaned against my side affectionately. It was touching, how much she loved her aunt.

"You shouldn't be so obvious," she said.

"What?"

"Around boys."

"I shouldn't *what?*"

"Be so obvious. You're all ooly over him."

"Obvious? Do you even know what that means?"

"It means," she said, haughtily, "you have a crush on Ian."

"I'm a grown-up. Grown-ups don't get crushes."

"Well, *you* do."

"I don't."

"Do!"

"Don't!"

"Do-do-dooooooooooooo!"

I refrained from sticking my tongue out at her. "What about Uncle Rip?"

Hannah rolled her eyes.

"Let's check on the cake," I said.

"Does *Ian* like cake?"

"Stop it," I said. "Little hellion."

"Or what?"

"Or I'll drown Bath Barbie."

The cake was adorable. The caterers had done a beautiful job, which was only improved by the hodgepodge of sloppy frosting-writing and pictograms Charlotte's kids had scrawled on top.

"Is that a dog or Mommy?" David asked the boys.

It was a monkey.

The caterers set the cake in front of Charlotte, with plates and a silver server. Thirty-five candles. Charlotte beamed around the room, her big blue eyes warm with love. She cut the first piece and said, "It's so wonderful having—having everyone—" And she started weeping. Not in joy, in sorrow. Great, gulping tears welling up from a mile underground. "I'm sorry," she choked. "I'm sorry."

She ran from the room, and Emily and I both stood to follow. Dad caught our eyes and shook his head, so we just stood awkwardly as David went after her. Then Emily cut the cake and I started teasing Rip about the phallic cactus, and the party continued as if nothing had happened.

But something had happened. Something awful. If Charlotte Olsen was unhappy, what chance did the rest of us have?

After everyone left, I put the kids to bed. The boys were exhausted and coated with a fine mist of sucrose from all the dessert they'd eaten. I bullied them through the face washing and the tooth brushing and deposited them in their beds. They'd been basically sleepwalking for the past half hour, so they were snoring before I left the room.

Hannah put herself to bed these days, but still demanded a good-night kiss. I thought she'd be asleep, too, but she was sitting against her headboard waiting for me.

"Why was Mommy crying?" she asked.

A good question. I was stumped. I couldn't think of a single reason. Charlotte had reappeared five minutes after her weepy exit, fresh-faced and claiming she was just nervous about the *Organic* photo shoot, because she hadn't worked in a while. But she'd never been able to lie convincingly. Not to her sisters, at least.

"Sometimes mommies just need a good cry," I said.

Hannah considered. "What makes a cry good?"

"If you feel better afterward."

"Then I always have good cries," she said. True enough—she was a fit-pitcher of the first order, and usually got her way in the end, which would make *anyone* feel better.

I kissed her forehead and turned the light off. I was still stuffed from dinner, but had the anxiety nibbles. Emily was carping, Charlotte was crying. And they were the successful sisters. My chances for happiness seemed impossibly remote if even they couldn't achieve it. So just one more bite of the *b'stilla* (chicken and almonds stuffed in sweet buttery pastry) and I could relax. Nothing calmed me so well as gluttony.

I crept into the kitchen, and found David putting the last few dishes into the dishwasher.

"Thanks, Anne," he said. Meaning for putting the kids to sleep.

"No problem." I opened the fridge and rummaged through the leftovers. What was the best snack to soothe my worries? Gossip, probably. "Hannah wanted to know why Charlotte was crying."

"Oh?"

I nodded, grabbing the *b'stilla*. "She was waiting up."

"What did you tell her?"

"That mommies need a good cry, sometimes."

"Can't argue with that."

"Even *she* couldn't argue with that!"

He smiled and finished loading the dishwasher.

"But, um…" I set the food on the counter and dug into it with my fingers. "I dunno what I'd have said if, y'know, she'd pursued it."

"I'm sure you would've thought of something."

"Yes, but—I wonder what, exactly. I mean…" I let my voice trail off, hoping he'd fill in the blanks. "I wouldn't want to say the wrong thing."

"No fear of that."

"David! Why *was* Charlotte crying?"

He dried his hands. "Mommies need a good cry sometimes," he said, and tossed the dishrag at me as he left the room. "Night, Anne."

Ny was waiting on my lawn when I got back to the cottage—the kids must've let him out. He hippity-hopped over to greet me, leading with his tongue. After the sponge bath, he turned his olfactory attention to the package in my hand. I set the bowl of lamb stew on the ground, and Ny did what he did best.

I watched him with satisfaction. Maybe David would refuse to share marriage secrets, but I got my revenge. No leftovers for him.

"Okay, fatboy," I said when Ny was licking the bowl clean for the second time. "Wanna go for a walk?"

"Sounds great," a voice said in my ear.

I leapt out of my skin and clutched my pounding heart.

"Sorry I was late," Rip said, wrapping his arms around me from behind.

"You killed me!"

"The party was that bad?"

"I'd tell you all about it, but I'm dead."

"Lucky for you, the doctor is in…" He turned me in his arms and resuscitated me.

I breathlessly said, "Necrophiliac."

He nuzzled my neck. "For you, Polliwog, I'd even give the kiss of life to—dog."

"To *what?*"

He pulled away, glanced downward. "The dog."

Ny was at our feet, watching intently. His tail was wagging softly in lazy pleasure. Rip removed his hands from my good bits and looked abashed.

"He's a *dog,* Rip!"

"He's got that look in his eyes again. That glint. He's positively Machiavellian. Look at him. I swear he's plotting something."

I laughed. "He's plotting a walk."

"Then let's walk. Anything to keep him happy."

"You want to come with us?" I was suspicious. Usually Rip would suggest that we close Ny in the kitchen and finish what we'd started. But this time he assured me he did want to walk. Probably to placate me. He had been three hours late, so I suppose I had every right to be miffed. But I'd been a little too Emily of late, and the truth was, I wasn't mad at all. In fact, I hadn't even missed him. Ian and I had been keeping each other amused, and—

I stopped suddenly. That wasn't right. Yes, Ian was appealing. But so was Rip. The only reason to prefer Ian was an acute case of VD. Which I didn't have.

So I cut the walk short, and proved that I was, in fact, satisfied. And proved it again early Saturday morning. I loved sex on Saturday mornings. Lazy and decadent, like the day was meant for pleasure. Rip agreed, and we drifted from bed to brunch. There was a newish restaurant downtown called Mississippi Junction. Not Southern Californian so much as Southern/Californian. The waitresses wore overalls and served chicory coffee. You could order fried green tomatoes and grits and biscuits (all delicious) and even okra (questionable, but tasty). Sort of southern nouvelle cuisine.

I sipped my chicory and sighed in happy contentment. Rip was perfect. He was loyal, smart, handsome. And he really did ring my bell. I liked him better than any other man.

Rip glanced up from his menu. "What are you gonna have?"

"The potato hash with bacon and scrambled eggs," I said.

"You hate eggs."

That was true—I'd only said it to test him, and he'd passed. "What do you think I should have?"

"French toast. Vanilla-dipped with homemade berry syrup and fresh whipped cream. And a mimosa."

He'd even passed the extra-credit question! "Sounds good."

I *was* satisfied. And Dad and Wren were right: it was time to stop fooling around. To settle on something. Anything. Or anyone. No, not just anyone—Rip. He was special. I imagined us sitting at the breakfast table like this, twenty years in the future, and it didn't feel so bad. It felt…hmm. It felt something. Scary. No, no—settled. That's how it felt. Settled.

We ordered and ate and, basking in the warmth of my feelings for Rip, I wondered how I could've been so silly over Ian. Well, it's not like I threw myself at him. Although Hannah noticed. Of course, Ian and I were the only two single people in the room, so naturally she would pair us. Any seven-year-old would do the same. They were obsessed with crushes and cooties. Not like us grown-ups.

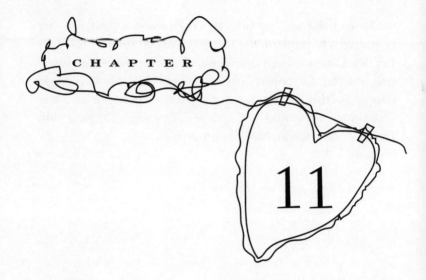

On Sunday afternoon, Rip had an open house on the lower east side. The house had been a rental and was now vacant and sad—and the gray storm clouds shutting out the sun didn't help. We stopped by the office for the plants we kept for just this reason. We loaded the bed of my pickup and decorated the house with ficuses and African violets and the yard with roses and geraniums. Rip dotted a baking sheet with chocolate-chip cookie dough and popped it in the oven. Not only would he have a fresh-baked snack to offer, but the house would smell delicious.

I left Rip, promising I'd be back at four to retrieve him and the plants, and decided to try again for Charlotte's gift. Might as well get it over with—then I could be done with Ian for another decade. And definitely a good idea to meet him while I was completely enamored of Rip.

I parked on the roof in the lot behind Borders Books. I stepped out of the truck and the heavens opened into a tor-rential rainstorm. Bad news for Rip's open house: always harder in the rain, plus the carpet would get filthy. On the bright side, the geraniums and roses would be watered.

I didn't have an umbrella, so I raced down the parking garage stairs and dashed the block to El Paseo, avoiding puddles and car-splashes. I darted toward Ian's shop through the monsoon. His door was a blurry rectangle, vaguely visible behind sheets of water, like it was being filmed through a Vaseline lens.

Gasping for breath, I clutched the doorknob and yanked. It was locked. And, wiping the deluge from my face, I saw a closed sign taunting me through the window.

"Hoy!" I yelled. "Ian!"

I pressed my face to the glass. There was a light on in the loft upstairs. If it hadn't been raining, I probably wouldn't have knocked. But it was pouring, so I pounded. A shadow moved upstairs. I pounded harder.

Ian came to the door. "We're closed," he said through the glass, pointing to the sign.

"It's me," I yelled.

He opened the door a crack. "Sorry, Anne, we're closed."

"I'm drowning!"

"You can't come back?"

"I don't want to come back." I pushed my way inside and stood dripping on his oriental. "I'm soaking wet."

"Don't worry about the carpet," he said.

"Sorry." I sloshed to the safety of the stone floor. "Me and old rugs don't mix."

He lifted a half-full tumbler of some amber liquid. "Like me and old Scotch."

"Drinking alone on a Sunday afternoon?" Then I realized: "*Are* you alone? Oh, God. I'm sorry. It's just if I hadn't grabbed your doorknob, I'd have been swept away to the Gulf."

"And?"

"And um…" I wasn't sure what he was asking. "And I didn't want to be swept away to the Gulf?"

He shook his head. "I'm alone. Come up and dry your…" He looked me over, a bit too blandly. I was all wet and clingy, he could have at least raised an eyebrow. "…self."

I followed him upstairs, dripping self-consciously. The loft was soft polished wood with diffused light glowing from the windows. It was cozy in the rain, and probably cheerful in the sunlight. I liked it. The décor, of course, could have used some work. There were a couple tatty old rugs on the floor, in burnished muted colors. Some Chinese vases in the corner which had undoubtedly been night-soil pots in previous lives. A collection of not-new weathervanes were mounted in two rows on the wall, providing stark contrast to the creamy white. And an antique desk dominated the room, an anchor amid the hodgepodge of other *objets d'old*.

Ian showed me to the bathroom, and gave me a fresh towel—bought new at Macy's, I noticed, and not circa 1200—and headed off. I dried my hair and repaired some damage and snooped in the cabinets. I learned nothing. I wasn't even sure what I was looking for.

Back in the loft, Ian was lounging at the desk, sipping his Scotch. The desk was ornate and old world and clearly a prized possession.

"That's really—" I wanted to say it was a nice desk, but was afraid he'd show me the urine stains from when Louis XIV's Pomeranian lifted a leg "—a big desk."

Ian nodded. "That's the technical term. Early American Big. You're here for Charlotte's cosmetics box?"

"Yeah. Sorry, I didn't know you were closed Sunday."

"Not usually. My assistant's out of town. I've got the box here somewhere—" He glanced toward a stack of parcels in the corner. "Care for a Scotch while I look?"

I checked my watch. Quarter to two. "It's a little early."

He nodded, looking slightly embarrassed to be caught drinking.

"But it *is* Sunday," I said, being polite. "I suppose one little Scotch couldn't hurt."

"Food for the soul." He stood and poured me a glass. The glass looked old and hand-blown and was tinted greenish. I managed to ignore my fear and loathing and took a slug, figuring the Scotch would sterilize any germs. It tasted pretty good. A warm glow started in my stomach.

I wanted to say something nice, to make up for barging in. "It really is a lovely desk," I said. "I mean, as well as being big."

"I bought it in an estate sale in Boston." He ran his fingertips over the polished top. "It's Hepplewhite, from the Colonial period. I really should sell it—it's not like I couldn't use the money. But I love the old thing."

I nodded in counterfeit understanding. They sold perfectly good desks at Pottery Barn. To ensure I didn't say anything offensive, I knocked back more Scotch.

"It's one of the problems with this business," he said. "You never want to part with the good stuff."

"Oh, um," I said. What good stuff? Everything was so used. The only new thing was a small TV playing ESPN in the corner. I looked around for a place to sit, and recoiled from an armchair upholstered in yellow chintz, instead choosing a wide wooden chair by the wall. That chintz had been the resting-place of a thousand asses—the wooden chair, I figured, retained previous buttage far less than fabric. "That's sort of the problem with real estate, too," I said. "Well, it's not parting so much as you hate the rich people who can afford your dream home."

"Charlotte's home is fairly dreamy," he said, settling into the yellow ass-chintz and not bothering to look for the lacquered box. "You hate her?"

"That's the most annoying thing about Charlotte. She's impossible to hate."

"Yeah, and still manages not to be one of those saccharine people who are too sweet to bear."

"You are *so* in love with Charlotte."

"Me? Charlotte?"

"You know you are."

"Sure. Me and ninety thousand other men. And not a few women, too, I'd imagine."

"That's true," I said, as he refilled my glass. "David even got a few threatening letters when they got married." I folded my legs beneath me and grabbed the remote from the desk. "What're you watching?"

"The game is—"

I clicked.

"Nothing, apparently," he said.

"Sports, feh." I changed the channel until I found an *Iron Chef* rerun just starting. "Fukui-san! Oh, the shrimp is so pink!"

Ian looked at me.

"Oh, it's like Italian gyoza!" I said. "Fukui-san! I am settling in to watch this show!"

"You like *Iron Chef?*" Ian asked.

"How could you tell?"

"Had you pegged as more the *Fear Factor* type."

I made a face, even though I loved *Fear Factor*. "I have very elevated tastes. Unlike you—you only have elevated prices."

Ian chuckled and we companionably sipped our whiskeys and watched the show. The host, Chairman Kaga, was in a jumpsuit designed for Ming the Merciless to wear to Liberace's pajama party. The episode was "Battle Eel." The Challenger took an eel and hammered a nail through its head into the chopping block before cutting out its spine. That sort of set the tone. The rest of the show was basically a series of too many close-ups of thinly-sliced eel head.

It was fun.

"Fukui-san!" I said. "Nakamura says he's using the pig's ear to make ice cream!"

Ian said, "This is worse than *Fear Factor.* Pass the Scotch."

"Fukui-san! The Challenger doesn't know the rules of the contest!"

"The Scotch, Anne."

"Fukui-san! I won't pass the Scotch until you start every sentence with Fukui-san! It's like Simon Says."

He was pretty well toasted by this point. He said, "Fukui-san! You anger the mighty Kong."

"What are you talking about?" I said. "I mean, Fukui-san! What are you talking about?"

"Fukui-san," he said. "Pass the Scotch before I put you over my knee."

Well. I was just buzzed enough for that to sound tempting. But I never played Secretary with two men at once. So I topped my own glass, then handed the bottle over. "The Challenger got robbed," I said, to change the subject. "He owned that eel."

"Yeah, nothing like hammering a nail through its head to drive that point home."

The next episode featured pumpkin. I sighed, as I'd been hoping for the Bobby Flay rerun, where he gets his butt kicked after jumping on the table in triumph. Still, I directed my attention to the TV and said, "Fukui-san! He's using pumpkin rind to make paste for his egg rolls!"

"Would you stop that?"

I guess it was a little annoying. "Oh, sure," I said. "Fukui-san!"

He shook his head in resigned amusement, and we fell silent, watching. The rain lashed down outside, which high-

lighted how warm and dry and comfy it was in the loft. It
smelled nice, too, like wood polish and lavender. The stuff
was old and moldering, but it did lend a sort of atmospheric
glow. It felt almost magical inside, like a little corner of the
world that time forgot. A tree-house hideaway, with the
Scotch, the pumpkin, and the company.

The Iron Chef triumphed, and I clicked off the televi-
sion. The image blinked and faded. The room was quiet except for the patter of the rain. I was still in the wood
chair—it was wide, and not uncomfortable—and Ian was
lounging on the chintz, legs propped up on an old trunk.

He passed me the jar of cashews he'd pulled from his desk
drawer. I chewed thoughtfully. "How long have you been
back in Santa Barbara?"

"Almost two years now."

"You didn't like New York?"

"I'm a Santa Barbaran. You know how it is—wherever we
go, it's never as good as home."

I laughed, slightly tipsily. "I went to Hawaii a couple years
ago, and complained the whole time."

"Oh, I don't know if I can believe *that*."

"Well, at least I didn't reject all of New York."

"Only because you haven't had the chance."

I grunted, because he was probably right.

"I liked New York," he said. "But I thought Santa Barbara would be a great place for an antiques shop. There's
lots of money here. And *some* people appreciate the finer
things."

"The older things," I said.

"With age comes wisdom."

"And decay."

He tossed a cashew at me, but I handily caught it and
popped it in my mouth. He laughed. "You're incorrigible."

"Why'd you call it Tazza?"

"A tazza is the first thing I sold. An eighteenth century glass cup with a stem and a—"

"So, where's Brianna?"

"—folded foot. Who?"

"Your fiancée."

"Helene. She's working."

"On a Sunday afternoon?"

"She likes to work," he said, sort of flatly. "She called, though. Around noon."

I wanted to make some disparaging remark about people who liked to work, but I sensed Ian was gonna confide something, and didn't want to mess it up by interrupting.

He took a slug of Scotch. "She set a wedding date."

"Oh! Well. Congratulations?" I raised my glass. "I mean, congratulations!"

"Thanks."

"You don't seem…"

"No, no. I'm happy. I am. I just—I thought we'd make an event over it. I wasn't expecting a call between her meeting with HR and her big presentation."

"She has a big presentation on a Sunday?"

"I don't know what she has," he said, a bit snappishly. "I'm just saying, she called from work to set a date to get married. Isn't that a little odd?"

"So she had to check her calendar. So she keeps her day planner at the office." Why was I defending this woman? "Vice presidents are busy people."

"I suppose." He nodded and swirled his Scotch. "What about you? Gonna marry Rip?"

"Maybe. I don't know. He hasn't asked. Maybe. I'm not sure." But hadn't I decided just yesterday that I was satisfied? "Yes. Yes, I might. Definitely. Yes."

"Well, now you've decided," he said, his humor returning, "there's the phone. Give him a ring."

"God, what would he do, if I just called and asked him to marry me? He'd probably faint." But he wouldn't faint. He'd say yes. Oh, God. "Oh, *God*…"

"He'd say yes, huh?"

"Oh, God. He *would*." The untrustworthy backstabbing conniver. "He really would."

"And he seems like such a nice man."

"I *know*. But what kind of—" I realized Ian was teasing and tossed a cashew at him. It hurtled over his shoulder and landed somewhere downstairs.

"Guess you're not quite ready, huh?"

"I am. I'm ready." I definitely was not ready. "Why wouldn't I be? I think there's something wrong with me."

"There's nothing wrong with you."

"Then why have I never been in love? I've had loads of relationships. Plenty of opportunities. And yet…" I looked at my hands. I'd never even said "I love you" to Rip. "I don't know…."

"What?"

"You have to give in, don't you? To let go, I guess. Maybe it's because of my sisters—I'm afraid of being overshadowed." We were silent a moment, and I realized this was turning kind of serious. I wasn't usually a maudlin drunk, so I said, "I *should* ask him, though. Yeah. I would've asked him today, but he's working."

"Sure. He's probably at Brianna's big presentation."

I laughed. "No, he's got an open house over on the—ohmigod! What time is it?"

"Four-thirty."

"Oh, shit! Shit, shit! I'm late. Shit!"

I stood and stumbled downstairs and lurched outside and plowed through the rain back to the parking garage. I was unlocking my truck before I realized I hadn't even said goodbye. Or picked up Charlotte's gift.

★ ★ ★

I'd forgotten my cell phone in the truck, so I missed Rip's two calls. He'd left messages: wondering where I was, and telling me he was leaving. Oh, and he hadn't sold the house, but the cookies had been delicious.

I dialed him. "It's me. I'm so sorry! I stopped for Charlotte's gift and—"

"Got stuck there, huh? She wanted to talk about the other night?"

"Uh…well, actually—sort of a funny story…" I didn't know how to tell him I'd been watching TV and drinking whiskey with Ian. He probably didn't want to know I'd been hanging out with another man all afternoon. Well, he probably did, but that didn't mean I wanted to tell him. Still, even if I couldn't say "I love you," I was always honest. "I, um, it turns out—"

"It's okay," he interrupted. "You don't have to tell me. Sisterly confidences. I'm glad you were there for her—I've never seen Charlotte cry like that before." He paused reverently for a moment, then continued. "We can pick up the plants on the way to work tomorrow."

He was being so sweet, I didn't have the heart to tell him the truth. And anyway, a white lie of omission wasn't a *real* lie. It was more a public service. Rip was an only child, and tended to idealize sibling relationships. He'd feel foolish that he'd said all that about "sisterly confidences" if I told him I'd actually been nestled in another man's cozy lair, drinking heavily while wearing dampened skirts.

"What about dinner?" I asked. "I can stop at the store on my way home."

"I thought you *were* home."

"Oh. I was." Which was, technically, true. I'd been home just that morning. "But I left." Also true. "I feel real bad I missed you." Still true. "I want to make it up to you. How about I cook you something special for dinner?"

"Steak?"

I'm not a big meat eater, and I'd used up my flesh quotient for the week with Dad's pork chop. Still, I owed Rip. "Sounds great." Finally, a lie! "I'll stop at Lazy Acres. I'm totally in the mood for beef."

"Liar." His smile was audible in his voice.

"I'm not lying!" I said. "I really will stop at Lazy Acres."

"Well, if you don't mind…"

"Steak it is. You know, I really do love—" I almost said *you,* but choked at the last moment "—being with you. I mean, cooking for you. Dinner with you. I mean—oops! Better run before the market closes."

In the end, Rip had steak and I had a veggie burger. Actually my total contribution to dinner was buying the meat, garden patty and beer, and encouraging Rip as he squirted lighter fluid on the charcoal briquettes. Four months ago, over my strenuous objections, he'd bought a GrillGod Steakerator from an infomercial. Just ninety-four simple payments, and it darns your socks, too. Of course, he'd never once regretted it. Mostly, because he liked the way it looked on his deck: sort of futuristic-macho.

Beyond the Steakerator, the view was spectacular. Rip's house was on the lower Riviera, overlooking the city. The rain had finally stopped, and we could see past the harbor to the Channel Islands.

The view was beautiful. The grill was impressive. But the house was funky. Not what you'd expect from a successful Realtor. Nothing had been updated for thirty years. You opened the front door and stepped into 1975. The walls were papered in a brown floral motif, the carpet was rust shag, and the kitchen was avocado green. There was a sunken living room with built-in couches. One bathroom had blue foil wallpaper and a baby blue toilet, the other a red roses motif and a marbled-pink sink, toilet and bidet.

"I know exactly what to do with your commission," I said, as I finished my burger. "From the Knox Tower sale. The Keebler money."

"Invest it," he said, as I said, "Redecorate the house."

"Invest?" I said.

"The house?" he said.

"It's a very bad time to invest," I told him. "I almost became a stockbroker. I know these things."

"What's wrong with the house?"

"You mean besides the obvious?"

"The roof is new. The foundation's solid. Everything works great. If it ain't broke…"

"You told me the first time I came over that the minute you got cash, you were gonna remodel. That until then, it was the view that kept you here. If I'd thought you were happy with this Shag Palace, do you think I'd ever have—"

"Shag Palace?" He leered.

"I mean the carpet." I pointed my beer bottle at him. "Don't push me."

"It's grown on me. The '70s are back in."

"Sure, and paisley is the new pink. Listen, it's simple. Tear down the wall between the kitchen and the living room— turn that into a great room. The kitchen needs cabinets, counters, sink, appliances, new floors, and lighting figures. Besides a good exorcism."

"What about the microwave?"

"Rip, it's not even a microwave. It's a Radarange. Then gut the bathrooms. Actually, gutting is too good for them. Disembowel them. Draw and quarter them. Rend them limb from limb. Then maybe wood floors instead of carpet.

Even berber is cliché, now. There's this grass matting I saw at Apoliné, though. Delicious."

"You're delicious," he said.

"Does that mean we can do it?"

"We can paint. Then we'll see."

It was a major concession. The truth was, Rip did want to redo the house. He knew he lived in the ugliest three years of the 1970s, but was afraid of change. Like he thought his house was a totem, and if he kept it perfectly kitschy it somehow protected him from the vagaries of the real estate market. I guess he felt in control—make a sacrifice here, gain control there.

It was like me not being able to say "I love you." I guess I sacrificed that for control of...something.

I swirled the beer in my bottle thoughtfully. Not sure it was a sacrifice I wanted to make. Maybe Ian was right. Maybe I should give the love thing a try with Rip.

We sat in our deck chairs, watching the sun disappear over the mesa and the lights flicking on downtown. I looked at him. He was leaning back in his chair, his eyes closed.

"Rip?" I said.

"Hmm?"

"I, um—"

There was a long pause.

"Thing is," I said, and my heart started pounding. My throat clenched. "I think I, um..."

He opened his eyes, and was looking directly at me. His brown hair was mussed and his green eyes were warm and there was a tiny speck of BBQ sauce on his chin.

"I love you," I said. I felt myself turn scarlet—blotchy and mottled. My face was burning, and I didn't know where to look. At the view? At the floor? At my beer bottle? But somehow I couldn't look away from his eyes.

He said, "And I love you, Anne," like it was the most natural thing in the world.

"Well, you could have told me!" I said. How could he be so calm?

"You'd have hated it if I told you first."

"Yeah. Yeah, well—I love you." There. I'd said it twice, now, and I hadn't burst into flames. "I love you."

A slow smile spread across his face. He stood and put his beer aside and squatted next to my chair, his face a foot from mine. He kissed me.

"I love you," I said again, in case he missed it the first three times.

It was sort of anticlimactic, after I'd had such fear of saying the words…but also a tremendous relief. I was exhausted and exhilarated, like a marathon runner crossing the finish line. I was damp with nervous sweat, and couldn't stop smiling.

I didn't know what the big deal was. It was just three stupid little words.

I love you.

CHAPTER

12

Three little words, and the floodgates opened.

Monday morning, Rip stepped out of his office, and I chimed, "I love you!"

His clients, the Brenners, stopped and stared. She was a pinch-faced woman wearing too many flowing layers, and he was perfectly gray, from hair to eyes to teeth to suit. They sort of inspected me for a moment and—true to form—sniffed.

Rip said, "And I love you." He turned to the Brenners. "Happy secretaries are productive secretaries."

Mrs. Brenner giggled horribly as I plotted my revenge for being called a secretary. Maybe tonight I'd be the demanding boss, and Rip would be the guy who delivered water. The phone rang before I could say anything, and I was *this* close to greeting the caller with "Love you, Parsons Realty," but nipped my ardor in the bud, and merely took a message for Mike. Then clattered at my keyboard for forty minutes, daydreaming happily, until Rip headed out for a market analysis. As he passed, I love-bombed: "Hey Rip? I love you!"

He kissed me on the head. "Me, too, Anne."

I was so bubbling with love, I even loved my job. I applied nose to grindstone for the next hour. Updated the Web site, answered the phone, put together a presentation package, and only stopped when Rip returned. "How did it go?" I asked. "I love you!"

He laughed. "Went well. And I still love you, too."

Fifteen minutes later, he poked his head out the door. "You have the Sharones tonight?"

I nodded. He meant Shannon and Shayla, friends from the title company. We go bar-hopping every month or so, a fairly tame girls' night out. Shannon's a bubbly customer-service rep, and Shayla's a pleasantly plump title officer, and I wasn't quite sure why I'd started calling them the Sharones. "Don't wait up," I told Rip.

"I won't—Frank just called."

"No lap dances!" I said. Frank was a city planner friend of Rip's, and the original perv. He elevated lechery to a lifestyle. The only thing that saved him from being completely awful was that he knew how awful he was. "Not even sitting on your hands."

"No lap dances," Rip agreed. "We're going to the Brickyard, anyway." A sports bar. "To watch the game."

"Frank would ask for a lap dance at Chuck E. Cheese."

Rip grinned. "I'll keep him out of trouble."

"I don't care about him. It's you I love."

"And I love you," he said. "Not some nineteen-year-old hotbody, naked and oiled and swinging around a pole."

Well, that was reassuring. But there was no chink in the armor of my love. He could talk about naked teenagers all he liked. To prove my undying devotion, I caught him a half hour later, as he was heading back from the bathroom.

"I love you!"

"Uh-huh," he said. "Did you run the Lewis search yet?"

I handed it over, lovingly.

"Thanks." He shut himself in his office.

By that afternoon, he was absently responding to my professions of love with *I know*. Hmm. Too much of a good thing?

So I called Emily at her office and told her I loved her. She said, "Broke up with Rip, huh?"

"I most certainly have not!"

"There's a grad student here, Sibaj Chakrabarti. Indian. Gorgeous. Smart. Single. Want me to give him your number?"

"Chakrabarti," I said wistfully, because it was a lovely name. Then I shook myself. "I love Rip. I'm in love with Rip. Rip and I are in love, Emily. What God hath bound, let no Chakrabarti rent asunder."

"What God has joined together, let no Chakrabarti put asunder. Not rent. Put."

"You're such a know-it-all."

"So where did this come from? All this love?"

I almost said from drinking with Ian. Instead, I said, "From the heart, Em. Anyway, I got to get back to work. Just called to say I love you."

"I love you, too, Stevie Wonder."

I called Charlotte, but there was no answer so I left a loving message. An individually tailored message for each of them. I'd call Dad, but he'd be worse than Emily. He'd assign my love some dreadful acronym: Professing Anne's Passion. He'd be teasing me about my "PAP" in crowded elevators.

So I called Wren, and was quite subtle. We chatted for a while, and I asked if she was going to join me and the Sharones tonight. She sometimes did, despite her flirting impairment. But Shannon had teased her a couple months ago, after she'd sat on a plate of mozzarella sticks while trying to girlishly perch on a table for a flirt. She hadn't really recovered. Anyway, I waited until we were hanging up before saying, "Love you. Bye."

She said, "Have fun!"

Hmm. No return of affection.

I had better luck with the Sharones. We met at Elsie's, a laid-back bar downtown. We sprawled on one of the ratty couches, plotting our evening over preparatory drinks. There'd been a time when no plotting was necessary, we'd just make ourselves beautiful and stomp on the accelerator. But with age came wisdom, or at least caution. Plus, I wasn't single anymore. So we needed to discuss if we wanted a man-hunt for the Sharones or a quiet evening of gossip. As always, we decided on the former.

By midnight, they'd both struck out miserably. We should've known—Monday night was not good for the man-hunt. But despite the abject failure, they got to hear *me* tell them I loved them. Repeatedly. At alcohol-fueled length. Lucky girls.

And it only got worse. I couldn't hold a conversation without professing love. Hannah said I was boy-crazy. Emily accused me of decentering the primordiality of maternal transference. Only Ny didn't seem to notice a difference. Although I did catch him glancing at the cabinet over the fridge more often, where I kept his rawhide treats.

Late one night, several days after my love epiphany, I pulled out a picture I kept in my bedside table. My favorite picture of Mom, before any of us was born. She was on the beach, her hair lit by the sun and swirled by the wind. Of the three of us, I looked most like her—it was almost like looking in the mirror. She was twenty-two, wearing a green bikini and smiling and squinting lovingly into the camera.

Or at Dad, behind the camera. I glanced at the back of the photo, where he'd written _Amelia, 1968_. She was so young— not yet married, not yet a professor or a mother. But I felt I could still see what she'd become—seven years younger than me, and she still looked like Mom.

I said "I love you," and had the best night's sleep of my life.

Wednesday after work, I met Wren at Element. She was supposed to finish at five on Wednesdays, for dinner and sculpture, but always had one more thing to do before she could leave. So I riffled through the racks as I waited.

I'm not sure exactly when it happened, but there were suddenly piles of beautiful clothing that were too young for me. Whole lines. Entire looks. I'm twenty-nine, but micro-minis, lingerie-inspired tees, and transparent blouses made me feel like—as Dad would say—mutton dressed as lamb. I told myself that it's not like I _couldn't_ wear them, I simply chose elegant maturity. I sulked over to the matronly sec-tion, and flipped through a stack of velour sweatsuits.

"Can I help you?" one of the Element girls said, sleekly materializing at my elbow. She was new, or she would have recognized me as the Wednesday Night Window-shopper.

I turned with a smile. "Just looking, thanks."

"Anne?" she said. She was maybe five years younger than I, and five sizes thinner, and looked like a girl who worked at Element. But not like anyone I knew. "Anne Olsen?"

I flushed in fear that my credit card had been rejected, and started mentally preparing excuses. This was a favorite free-floating anxiety of mine, despite the fact that my card had _never_ been refused—and I hadn't shown anyone my card, anyway.

"It's Jenny," she said. "We worked together, back at—"

"Banana Republic!" I was hit by a wave of girlish nostal-gia. "Jenny! I didn't recognize you—you look _exactly_ the same!"

She hadn't aged five minutes. She was wearing the young stuff and pulling it off.

"You look great," she said, no doubt meaning for my advanced age.

"You, too," I said, and we chatted for a few minutes. She was funny and bright, and I said, "God, I love you!"

She cocked her head.

"I mean, I love seeing people I haven't seen in a while. It's like a—a window into the past. I love the past! I mean, um…"

In answer to all my silent prayers, Wren emerged from her den, and signaled to me. I gave Jenny a jerky wave and raced away, babbling farewells.

"Oh, my God," I said, when the door closed behind us. "You hired Jenny Republic!"

"Yesterday. She came in to fill out an application and I recognized her."

"Why wouldn't you?" I said bitterly. "She looks exactly the same."

"She's great. I have no idea why we didn't like her."

"For me, it was apparently repressed lesbian lust. I just told her I loved her."

Wren laughed. "You're gonna have to stop with that."

"I can't. I've tried. I'm like a walking Hallmark card."

"A walking, *talking* Hallmark card."

She was enjoying this a bit *too* much. "Maybe I'll tell Naked Kevin tonight that *you* love him."

"Don't you dare!"

I said, with gravitas, "Wren and Kevin, sitting in a tree…"

"He's gay!"

"He checked you out from stern to bow, baby. And I think I saw movement." I wiggled a finger. "You know. Up periscope."

"You did *not* see movement. Stop that. I won't even be

able to look at him now. Oh, this is great. Up periscope—I'm lucky if I don't ask if he likes submarine movies."

"Don't you want him to hunt for your Red October?"

"Stop it! You know how hard it is for me—stop it, Anne. Really."

"Oh, Wren. I love you."

Wren survived class without undue disaster, by the simple strategy of avoiding Naked Kevin. She rolled her sculpture stand to the back of the room, and glanced at him only occasionally. She still somehow managed to capture his perfect likeness, from the tousle of his hair to the curve of his butt.

During the break, Kevin wandered around the room, looking at the clay images of himself. He stopped in front of mine. "My feet?" he asked.

"They're very expressive."

He chuckled and looked at Wren's sculpture. "Wow."

I turned to encourage Wren, and she was gone. Vanished in a flash of flirtphobia. "That's Wren's."

"She's good."

"She *is* good."

He furrowed his brow. "That's what I said. She's good."

"No, no—" I shook my head. "She's not good. She's goooood. Are you gay?"

He gave me an off-center smile. "Nope."

"Didn't think so, except you have those abs."

"My ex-girlfriend was a personal trainer. I'll have my hetero beer gut back in no time."

"How long have you been broken up?" Because I didn't want Wren to be a rebound hook-up.

"Five months. No—must be six, now." He scratched his chin. "Or seven."

A sufficient length of time, and he got extra points for not knowing exactly how long it'd been. Meant he was over her. "Seeing someone new?"

"Nobody serious." He gave me a curious, assessing look.

"Not me! I'm engaged!" I said. "Actually, I'm in loooove. True love. I was just...wondering."

"What about her?" he asked, glancing at Wren's sculpture.

"I don't know what you're talking about," I said. "But she's single and she's wonderful. She's the best." What did men tell each other to recommend a woman? I knew I shouldn't say she had a great personality, even though she did, but beyond that I was baffled. So I kept it simple. "I know she flirts like the Keystone Kops, but—"

"I like how she flirts."

"You do?" I said, and I was so careful not to say "I love you" that what came out of my mouth was: "Then you ought to ask her about the Yellow Submarine."

It was Thursday when I decided to finally get Charlotte's gift from Ian. I'd spent all day telling Rip I loved him because I wanted to be sure I'd purged every drop of love from my system before seeing Ian. An accidental love-burp in front of him would be even more embarrassing than declaring my devotion to Jenny or Kevin.

Rip scurried out of the office at four-thirty. He claimed he had an appointment, but I'm pretty sure he was just avoiding the mad love-bomber. I steeled myself to not say "I love you" as he grabbed his jacket and briefcase. Just once today, he should be able to leave my presence without hearing the dreaded refrain.

"You're okay to lock up?" he asked.

I nodded.

"Oh, and see if you can't get Mike to call the Sima people. But tell him to watch his mouth—they've got a new guy there now. Mike shouldn't call him dickhead until after they're friends."

I nodded.

"Web site updated?"

I nodded.

"See you tomorrow, then."

I nodded.

He was at the door. I was silent. His hand on the knob. I remained quiet. He opened the door. I said nothing. He turned and said "I love you."

I gritted my teeth.

He closed the door and walked toward the parking lot. I waited until I was sure he was out of earshot.

"I love you!" I shouted, triumphantly.

At the fax machine, Mike said, "The hell are you talking about, you crazy bitch?"

"I was talking to Rip," I said. I didn't mind the "crazy bitch." Mike addressed his Mother's Day cards: *To a fucking harpy* and signed them, *Your loving son,* so you had to take his words like bulletins from another planet.

"Rip has left the building," he said.

"You're suppose to call Jeremy at Sima. And not call him a dickhead."

Mike nodded. "He's not a dickhead."

"I'm glad to hear it."

"He's a fuckwad."

So I explained appropriate language to Mike for twenty minutes, then ushered him into the expletive evening. I locked the door. Checked the lights and computers and took a few moments in the bathroom to buff and polish, in preparation for the Ian visit. In a purely platonic way—I just wanted him to know that I was not, normally, such a mess. I mean, I didn't normally ask high school boys to get lei-ed, I didn't normally wrestle mannequins in shop windows or sleep with dust bunnies under Hannah's bed. I didn't normally get caught in the rain and pick the wrong gift and track mud all over the carpet while wearing bloat-tastic soccer shorts.

Ian was locking the door as I got to Tazza Antiques. He turned at my approach and watched me catch my breath and shove a hank of untidy hair behind my ear. I'd had to fight traffic to get here, and I wasn't exactly the picture of cool glamour I'd intended to portray, since I'd run to catch him. Anyway, it wasn't like a man noticed what you were wearing—in fact, he probably had no idea I'd been encased in a pair of Sta Puft shorts last time.

"Here for the box?" he asked.

"No, I just happened to be jogging past…."

"Should've worn your soccer shorts."

Great. "If you can't jog in Juicy Couture, you should stay off the roads."

"Is that Juicy?" He picked a scrap of rawhide off my cashmere sweater. Ny had been in the front seat again, and apparently left part of a chew clinging to the headrest. "No doubt from their 'Old West' line."

"Anyway," I said, smoothly changing the subject. "Charlotte's gift?"

"She beat you to it."

"What do you mean?"

"She picked it up Tuesday."

"Charlotte did? She came here?"

"She didn't tell you?"

Tell me what? What had happened, exactly? How long had she stayed? Did he take her to his loft and feed her whiskey? She didn't like *Iron Chef*. Did he know she didn't like *Iron Chef*? Not that I cared. I was in love with Rip. I was just saying. It wasn't right—Charlotte whiling away a Tuesday in her ex-boyfriend's love nest. She was a married woman. She should be ashamed.

Then I realized, with the gift out of the way, I had no reason to be talking to Ian. So I opened my mouth to say I'd see him next decade and he said, "Drink?"

I said, "Love to."

We walked across the street to Red, a restaurant and bar at the corner of State and Paseo Nuevo, the outdoor mall. But not your average mall—Paseo Nuevo has terra-cotta roofs and cobbled streets and sidewalk cafés. And Aveda and Nordstrom and all the other regulars, including the new Women's Banana Republic directly across from Red, to spark not-entirely-fond memories. We sat upstairs, on the balcony overlooking the street, and ordered bizarre drinks off the happy hour menu. Mine was called an All Around the World and consisted of banana liqueur, whiskey, Cointreau, and orange juice. Ian chose the Blue Lagoon, which had vodka, blue curaçao, fresh cream, and lemonade.

"So I decided to take your advice," I said, when our drinks came.

"You're going to challenge the Iron Chef?"

I tasted my cocktail and barely managed not to gag. Ian tried his and had the same reaction.

"Switch?" I asked.

He nodded, and we exchanged drinks. Sipped cautiously.

"Forget *Iron Chef,*" I said, grimacing. "These are *Fear Factor.* But I meant I took your real advice. About looooove."

"I don't give advice about loooove."

"You did! You told me I should tell Rip I loved him."

"I never said that."

"Did, too. I remember distinctly." Didn't I? "No, I'm sure you said something. We were talking about love. And that's when you said—"

He sipped and flinched. "You were drunk."

"*I* wasn't the drunk one."

"You were throwing cashews over the railing."

"Soberly."

He shook his head. "So, how did it go? You told Rip?"

"Yes."

"And?" he prompted.

"And my best friend. And Charlotte and Emily, and their husbands and kids. And my aunt Regina, and the Sharones, and this guy I dated in college who called the other night—boy was *he* shocked. And a telemarketer—he was happy, I think he was calling from jail. He asked what I was wearing." I paused to sip. "And a salesgirl and a naked male model. So things may have gotten a little out of hand, thank you very much."

Ian choked on his Around the World.

"I told my dad," I said, "and he felt my forehead to check if I was feverish. He acted like I'd never told him I loved him before."

"You tell him often?"

"Well…it may have been a few years."

"How many?"

"He *claims* the last time was after his car crash."

"Which was when?"

"Maybe seven years ago?"

Ian laughed, and shook his head.

"You created a monster," I said.

"I had nothing to do with it," he said. "But it's not enough to say you love someone, Anne. As I understand, you're supposed to actually mean it."

"Like when you tell your fiancée?"

He took a moment to drain his drink. "In a way."

"What way?" I asked, a little blurry from the Blue Aqua Velva, or whatever it was I was drinking.

"Helene likes to hear it," he said. "And I like to make Helene happy."

"That's terrible. That's worse than me. That's a pity 'I love you.' You really *should* mean it. Why am I even listening to you? You're a big creep."

"Do as I say," he said. "Not as I do."

I was about to press him for details about Helene when the waitress arrived. I glanced at my drink. It was inexplicably empty. "Those were the most repulsive drinks to which I have ever been subjected," I told the waitress.

"Revolting," Ian added. "Horrible."

"Another round?" the waitress asked.

"Please," we said.

Saturday afternoon, Rip and I met for lunch at the Italian place across the street from the office. Rip had a meeting with a couple from Springfield, Illinois, looking for an affordable condo in Santa Barbara. He was showing them a two-bedroom in the Highlands for $449,000—the bottom of the market—and hoping they didn't keel over.

The restaurant had once been an ice cream parlor, and the décor retained that olde-fashioned ice cream feel. The same etched glass dividers lined the dining area as when I was a child and my father used to cry highway robbery at the fifty-five-cent cones. But despite the ambience, the food was excellent. We ordered bruschetta and salads—I was watching Rip's figure—and sat at a table in the corner.

"Something's different," Rip said. "Not your hair…"

"I've lost weight?" I said hopefully.

"No, it's not that."

"Well, it *could* be."

"Maybe it *is* your hair."

I sighed. "I've stopped saying…you know."

"Oh! Oh, you have. You're right." An expression of relief suffused his face…then was marred by concern. "But this doesn't mean—?"

"No, no. I'll still trot it out on special occasions. I just—I decided I needed to take the edge off my euphoria."

He nodded.

"And get my ass in gear. I called the sea hag again."

"The sea hag?"

"Melissa Kent. About the Cypress Road property where I walk Ny."

"Did she tell you anything?"

I nodded. "It's owned by a corporation. Apparently just some guy, actually, but he's got all these corporate blinds, or shelters, or veils or something."

"Why do you even care? You have a file full of potential deals..."

Meaning that I've never followed through with any of the others. "I don't know. I can't stand that she won't tell me. And Ny and I have been walking there forever. What gives them the right to sell it?"

"They own it?"

"Other than that."

"There *is* no other than that. You're just lucky they allowed trespassers all this time."

I grunted. I'd have to find out on my own. The thing was, the Cypress property was more real than my other Recent Developments. I knew it. I'd walked every corner of it, every week for years. The trail up to the ridge, the meadow and the view and the sound of honeybees buzzing through the clover. The serenity and the calm. Plus, Ny had peed on every individual tree. We owned that damn land.

"Maybe if you tell Melissa that you love her..." Rip teased.

I blushed and fiddled with my salad.

"You didn't!"

"That's why I decided to go cold turkey. I am officially a love-free zone."

"So no nooner today, huh?"

"That's not love," I said. "That's exercise."

But we had no time, anyway. Rip had clients, and I had to meet Wren at the zoo with Hannah and the boys. We finished our meal, and glancing at the etched glass, I had a sudden yen for ice cream. Good thing they sold gelato. I bought a scoop to go. Dad would have fainted at the price.

Wren was often pressed into duty as an auxiliary aunt. The kids loved her—more than me, because she never said no. And why would she? She didn't have to live with the spoiled little monsters.

We strolled around the zoo as the children bounded in front. Wren and I talked of this and that. Girl talk. Nothing important. Then I casually mentioned going to Red with Ian. Sharing the awful drinks. And buying a second round.

"Does Rip know?" Wren asked.

"Know what?"

"That you've been meeting Ian for drinks."

"I'm not meeting him for drinks. We just happened to… meet."

"For drinks."

"It's not like I'm making a habit of it, Wren."

"First *Iron Chef,* now this. You're living a secret life."

I'd forgotten she knew about the whiskey in the loft episode. "There's nothing secret about it."

"So Rip knows?"

"No."

"Anne—" She paused as I bellowed at Hannah not to encourage her brothers to crawl into the monkey cage. "It's not appropriate."

"It's only drinks."

"It's not lemonade. I know what happens when you drink." She thought just because I often kissed strange men when I was drunk, that was a problem.

"What did you wear?"

"The Calvin Klein you sold me."

"The one with the cleavage?"

"I'm glad *someone* noticed," I said, trying to distract her. "Nobody else has said anything. Well, except for David, which wasn't exactly—"

"Are you serious about Rip, or not?"

"I told him I loved him, didn't I?"

"Anne, you said 'I love you' to the guy at Starbucks for giving you extra foam."

"I like foam."

She looked at me.

"Okay, so I was having a little verbal-tic problem. But I meant it with Rip."

She continued giving me the look.

"Ian's a friend. We had drinks. It's not like I'm screwing him."

"Not yet," she said.

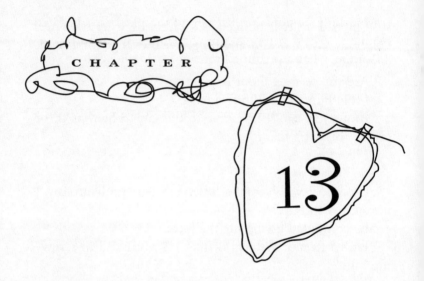

CHAPTER

13

The next day, I helped Charlotte in her garden, a half acre of land descending from patio to pool to plantings of roses, lavender and Mexican sage.

"Tell me again why you don't hire gardeners," I said, slaving over thorny rosebushes and potting soil.

"To teach the kids a lesson."

I glanced toward the pool, where the kids were splashing with David. "Uh-huh. So, was it weird to see Ian after all that time?"

"Why would it be weird?"

"First love and all. You're not still attracted to him?"

Charlotte unleashed a trademark Charlotte Olsen smile, and the roses spontaneously blossomed. "He looks good, doesn't he? He's kind of…filled out. And he's so charming. He always was. Even when you asked him to—"

"If you like him so much," I muttered, shoving a rose into the ground. "Maybe you should have married him."

"What?"

"Nothing." I tamped dirt around the plant in a pointed manner. "Why'd you break up with him, anyway?"

"Anne, what are you talking about? Is this part of your love thing?"

"Just answer the question."

She put her trowel down and looked at me. "He was a high school boyfriend."

"He's still in love with you."

"You weirdo. He is not."

"I saw him looking at you."

"Well, *if* he was looking, it was just because of all…this." She gestured to her house and grounds, but she really meant her beauty and celebrity. "But he wasn't. Honestly, Annie, by now I can tell when a man's interested."

"The thing is, now that you've met Ian again—" I pricked my finger on a thorn. "Ow! It's like your first love is back again. Back in your life. Young love. He's all…him. And you're all…*you*. And what does it mean, he's filled out? Filled out? What is *that?*"

Charlotte grabbed her trowel and started digging. "I dated him eighteen years ago, Annie."

"Just tell me—are you going to have an affair with him or not?"

"No, you freakazoid. I am not going to have an affair with Ian. Okay? I've fucked up my life enough, without adding that to the mess."

Charlotte *never* swore. "What? You what? Charlotte, your life is perfect."

"Stop saying that. I hate when people say that."

"You're beautiful. Famous, rich. Your husband loves you. You have a great house. Fantastic kids—" I got hit by a sudden anxiety. "You're not sick, are you? Nobody's sick?"

"Everyone's fine. Except me. I'm stuck home with the kids, and I'm starting to hate it. I'm picking fights with

David. Because he has a career, he gets out of the house, he actually does something. Aside from *Organic Style,* I haven't had a real job in…well, years. I'm just coasting on my—my reputation or whatever, *Sports Illustrated.* I haven't actually done anything else."

"You garden," I said.

"Don't patronize me, Anne."

"You…you redecorate?"

"You redecorate twice, then you're either done or you're obsessive."

"You haven't done the guest house. Maybe you could—"

She gave me a look.

"No. No. We're tired of redecorating," I said. "But Char-lotte—you have three kids. You're raising three kids."

"Yeah, me and a cast of thousands."

"You don't have a staff."

"The kids have activities all day. All I do is drive. I need something for *me.*"

"You want to do more modeling?"

She shook her head. "I can't see myself losing twenty pounds to advertise beer. Besides, I always hated it."

"What?" Another shocker. "You never complained."

"You weren't the only one who wanted new clothes, Anne. And if I'd ever said anything, Dad would've made me stop. Then my career took off…and well, you don't really turn that down."

I was stunned. All this time I'd thought Charlotte was per-fect and happy and perfectly happy. "Oh, Charlotte…"

"I just wish I'd gone to college like you and Emily. In-stead, I'm driving the kids to these weird rich-kid activities and locking myself in my room sewing swimsuits."

"Swimsuits?"

She nodded towards the pool where Hannah was wear-ing a red one-piece. "I did Hannah's."

"Cute," I said. I didn't know what to say about the locking-herself-in-her-room bit. That was not cute. That was depressing.

"You want one?" she asked.

"Sure." I didn't, but I couldn't say no. "But Charlotte, what are you going to do? Locking yourself in your—what about therapy?"

"Maybe I should get a part-time job." She glanced into the distance. "You like working, don't you?"

"No."

"No." She went back to digging. "It doesn't matter. You're right. I have the perfect life. I shouldn't complain."

"Complain all you want, Charlotte. Why let me and Emily have all the fun?"

I hugged her tight as she gave me a brave face. "I'm okay. Really. It's just turning thirty-five. I keep thinking, I'm gonna live another fifty years. How am I going to fill all that time?"

We finished the roses and sat in our dirty clothes on the deck, drinking iced tea. We watched the kids and David frolicking, but didn't join them.

"You like him, don't you?" Charlotte said.

"Of course I like him. I love him. You're not thinking of leaving him? That will not make you happier, Charlotte."

"I meant Ian."

"Oh. No. Yes. As a friend. He's comfortable. I like him."

"You always did," she said. "Must be why you asked him to your school dance."

"I felt sorry for him."

"Anne, you were thirteen. He was almost eighteen. Asking him to get lei—"

"Don't say it!"

"I think you were trying to steal my boyfriend."

"Well, I felt sorry for him, stuck with you in your gawky phase."

She smiled. "You were so cute in that grass skirt. Pity Dad wouldn't let you wear the coconuts."

"He could only handle one sexy daughter."

She jingled the ice cubes in her glass. "You always felt like old news, didn't you? I mean, the third of three..." She sounded so sympathetic, and it was so true. "Like the whole daughter/sister novelty had worn off by the time you came around."

I nodded.

"Well, I don't blame you," she said. "I'd have felt the same."

Hearing that was such a relief that I told her I loved her.

"Not that again," she said.

"No, really. I just say it when I mean it now. Everything in moderation."

She shot me a dubious look. "You have only two speeds with love, Anne—full stop, and full tilt."

"I'm on easy medium now. Anyway, when was I ever full tilt?"

"When we were kids. Everything was 'I love you.' You stopped after Mom died."

"I did?"

"You used to say it all the time. Kind of like the past few weeks. But then she died and...well, you just stopped."

I pressed my hand to my mouth. "Really? You noticed?"

"We all did."

I left my chair to sit on the deck at Charlotte's feet, wanting to be close. I leaned my head on her knee like I'd seen Hannah and the boys do. She put her arm around me, and I suddenly envied the children their mother. "Even though I never said it, it didn't mean—"

"I know." We sat there for a while. "Can I ask you something? What changed? Why are you saying it now?"

"Rip," I lied.

★ ★ ★

Back in my house, I was suddenly ravenous. I opened a box of Oreos and ate half. Then drank an enormous glass of milk. Then I wanted something salty so I ate a bag of chips. Then I was ready for sweets again, so I finished the Oreos. And the milk. Luckily, there was only lettuce left in the fridge, otherwise I never would have stopped.

I wasn't in love with Ian. It was an infatuation. It was nothing. I was in love with Rip. Ian happened to be there during the formative years, so I was fixated on him. Plus, I liked him. We laughed at the same things. We were friends.

Ian of the dirty blond hair. Ian of the dirty antiques store, and the dirty pretend remembered sex. Ian who'd helped me say "I love you" again. Ian—Charlotte's ex. Her old boyfriend. Her used, ex, previous, moth-eaten boyfriend.

It was disgusting. I couldn't like Ian. Not romantically. I wouldn't. I didn't.

Fine. Good. Settled. It's all about the power of the mind.

Five minutes later: I still kinda liked him.

Decided to call Rip, to wipe Ian from my brain.

"Hi, baby," I said, when I got him on his cell phone.

"What's up?"

"Nothing."

"Anne, I'm with clients."

"I think we should ask Ian to dinner. And his fiancée."

"Ian? Charlotte's ex-boyfriend?"

"Yeah—you met him at her party. She says she doesn't love him anymore. But I think *he's* in love with her. So I've got to check out this fiancée. Can't have some old flame reappearing in my sister's life without—"

"Anne, I really don't have time for this."

"That's okay, I'll arrange everything."

"I don't think I—"

"Bye, sweetie!"

It was a great plan. All I needed was to see Ian with his fiancée, and I'd get over this silly obsession. Now I just had to call him. I didn't have his number at home—I didn't even know if he had a home. Far as I knew, he dwelled in the whiskey-lair above his shop. So I called him at work.

The machine picked up and told me I'd reached Tazza Antiques. I told it: "Ian, it's Anne. Olsen. Anne Olsen. Um…we had drinks the other night? I'm Charlotte's sister? Okay, I guess you know it's me, now. Anyway, Rip and I were wondering if you and your fiancée want to have dinner. Maybe this week? Okay, it's um, Sunday afternoon. You should be working. Why aren't you there? Maybe you are. Maybe you're with a customer, and you're both listening to this message. Hello, customer. Anyway, I better make this short. When you two have a free night, we should go to dinner, okay? Call me."

I left my number and hung up before I could say anymore. It's all about the power of the mind. And the power of my mind was telling me I'm an idiot.

Ian called Monday morning. Rip and I were in bed. Ny was shut in the kitchen.

When I answered, Rip called me a rude name.

"Anne, it's Ian. Ian Dunne. We had drinks the other night. I'm Charlotte's ex-boyfriend."

"Yeah, yeah. Very funny."

"Just got your message. How about dinner tonight? Or is that too late notice?"

"Let me check with Rip." I covered the mouthpiece with my hand. "Are you up for dinner tonight with Ian and his fiancée?"

He pointed his morning two-by-four at me. "*No.* The only thing I'm up for is—"

"We'd love to," I told Ian.

"Great. Helene likes Vina, in Montecito. Is that all right?"

"I love Vina." Italian place, fantastic pasta. "Six o' clock?"

"Well, Helene is…we're kind of into eating later, at eight or nine."

Nine? It was a Monday. I liked to be home by nine on weeknights. "Eight's great," I said. "I love a late dinner. See you then."

I hung up and turned to Rip—who'd rolled out of bed and was getting dressed in a huff. "Where are you going?"

"I can't believe you just did that," he said. "Answered the *phone.*"

"I thought it might be my dad."

"And that makes it better?" he asked, incredulous.

"No, you're right. I'm sorry. I don't know what I was thinking. Forgive me?" I forgot how much men hated to be interrupted. They're like fanatical tree-huggers: they must preserve the wood at all costs. "I just thought maybe we needed more friends or something. Try something different." I glanced at the clock. "Like playing Office Manager."

"What's that?"

"It's Secretary, but with a better job title."

"You think sex is gonna make up for it?"

I gave him my best naughty schoolgirl look.

He started undressing. "Good point."

Dinner was a fiasco.

First, Helene was gorgeous. You'd think I'd be used to that, growing up in the shadow of Charlotte, but no. It hurts every time, like a bikini wax or having someone rap you sharply on the forehead with a ball-peen hammer. And it didn't help that every light in Vina had been personally adjusted by the headwaiter to shine directly on the fabulous fiancée. She sat there in a nimbus of white light, looking like Reese Witherspoon playing a come-hither angel. I, on the other hand, was sitting in a sucking black hole, looking like Cameron Diaz—in *Being John Malkovich*.

Second, Helene was smart and friendly and charming. Very vice presidential. But I guess it was a good thing that Helene was so mesmerizing, because Rip and Ian had nothing in common. It wasn't that they disliked each other— more that they were from different planets. For example, Rip was from the planet of the Men Who Order San Pellegrino, while Ian was a member in good standing of the Intergalactic Association of Martini Drinkers.

So I ordered a Negroni. I had no idea what a Negroni was, but the restaurant was Italian and the Negroni seemed *molto Italiano.* Plus, I didn't want Ian to feel awkward at being the only one with a drink.

Helene asked Rip about Santa Barbara real estate. She and Ian were thinking of looking for a house, as a wedding present for themselves. "But we're afraid of buying at the top of the bubble."

Rip perked up at his favorite topic. "In Santa Barbara, there is no bubble. Real estate just goes up and up and up and up."

"Like Internet stocks," I said.

"No, Anne," Rip said. "Internet stocks were based on nothing, which is why they bombed. But Santa Barbara? You've got a small strip of land between the ocean and the mountains—they're not making any more of Santa Barbara. Prices are completely crazy, it's true. But there's nowhere to go but up."

"Where would you buy?" Helene asked, her naughty-angel face bright with interest.

"The west side," Rip promptly answered. "Bottom of the market—get a place for five or six hundred thousand. Put some money into it, fix it up—"

"A fixer-upper at six hundred thousand?" Ian said.

"Don't think of it as dilapidated," I said. "Think of it as antique."

A silvery laugh from Helene. "Oh, well said! Ian will fall in love with anything, so long as it's old."

Well, that was too good to ignore. I was about to say *he must love you very much* when the horrible woman continued. "It's why he loves me so much."

"My aged crone," Ian said fondly, laying his hand over hers.

Rip, on cue, loudly refused to believe that Helene was three years older than Ian, while I marveled at the sheer confidence of the woman. Of course, it couldn't be hard to admit you were almost forty when you looked twenty-seven.

I huddled in my gloomy corner and smoothed my sackcloth skirt, feeling self-conscious about my hunchback. The waitress brought the Pellegrino and martini and Negroni—and a glass of the *Au Bon Climat* Chardonnay for Helene. Great. I definitely should have ordered Chardonnay, even though I didn't like white wine and would've pronounced it "climate" instead of "cleemaht." Odd that a native of Notre Dame such as myself couldn't speak French.

Ian raised his martini glass. "To new friends…and old."

Helene brightened at the toast—she thought "old" meant her. I brightened, too: I knew it meant me. We all clinked glasses.

Helene sipped her wine elegantly and I took a consoling swig of the Negroni and coughed until I saw stars.

Rip pounded my back. "Are you okay?"

My eyes were watering and I couldn't breathe. I finally squeaked, "Wrong tube."

Ian looked amused. "Speaking of which, how's the penne here?"

I shot him an evil look, but was thankful he'd diverted the attention away from me. He asked Helene what she was having. I lost my silent bet with myself when she didn't say "the dinner salad." She was having her favorite, fettuccine Alfredo. About 3,500 calories, she blushingly admitted, but she was one of those people who just couldn't gain weight, no matter how much she ate. Must be all the running around she did for work. Poor thing.

Rip asked about her job, and she was deeply humble about being such a high-powered executive. "All I do, really, is have those awkward conversations the CEO would rather avoid. Negotiating leases and firing employees, flying to D.C. to speak with congressional panels. That sort of thing."

I gulped my Negroni. Maybe if I numbed my frontal lobe, this would go better. But I knew I couldn't finish it. It wasn't Blue Lagoon awful—so bad that it was good—it was bittersweet and repellent, like bug spray with saccharine.

So I switched drinks with Ian.

"Congressional panels?" Rip asked.

"Oh, the SEC, the Fed. All very boring. Though legislative sessions can be quite…"

Ian's martini was far better than my Negroni. Usually I didn't like martinis, but I knocked this one back in a twinkling. Desperate times called for desperate manners. Ian appeared not to notice the drink-switch. He merely sipped the Negroni and pronounced it good.

"…before I was sent to San Jose to direct the Value-Added-Branding project…"

"You can drink that?" I asked Ian.

"It's good. The Negroni is my third favorite drink."

"After Scotch and martinis?"

"Scotch and beer. Martinis are a mood thing."

"…we're opening an office in Chicago, and the telecommunications initiative was in tatters, so the CEO asked me to…"

"What mood is a Negroni? Bitter? It's worse than an Around the World."

"Only if you have a taste for the simple."

"I have very complex tastes."

"Which is why you shop at Bed Bath & Beyond."

"…loved me in Chicago, but I had to lay off half the I.T. department…"

"I never shop there!" I lied. "Besides, there's some really sophisticated stuff in Beyond."

For some reason, I found this funny. Maybe because I hadn't eaten since noon, and was drowning my awkwardness in vodka.

Ian offered a Negroni-fueled chuckle. "You *are* beyond."

I was oddly flattered. I was going to tell him that he was bed and bath—whatever that meant—when I noticed Rip and Helene were silently watching us.

"Chicago!" I said, digging in my memory for a key word from their conversation. "I loved that movie!"

"You did not," Rip said.

"Well, none of them can sing or dance. Why wouldn't they hire actors who'd actually been on Broadway? Can you imagine how you'd feel if you were a real theatre person, and they gave all those roles to Hollywood?"

"But you just said—didn't you just say you loved it?" Helene asked.

"Oh, I did," I explained.

"What about buying in Goleta?" Ian asked Rip. "Maybe up north, off Glen Annie or Storke?"

That kept us going through dessert.

Rip drove home. I slumped in the passenger seat, demolished by the second martini and uncounted glasses of Chianti.

"They're not going to buy," Rip said.

"Mmm?"

"A house. They're not serious about buying."

"You think?"

"I know."

Well, he did have a feeling for these things. "Good," I said.

"Good? Why good?"

Oh. Hmm. An excellent question. "Because of the bubble?"

"You have a crush on Ian," he said.

"I do not! Of course I don't. On *Ian?*"

"You are utterly crushed."

"I'm not crushed! I don't have a crush. He's so..." I couldn't think of anything disparaging. "You know."

"He's so what?"

"He drinks too much!" I hiccuped.

"Of *your* drink."

"Well, I—I don't like Negronis. I knew you wouldn't want it..."

"It's okay, Anne. I don't mind—you can have a crush on anyone you want, long as you come home with me."

"Well, I *don't* have a crush on him," I said. "You really don't mind?"

"Course not." He tapped the turn indicator. "It's like me and your sister."

"You have a crush on Charlotte?"

"Sure I do," Rip said. "I used to have her poster on my wall. The one where she's under the waterfall wearing—"

"I *know* which poster, Rip." The poster that every boy had on his wall...if his parents let him.

He shrugged. "All I'm saying is, it's okay you have a crush. It's kind of cute."

"I don't have a crush on Ian!"

"You were glaring at Helene all night."

"I was squinting. Because of her halo."

He glanced at me, decided not to follow that up. "And you switched drinks with him."

"Well, I…"

"And *then,* you groped me all through dessert."

"Because I have a crush on *you,*" I said, rolling down the window because I was suddenly hot. Maybe Wren was right; I did lose the tiniest bit of control when drunk. At least this time it hadn't been a strange man, but it's true I'd tried to climb into Rip's lap between the tiramisu and the coffee. And as the cool breeze hit my face, I remembered: before dessert, I'd pretended to be the *Flashdance* woman who eats lobster so sexily. It hadn't worked so well with *fettuccine al limone.*

"Oh, Rip. I'm sorry. I don't know what got into me."

"It's only a crush, Anne. Probably left over from when you were a kid."

"Yeah," I said. "My inner thirteen-year-old."

As Rip turned onto my street, I thought about it: my crush could only be a fear of commitment. I was nervous about getting closer to Rip, so I transferred my feelings to Ian. I explained this to Rip. "And now I've figured it all out, I can really commit. I mean, we can take our relationship to a whole new level."

"You're drunk," he said.

"In vino veritas," I replied. "Did you notice that Helene's nose is sort of funny?"

"Nope."

"It is. It's funny."

"Didn't notice."

"Well, it was hard to see, with the glare."

"What are you talking about?"

"You have such a crush on Helene!"

He laughed. "She is pretty cute."

"Except for the nose," I said.

I woke the next morning without a hint of hangover—it was my resolution to truly commit to Rip that was ringing in my head. My fascination with Ian made sense, if you considered it psychoanalytically. He was my version of the seven-year itch: roughly every seven years he appeared, and I itched. I was only using him as a way to keep from committing to Rip.

Well, no longer.

Just thinking about it differently made all the difference. Even work—with the tedious secretarial tasks—took on new significance. I was totally committed to Rip. We were partners in life, so we should be partners at work. I was no longer the Office Manager, I was the co-owner. Or at least the owner's significant other, which was pretty close.

And it was enough. I took a proprietary interest in the job, updating the database, answering the phones, taking messages—all quite enjoyable when you're part of the management team, and no longer a downtrodden lackey.

I'd basically promoted myself to Vice President—or

maybe Co-President, so I could outrank Helene. I was also, if I say so myself, even more charming than usual. Bright and enthusiastic, without being chirpy. I'd gotten sick of taking phone messages, but today I hand-delivered them with a smile, and even checked that they were legible. And not a single made-up phone number because I'd forgotten to ask.

Mike was the first to comment on my newfound enthusiasm. He said, with his customary aplomb, "The fuck is up with you?"

Now that I was virtually half owner of Parsons Realty, I wasn't sure I should condone that sort of language. "Pardon me?" I said. "To what are you referring?"

"You. You're all namby-nice," he said. "The hell have you done with the real Anne?"

"I'm still uncertain as to the nature of your inquiry."

"And what is this shit?" He waved a stack of neat, legible messages at me. "Freaked me out."

"Those are messages, Michael," I said. "If you read them closely, you'll see a note, along with the time and date it was left. Additionally, you'll find them color coded. The cool colors, blue and green, are least urgent. Yellow and orange lead to red—most urgent."

He used the stack of messages to pick at a scab on his forearm. "Does Rip know what you're up to?"

"I'm merely optimizing corporate communications." A direct quote from Helene. "It's my new paradigm."

"Poor bastard." Mike shook his head. "You were bad enough surly. Now he doesn't stand a chance."

"A chance at what?"

"Freedom. You set a date yet?"

I refrained from flicking a paper clip into his eye. "Just because we're a small agency doesn't mean we can't act professional."

"And here I thought you'd never settle down," he said.

"Thought you were the original rolling stone. Love 'em and leave 'em."

"Rolling stone? I don't—"

"Yeah. Never figured you and Rip for the long haul. The old ball and chain. A cell block built for two."

"What makes you think—?"

"You shitting me? The whole Mrs. Cleaver show, here. You're acting like the Stepford Anne."

"Fuck you, Mike."

He smiled. "That's better."

Emily and Jamie lived in a charming Spanish bungalow in the chi-chi section of the upper west side, just off State Street. I rolled up around six, to baby-sit Zach. It's the Single Sister's Burden—Emily and Charlotte had long ago stopped even pretending to call baby-sitters before they asked if I had the evening free. It had never bothered me. I loved their kids, and we'd always been a close family.

I found Emily and Jamie in the kitchen, where she was putting the final touches on the note she always left me.

"I *know*," I said.

"Just in case something happens," she said, adding an annotation.

"What's gonna happen that the police and firemen can't handle? I've memorized 9-1-1."

Emily scribbled a phone number. "This is where we'll be."

"If a guy with a knife breaks in asking questions about Foucault, I'll know who to call."

"Watch for the plants. Zach almost poked his eye on the *chlorophytum* the other day, looking for bugs."

"Emily," Jamie said. "She has it under control."

"You didn't grow up with her," Emily said.

"She's watched Zach once a month for six years," he said. "We have to go through this every time?"

I opened the fridge. We *did* have to go though this every time. Consistency was part of Emily's charm. She started explaining, at length, why this time was different, and I said, "Are we having a publication party for your new book?"

A sharp exhalation. "No."

"We should. Remember the last one?" The last one, when I'd propositioned Ian and he'd said no. Why? Why? Any man so eager to have imaginary skinny-dipping sex should be equally eager for real sex. But apparently not with me. I felt myself flush, and blustered onward. "With the photographers, and the magazine and—"

"I remember, Anne," Emily said.

"Oh, of course! That's when you and Jamie got together. We should have another one."

"Must this family throw a party to commemorate *every* marginally significant event?" Emily asked. "Why can't we celebrate quietly, instead of making a fuss?"

"Because fusses are fun?"

"They're messy," she said sharply. "We don't need a party for every little thing."

"Emily," Jamie said.

"It's obsessive. It's ridiculous. It's juvenile, and I won't have any part of it."

What the hell was this? Emily loved parties—especially those in celebration of her. She always stretched her birthday into a week-long event. "I guess we don't *need* a publication party," I said.

"No," Emily said. "We don't. Because it's ridiculous that we see the incommensurability of the private and the public spheres as a personal affront and—"

"Okay, Em," Jamie said, shepherding her to the door. "Anne gets the point."

"I'm not sure she does."

"Emily," Jamie said. "We're gonna be late."

"I just want to explain—"

"Bye, Mommy," Zach said, standing at the front door with his favorite video, *The Little Mermaid,* in his hand. "Me and Aunt Anne are gonna watch Sebastian."

Emily visibly softened at Zach's eager face—and gritted her teeth at the video. She had one thing to say about *The Little Mermaid:* "A mermaid needs a man like a fish needs a bicycle." But she let Zach watch it despite the scaly sexism, because he loved it. And, thankfully, he was one of the few earthly forces that could avert one of her tirades.

"Good night, sweetie," she said. "Be nice to Aunt Anne. And stay away from the *bryophyllum.*"

"See you at eleven," Jamie said, and dragged Emily out the door.

Despite Emily's worries, Zach was always well-behaved. He was only a month older than Charlotte's Kyle, but far more mature. Either because he didn't have a younger brother inciting him to mischief, or because Emily was the Evil Queen to Charlotte's Snow White.

Okay, she wasn't that bad—but nobody could push my buttons like she could. She needed to leave an instructional note? She suddenly hated book parties?

Zach and I watched the video. He sang along with "Under the Sea" while I wondered if I'd give up my fins for Rip. Answer: no way. All that swimming had really tightened Princess Ariel's butt. Two years on land, she'd have a big floppy ass.

I made rice pilaf and broccoli for dinner and we ate at the kitchen counter. I wasn't as close with Zach as with Charlotte's kids, because I didn't live three hundred feet away, so we sometimes had a kind of polite reserve. Still, even polite six-year-olds liked to gossip, right?

"Your mom seemed a little grumpy tonight," I said, testing the waters.

"Mommy's book is getting bad reviews."

Jackpot! "Oh...where'd you hear that?"

"She's been crying about it all week."

"Do you know what that means?" That Emily's a big fat failure, like me! Ha! Ha-ha!

"Well, *Spy Kids 2* got bad reviews," he said. "But I thought it was pretty cool."

I smiled. "I thought it was cool, too."

Shortly after dinner, Zach collapsed into bed and I had two hours to kill before Emily and Jamie returned. There was nothing on TV. Their bookshelves were filled with academic treatises and the esoteric stuff Jamie published. "Literary" fiction, unlike all those nonliterary novels you see out there. All I wanted was a nice mystery, but the closest they had was a Dorothy Sayers I'd already read.

I rummaged in the shelves for a while, and found myself absently tidying. The house was a mess. Jamie and Emily both worked insane hours, and Zach, being six years old, was a miniature tornado in footsies. Looked like their weekly cleaning had been put off for a month. So I decided to clean house. In penance, mostly—for my delight in Emily's bad reviews. Sometimes I was too eager to embrace my inner *schadenfreude*. So I did the kitchen. I did the living room. The front hall and the dining room. I did the bathrooms—even the toilets—and was flushing triumphantly when Emily and Jamie walked in the door.

"Good God!" I heard Emily say, in amazed reverence.

I strode out of the bathroom, toilet brush held high, prepared to accept the gushing accolades.

"So the truth comes out," Emily said.

"Yes!" I brandished my toilet brush like a scepter. "I am the Queen of Clean!"

"No—you think I'm a bad mother."

"What?" My scepter fell to half-mast, reverting to a toilet brush. "I, um—I cleaned the house?"

"You think Charlotte's a better mother than I am."

"What are you talking about?"

"You heard me."

"Emily, I never said Charlotte was a better mother."

"Obviously you think it, or you wouldn't have cleaned."

"Jamie?" I said, hoping he'd manfully intercede.

"I'll be in the bedroom," he said, and slipped past.

"I can't believe you." Emily tossed her keys onto the kitchen counter. "You do. You think I'm a bad mother. Why not just say it?"

I refrained from tidying her keys. "Emily, you're a great mom. Zach is a great kid."

"You never liked him as much as Tyler and Kyle."

"Jesus. How was *your* evening?"

"Oh, it's just high-strung Emily going off again, isn't it?"

"Um—yeah?"

"Then why clean the house? You think I neglect the private sphere."

"Emily, I'm this close to shoving a toilet brush up your private sphere. I cleaned your house because I wanted to cheer you up. I wish someone would clean *my* house. Besides, I said you were a good mother—I never said you weren't a slovenly pig."

She glared, and I threatened her with the toilet brush, and she cracked a reluctant smile. Thank God. "I'm sorry," she said. "I'm a little…*God*…do you want a cup of tea?"

I wanted to say no. It was already eleven, and I had to work tomorrow—and it was exhausting being the bright and efficient Co-President in Charge of Everything. But Emily needed to talk, so I put the toilet brush away as she filled the kettle and set it on the stove.

"It's my new book," she said.

"You're not happy with it?"

"No, I…it's the reviews."

I nodded. "Yeah."

"Did Jamie tell you?" she asked.

"Zach."

"Yeesh. We haven't said anything to him, but he's got kiddie radar. He's so smart." She smiled. "I guess I'm not doing *everything* wrong."

I told her what Zach said about *Spy Kids 2,* and she laughed.

"It stinks," she said.

"It wasn't that bad. Anything with Antonio is worth watching."

"My book, Anne. It reeks. We sent it out for pre-pub reviews. Everyone hated it. Academics, film critics, the popular press. *Cosmo* hated it. It's universally despised."

The kettle whistled, and Emily made two cups of chamomile and we sat at the kitchen counter. She looked sad and baffled. She'd never really failed before, not publicly.

"I don't know what to do," she said.

I blew on my tea. "But plenty of great books get crappy reviews, right?"

"Not this crappy. One reviewer called it 'a sodden mess of wasted paper pulp.' Sidra Lorne said it combined the best of two worlds, but unfortunately those worlds were both pedestrian and deeply flawed."

"I never liked Sidra Lorne," I said. "Stuck-up bitch. Besides, it's just one opinion. She probably didn't even understand your points. Who is she?"

"She chaired my doctoral committee!" Emily wailed.

It was strange—I was finally in a position to give Emily advice based on my own experience: Failure. But I wished I wasn't. So instead, I listed the top seventeen reasons why I despised Sidra—whom I'd never met—while

Emily caught her breath. If there was one thing I was good at, it was the invention of extemporaneous grievances. Then I said, "Well, it's not published yet, right? I mean—and Jamie is the publisher, so... Can't you edit it or something?"

"See?" She sniffled. "You hate it, too."

"I hated *Porn Is Film*. If I hate it, that means it's good. Do *you* like it?"

"Oh, God," she said, her face crumbling. "Oh, God...it's just *awful*."

"Good," I said. "Start over. Write something different."

"I can't start over."

"Why not?"

"It took years..."

"Yeah, but you ended up with crap and—"

She started crying. Maybe "crap" wasn't the best word.

"Listen, Em," I said. "It's just the sophomore slump...."

"I can't start again," she said, her voice ominously soft. "I can't because I'm a fraud. This was supposed to be my non-porn book, but I...I wanted to combine sex-positive post-feminist theory with a form of popular cinematic discourse which—" She shuddered, was quiet a moment, then continued. "I spent so much time on film and porn, because I needed to make a reputation for myself—and then I needed to live up to that reputation—I just don't have the grounding in theory anymore..."

"Emily—you're so theoretical, you're basically your own *ism*."

"I'm a time capsule—theory of the '90s. Everything I say, it's just jargon and bullshit. Sidra's right."

"So brush up on your theory. I know you can do that—you can do anything. Your mind is still a lethal weapon."

"Shooting blanks."

"So forget this book and write another about porn."

She shook her head. "I swear, Anne, if I have to sit through one more blow job, I'm gonna die."

"Weird," I said. "That's exactly what Rip says."

Had trouble sleeping that night, and not just because I was sharing my bed with a flatulent cover-hog. I plumped my pillow in a meaningful manner, and muttered about my feet being cold. To no avail. So I yanked the covers roughly back to my side of the bed and he gave me a doleful look, like I'd stolen all the comfort from his world.

"I don't care," I said.

He turned his head away and farted.

"Oh, God!" I fanned the covers, but that only made it worse. "What've you been eating? Brimstone?"

Ny wagged his tail hopefully, as if *brimstone* were another word for *walk*.

"Forget it, fatboy. Go away. Get off—go!" I shoved him toward the edge of the bed. He rolled onto his back and put his paws in the air. Great. He knew I couldn't resist him playing dead.

And I wasn't pissed at the dog, anyway. I was used to his sulphuric emissions and mattress annexation. I was thinking about Charlotte and Emily. How their lives weren't perfect. I mean, of course they weren't *perfect*. But their lives had always seemed, at the very least, like a couple walks in a particularly pleasant park. Early success—beauty and brains and fame—loving husbands, great families. How hard could it be?

But both were struggling, both were lost and confused and hurt. It was sobering, and it defied everything I thought I knew. I mean, I was struggling, too—but I was *always* struggling. Unlike them, I knew how to struggle. I knew how to live with embarrassment and failure and Vague Dissatisfaction. They were babes in the woods of inadequacy. They hadn't come to terms with their limitations. They weren't old friends with procrastination and obsessive lotto-fantasies.

Part of me wished I could take all their struggles and pain into my own life, where they belonged. Wished I could erase their problems and restore the balance of the world. It was my job to be fucked up and their jobs to be perfect. They were screwing with the cosmic scales here.

But another part of me thought, *maybe now's my chance!* Maybe now that they were down, I'd seesaw upward. Like there were only so many Success Units per family, and if they lost a few, I'd gain some. Only problem was, I wasn't really struggling to be a success at anything in particular. I was just struggling in general. Struggling with my job, my relationship, my lack of ambition and my VD…and my fragrant dog, stealing the covers.

I tugged the blanket back to my side, and dozed for fifteen minutes before my alarm clock sounded. I'd set the damn thing for six o'clock, but it couldn't be six already. I hadn't slept. I summoned the energy to open one eye—6:07.

I planned on getting to the office by seven-thirty, to set an example for the employees, being virtual co-owner and all. At least I wasn't struggling with my relationship anymore. That one thing had been resolved. I was committed. I was settled.

So I bathed and dressed, fed and walked Ny and myself, and actually got to work as planned. I flitted around the office, opening shades and brewing coffee and tidying a bit—not in my job description, but we business owners must stoop low to raise high—and by the time the first Realtor arrived, I was exhausted.

It didn't help that the first Realtor was Mike, who'd never quite gotten over his boyhood routine of waking at dawn to swab the decks and gut the tuna, or whatever it was fishermen did. He was early-rising, but not even-tempered. He poured himself a cup of coffee and swore viciously when he splashed cream on his cuff.

"And good morning to you!" I said chirpily, to annoy him.

"It's too early in the morning for this shit."

"You should switch to tea. I recommend chamomile."

"Not talking about the coffee. Look at you. You're all…" He waved his coffee cup, spilling a bit more. "You look fucking gift-wrapped."

"Thank you, Michael," I said. "You're looking well yourself."

"Christ. Tell me when Anne gets in." Grumbling under his breath, he retreated into his office. "…fucking nightmare…"

For some reason, this reinvigorated me. I dug into the mountain of contracts that needed filing, updated the database, printed labels for a new direct mail piece, paid some bills, and by lunchtime had achieved more than I usually did all day. I told Rip I loved him—but privately, not with a singing telegram, troupe of clowns, or skywriter. And when an older couple came in with questions, I virtually sold them on a place myself—the open house from the rainy day. Rip made an appointment to show it to them that afternoon, and told me I should have lunch on him, as a reward.

I ate lunch at my desk, though, because I was working on a flow process chart. Rip had some business management books in his office, and this was featured in one of them. I was attempting to clarify our work flow, so any bottlenecks or log-jams were immediately visible.

Bottlenecks, log-jams, and dead ends. Hmm. I glanced at my Recent Developments file. That file was like my fixation on Ian. It was an excuse not to commit to my real situation. Ian was a daydream to avoid the reality of Rip, and the Recent Developments file was a daydream to avoid the reality of my job. Instead of immersing myself in work, I wasted time playing Developer. And there was no place on my flow process chart for *that* sort of behavior.

I took a deep breath. Grabbed the Recent Developments file. Took another deep breath.

And I dropped it in the trash.

CHAPTER

15

"I understand that's what the seller says he needs," I told the Realtor on the phone. "I need a million four, too—but I'm not gonna sell my truck for seven figures, no matter what I need—because it's simply not worth that much. Your seller's dreaming.... No, it's not *his* job to be realistic. It's your job. You think a buyer cares how much your seller needs?... Well, show us the comps... Yeah, we got the package. *One* comp? And for a house that sold at a million one anyway, *and* it's twenty percent bigger... Well, look at the taxes. Divide the price by—no, I don't think I'm an appraiser, I think I'm interested in real estate in Santa Barbara. Just like your average buyer."

Rip came and leaned against my desk, and tapped his watch. I put a finger in the air, telling him to wait a second, as the Realtor squawked in my ear.

"Of course it's the seller's decision," I said when the Realtor finished. "Of course you can't lower the price yourself. But you can refuse the listing at that price. And why wouldn't you? You like wasting your time? His time? That's fine. But you're wasting the time of my agents and our clients. Try professionalism. Try honesty. You know it's not gonna sell at one point four. I know it. Everyone knows it but the seller.... Uh-huh. Well, then have that difficult conversation. Believe me, you'll feel better. Yeah. Yeah? Good. You, too. Give me a call after? Great. Bye."

I hung up and caught Rip staring at me with incredulous awe. "What was *that?*" he said.

"You said the market analysis came in at a million even."

"Yeah, but—"

"You know you hate when agents buy listings." Agents "bought" listings by letting the seller set hugely overinflated prices, even though the Realtor (and everyone else) knew it would never go for that.

"I didn't mean for you to call the poor guy and scold him. He's not about to insist the sellers lower the price."

"He's calling them right now."

"Really?"

I nodded. "They don't lower, he's gonna drop the listing."

Rip chuckled. "Well, then—keep doing what you're doing. Except...let's do it over dinner. Alcazar?"

"Well, I have a few more things here...."

"C'mon, Polliwog. All work and no play."

Which was the very first time anyone ever said that to me. So I organized my work for tomorrow and we left. "Not Alcazar, though," I said. "How about we pick up movies and I'll cook?"

"How about we pick up movies and *I'll* cook?"

"Deal." Which just proved how right I was to commit. Rip realized how hard I'd been working, realized I didn't want to go out to dinner, and found the perfect way to treat me.

We rented a few movies at the Wherehouse and went next

door to Gelson's Market for dinner stuff. That's where things started to go wrong.

I suggested pasta, because Rip had the mysterious ability to cook sauces which actually stuck to the pasta—my sauce invariably pooled at the bottom of the pan. We agreed that my contribution would be salad and garlic bread, as I had no problem getting butter to stick to toast or dressing to lettuce.

There was something about shopping together which put me in an entirely domestic mood. I loved doing errands as a couple. My idea of a perfect relationship was one in which I never had to go to the post office or the dry cleaner's alone. And here we were, after a day in the office together, shopping for lettuce (him) and bread (me), on our way home (mine, but soon perhaps "ours?") for dinner and a couple movies. Did it get any better?

I grabbed a loaf of San Francisco sourdough, which sparked a thought. I called across the aisle from bread to produce. "We should go to San Francisco this fall. Drive up, stay in a nice hotel." Spend some of that Knox Tower money. "Maybe a day in the wine country…"

Rip, bent over the various lettuces, said, "Mhl vimmor hrhr."

"What?"

He stood, a bag of mesclun in his hand, and said, "Well. Um…"

"You love San Francisco."

"Um, yeah, but…"

"We could go somewhere else. Hawaii? What's wrong with San Francisco?"

He mumbled.

"Or Mexico!" I said. "Cancún or something. I still think San Francisco."

"I just dunno about this fall…." He tossed the bag of mesclun into the shopping cart.

"What, you're busy the whole season?"

"No, I just…"

"You just *what?*"

He sort of sighed. "I doubt we'll still be together."

I laughed. "Right. Now that we're totally committed, we're not gonna make it through the fall."

"I'm not kidding, Anne."

I calmly said, "You're not kidding about what?"

"I don't know how long we'll be together."

The shopping cart leapt from my grip and rammed a shelf of canned beans. "You want to break up with me?"

"No, I don't want to break up with you."

"Well, nobody's fucking making you."

"I'm not breaking up with you. I don't want—" He shook his head, his eyes sad. "I just think you're not taking our relationship seriously."

"What? Where have you been? I've never been this committed—I, I'm totally committed, we're taking the relationship to a whole new level. Haven't you noticed?"

He said, very gently, "Annie, the harder you try, the clearer it becomes—you're not ready to commit."

"I am totally committed!"

A can of garbanzos fell to the floor, emphasizing my words with a crash.

"Anne, I love you. But I want to settle down, I want to start a family. I'm not getting any younger."

"Listen to me carefully, Rip. Can you hear me? Can you see my lips moving? I am totally committed to you, to us, to this relationship. I have never been this committed before."

"Then let me ask you: will you marry me?"

"What, here? In the middle of Gelson's?"

"Will you marry me, Anne?"

"You can't ask this—not while we're fighting. It's not fair."

"Would you settle down with me, spend the rest of your life with me? Have children with me? Would you?"

"I told you I love you."

"I know. But you're not ready to—"

"I've never said that to a man before." Except the guy who makes my smoothies at Blenders, everyone at work, the cop who pulled me over… But I *meant* it with Rip. "You're the first."

"And I'm honored," he said. "But it's not true. Not the kind of lifelong love I—"

So I rammed the cart into the bean shelf again, causing a hail of chili beans. "Oh, it's true! It's true, goddammit! I love you! *I love you!*"

"Annie…"

"I love you!"

"Polliwog—"

"I *love* you!"

Some guy poked his head down our aisle, and I turned on him. "What the fuck are *you* looking at? Never seen a woman in love before?"

Turned out he was the manager. So, in the end, we left the store without groceries.

Five minutes later. Standing in the parking lot. I'd never been kicked out of a grocery store before. Rip probably hadn't even been shushed in a movie theatre. Plus, we were sort of breaking up or something.

We looked at each other.

"So… Thai food?" I said.

"Sounds good."

That was the sum total of our conversation, other than debating if we should get a large Tom Yum Gai or a small, until we got to my place to watch the videos. We'd always watched a lot of movies together—but early on, after Rip brought home *Emma* and *American Psycho II,* I'd imposed Theme Night. The movies had to have some relationship. *Emma* could be paired with another Jane Austen film, period piece, or anything with Jeremy Northam. *American Psycho II* (despite being *American Psycho II*) was acceptable with *AP I* or another horror sequel such as *Final Destination II.* Hell, I'd even accept *American Psycho* with *Legally Blonde,* because they both had Reese Witherspoon. This had sparked a contest between us, to see who could come up with the most tenuous theme, a sort of six degrees of thematic separation.

But I'd been tired tonight, and uncreative. I'd chosen ethnic matrimony, with *My Big Fat Greek Wedding* and *Monsoon Wedding.* Apparently that had been a strategic error, as it got Rip thinking about marriage. Marriage and commitment and the pitter-patter of tiny feet. Men were supposed to be the ones who didn't want to marry. Sheesh. He should be counting his lucky stars to find a woman like me.

Anyway, I didn't know how he could say I wasn't serious about the relationship. I'd love to settle down with him. To marry. To have children. To spend the rest of our lives together.

"Anne? Are you okay?"

I nodded, hand to my mouth.

"You look green."

"The Tom Yum Gai's a little light on the *yum.*"

He eyed me suspiciously.

I swallowed, with some difficulty. "Let's do it. Let's get married."

"What kind of wedding? Monsoon, or big fat Greek?"

"I'm serious," I said. "Let's do it. I want to get married. I want to marry you." I took a deep breath. "Will you marry me?"

★ ★ ★

Thirty seconds later, I was standing over the toilet. I finished and rinsed my mouth. I splashed water on my face and looked at myself in the mirror. Yep. There I was. Then I crept timidly back into the living room.

Rip was pointedly watching the extra features on one of the DVDs.

"It was the soup," I said.

Rip pointedly began watching me.

"I think I'm allergic to lemongrass," I told him.

"Anne, you don't want to marry me."

"I do! Maybe I do."

"You don't."

"You can't tell me I don't. You're not the boss of me!"

He smiled, a bit sadly. "Okay, Annie. Let's get married. I'd love to marry you. I want you to be the mother of my children. I've loved you since the day you yelled at Mike, 'Talk to Charlie Tuna.' I still have no idea what that means, but I knew I was falling hard." He took my hand, and his voice was as intent as his eyes. "We're getting married. We're going to spend the rest of our lives together. How does that make you feel?"

I started to cry.

"Yeah," he said.

"I just n-need time…." I hiccuped.

"Anne, I'm ready to settle down. I'm ready now."

"It's just, I don't know if I want—"

"I know what you don't want," he said. "You've always made it clear."

"It's only been six months, Rip. Give me a chance. We could get engaged."

"Engaged *to get married?*"

"Engaged," I said. "Engaged like—you know. We'd be fiancés."

He considered for a moment. "You do love me. In your way."

"In my way? What does that mean?"

"It means I don't want to wait. And you might never be ready. Not with me."

"But—"

"I'd better go."

"No, stay," I said. I wanted to comfort him. To prove I loved him, prove we had a chance together. Prove I wasn't a commitment-phobic loser.

He kissed me. Then he left.

CHAPTER

16

What do you wear to work when you're no longer the Co-President in Charge of Everything? When you're probably the Boss's Ex-Girlfriend, but don't really know if you've been dumped? It's hard to plan an outfit around this stuff. Do you go for the Woman Spurned pantsuit? Offer a glimpse of Possible Reconciliation décolletage? Or wear your business-inappropriate Eat Your Heart Out miniskirt? And I don't even want to start on the hair issue.

Anyway, Rip apparently didn't spend much time trying to decode my black miniskirt, gray tights, and crimson sweater, although any normal person would know exactly what it meant. Instead, he treated me with a sort of overpolite courtesy. And I'm pretty sure he eyed Janelle, one of the female agents, with a certain speculation. Like he was mentally measuring her hips, checking her child-bearing potential.

"Want to borrow my calipers?" I mumbled, clicking my mouse and ignoring the phone as it started to ring.

"Um," he said. "Excuse me?"

"Nothing," I said.

"Okay. Um—could you run some listings for the Lockhearts? They want San Roque."

The phone kept ringing and I put the ten of hearts on the jack of clubs on my computer screen. "I'm busy."

"Oh. Okay." He glanced at the phone. "Um…"

"Yes?"

"Nothing." He opened the door to his office, then glanced at the phone again. "Could you take care of that?"

I smiled warmly. "Sure." I bellowed down the hall, "Someone answer the fucking phone!"

Rip slipped into his office and closed the door.

"Welcome back," Mike said, walking past.

I cheerfully threw a pad of sticky-notes at him. Oddly enough, by that afternoon I'd lost my sprightly good mood—and thirty-seven games of solitaire. This whole situation was bogus. I didn't even know if we were having a fight or the whole relationship was over. I was pretty certain it was somehow my fault, though. For what? For being more committed to Rip than I had ever been to any other man? For telling him I loved him, and for trying to be partners at work? What was his problem? His biological clock was ticking?

So I flung open the door of his office and stormed inside. *"What?"*

"Um…" He'd been saying that a lot today, and it was starting to annoy. "What, what?"

"You know what what. Don't you pretend you don't know what what."

"Um…"

"Shut up! I just want to know, Rip, am I dumped or not dumped?"

He looked confused. "Of course you're not dumped."

"So we're still together?"

"Well, no."

My turn to look confused. "We're not together, but I'm not dumped?"

"Exactly," he said, clearly hoping that would end the discussion.

"Rip, I'm this close to losing my temper."

"You're not dumped!" he hurriedly said. "I'd never dump you. I, um—my feelings for you—I still, you know. But it's not going to work for us. I want kids, marriage. You want... whatever."

"Whatever? What is whatever?"

He sighed. "You want sex and company, Anne."

"Oh, that is such crap! What I *really* want is—" What I really wanted was sex and company. "—is whatever. Love and...all that."

We were silent a moment, he trying to look solemn and me struck dumb by the sheer feebleness of my retort. Then I said, "So, what? We basically what? We grew apart?"

"Yeah," he said. "We realized it wasn't going to work out."

"And we stopped seeing each other?"

"Yeah."

"I'm not dumped?"

"Of course not, Annie."

"Maybe I can dump you?"

He laughed. "If you want."

"We just grew apart?"

"Nobody's fault," he said. "We're still friends."

"Okay. Good. That clears it up. Great."

"Good." Rip smiled. "I'm glad that's settled."

Fuck. I was so dumped. So I said, "I quit."

In class that evening, I told Wren the whole story, emphasizing the key bits about Rip throwing a tantrum at Gelson's and reading bizarre messages into *My Big Fat Greek Wedding*.

I was engaged in an extended fantasy about how I'd told Rip that we should still be friends when she spun her sculpture stand in a meaningful manner.

I stopped talking, and she gave me the eye. Clearly I was supposed to understand her sculpture stand charades.

"Less pantomime," I said. "More sympathy."

"You see this?" She spun her stand again. "It's called turnabout."

"Yeah?"

"Yeah. And it's fair play."

"What is that supposed to mean?"

"How many men have you dumped? Dozens. Well, this time the dump is on the other foot!"

"Gross," I said.

"You know what I mean."

"C'mon. He dumped me because—well, *if* he dumped me, which he says he didn't—it was because I'm not ready to marry and have kids. What is he, a girl?"

"No, he's a—"

She was interrupted by the teacher, Claire, making an announcement. "This is Kevin's last night with us, so finish what you're working on. We'll be firing the kiln next week—anyone who can help load, we'll meet at noon and—"

Wren turned to me in panic. "Help!" she whispered. "He's leaving. I'll never see him again. Oh, God. I should ask for his phone number. I can't ask for his number. How can I ask for his number? You know I can't ask for his phone number. What do you mean I should ask for his number? You *know* I can't ask for his number, Anne!"

I spun my sculpture stand in a meaningful manner.

"Anne..." she said warningly.

I smiled. "I'll take care of it. Don't worry."

"Promise?"

"I promise."

"You don't—now that you're single, you better not get his number for yourself. You still think he's gay, Anne. Remember? Okay?"

"Wren. C'mon, would I ever?"

She had the grace to look abashed. "No. You're right. But he's gonna put his clothes on and walk out of here in two hours and—"

"And you won't see him with his clothes off again, unless you take action."

"Unless *you* take action."

"Then watch my subtle magic, and be amazed."

I waited until class was over and Kevin was dressed, and waved him over to us. He admired my sculpture politely and Wren's enthusiastically. I glanced at Wren as if to say *watch the moves!* and said, "Hey, Wren and I are going out for a drink. You wanna come?"

"Sure."

Yep. It was that easy.

We ended up at a bar called Shika, a good place to go if you wanted to talk, because it was perennially empty. I hustled Wren and Kevin into a booth and monopolized the other side myself, so they were smooshed together. I was being completely obvious, but so what? It's not some complex mating ritual, like with bower birds or geckos. This was a man we were talking about.

The thing was, I was a bit conflicted. I wanted Kevin to like Wren, but I also wanted some company for my misery. What if they got together, and she was totally happy while I was morose? That would be wrong. Our relationship had always maintained a delicate balance. She excelled at her career, I was better with men.

So I flashed on this evil desire to sabotage things with her and Kevin. And immediately knew that I *had* to get them together. If I didn't, I'd always wonder if I'd undermined my best friend. And I might not be much, but I was there for my friends.

The first step in my Matchmaker Mode was a bit of conversation they could bond over, preferably about someone else's troubles. Like mine.

"So I have no man and no job," I told Kevin, after we ordered. "As of yesterday."

"You lost both the same day?"

"I never do things halfway."

"Wait, let me guess. You worked together?"

"I worked for him."

"You were sleeping with your boss?"

"No," I scoffed. "Of course not. I was working for my boyfriend."

He laughed. Wren laughed, too, and managed not to snort. She looked about to say something, so I glared at her until she started toying with a salt shaker that was on the table.

"What happened?" he asked.

"He wanted to get married and have kids and all," I said, disgusted.

"What is he?" Kevin said. *"A girl?"*

"Exactly! That's exactly what I said. Let me ask—are you interested in marriage? Children?"

"Not me," he said. "Not yet."

I looked to Wren. "Now *this* is a man. I'm telling you, I could go on Jerry Springer. My boyfriend was a girl."

"You're only mad because you got dumped for once," Wren said, and explained to Kevin, "She's always the dumper, never the dumpee. She's dumped like a hundred guys in the past ten years. That's ten a year. That's almost one a month. It's like one every five weeks or something. Maybe six weeks. No, five. Five and a half. I'm not very good at math." She giggled horribly, and turned a bright red. "Anyway, Anne's always the dumper. Not the dumpee. That's why she's mad."

"I'm mad, Wren, because Rip is an evil girl disguised as a man."

She fiddled with the salt shaker, clearly determined not to open her mouth. But I could tell the wheels were spinning.

"What?" I said.

"Nothing," she said. "I mean, nothing. Nothing."

"C'mon, Wren. I know that expression."

She glanced at Kevin.

"You can talk in front of Kevin," I said. "We have no secrets from Kevin. We spent the past three hours staring at his—"

"Well!" she interrupted. "Well, I—I'm sorry that you're hurt."

"Sheesh. At least call him a rat bastard or something."

"I know you don't want to hear it, but Rip has a point."

"What?"

"You were never going to commit."

Oh, she couldn't manage a single sentence while flirting, but she was fluent enough when she was scolding me. "That doesn't give him the right to break up with me."

"Of course it does. Anne, we're going to be thirty. You're the only woman I know—I mean, even some *guys* are ready at this age. And Rip's one of those guys."

"I can't believe you're taking his side."

"Not completely." She brushed a strand of hair out of my face. "I'm mad at him for making you sad. I hate to see you unhappy."

"Yeah, and it's not just Rip. It's the job, too." I moaned for another few minutes, until I figured I'd given them enough to talk about for days. Then I feigned checking the messages on my cell. "Oh, my God! I was supposed to meet my dad at the train station! I've gotta go."

"Oh, no," Wren said, in a sudden panic. "Can't you stay for one more drink?"

"And leave Dad out in the cold?"

"It's not cold—it's not that cold outside. He can call a cab—or not a cab, one of your sisters," she said desperately. "Emily can pick him up. It's not that cold outside. It's hot— it's pretty warm in here…."

"Careful you don't overheat," I said.

"We can but try," Kevin said, his eyes laughing.

"Anne!" Wren said, and twisted the salt shaker. The top popped off and salt spewed across the table.

I tossed a pinch over Wren's shoulder, bussed her on the cheek for luck, and left.

Over the next week, one thing was clear: my nearest and dearest had absolutely no family values. I refer to such Family values as the Mafia code of silence, as well as any slight trace of loyalty. Love, yes. Loyalty, no.

A few days after the breakup, I was standing in what Charlotte now referred to as her "sewing room," being fitted for a bathing suit I didn't want. And she was humming happily as she worked.

"Would you stop?" I said.

"Did I prick you?"

I told her that her good mood was needling me, and she went back to work, wearing a big grin.

"Okay," I said. "Why are you so happy?"

"You got dumped."

"And this is a good thing because…?"

"I don't know," she said, measuring my waist. "Because you deserve it?"

"For what?" I asked, looking at the ceiling so I wouldn't be tempted to check the tape measure. "For being loyal and loving?"

"For dumping all those guys over the years. For breaking hearts."

"I've never broken a single heart. Name one guy who—ouch!"

"Sorry."

"Name a single guy whose heart I broke."

"Nick? Alex?"

"Nick wore Mary Janes! Anyway, like you never broke up with a guy."

"Not like you. Remember Garret?"

"He doesn't count. He was balding and had a ponytail. Either one is fine, but both together?"

"That's what I'm talking about."

"Well, what about Ian?" I said. "You broke up with him."

"We were teenagers. He went to college. I went to model. We broke up with each other. It's not like you—you were in your twenties. And now you're looking down the barrel of thirty—"

"It's not like any of them thought I was serious."

"No," she said, glancing at me. "But you could've been. And not just with Rip."

"With who then?"

"I always liked Arthur."

"The plumber," I said. You'd think a famous swimsuit model would look down on plumbers, but of course Charlotte liked Arthur the best.

"Nothing wrong with that," she said.

"Except he was the kind of plumber who wrote letters to *Penthouse*. 'I never thought it would happen to me, but I got a call to fix this lady's toilet....'"

"He slept around? *Arthur?* C'mon, Annie."

"A woman knows."

She jabbed me. "The point is, you never give anyone a chance."

"That's not true," I said, angrily rubbing my thigh. "Rip left me. I'm the victim here. Why can't anyone see that?"

"Because nobody believes you ever would've married him."

I brought chocolate éclairs to Emily. I knew she'd be home with Zach, because Jamie was at a publishing conference, and after I was so good about her crappy book, I figured she owed me sympathy. I ran down the top ten reasons I was happy to be rid of Rip, ending with, "And he was always talking about real estate. Rates of appreciation and 7/1 ARMs and blah blah blah."

"That's his job, Anne."

"Yeah, but still."

"And you liked the real estate stuff. You know you did."

"That's not the point, Emily."

She wiped pastry cream from her mouth. "What's the point, then?"

"It's, um…he just never really rang my bell."

"It's always about sex with you, isn't it?"

Okay. I had no idea where this was going, but I knew I wasn't in the mood. So I told her I had a headache and left.

I got home and found a message from Dad: "He was one of the good ones, Anne." He'd left a second message an hour later: "How are you doing for money?"

Over the next week, my whole world basically weighed in with a resounding vote for Rip. So I called my ex-boyfriend Alex, in L.A. He'd been rejected enough times for his writing—still hadn't sold a screenplay—that I figured he could relate.

"Let me get this straight," he said. "Someone dumped *you?*"

"Yeah."

"That's too bad, Anne."

"Hey! I didn't laugh when your script about the Irish rabbi didn't sell."

"I've had a lot of interest in *Mickey Doyle, Irish Moyle.* I want Mike Myers for the moyle. Or you think Adam Sandler can play Irish?"

"Anyway," I said, unwilling to begin a three-hour conversation about the fantasy cast for his movie, "what are you doing this weekend?"

He sighed. "I wish I could, Anne."

"Wish you could what?"

"Come see you." He managed to leer with his voice. "Give you a shoulder to cry on."

Cocky bastard. "What makes you think I want—"

"You call every time you break up with someone. Just because you were the one dumped doesn't mean—"

"Are you gonna come, or not?"

"I've got a new girlfriend," he said.

"So?"

"Anne."

"She doesn't have to know."

"Anne."

"Fine," I said, sulkily. "I wouldn't want you to cheat on your precious new girlfriend."

"That's better."

Might as well *pretend* I was a grown-up. "So when do I meet her?"

"Actually I was gonna call about a double date with you and Rip. I guess that's off, though."

"Funny," I said.

Then there were the Sharones, my ex-co-workers Shannon and Shayla. I'd invited them to lunch to hear me complain about Rip. As single women actively dating, they should've been more than happy to drink mimosas and revile my ex. So I told them a version of the story in which a black-hatted Rip twiddled his moustache and said, "You must pay the rent" and "Curses! Foiled again!"

"Rip's single?" Shannon said, not really following my point. "Really?"

"Rrowr," Shayla said.

"He dumped me!" I said.

"He's one of the good ones," Shannon said. "If he were my boyfriend, I might even let him sleep around."

"He didn't want to sleep around," I said. "Worse. He wanted to get married and make babies."

They eyed me strangely. "And he's single again?" Shayla said.

"What does he have, green eyes?" Shannon asked.

"Would you two stop it? I'm dumped, I've been dumped. He's the dumper. He dumped me in the ketchup aisle at Gelson's!"

"Well, I think he's rotten to have broken up with you," Shayla said, coming to her senses.

"Thank you."

"I know what it's like to pour out all your love and caring, to invest everything you have in a man, and then be rejected, unwanted and unloved—"

"Shayla, he's a *cat* for Christ's sake," Shannon said.

"So? I feed him, I love him. And he moves next door, where they have Sheba with its fancy little containers and—"

And that's as much sympathy as I got. Hell, even my aunt Regina phoned to lecture me about settling down, and she'd never even liked Rip.

Nobody was on my side. Except Ian.

CHAPTER 17

I was home alone. It was evening. I was leafing through the newspaper, trying to ignore the dreaded section G: Help Wanted. Eventually, however, I had to admit that the funny pages simply weren't. So I cautiously opened the classifieds and was staring morosely at an ad for Office Manager—worse pay than Parsons Realty, and no benefits—when the phone rang.

I pounced, hoping it was a long-lost friend who'd actually side with me. And I guess it was.

"Thursday night," Ian said.

"Who's calling please?"

"You want to start with that again?"

He meant either the fake remembered reservoir sex or the awkward message I'd left on his machine. I wasn't sure which, but I wanted to start with neither, so I said, "Hey, Ian."

"It's Thursday night," he said again, as if it meant something.

"I know. I've got the newspaper in front of me, I even know the month and year."

"The newspaper? That doesn't sound good."

"I do read the paper, you know."

"Of course," he said. "What *is* that wacky Garfield up to?"

"Ha–ha." I circled an ad for data entry. "I'm reading the business pages, I'll have you know."

"The *Business Pages?* Is that by the same guy who does *Foxtrot?*"

"Oh, shut up and tell me about Thursday night."

"It's drinks night."

"Drinks night?"

"Thursday. Tonight. Drinks. Us. It's a tradition."

"Where's Helene?" I asked, crossing out the ad for data entry.

"Out of town on business."

I wish I were out of town on business. "I don't feel like it."

"Why not?"

"Um, well…I was going to spend the evening doing yoga. And reading Virginia Woolf."

"Because you got dumped, huh?" Ian asked.

My pen ripped a jagged tear through an ad for Library Director. "Who told *you?*"

"Rip."

"Rip told you? You were talking to Rip? You don't talk to Rip! He told you he dumped me? What's he doing—calling everyone in his Rolodex? Maybe he should just take out an ad, save himself the phone bill." Or maybe he called Ian because he knew I had a crush on him. Uh-oh. "He's a big fat liar, that's what he is. I hope you didn't believe one word he said. I don't know what he's saying. He really called you? *Rip?* Rip called you?"

"I'm coming over," Ian said, and hung up.

"No! Wait!"

Shit. Shit! Rip told Ian I was warm for him. Why else

come over? What if he was coming over to ring my bell? Okay. Calm. He wasn't coming to ring my bell. He still had a fiancée, he wasn't after sex. But she was out of town, so maybe he was. God, I hoped not. Not that I didn't want to— if he weren't Charlotte's ex-boyfriend, I'd take him in one hot steamy second. But I liked him, I didn't want him to be the kind of man who cheated on his fiancée. And I wasn't the kind of woman who slept with engaged men. Even if his fiancée was Helene. Besides, he was Charlotte's ex. It would be gross and incestuous.

Still, for purely aesthetic reasons, I brushed my hair into a high ponytail—wouldn't hurt for him to notice I was younger than Helene, though obviously not as beautiful—and added blush and mascara. I really needed lipstick, but didn't want to seem like I'd gone to any effort. I wanted to look like Meg Ryan, when Tom Hanks comes to the door. She isn't expecting him, but still looks flawless and vulnerable in a tank top and pajama bottoms. Of course, she has the unfair advantage of actually being Meg Ryan. So I went for a sort of second-rate Charlotte Olsen look—younger and not as beautiful as her, either—but clearly flawed and vulnerable.

I tidied away any items of potential embarrassment, such as a pair of Rip's boxers I'd been shredding, and an erotic romance I'd been reading, before Ian arrived with a bottle of Merlot and a white grocery sack.

"Ian!" I said, feigning surprise. "I didn't think you were really coming!"

"You've got mascara on your cheek," he said. "Kitchen's through there?"

I nodded dumbly, and followed him in. Ny perked a sleepy ear. One of his nostrils twitched, and he hopped off the couch, on the scent of something tasty.

"Hope you don't mind," Ian said, setting Chinese takeout cartons on the counter. "I haven't eaten."

"Ooh, Chinese!" I'd devoured the entire contents of my cabinets and fridge earlier, and was still starving. Getting dumped took a lot of energy. "What'd you get? Ny! Down!"

"Kung Pao Beef," Ian said, fending off Ny with a graceful knee. "Lemon Chicken and Veggie Lo Mein. Where's your corkscrew?"

"In there." I pointed to the drawer and pulled my favorite wineglasses from the cabinet. They were Baccarat cut crystal—a birthday gift from Charlotte—and maybe a little cliché, but looked gorgeous filled with red wine.

We ate in the living room and I caught an immediate buzz from the food and wine. This was so exactly what I'd needed. We even shared cartons, tossing rice on top of the dishes and dipping in with our chopsticks. And there wasn't any scary sexual energy. Possibly a faint hormonal hum in the background, but a normal amount for straight friends of the opposite sex.

I told him I didn't want to talk about the breakup, then made him sit through the whole story. There actually wasn't that much to tell anymore, so I embellished a bit: "…and he kept ramming the shopping cart into a display of canned tomato soups, screaming that he loved me."

"Uh-huh."

"It was a Campbell's soup explosion. The manager—"

"Were they stacked in a pyramid?"

"What? No."

"Wouldn't it have been cool if they were stacked in a pyramid?"

I glared. "*Anyway*—the manager came and kicked him out. He was a public nuisance. He was a danger to himself and others. That's the sort of devotion I inspire."

"Uh-huh. So you rented a bunch of wedding videos, he realized you'd never marry him, and he dumped you?"

"Yeah. Like I said."

He laughed and I refilled our glasses with Merlot. We finished the food and I poured the extra sauce in Ny's bowl, and we chatted about movies and Santa Barbara and New York. I told him about my Recent Developments file and he told me a few Sotheby's horror stories. Then he started making fun of my furniture.

He looked around the room with a sort of curious horror. "How many trips to Crate & Barrel did you make?"

"I don't know what you're talking about," I said.

"The couch, the bookshelves, the lamps…"

"Those are Ikea."

"Oh, *much* better. The linens and dishes—"

"Pottery Barn."

"And you're proud? It's a schlock showroom in here."

"Hey! I spent a lot of time getting everything the way I like it."

"Well, it's very…glossy. And everything matches."

"Thank you."

"But it's got no soul. Except for this." He stood to examine the old table Charlotte had given me. "This is beautiful. Victorian mahogany…" He swarmed over the pestilential old thing, muttering about its "birdcage" and "leaf-carved tripod base." Then he said, "Where did this come from?"

"Charlotte."

He nodded. "Of course."

"Of course? What does that mean? She gave me a used table for my birthday."

He murmured something soothing to the table, rubbing his hand over the top like it was a woman's hip.

"She knows I like new things," I said. "But she couldn't resist giving me that Goodwill special. I don't know why everyone says she's so nice. She's pure evil."

Ian shot me a sympathetic look. "I see what you mean.

She should've known the table wouldn't work in here. It makes your other stuff look awful."

"Everything else is new!" I said. "New is better."

"If it's made with love, maybe. This stuff—" he swept a disdainful arm at my furnishings "—has no integrity, no history, and no quality. It won't last. It won't age. You're just storing it between the factory and the junkyard."

"Yeah? Well—well, it's your fault Rip dumped me!"

"Really?" he said, cheerfully.

Uh-oh. "Not because I—it's not like you came between us." I made a sound somewhere between a snort and a huff. "Puh-lease."

"No?" He tore himself away from the table and sat beside me on the fresh, new, clean couch he hated so much. He leaned close. "I thought maybe I was a home-wrecker—and you and I were fated for an illicit rendezvous of..."

My heart started beating faster, before I noticed the teasing glint in his eye. "Shut up," I said, shoving him.

He grinned. "I don't know how else it could be my fault."

"That whole *I love you* thing."

"I never told you to start with that."

"You did!"

"All I said was, stop saying *Fukui-san*. Anyway, you should thank me. Rip wasn't right for you."

"How do you know?" I said. "You don't even know him. I was totally in love. Totally committed. Ready to take the relationship to the next level. I was—I was..." Okay, maybe I'd had a bit too much wine, but I could feel the tears in my eyes and throat, and I sort of wailed, "I was Co-President in Charge of Everything!"

Ian held me while I cried, and patted my back and made soothing noises. When I'd finished, and had wiped my eyes on his T-shirt, he said, "So maybe now you're the *President* in Charge of Everything."

"More like the CEO of Stupid." I looked up at him. "Have you ever felt like you made the right decision, but everyone says you're wrong? Rip broke up with me—why is everyone on his side? You start to think, What am I, crazy? Am I taking crazy pills here?"

"You stole that from *Zoolander*."

"It was on TV last night."

"You're sure you don't want to marry him?" Ian asked.

"Yeah, I'm sure," I said. "I don't want to get married. And I definitely don't want to have kids—not yet, at least."

"So wait—back up. You're sad because he dumped you?"

I sniffled.

"But he dumped you because you didn't want him," he said. "Right?"

"I guess."

"Well, if the reason for the breakup was a decision *you* made—not to marry him—then who really dumped whom?"

"Good try," I said. "But he really dumped me." Still, I smiled. I did feel better—and it wasn't just the Kung Pao and wine. "So—why did he call you?"

"To see if Helene and I were interested in a house."

"Oh! Oh. And are you?" I wanted to know more about Ian and Helene. He was so closemouthed about their relationship.

He shrugged. "She's not sure."

Well, I tried. "What did he say about me?"

"Just that you broke up."

"Did he mention we were still friends? That we'd grown apart?"

"I didn't really ask."

"Hmm." I wanted to believe that Rip was emotionally frigid, but he'd teared up watching *What a Girl Wants*. "So not only have I been dumped, but he's completely over me."

"He didn't deserve you, Anne."

"You mean like he didn't deserve to win the lottery, or like he didn't deserve to die of a painful wasting disease?"

He considered. "A little of both, actually."

"Oh," I said. "That's okay then."

We finished the wine and took Ny for a walk. When we got back, Ian—having scoured my kitchen for any crumb of dessert—whipped up some shortbread with flour, butter and sugar. Sweet and simple. Then he went home. No bells were rung. It was very innocent. It was very nice. It was like we were...buddies.

The next morning I cleaned the remains of the feast and took Ny for a long walk at Ellwood Park in Goleta, the town north of Santa Barbara. It was a half hour drive out there, an hour walk, another half hour back—plenty of time for mulling over my job hunt. But I got distracted by the fields and the cliffs and the beach. In the winter, monarch butterflies fly up from Mexico to mate or lay eggs or something—tens of thousands of them. There weren't any to distract me at the moment, but I still managed to spend a half hour wondering about them, instead of mentally polishing my resume.

I couldn't decide if the monarchs were to be envied or pitied. On the one hand, butterflies are about as aerodynamic as envelopes, and they had to fly two thousand miles just to get lei-ed. What, did they live with their parents? They couldn't get any butterfly nookie at home? It was ridiculous, going to those extremes for sex and company. So I pitied them.

On the other hand, they knew what they wanted. They knew what they needed. Somewhere in their pinhead insect brains, there was this driving urge to leave home for warmer climes, to romp with equally pea-brained creatures exactly like them in every way but one. Like college students on Spring Break. They had no Vague Dissatisfaction. They had no questions or worries or regrets. They just flitted for a couple thousand miles and bellied up to the bar. Enviable.

I walked down the path to the beach, and moodily tossed a stick for Ny. He ignored it, intent on the perfume of rotting seaweed. Maybe I shouldn't have quit. Rip gave me three weeks' vacation pay, so I was okay for money, and there were always temp jobs. But I wanted something real this time. Something that inspired me. And something that paid well. Maybe I could work at Mott & Kensig. Then Helene could fire me. That'd be neat.

I sulked along the beach, caught up in bright scenarios of unemployment and failure, until we got to the Bacara. The Bacara was a huge luxury resort squatting among the sand dunes that always reminded me of the resort hotels in Mexico or Hawaii. It was perfect for people whose only desire was to nap by the pool or play golf. I always wished it were more like Esalen in Big Sur, with oceanside hot tubs and yoga classes and human development programs and macrobiotic cooking. More of a retreat center. Nobody was better than I at retreating.

Daydreaming of a new job as social director at Bacara, once it spontaneously transformed into Esalen South, I headed back to the car. We got home and I hosed Ny down outside. Hosed myself down inside, got dressed and was looking at my big ass in the mirror when the phone rang.

"Guess what?" Wren said.

"Objects in mirror are larger than they appear?"

"What? No." She emitted a noise of pure contentment. "But some objects are larger than at first sight. Kevin and I…"

"You didn't?"

"We did!"

"And?"

"And! And *and!*" She paused for breath. "And all I can say is, man alive."

"Man alive?"

"Man *alive!* Hoo boy. Yamma hamma."

"Okay, Wren. You're scaring me."

"It's been eleven months, Anne. But I'll tell you—it was worth the wait. Kevin's wonderful. He's wonderful. We talked about everything. He actually reads books—real books, not graphic novels—and we both like *The Amazing Race* and he listens when I talk and…"

And on and on. I told her how happy I was, and how lucky she was, and then we hung up and I cried.

By four o'clock, I was sick of myself. The only thing I liked less than work was inactivity. So I went to the Farmer's Market downtown and bought enough veggies to last three weeks, and pistachios, avocado honey, and sunflowers. Ny made himself useless, as always, and was petted and cooed over. I made myself useful, and was not.

The Farmer's Market was usually a good place to troll for men, but I wasn't in the mood. Plus there were a half-dozen girls there already, who happened to be wearing skimpy skirts and cute little tops for veggie shopping. I didn't want to become a cliché.

I tossed my shopping bags in the back of the truck and my dog in the front, and drove to the upper east side. Dad was teaching a class, so I let myself in and started dinner. Spaghetti and green salad and chocolate chip cookies. Nothing fancy except the sauce was a complicated rustica which involved roasting red peppers and caramelizing onion. I made the cookies while the sauce simmered, and was just setting a second pot of water on the stove to boil when my father walked in the door.

"Hey, Dad," I said. "When are you gonna buy new pots and pans?"

He had the same ones since we were kids—you can imagine how old and encrusted they were. I'd had to boil an initial pot of water just to detoxify the thing. It would've been a waste, tossing the water out—but it detoxified the sink, too.

"Actually," I said. "You could use a whole new kitchen."

Dad put his briefcase on the kitchen table and sang, *"Make new friends, but keep the old, one is silver and the other gold."*

"Were you always a freak?" I asked. "Or are you just getting doddery in your old age?"

It was a rhetorical question. He'd always been a freak. But he said, "Old? To quote Frank Sinatra…" And he sang again. *"Fairy tales can come true, it can happen to you, if you're young at heart."*

"Okay, okay," I said, laughing. "I give up."

But he didn't. He sang the Sinatra song through to the end.

"You're in a good mood," I said, when he'd finished.

"Dinner on the table does that to a man." He lifted the top from the saucepan. "Smells good. Spaghetti?"

"Capellini."

"You young people with your crazy pastas."

"It's angel-hair." Mom's favorite.

"Exactly," he said, dipping a spoon in the sauce for a taste. "So what brings you?"

"Does a loving daughter need an excuse to cook for her father?"

"Need money, huh?"

"No—"

"Depressed about Rip? That doesn't sound like you." He wrinkled his brow. "Ah! Looking for a new job."

I grimaced.

"Give it another week," Dad advised. "Then get temp work."

"Yeah," I said, resigned. "Except this time I want to find a real career instead of taking the first office job that comes along." But there was too much of my father in me—I couldn't stand having no income for more than a few weeks. The idea of getting behind on bills terrified me, even if I was sure Charlotte and David would forgo rent. They hardly needed the $400. Sometimes I wondered if they just cashed my check and gave it to the kids.

Dad sat at the table and opened the evening paper. "That's why they call it temp work. Between jobs, you can look for something permanent."

The water started to boil and I added the pasta. "But what? I don't know. Maybe I should go back to school."

"Grad school?" he said, surprised.

"Well, why not? You and Emily are both professors. And Mom."

He closed the paper. "What would you study?"

"Literature?"

"Your favorite author is Stephen King."

"That was high school, Dad. I outgrew Judy Blume, too."

"How about history?" His subject.

"Yuck. I was thinking, maybe…library science."

"A librarian?"

"No, a library scientist. Of course a librarian. I like books."

He nodded. "This is true. And you could specialize in new books."

"There's a specialty in new books? Oh, man. That'd be great." Because my only hesitation about working in a library was the greasy, old, disease-ridden, pungent archives. "I'd be perfect for that. Really? New books?"

"No, not really, Anne. If you want to specialize in new books, work at Borders."

I deflated. "Oh, that helps. Thanks a lot."

"Annie—if you want to find a job you love, you can't follow some whim. You can't pick a new career out of a hat. You have to think, what is it you like doing? What have you liked about your other jobs? What do you like doing when you're *not* working? Then find the job that matches all that."

"Follow your bliss," I sneered. "Blah blah blah. I don't *have* a bliss. All I have is a blister."

He looked at me. "A blister?"

"Yeah, a minor irritation instead of a vocational calling."

He lifted the newspaper to wall himself off from me and my mood. I checked the pasta. It was *al dente,* but I cooked it another two minutes, because Dad liked it ready to revert back to flour. I stirred the sauce and adjusted the spices. Set the table, poured the OJ and served.

Dad put his paper cautiously aside and dug in. "Delicious," he said. "It's sort of sweet and sort of smoky."

"The sweet is caramelized onions."

"And the smoky?"

"Burned peppers."

"Did you see the article about the dog-walkers?" He tapped the newspaper. "There's a picture of the Cypress property. Did you know they were selling it?"

"Yeah."

"It'll be a great loss to the community."

I couldn't tell if he was teasing me, so I just said *yeah* again and concentrated on dinner. The sauce was pretty good. The pasta was overcooked, but Dad was happy. The OJ was OJ. And after pasta and salad, the cookies were wonderful— warm and gooey. We finished, and cleaned the table. Washed and dried the dishes and moved to the living room. I was clicking the remote when I suddenly hit the off button.

"I think I've decided," I said.

"Anything but *The Sopranos.*"

"No, I mean what I want to do with my life."

"What?"

"I wanna find out who owns that damn Cypress property."

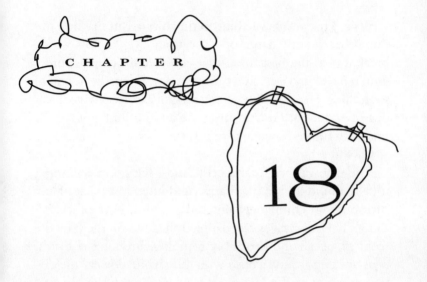

CHAPTER

18

First light the next morning found me at Cypress Road. I pulled into my normal spot under the oak tree and Ny scrambled over me out the door. He pissed happily on the For Sale sign—"Good dog!"—then lifted a furry leg on the other sign. The new sign: No Trespassing.

No trespassing? *No trespassing?*

This meant war.

There were no other cars parked nearby, so I glanced furtively over my shoulder and sauntered toward the sign. I stopped a foot away, facing the other direction, and kicked backward like an ill-tempered mule. Direct hit! The sign wobbled, but remained upright. I gave it another dose of the cloven hoof. Another hit, another wobble.

I turned around and stomped the fucker into pulp.

Woo-hoo! Ha-ha! It was liberating. You can't fence *me* in! Born free!

I caught my breath, stepped away from the broken, battered sign, and moseyed up the trail.

Well. That was a wee bit too much fun. But maybe I *was* the President in Charge of Everything. Maybe this whole breakup was the best thing that could've happened. Sure, I didn't have any *real* direction, but I was on the scent of something. I was like Ny after a seagull carcass. My goal was out of sight, but I'd trust my nose and I'd fluff my tail. I'd track my future down and roll in it.

Or something.

The day was bright and crisp, and I felt good walking. I usually found hiking meditative, and often lost track of my surroundings completely, but today I took note of everything. The way leaves cast dappled shadows on the trail, the scent of ocean and earth. Ny romping through the brush, bees buzzing around a bush with little white flowers, the distant drone of traffic. When I'd reached the top, the sun beat clean and bright on my face. I looked across the city to the ocean. Life was good.

Finding the owner of the land would be tricky, but worth the effort. If I could drag him along on one of my walks, there was no way he wouldn't fall in love with this land. And how hard could it be, asking him to take a hike?

"Can't be done," Kevin told me. "Stop staring."

"I'm not staring."

"You are."

"Well, it's weird," I said. "Seeing you with your clothes on. And what do you mean, it can't be done?"

"It can't be done. At least not by you."

"Anything can be done. Everything's done all the time. You're telling me there's no way to put a name to this corporation?"

"Oh, is *that* all you want to do?"

I nodded, relieved. "Yeah. Yeah. That's all."

"In that case—it's impossible."

"Impossible like a violation of the laws of physics, or impossible like President Schwarzenegger?"

He thought about it for a moment. "Schwarzenegger."

It'd been a week and I was no nearer to finding the owner of the land on Cypress. I'd been to the city clerk. I'd been to the tax assessor. I'd been to every room in the courthouse, basically, begging for help. The sum total of my newfound knowledge was that the land was owned by a corporation called Little Lamb, Inc., based in L.A. I checked the address. It was a twelve-story law firm on Wilshire.

So I checked everything called "Little Lamb," from Goleta to L.A. That's a whole lot of Christian preschools. None of them admitted to owning the land on Cypress, and I can't say I thought they were lying. My second-to-last-gasp effort had been coming to the law library to get some free legal advice from Kevin. The price was right, but maybe if I paid someone, they'd be willing to tell me what I wanted to hear.

"Schwarzenegger," Kevin repeated, "because it is theoretically possible for you to find out who owns Little Lamb, but—"

"Wren told me she knew." I tried to imitate her voice: "*You know who owns Little Lamb? Mary!* Ha-ha."

He laughed. "She's so—"

"Lame."

"Cute. Anyway, it'd cost money and it'd take time—and you still might not get the name you want."

"Why would anyone go to all this effort to hide the fact they owned some land in Montecito?"

"Because people like secrets."

That gave me an idea. "How about this? You find out who owns that corporation, and I'll tell you all Wren's dirty little secrets."

"Not all of them, Anne." He laughed throatily. "We make new ones every day."

★ ★ ★

Great. Wren was accumulating brand-new secrets by the unspeakable boatload, while I didn't even have a boyfriend. At least I'd played Secretary with Rip—that was a naughty secret, right? Of course, I had told Wren, but still. It was a secret in the larger sense.

I couldn't believe how well she and Kevin were getting along. Despite looking sort of funny clothed, I had to admit he was great. Pity he couldn't help uncover the identity of this shadowy landowner. I guess that meant Plan B. It was a good plan in a sort of risky and juvenile way, which involved certain quantities of deception and skullduggery. All I needed was an evil minion to do my bidding.

But first back to work—my lunch break was over. I'd hit the breaking point last Monday, and called my old temp agency. It took them exactly one day to find me a job. With my experience at the title company and having worked for Rip, I was a shoo-in for any real estate job. So on Tuesday I'd reported for duty at Quality Escrow, where I filed and phoned and filled forms—all with a great deal of efficiency and alliteration.

I left the law library and was back at Quality in ten minutes, working as the assistant to the assistant of an escrow officer. I slipped away exactly at five, took Ny to Butterfly Beach and was faced with a serious ethical dilemma: it was Thursday.

Thursday was Drinks Night. Ian and me. Together. Drinking. It was tradition.

But what if Helene was back from her trip? She couldn't come along, could she? Well, why not? We weren't doing anything illicit—just having drinks. Like a couple of buddies. Which we were. Buddies. So there was no reason Helene couldn't join us—except…yuck. But why *yuck?* Well, because it was like boys night out. You couldn't have the fiancée tagging along, girling the place up. She'd probably wear some little dress with spaghetti straps and hog the entire spectrum of visible light. Plus, if she came along we couldn't scratch ourselves manfully, and spit on the sidewalk.

Back home, I listened to my messages—nothing from Ian—and stared into my closet. What if he didn't call? I should be willing to call *him,* that's what. We were buddies. Buddies didn't stare at the phone, waiting, anticipating. Buddies called. But what did they wear? Nothing designer, obviously. Sneakers and jeans and a T-shirt. And if the T-shirt was the red sweater that revealed the cleavage, so what? Buddy didn't mean ugly. I checked myself in the mirror. I looked okay. Like the Girl Next Door as played by Charlotte Olsen's homelier sister.

I stared at the phone. It didn't ring. So I made my bed, and read the first three pages of a Fay Weldon novel that had been floating around my house for months, before deciding I couldn't concentrate due to all the silence. So I went outside and tossed a ball for Ny. In a few minutes, Hannah and the boys came over and we took turns throwing the ball, and in no time the phone rang.

I casually galloped inside. Took a few calming breaths: "Hello?"

"I bought you a cashmere sweater," Wren said.

"Oh."

"What, oh? You love cashmere!"

This was an exaggeration. *Wren* loved cashmere. "A cashmere sweater? Really?"

"It's a blue TSE. You won't believe how soft. They came in today, and I knew you'd want one."

"Great. Thanks. Oh, I saw Kevin today, did he tell you?"

"No, we're not meeting till later."

I filled her in on our conversation.

"He's incredible, isn't he?" she said.

"Godlike," I said.

"You're so jealous!"

"I'm not going to dignify that with a response." Only because it was true. "So...I hear you've been keeping secrets from me."

"What? Me? What? No I haven't. Me? Secrets? From you? No. What?"

"Wren," I said, because I'd clearly stumbled on to something that called for further digging. "I can't believe you're not telling me!"

"I don't know if it...I'm not sure if—"

"If what?"

"I can't talk about it yet!" she said, and hung up.

I stared at the phone, listening to the distant sounds of Hannah organizing a game of hide-and-seek with all the gentle charm of a drill sergeant. What secret? Wren had a secret from me? We didn't have secrets from each other. Well, at least *I* didn't. Not important secrets. Not the sort of secret which led to extended phone-babbling and hanging up.

I was about to dial her number for a little Anneish Inquisition when the phone rang in my hand. "What secret?" I demanded.

"My middle name is Stanley," Ian said. "This is an odd game."

"Oh! Hi."

"What if I'd been a telemarketer?"

"I thought you were Wren," I said, then immediately realized I shouldn't have.

"She has a secret?" he asked.

"No."

"Ah. I see." A short pause. "It's Thursday."

"I was about to call you. We still on?"

"If you're free."

"You bet. I mean—I guess. Um…is Helene back? Can she join us?"

"Still in Chicago. They keep putting off her return date."

"Oh, that sucks. That totally bites. That both sucks *and* bites. Like a vampire giving a hickey." Okay, I was way too happy. Must dampen the happiness. Must think *buddies.*

"I was thinking we could meet at Durgan's," Ian said.

Nice Irish pub, between a parking garage and a movie theater. Good place for buddies. We could do an Irish thing, drink whiskey and listen to Van Morrison and be morose. "That sounds great—like in a soulful Gaelic way." *Soulful?* Hardly buddy. I tried again. "Man, I'm beat from work. All's I want is a few beers and a TV. I'm gonna be, like, no fun." Oh, God. What did buddies *say* to each other?

"Rough day?"

I suspected he was laughing at me. "Anyway," I said. "Half an hour? I'll just come as I am."

"I wouldn't have you come any other way."

So I was sitting on a bar stool in Durgan's thinking, what did *that* mean? Was that some kind of double entendre? Or was he just saying I shouldn't make an effort? God, he was so confusing. Why couldn't he ever just say what he meant?

I caught the bartender's eye and ordered a double.

"A double what?" he said.

"Um, whiskey?"

He recited a dozen kinds of whiskey, each with a stranger name than the last, like *White Bush* and *Orangie* and *Something-frog.* I listened attentively, then asked him to tell me again. He was Irish, possibly Durgan himself, and had the prettiest accent, so I was going to ask for a third recitation when Ian came in the side door. He was wearing a pale blue shirt and jeans, looking like he'd stepped out of the J. Crew catalog.

"Oh," I said. "Maybe I should see what my buddy's having."

The bartender and I watched Ian approach. He looked good, approaching. I almost bragged to the bartender that he used to date Charlotte Olsen, but restrained myself.

"I was just going to order," I told him as he slid into the next stool.

"Black and tan?" he suggested.

"I was gonna have a lap-dog," I said. "But a black and tan sounds good."

The bartender bustled off to combine something black with something tan and I realized, "Hey, that's like the Irish version of *Ebony and Ivory!*"

Ian laughed. "I have no idea what you're talking about."

"The black and tan. It's striking a blow against racism. Ebony and ivory, together in perfect harmony. They should have an ad campaign—" I lowered my voice to TV-announcer levels. "'Jesse Jackson says...fight racism, drink a black-and-tan.' You know, because the Guinness is black and Harp is tan, together in perf—"

"I think it's Bass," Ian said. "Not Harp."

"Well, *whatever.* Literalist."

"And they don't mix." He nodded at the glasses as the bartender placed them in front of us. "They separate."

"Oh, right. Hmm. That kind of ruins it. Maybe a black-and-tan blended. Like a mocha blended—oh! The mocha blended, of course! Al Sharpton says..."

He laughed again. "Are you always like this? Or only when you're totally beat?"

"I have ideas, is all. So, how was *your* day?"

"Fifty-six dollars."

"From the shop? Total? That's all you made today?"

He nodded again. "Pre-tax, pre-payroll, pre-rent, pre-everything. So I actually lost money."

I shook my head and raised my glass. "Here's to business."

"To business," he said, and we drank.

"Are you worried?" I asked.

"Well, some days I make a few thousand, and that carries me. But yeah—if I go too long without a big sale, things start looking pretty grim. One of the benefits of self-employment."

We moved to a table, chatting about his business. It was surprisingly interesting, because if you could overlook that he was a debris-dealer, he basically owned his own boutique. Plus, Ian was a good story-teller, and clearly loved his job. His eyes shone when he mentioned his Belleek lotus vases. And he waxed positively poetic about his collection of—I kid you not—muffineers.

"Muffineers?" I said. "What's that, a buccaneer who steals muffins?"

"It's a—"

"A baker who revolts? Like *Muffiny on the Bounty*."

"A muffineer," Ian said, "is a caster for sprinkling sugar or spice on a muffin."

"Alternately, it's the ear of a muffin. If you can have a muffin-top, why not a muffin-ear?" I sketched a muffin in the air. "The bits that overhang."

"You're a muffin-head," he said, and his cell phone rang. "Oh, sorry. I'm expecting Helene."

"Oh." I said. "Okay."

He answered. It was Helene. They exchanged fairly loverlike greetings, then Ian said, "We ended up at Durgan's. No, just me and Anne." He listened for a bit. "He did? Well, what'd *you* do? Uh-huh. And Lincoln fired him? Yeah... Uh-huh. Uh-huh. Well, don't have *too* much fun. Uh-huh..."

I sipped my beer, flagrantly eavesdropping—because there were no rules against eavesdropping on cell phones—

stunned that he'd openly admitted to the fiancée that he was out with another woman. Granted, we were buddies. Granted, it was entirely innocent. But how did *she* know? Did she think I wasn't even *potential* competition?

Ian finally hung up and apologized again. "I never answer in public, but I knew she'd be calling. There's some kind of office politics going on, and the CEO wants her there until it gets resolved." Then he told me the theory of Helene's office politics: She was always right, everyone else was always wrong, and in the end she'd prevail.

It made me long for the muffineers.

Still, I nodded politely until such time as I could change the subject. I quizzed him about his family—hardly fair that he knew mine and I didn't know his. Then we spent a while discussing movies and music, until, on beer three, I got morose.

"I don't know why I even care. I'm never gonna find the guy who owns the land on Cypress. And I couldn't convince him not to sell, anyway." An alcohol-sodden bell rang distantly—I knew I was supposed to be enlisting Ian's help for something, but I'd forgotten for what. "It's just another distraction from the real problem—getting a job I care about. I'll keep working at Quality Escrow. Maybe they'll hire me permanently."

"You like it?"

"Of course I don't like it. What's there to like?"

"Well, maybe—"

"Easy for *you* to say. You love your job. You love rooting around in your old rubbish heaps of rubbishy rubbish! You're like a…a guy who loves old rubbish! You know who you are? You're Golem. *Oooh, precious, my precious muffin-ear.*"

"Well, maybe you have to—"

"Zip it, Smeagol! You found your bliss."

"Maybe—"

"You know what my real problem is?"

"That third beer?"

"My problem is Charlotte."

"Your sister Charlotte?"

"Don't say it like that! She's not a saint. St. Charlotte of the Swimsuit. Our Lady of C-Cup. Oooh, sometimes I just—" I was gonna say *hate her*, but that was too strong even in my half-drunk state. "I just can't stand being her sister. She's so perfect and good. It's impossible. What am *I* supposed to do? You can't compete with Charlotte Olsen—why bother trying?"

"Yeah," he said. "So?"

"So what? What, so?"

"So stop competing."

"What's that supposed to mean? 'Stop competing.' I don't compete with Charlotte—I *can't* compete. That's the problem. And it's not just now. It was growing up in her shadow. Always being Charlotte Olsen's little sister. And Emily hasn't helped matters. I'm like the fifth Baldwin brother. The third tenor. The fourth Arquette. I'm—"

"Kato Kaelin."

"What?"

He nodded. "You're Kato Kaelin—living in the shadow of celebrity. In the guest house, even."

I used the condensation on my glass to make Olympic rings on the table. "You have a point?"

"Yeah, Anne. Stop complaining about Charlotte. Let it go. You and a billion other girls will never be Charlotte Olsen. Was it harder for you? Yeah. But do you get to live in the guest house? Yeah. Stop using her as an excuse. You're blaming your lack of—whatever—on the fact that Charlotte looks good in a swimsuit. This is what defines your life? Her bikini? You can't have it both ways. Either live in the shadow of Charlotte—the actual shadow, a hundred feet away—or don't. Either be Kato or be Anne." He shook his head. "You've got more to offer than that. You're about the smartest, funniest—you've got humor, looks, everything. You talk about what a failure you are, but you've never actually failed at anything you cared about, have you?"

I didn't respond. I didn't know where to start. Oh, wait—yes I did: "You're being an asshole."

"I'm being your friend. I think you're great, Anne. But you've got this defeatism, like you can't change your life, you can't make it happen for yourself. It's not right. You can make it happen, whatever *it* is. Or hell, at least you can fail, trying." He raised his beer glass. "Fifty-six dollars."

I wasn't sure if I should be mad or sad or both. But I guess he finally told me what he really meant. So I clinked my glass against his. "Fifty-six dollars," I said. "And counting."

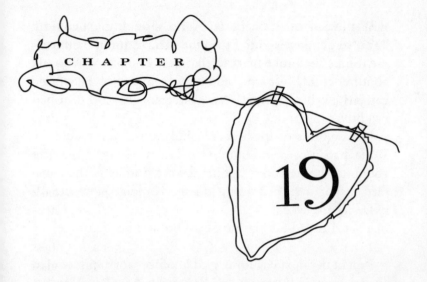

CHAPTER

19

When I got home the next evening—after an interminable day at the escrow company, sick with hangover and preoccupied with thoughts of Wren's secrets and whether or not Ian hated me—I found a small square box on my welcome mat. It was wrapped in pale lavender paper, with a creamy French ribbon. I opened the front door for Ny, who was scrambling to be let out, and ripped apart the wrapping paper.

Inside: a raspberry muffin.

There was no note. I tore the muffin-ears off and ate them, and gave the muffin body and muffin-head to Ny. We wagged. After the dog-walk and dinner, I curled up with the phone. I planned on having a long chat with Wren, excavating all her secrets and mysteries. I dialed, but she didn't answer. I said, "Hello? Wren? It's me," to her answering machine, and had the horrible suspicion that she was screening me. But she was probably just out with Kevin, discovering new secrets faster than she could describe them. So I left a message claiming we'd made plans with the Sharones weeks ago, for a shopping expedition. "You remember, right? In honor of…Shannon's anniversary. Since she broke up with that guy. The one who didn't treat her right." Which could have been any of Shannon's various ex-boyfriends. "See you tomorrow," I finished brightly.

It wasn't one of my best confabulations, but it would do. Wren had missed sculpture class last week, now that she could stay home and sculpt her favorite model in the comfort of her own bedroom, and she couldn't blow me off twice in one week.

Then I called Shayla and Shannon, and begged.

I spent the next day immersed in office work and focused all my emotional energy on Wren instead of Ian. Not that I was consciously *not* thinking of Ian. I just wasn't thinking of him. I happened not to think of him all day. He simply didn't come up in my thoughts. He could court me with baked goods of every variety, but that didn't mean I had to think about him. Because I didn't.

Ian was probably thinking about me though. Probably weeping into his pillow because he'd been so mean to me. I bet he was calling Helene and telling her that I'd never failed at anything I cared about. What kind of thing was *that* to say about somebody?

So I was standing over the fax machine, not thinking about Ian, when a familiar voice said, "How the fuck are you, Olsen?"

I turned, unreasonably happy to see him. "Mike! What're you doing here?"

"Could ask you the same question. Been a fucking funeral dirge at Parsons since you quit."

"Really?"

He nodded, offering me a toothpick. "Rip spends every morning crying into his coffee."

"That's terrible," I said, with a very nearly straight face.

"I'm lying," Mike said. "He's got a new girlfriend."

"What?"

"Yeah, she's some Realtor."

Probably that baby machine with the battleship hips. Jesus. It'd been like twenty minutes since he'd dumped me. "In the office? Janelle?"

"Nah, at Coldwell Banker or somewhere. Every morning with the phone call. 'Hey, Polliwog—I miss you already.' Makes me wanna puke."

"Polliwog? He calls his new girlfriend Polliwog?"

"All the fucking time—the hell is up with that? She an amphibian? She sprouting legs?"

"He called *me* Polliwog!"

Mike glanced at my legs. "With you, it makes sense."

"He can't be calling some other woman that—that was his special love name for *me.*"

"Polliwog?" He wiggled the toothpick between his lips. "Rip's such a hosebag."

"He is a hosebag! That's my special love name for *him.*" Starting now, it was. I couldn't believe he was calling his new girlfriend Polliwog. I couldn't believe he *had* a new girlfriend. I bet he already told her he loved her. Probably already proposed. God, what if Rip was getting married?

I steadied myself against the fax machine and hyperventilated.

"You free for lunch?" Mike asked.

"What?"

"Lunch, Anne. You free for lunch? Drown your sorrows in food."

Hmm. Something about his tone. And he *was* looking extra spiffy, with his hair slicked back and a clean tie. "Like on a date?"

"Like on a lunch."

"You won't ask me to marry you?"

"Relax, Polliwog," he said. "For all I know, you're a lousy lay."

That night at Nordstrom's, Wren subjected a Donald Pliner boot to a cursory inspection as we all clustered around the sale racks. Shannon and Wren were in the size sixes, while Shayla and I were in the eight-and-a-halfs.

"So who was this guy?" Wren asked Shannon, putting the boot back on the rack.

"Which guy?"

"The guy in whose honor we're shopping here today."

A fine question, but the convolutions of Shannon's love life were far too complex to discuss when the real issue was Wren's secret life. "He's a secret guy," I said. "Shannon can't talk about him. Because he's a secret."

Wren shot me a look.

"He's a riddle," I said, "wrapped in an enigma."

"Oh!" Shayla said, looking up from trying on a Kenneth Cole heel. "You mean Devon! The enema guy."

"*Enigma,* Shayla," I said. "What enema guy?"

"High colonics," Shannon said. "Devon the colon hydro-therapist. You remember. The Irrigator."

"The Irrigator! I never knew his real name. Devon. Well, that's *one* secret brought to light. I wonder if Wren has any good ones hidden away."

Shannon and Shayla looked at Wren. She grabbed the sports sandal Shannon was holding. "My secret is—these're way past the sell-by date."

"She and Kevin," I said. "They've been doing dirty deeds."

"That's no secret," Shayla said.

"Are they?" asked Shannon, meaning the shoe. "I thought it was cute. Looks comfortable, too."

"But she *does* have a secret," I said. "A juicy one."

"Comfortable," Wren said. "But nobody will be wearing them in three months."

"He had an enigma table and everything," Shayla said. "Devon did. I remember when I saw it I thought, What on earth is *that* for?"

I eyed her suspiciously. Was she joking? "There's no telling, with an enigma table."

"Oh, but it was for colonic irrigation," she explained.

Shannon nodded. "And sex."

I had to stop this before we got too sidetracked. "On an enema table?" I accidentally asked, in horrified fascination.

"Wet 'n' wild," Shannon said, and monopolized the conversation for a while. In fact, we were done with shoes and busy looking for cheap T-shirts in the teeny-bopper department when I managed to steer things back toward Wren's Riddle.

"That's a great secret," I finally told Shannon. "Almost as good as Wren's."

"Wren has a secret?" Shayla asked.

"She does," I said.

"Wren does?" Shannon asked.

"Big fat secret," I said. "Top, in fact. Confidential. For your ears only."

My point made, the Sharones and I hectored Wren until she finally spilled. "Fine," she said. "Fine, if you *must* know, I've been meeting an engaged man for drinks every Thursday night. We have a standing date."

"Wren!" Shayla said. "You home-wrecker."

"I know," Wren said, in mock sorrow. "But I can't help myself. I'm in love."

"All's fair," Shannon said.

"He's *engaged,*" Shayla said.

"It's not that bad," I said. "What's a few drinks? I mean, if you're buddies with a man. And the fact that he's engaged makes it totally innocuous. He's taken. It's like having a drink with your brother-in-law."

"My brother-in-law?" Shannon said. "You mean Horn-dog McBoner?"

"Yeah, what *is* it with your brother-in-law?" I said, a little desperately, because I didn't like where the conversation was heading.

"No, let's talk more about going drinking with another woman's fiancé," Wren said. "Every week. Just the two of us…"

"Well, I can't believe you're doing it," Shayla said. "Especially now that you have Kevin."

"Yeah, but it's not me—it's Anne." Wren smiled. "She's been seeing this engaged guy who used to date her sister."

"Sibling rivalry," Shayla said. "Which sister?"

"No, it makes sense," Shannon said. "He already knows what the Olsen girls like, so Anne doesn't have to train him on which buttons to push."

"Eeew!" I said. "There's no button pushing going on. That's disgusting. He's like—I've known him since I was thirteen. He's like family. He's been with Charlotte—so, yuck. It'd be like sleeping with David or Jamie." I shuddered. "Just…wrong."

The three of them looked at me. Then they looked at each other.

"She's in love," Shannon said.

"Yeah, that changes everything," Shayla said.

"Jesus," I said. "I'm not in love. We're buddies."

Shannon said, "Anne's in love with her buddy."

"I'm *not!*"

"It's a secret love," Wren said.

"I'm not!"

"Every Thursday?" Shayla said.

"They call it 'Drinks Night,'" Wren said. "They secretly meet at her house, or in his loft—"

"Does he show you his etchings," Shannon said.

"—or a candlelit bar somewhere. They just talk, you know."

"Sure. It's a platonic affair. They do nothing…." Shannon paused meaningfully. "But."

"But what?" Shayla asked.

"*But* who knows what the future holds?"

"It holds his wedding," I said. "To his fiancée. C'mon. We're friends is all. We talk about *antiques,* for chrissakes!"

They looked at each other again. "You're a goner," Shannon told me. "Game over. Just watch he doesn't start talking about intestinal hygiene."

"Speaking of which," I said. "I need the bathroom." And I left them there, giggling. When I returned, they'd moved on to business wear, and my Ian-crisis was averted. We shopped for another hour, before going to the café for dessert. Wren and I preserved an uneasy truce, neither of us mentioning secrets—until, on the way out the door, shopping bags in hand, she turned to me and quietly said, "Ha!"

The next day was my last at Quality Escrow. When I left, they threw me a big goodbye party, with a cake and gag gifts and everything. Or maybe they just signed my time card and showed me the door.

I didn't have a job tomorrow, so I was free. Free to sleep late, to enjoy the weather, to laze around at home. Free to be incredibly anxious, as every day without a job was another step toward bankruptcy and starvation. The woman at Superior Employment wanted me to apply to some temp-to-perm jobs she said were perfect for me, but I wasn't ready for something long-term. As I said to Emily that evening, after she'd presented me with the note of emergency numbers just in case something happened while I was baby-sit-ting, "Fuck off! I *still* know 9-1-1!"

No, actually I told her I was going to take my time. I was going to patiently wait for the job that really felt *right*.

"That's a great idea, Anne," she said. "If you can do it."

"Of course I can do it."

She gave me the Emily eye.

"Maybe," I said.

"You're not good with uncertainty," she said. "I know, be-cause I'm worse."

"The book?"

She nodded. "We cancelled the publication. Stopped the presses and everything."

"Sometimes it's good, sleeping with the publisher."

She tried to smile. "I'm sick about it. I don't even want to think what it cost. Jamie says it's okay but…I can't believe I did that."

"Are you still working on it?"

"I'm taking a step back, starting again. I don't know. It's all up in the air. We'll see. I'm kinda panicked, but also re-lieved. The thing is, I'm trying to take my time, too. Figure out what I really want to say."

"You gonna brush up on your theory?"

"I don't know. I break out in hives, thinking about Der-rida." She nibbled on the cap of her pen. "I want to get some thoughts on paper, see what happens. It feels like a dead end, not knowing what to write. I had it all planned, my career and my books—and then this happened. But I guess some-times it's the dead ends that have the best view."

"And the roadkill."

"You're a comfort, Anne."

So I hugged her and told her everything would be okay, and she told me the same. How come it was so easy to see that the crises in other people's lives were only molehills?

By midnight I was back home, preparing myself for another lonely night in my cold bed. As I brushed my teeth and removed my contacts, I thought, *sometimes the dead ends have the best views.*

Well, why not? I had the scent of this thing. I had the cunning plan. I had the evil minion, if he'd play along. Fuck it. Might as well fail hugely. Might as well fail at something I really cared about.

I called him at work. "Ian, it's Anne."

"Anne who?"

"Olsen. You know, I'm Charlotte's—"

He laughed. "Has anyone told you how endearing your insecurities are?"

"Actually, I think people find me abrasive and overconfident."

"Then they don't know you like I do."

I shivered at his tone. I recognized the giddy, goose-bumpy feeling…but Ian was Charlotte's ex. Ian was engaged. So I kept my tone businesslike. "You up for lunch tomorrow?"

"You're buying?"

"Sure I'm buying—I make more than fifty-six bucks a day temping."

"How about the Wine Cask, then? They have a Carina Cellars Syrah I've been wanting to try."

"You ever wonder if you drink too much?" I asked.

"Only when I'm with you."

"You only wonder when you're with me, or you only drink too much when—"

"The latter."

"Why do you think that is?" I asked.

"It's one of life's great mysteries."

"Hmm," I said. "And dress nice, okay?"

"I always dress nice."

"Wear a suit. Do you have a suit?"

"They don't make you wear a jacket at the Wine Cask. I can't think of any place in Santa Barbara that does. Maybe one of the country clubs in Montecito. You'd know better than I."

"Wear one anyway."

"Why?"

"Because I'm asking you nicely."

He paused. "You're a bit eccentric, aren't you?"

"It's just I'm going to dress up, so it'd be nice if you did, too."

"What's this about? You get a new job?"

"Just wear the suit."

"Yes, ma'am," he said. "I'll meet you there?"

"No, let's meet at your shop. One forty-five."

"One forty-five? What kinda time is that for lunch? I'll have eaten my newspaper by then."

"A late lunch," I said. "It's cosmopolitan. Sophisticated. Romantic."

"Romantic?"

"In the metaphorical sense."

"Ah," he said. "Quarter of two then. In honor of metaphorical romance."

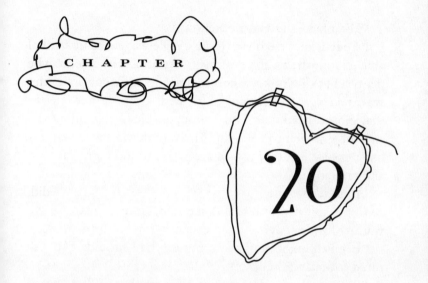

CHAPTER

20

The bell jangled when I opened the door to Tazza Antiques. I took a deep breath of the freshly oxygenated air outside, and stepped into the stuffy musk of the past. Well, the shop actually smelled pleasantly of lemon blossoms and beeswax—on the surface, at least. Lord only knew what festering odors lurked beneath.

My heels tapped on the stone floor—I avoided the Persian rugs—and I paused to eye the fresh roses in the blue-and-white vase, faintly surprised Ian didn't prefer dried. I stopped to smell the flowers—because that's the sort of girl I was—and Ian's head poked over the wall of the loft. I raised a hand in greeting, and his head disappeared. Putting on his suit, I hoped.

There was a pretty young woman behind the counter—a few inches shorter than I, more than a few years younger, and round-faced and chubby. The mysterious assistant. "Can I help you?" she asked.

"I'm just waiting," I said. "Thanks."

"Oh, okay," she giggled nervously.

I smiled, because her nervous giggle was adorable. Adorable girls in their early twenties are not usually my favorite people, but she looked like a pudgy and ebullient pixie. She was wearing a funky pink skirt, with a purple net overlay that grazed her knees, and a short purple T that allowed a strip of stomach to peek out. She was plump, but it was just baby fat—still at that nubile age when round flesh was firm and enticing.

I missed that age.

I checked my watch and she said, "Um…what are we waiting for, exactly?"

"Ian. I thought he saw me, but maybe I should…" I gestured toward the stairs.

"Oh, no. He doesn't like customers up there. I'll call him." She dialed the phone on the counter, and we listened to the phone ring in the loft.

It cut off, and upstairs Ian said, "Hello?"

I said, "This is ridiculous."

"Mr. Dunne," the girl said. "There's a customer here for you."

"I'm not a customer," I said.

"Be down in a minute," he said.

"I can hear you!" I yelled upstairs. Then I asked the girl, "He makes you call him Mr. Dunne?"

She giggled again.

"Mr. Dunne!" I called upstairs. "It's your lunch appointment."

"Anne?" He poked his head over the wall. "Is that you?"

"In the flesh." I pirouetted. My aged flesh might not be perfectly firm and enticing but I was looking pretty fine in a pinstripe Dolce & Gabbana suit I'd borrowed from Charlotte. The pants were a gorgeous drapy cut, the jacket nipped at the waist, and I wore a lacy camisole underneath. I was even wearing my best heels—the pair of Blumarines I'd bought at Element. Charlotte had assured me she'd never worn the suit, though I think I would've borrowed it even if she had. Anything for the cause.

"Oh, so *you're* Anne," the salesgirl said, and her pixieish ebullience brightened.

"Whoa," Ian said from the loft, before I could determine exactly what the girl had meant. "I didn't recognize you."

"Perfect," I said, because I was in disguise. "C'mon, we're gonna be late."

I'd planned on arriving earlier, but makeup had taken longer than usual, as I'd dyed my hair dark auburn. The new shade required a different palette, and there'd been an extended period of trial and error. Charlotte and I had finally decided on eggplant eye shadow, tawny blush and a burgundy lipstick. I'd barely recognized myself when I looked in the mirror—which was precisely the point.

"It's a thirty second walk," Ian said, from above.

"That's what you think," I muttered.

"What?" Ian said.

"Would you come down from there?" I said. "I'm getting dizzy."

"Hey, this is metaphorically romantic. You're supposed to say *'Romeo, Romeo, wherefore art thou.'*"

"Just get your Capulet ass down here."

He laughed as his head disappeared.

"Actually," the pudgy pixie told me, "Juliet was the Capulet."

"Well, Ian has a girlish figure," I said, fudging matters somewhat. As was made immediately clear when he came down the stairs. He looked good. Clean-shaven, freshly brushed, and wearing a beautifully cut, beige linen suit. A little conservative, a little classic, and more than a little masculine.

He stopped at the base of the stairs and returned my examination. "Very nice," he said. "Glad I dressed appropriately. We'll be the best-dressed couple at the Wine Cask."

"We're going a little farther than that."

"So no Carina Cellars Syrah?"

"Later." I took his arm and ushered him toward the door. "I need you to do me a little favor first."

He dug in his heels. "How little?"

"Extremely little. Tiny."

"Tiny?"

"Infinitesimal." I tugged his arm.

"Okay, okay. Stop pulling. Libby," he said to the salesgirl. "I'll be back in—" he turned to me "—how long?"

"Maybe you should close up," I told Libby.

"If I'm not back by six," he said. "Panic."

Out the door, I said, "I can't believe you make her call you Mr. Dunne. Can we take your car?"

"I don't, and where are we going? What meal could possibly take four hours?"

"It's not the meal," I said. "It's the favor. You parked nearby?"

"I thought you loved your truck."

I growled.

"Around the corner," he said. "Maybe we should feed you first."

"I'm just nervous. It's a big favor."

"You just said it was small. Infinitesimal. What is it, exactly? Have you—" Blah blah blah. He talked as we walked around the block and into the parking garage, where he pointed to an old Jeep Wrangler with the plastic windows removed.

"That's your car?"

"What's wrong with it?"

I sighed. "I figured you'd drive an SUV or at least a—something more professional than a pickup truck or a Jeep."

"Now you're scaring me."

I ignored him, deep in thought. Should we go back and get my truck? It was hardly better, and would take another ten minutes. We were already late. Looks like I was stuck Wrangling. "Can I drive?" I asked.

"You want to drive?"

"That's what it means when I say *'Can I drive?'*"

"Where to?"

I pointed in a direction I judged to be southeast.

He shook his head and tossed me the keys. We got in the Jeep and I squitched the seat forward. "This isn't so bad," I said, pulling out of the parking garage.

"What's with the new look?" Ian asked. "Some post-breakup thing?"

"I just wanted to look different." Unrecognizable, in fact.

He fingered a lock of my hair. "I like this."

I smacked his hand away. "You'll mess it up."

Whoever invented the poker-straight style should be shot. My hair was naturally wavy and the dye added even more body. As part of my disguise, I'd blown it straight and hadn't touched it since, afraid it would crink up at the slightest contact. And if I couldn't touch it, neither could Ian, despite… you know. The sexy factor. Actually, he couldn't touch it specifically because of the *you know*.

"So what's this favor?" Ian asked.

My stomach tightened nervously. "I'll tell you later."

"Later than what? We're already on the road."

I saw no reason to answer.

"Are we at least having lunch first?" he asked. "I'm hungry."

"I'll feed you later, too."

"Where are we going?"

"You'll see."

"Would you just tell me?"

"I can't talk while driving." This was a terrible idea. One of my worst. And there was no way I could avoid explaining the whole thing to Ian. He was the key. It wasn't until I pulled onto the freeway that I spoke. "Okay. Remember what you said about being friends?"

"Whatever it was, I take it back."

I glared at him. "Well, you know that property I'm interested in? Off Cypress?"

"Where you walk Ny."

"Yeah." Then I ran out of momentum, and fell silent.

"Well?" he finally asked.

"Well, *you're* the one who recommended failure. I want you to remember that. So this is basically all your fault."

"Is this like the love thing again?"

"Here's the deal. I'm a Realtor." I stared straight ahead, but no explosions ensued from the passenger seat, so I continued. "I'm a Realtor, and I called this other Realtor, Melissa Kent from Villa Realty, and I told her—"

"Wait, wait—but you're not really a Realtor."

"Of course not."

"Right. Just checking."

"So I called this sea hag Melissa—"

"Kent."

"Would you stop interrupting? Yes, Melissa Kent. And I told her—"

"Is *she* a real Realtor?"

"Of course she's a real Realtor! Focus, Ian. I called her—"

"Melissa Kent."

"—and I happened to mention that I was a Realtor from Ventura named Senna Leon who—"

"Senna Leon?"

"It's an anagram."

"For what, *deranged Anne?*"

"Close. I told her I had a client. From abroad. Because *Leon*—" which I pronounced Lyon, like the city in France "—sounds foreign. So that's how I got the idea the client should be foreign, too."

"From Ventura."

"What? No. From Germany."

"You said Ventura."

"I'm from Ventura. Senna Leon's from Ventura." I gripped the wheel tight as I took the East Valley Road exit into Montecito. "Herr Daunen is from Germany."

Nothing from the passenger seat.

"Daunen is an anagram for Ian Dunne," I explained. "Well, minus the I and an N."

Silence.

"Which means you're Herr Daunen," I explained further.

Still nothing, and I was afraid to look.

"You're a German investor interested in buying the Cypress property." I peeked at him. He was expressionless, staring straight ahead. "Herr Daunen?"

He turned to me and his face was sort of stiff. For a moment, I thought it was from anger. Then I realized he was trying not to laugh. "You are, without a doubt, the most—"

This time *I* interrupted. I didn't want to know. "So you'll do it?"

"But *why?*"

"I need to speak to the owner. I can't get his name any other way. I've got to convince him not to sell the land."

"How?"

"If he walks up the trail with me, if I talk with him…I don't even know why he's selling. Maybe he doesn't realize people use it, people love it. I'm gonna try to convince him not to sell. I *am* going to convince him. This is something I really *do* care about, so I'm not gonna be defeatist. I'm gonna go for it."

"But why the new hair and everything?"

"In case Melissa Kent and I have met, like at a Board of Realtors meeting or something. I don't want her to recognize me. I don't *think* we've met, but…"

"Can I be French?"

My heart jumped. "You'll do it?"

He smiled, and the sun grew discernibly warmer. *"Mais oui."*

"That's fantastic! Thank you, thank you, thank you!" I turned onto Cypress Road. "But you have to be German."

"But I want to be French."

"But I told her you were German."

"The only word I know in German is *Nein*."

"How about *Achtung?*"

"Well, yeah. And *Ich bin ein Berliner,* my little *Schmetterling.*"

"You don't have to speak German, just do a German accent." I slowed as we approached the property.

Melissa Kent was already there, with her late-model Jaguar. She waved to us from the base of the trail, where she was trying to set the No Trespassing sign upright. As she waved, it fell over again and she sort of lunged at it.

"What is she *doing?*" Ian asked.

I choked back a laugh. "Someone must have knocked the sign over."

"You didn't," Ian said. "Tell me you didn't."

"Vandals." I parked the Jeep at a slight distance. "Quick, let me hear your accent."

"Weell ziss do? I am *un* Frenchman, *non?*"

"German," I said. "You're German."

"I can only be French," he said, stubbornly.

"Fine," I said, getting out of the Jeep and slamming the door. I saw no reason for him to be so difficult. "Have it your way."

"Merci." He climbed from the Jeep and minced toward Melissa. *"Bonjour, mademoiselle."*

Why was he *mincing?* I said he could be French, not gay.

"Oh!" she said. "Hello. I was, uh—the sign is broken."

Ian took her hand and kissed it elegantly. *"Enchanté."* He gave her a look that visibly melted her. Ah, he wasn't pretending to be gay. Just European. "I waz starting to dezpair of ze American wooman." He gestured towards me in a disparaging fashion, then turned back to Melissa with a smile. "Zen I find you."

Melissa blushed furiously as I gritted my teeth into a smile. She was just how I'd pictured her. Pale blond hair, horsey face, good teeth, and verging on anorexic. After years of watching Charlotte weigh herself, I could judge a woman's weight to the nearest half pound. Melissa was about five four, and exactly one-hundred-and-one pounds. Her hips and shoulder blades jutted from her black slacks and sweater like they were making a break for it.

"You must be Senna," Melissa said when she'd finished simpering over Ian. "I'm Melissa Kent."

I put a little swing into my hips as I stepped forward to shake her hand—let her see how a real woman fills out a suit. Sadly, a real woman doesn't wear three-inch Blumarines on a dirt path. I nearly toppled when I got stuck in the mud.

"Watch ze walking!" Ian said, enjoying himself way too much. *"Sacre bleu!"*

"Those're hardly hiking boots," Melissa said, extending a skinny leg to show off her own pair of practical Timberlands. "And I thought Herr Daunen was German? Well, *Herr* Daunen."

Yikes. To buy time, I said, "I was going to wear my sneakers, but they didn't go with the suit—of course not, ha-ha!—so I had a pair of flats which I just bought at Nordstrom's, but they weren't right either and…" And I had the perfect brainstorm. A rush of sheer genius. "Swiss! He's Swiss. I thought he was from the, uh, German side, but of course I was mistaken. Zurich, you know. Why is it they call you 'Herr,' Herr Daunen?"

He gestured Frenchily. "Oh, ze tradition, *n'est pas?* One answerz when one is addrezzed, *non?* For the sake of the politeness."

"Of course," Melissa said. "But do you prefer *Monsieur* Daunen?"

"Herr is fine," I said quickly. "Anyway, um—we're supposed to be meeting the owner, no?"

"Oui," Ian said, importantly. "I require ze owner."

"He just phoned." Melissa held up her cell for proof. "There's a bit of a problem."

My knees almost buckled in relief. Thank God! The owner couldn't come—and I'd escape from this ridiculous situation without major catastrophe. Best I could do now was cut my losses. Tuck tail firmly between legs and scurry back to lair. Maybe have lunch at *Trattoria Mollie.* Maybe Ian would buy...

I attempted an expression of offended disappointment and was about to say *This isn't how things are done in Switzerland* when Melissa continued. "Mr. Montague got off to a late start. He'll be a few minutes late." She offered her bony arm to Ian. "But shall we proceed? He said he'd meet us at the top."

Wonderful. To make matters worse, I'd never walked the trail in a D&G suit and stilettos. It was seven times its normal length, every inch excruciating. I was thoroughly disheveled by the time we reached the top, and I missed Ny. Strange to be here without him. It made me sad that someone else might one day own all this, and we wouldn't be able to come.

But no. I wouldn't let that happen. I may have been disheveled and sweaty, but my resolve was strengthened.

I hobbled toward Ian and Melissa as they looked out over the foothills and Ian said, "Wow, this view is awesome!"

True enough, but he'd been so impressed he'd forgotten his French accent. He sounded exactly like the surfer he'd been in high school. I was just grateful he hadn't said *"Tubular!"*

Melissa glanced at him, a slight frown marring her horsey features.

"His English is excellent, isn't it?" I said.

Ian tried to cover. "I've svent many times in your country."

"Didn't you spend a year at UCSB when you were in college? Learning how it is to surf, as you said."

"Exactement! This is when I fell in love with your Zanta Barbara and vowed one day I must return. I knew that one day, I must buy land. Big land. I did not know how, I did not know when, but one day I knew—"

"That's a very moving story," I said. "So, Melissa—can you tell us about the zoning? Building permits? Is there an environmental impact report?"

I guess I'd learned a few things as an office manager. I was hoping Melissa would tell me that there was trouble with the permitting or the EIR had shown that this was an official habitat for endangered red salamander—any ammunition I could use to convince the owner not to sell.

But she said, "Good news all around. Soils test looks great, and we've got preliminary go-ahead from the Board on cluster zoning. Should be sub-dividable, no trouble with water or waste disposal. You never know until you're in the process, but it looks like clear sailing to me."

"Oh great." I turned to Ian. "Isn't that great?"

"Oui," he said mournfully. *"Wonderfulment."*

"Well…" I glanced at my watch to cover my disappointment. "We must be getting back."

"Don't you want to meet the owner?" Melissa asked.

"Yeah," Ian said, forgetting the accent again. "Don't I want to meet the owner?"

"He should be here any moment," Melissa said.

But everything was set to be developed. There was no way I'd convince the owner not to sell. "Herr Daunen is a busy man," I said.

"May I have *un* moment with *Mademoiselle,* um, Senna?" Ian asked Melissa, and dragged me far enough that she couldn't overhear. "I thought you were crazy to be so obsessed with this land," he said, "but now that I've seen it— you're right. It's special. It should be a park or reserve. Let's meet the owner. Maybe we can convince him not to sell. We have to try."

"You're going to help? You don't think I'm just a silly stupid waste of time?"

"Never a waste of time," he said.

Melissa said, "Ah, here's Mr. Montague."

A dapper older man in a pale suit, yellow tie and straw fedora approached from the trail, hardly winded. He looked like something out of *Guys and Dolls,* a snappy dresser from sixty years ago.

"Mr. Montague!" I waved, gearing myself back into sales mode. "I'm so pleased to meet you."

"Anne, no!" Ian whispered. "Retreat! Retreat!"

"Losing your nerve?" I hissed, through my smile at Mr. Montague. "C'mon, we can do this."

Ian tried to back away, but I tugged him along, and Melissa started the introductions. "Mr. Montague, this is Senna Leon, of Nouveau Brokers. And this is her client, Herr Daunen. From Switzerland."

I shook Mr. Montague's hand as Ian stood frozen.

"Herr Daunen?" I said.

"Daunen?" Mr. Montague said. "I thought the name was

Dunne. You're the antiques dealer who sold me that tallboy last month."

Ian opened his mouth to respond and I said, *"Nein! Nein! Achtung!"*

A couple minutes later, Melissa was ranting. "Antiques dealer? What's going on here? First he's a businessman from Germany, then you tell me he's Swiss. Yeah, like a cuckoo clock. And what're you—Senna Leon? Is that supposed to be French? You're about as French as iceberg lettuce. Who do you think you are—oh, my God! You're Anne! Anne Olsen. I thought I recognized your voice, from all those insane phone calls. Senna Leon, my ass. You look like an Anne. *Anne.* You're not even a Realtor. There are laws about this sort of thing, you know. There are—"

Mr. Montague interrupted her with a hoot of laughter. "Falsely impersonating a Realtor! Swiss as a cuckoo clock!" He laughed and shook his head. "Oh, that's just what the doctor ordered. Senna Leon and Herr Daunen."

"You're enjoying the tallboy?" Ian asked politely, as if we'd met over tea.

"This is the most unprofessional display I've ever seen," Melissa said, sticking her bony finger in my face. "I'm going to report you to the Board. They'll yank your license faster than—"

"If she's not an agent, Melissa," Mr. Montague said. "She doesn't have a license."

"No license," I agreed.

"Couldn't pass the test," Melissa said, with more venom than strictly necessary.

I loftily ignored her, and addressed Mr. Montague. "I'm sorry, sir. I didn't mean to—to make all this fuss. But I wanted to speak with you, I've been trying to find the owner of this land for months, but Missy refused to give me your contact information."

"Afraid those crazy dog people would call me," he said. "You see what they did to the sign, down below?"

Ian choked, but I soldiered onward. "Awful, the way some people behave. But actually—I come here myself, I love this property. I walk here three or four times a week. I can show you the spot where the wild bees started a hive two years ago—the trail loops around now, even though the bees are gone. Like the land remembers. And *we* do remember. I mean the people who've been walking their—who've been bird-watching here for years. We're a community. I can show you where the lupine blooms in the spring, I can show you the stream where I saw mule deer tracks, I can show you the best views of the ocean and my favorite place for a picnic. But now someone's going to build a monster oversized house and put up the private property signs. Too much of Southern California has disappeared already. Is this Montecito, or Laguna Beach? Why sell now? Why sell now when you can preserve the land for this and future generations?"

Okay, so I got a little carried away. But I meant that last bit rhetorically. Still, Mr. Montague answered. "'Cause I need the money. That's the way the cash flows."

"Oh," I said. "Right."

"You've wasted enough of our time," Melissa said. "I'm so sorry, Mr. Montague."

"Not at all," he said, looking out over the city. "She's got a point."

"I do?" I said.

"She does?" Melissa said.

"She does," Ian said.

"That *is* what'll happen to it," Mr. Montague said. "One of them Ponzi dot-commers will buy the parcel, put up six thousand square feet of god-awful Italianate mansion and never set foot outside. It's a darn shame." He inhaled deeply. "Smell that? Manzanita."

I waited with renewed hope. Could it be so simple? One middling-passionate faux-Oscar speech and he'd donate the land to the county? "So you'll consider preserving the land?"

"No," he said. "I still need the money."

"You don't!" I said. "You can always sell that damn tall-boy. I can get you a new bureau for two hundred bucks. Ikea. You don't really *need* the money, do you?"

"I do," he said. "Don't look like that. I'm a real estate investor. I invest in real estate."

"And a collector," Ian said. "In fact, I might be able to locate an early American occasional table which—"

"Herr Daunen!" I said, "please, let me finish." I turned to Mr. Montague. "So you need money, right?"

"Like a flea needs a dog."

"Well, what about donating the land to the Land Stewardship Group? I looked into this. They give you an annuity—wouldn't you rather have all the cash and none of the hassle? Plus, you'd be doing a good thing. You want to live in Laguna Beach? Not me. Me for Santa Barbara. Me for Montecito. Me for the open land and the views, for the birds and the bees—" which wasn't exactly what I meant, but I was on a roll "—and the manzanita trees. When all's said and done, what's more important? This view, this meadow, this unspoiled land…or some balance sheet somewhere? At the end of the day, would you rather have the—the money, or the *love?*"

We were all silent a moment—from various degrees of embarrassment and incredulity. Finally, Mr. Montague turned to Ian. "What're you doing involved in this? I'd pegged you for a reasonable man."

"Reasonable?" Ian said. "No, I'm with Anne. *Il faut beaucoup de naïveté pour faire de grandes choses.*"

What was that, an ancient Swiss curse? "Thanks for the vote of confidence," I said, as if I'd understood.

"You make a good point," Mr. Montague told me, ignoring Ian. "And you're a charming young lady—and I applaud your effort here, even if it's ruined my shoes. But no—I'm sorry. I won't donate the land. I won't preserve the land. I won't gift the land. I'll sell the land to the highest bidder, Italianate mansion be damned. That's what I do."

"Perhaps if you come back with a client?" Melissa told me. "And a license. And a *brain?*" She held out an arm to Mr. Montague. "Shall we?"

"I suppose." Mr. Montague tapped the brim of his hat. "But the old man needs something with a little more heft to hold on to." He gestured to me. "Name's Anne, isn't it?"

"Heft?" I said.

"Men of my generation," he said. "We like the well-fed woman. Not like these young fellows."

My God. "Women of my generation," I told him. "You call us hefty, we kick your sorry butt off a cliff."

He cackled and offered me his arm. So I slipped off my Blumarines and walked barefoot down the trail beside him.

"Anne Olsen," he said. "What do you do with yourself when you're not pretending to be a Realtor?"

I told him I used to work for Parsons Realty. Told him why I quit. Told him my whole work history, actually—back to The Ask It Basket. "No idea what I'm gonna do now, though," I finished.

"Don't look so glum. You'll find something."

"How about this?" I said. "The Land Stewardship Group has a trust program. A sort of reverse mortgage thing…"

"You're some kind of pit bull, aren't you? You've got the personality of a developer. Everyone else sees a red flag, you see a red cape. Put your head down and charge."

"Some people say I don't try hard enough."

"'Cause you haven't seen the right red cape. Give it time."

"You think?"

"Used to be the same, myself. Now I leave all the head-aches to younger folk. It's why I'm not developing the land myself. Besides, no way to make a dime on low-income here, and I hate building for the rich. They're wankers."

"Mr. Montague!" I laughed.

"Call me Monty," he said. "And it's true. Bottom of the market's the place to be. Of course, I just built a new condo complex on Las Positas and my head's deep in the alligator, with maintenance and—"

"Las Positas? The ones that look like storage units?"

"They don't look like storage units. Look like affordable housing."

"I'm sorry, Monty—no amount of pastel paint can make them look like anything but plywood boxes."

"Pastel? No, mine are the ones next door. But you know who built *those,* don't you?" He dished about a local devel-oper until we arrived at the bottom of the trail. Melissa and Ian arrived at the road a minute after we did. Melissa was looking less than picture-perfect, her blond hair awry and her pale face blotchy. Ian, however, had taken off his jacket and rolled up his sleeves and appeared sort of business-outdoorsy, like a well-dressed CEO who'd been on a metaphorically romantic picnic lunch.

"Well, it's been an experience," Monty said, as they ap-proached.

"Like dental work," Melissa said.

"*Something's* making me want to rinse and spit," I said, and wiped the mud off my feet on the No Trespassing sign.

Ian put a hand on my shoulder to keep me from toppling, and Melissa shouldered bonily past. She grabbed the sign and jabbed it back in the ground. "Come back here," she said, "and you *will* be breaking the law."

"Anne's always welcome, Melissa," Monty said, jangling his car keys in his hand. "Until the sale goes through, at least."

She offered a skeletal smile. "Then I'll work doubly hard to find a buyer. A *legitimate* buyer." She slid into her Jaguar and screeched away.

"She has a temper," Monty said. "But I like a spunky woman."

"I bet," Ian murmured. Then, louder, "Shall I call you about the occasional table?"

Monty said he should, and got in his Mercedes. "Been a pleasure." He considered, watching us through the open window. "Oddly enough, it has."

"Hey, Monty!" I called. "Why *Little Lamb?*"

"'Cause it's all about the fleecing," he said, and roared off.

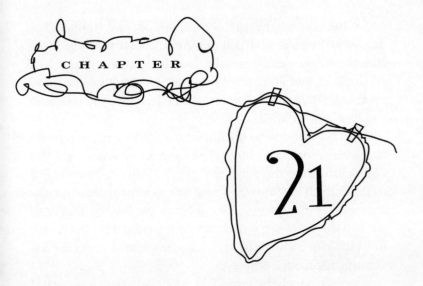

21

I slipped my Blumarines back onto my dirty, aching feet. "That went well."

"Could've been worse," Ian said.

"How?"

"Monty has a thing for young hotties. If you weren't *you,* he might've been pissed."

"How do you know what he has a thing for?"

"When he came to the shop, his assistant was there. She's like Salma Hayek, but prettier. Then he's got Melissa as his Realtor. And, the way he reacted to you. I think old Monty has a thing for the PYT."

"Melissa? Yuck." I kicked the No Trespassing sign over again. "She's so skinny she's transparent."

"Transparently hot."

"You could paper cut yourself on her hipbones."

"I could? You think she liked me?"

"Oh, shut up. She did *not* like you."

I tossed him the keys and we climbed into the Jeep.

As Ian started the car, the image of him saying *Oui, exactement!* suddenly struck me. And Melissa frothing at the mouth, and the fact I'd actually done it—I'd found the owner of the land, and I'd conned him into meeting me and...everything. I glanced at Ian. He glanced at me. And we sat in the Jeep and laughed.

After we caught our breath, we decided we needed cocktails even more than food. The afternoon was sunny and cool, perfect for the patio at Café del Sol, a restaurant five minutes from East Beach. The first round of margaritas disappeared as if by magic. The second went down slower, as we had the extra-large nachos to contend with. I licked salt from the rim of my glass, still marveling over our recent adventure. Or fiasco. Whatever.

"French as iceberg lettuce?" I said. "What's that supposed to mean?"

"I thought it was kinda funny."

"Well, you didn't have her bony finger an inch from your eyeball. I was scared to death."

"Yeah, you looked scared—the way your eyes were glowing and flames were issuing from your nostrils. I thought you were gonna punch her."

"I can't believe you think she's hot."

"She *is* hot."

"You're an engaged man. You can't be thinking these things."

"Thinking is all I can do. Well, and looking. I'd never actually touch another woman."

A nacho got caught sideways in my throat, and I coughed until my face was red and there were tears in my eyes. I gulped the rest of my margarita. "And I look like an Anne?" I said, when I could speak again. "What is that supposed to mean?"

"That you're plain and homely."

"I am not plain and homely!"

"I never said you were."

"You just said—you said I'm plain and homely." Now he'd *have* to say I was a hottie again.

"Hmm. I guess I did." He stuffed his mouth with a chip smothered in beans and cheese. "So what's our next move?"

We don't have a next move, Ian, because you'd never touch a woman who wasn't Helene. "What next move?"

"With the Cypress property."

"Oh. That. I've failed. I'm done. That's it. I cared, Ian. I really did. I love that land. Are you happy now? I really cared, and I tried, and I failed. Great. I feel better now. Thank you. Wonderful. What a friend. What a buddy. Oh, this is terrific. I don't know how I—"

"So you're giving up?"

It hadn't occurred to me not to. It wasn't giving up so much as acknowledging failure. But when he said it like that, it seemed somehow wrong.

I said, "Hell, no."

But I couldn't think of a next move.

I spent the following day in a Buddha-like state of deep introspection, turning over every possibility and examining each potential approach with meticulous care. In other words, I cleaned my house. I needed something to occupy my hands as I tried to figure out how to save both the Cypress property and my rapidly diminishing sense of self-worth.

I'd tied my hair back with a rubber band and put on a sweatshirt and pajama bottoms decorated with dancing dogs—my normal cleaning outfit. When I'd finished the floors, I'd accumulated a pile of Ny-hair large enough to construct a second Ny.

I also ended up with a pile of Rip's stuff. His magazines,

toothpaste, CDs and a corkscrew. Poor Rip. All he wanted was a wife and children, and he got me instead. It was kind of true. We *had* grown apart. It was nobody's fault. We'd just realized it wasn't going to work. Because we wanted different things.

The problem was, Rip knew what he wanted. I knew what he wanted. So why didn't I know what *I* wanted?

I only knew what I didn't want. The jobs I could get weren't the jobs I wanted. And the man I could get wasn't the man I wanted. The Cypress property honestly mattered to me, I loved that land—but it was hardly a job. I scrubbed the grout between the tiles in my shower—at least I could win *that* fight.

There was a knock on the front door, and Charlotte called, "Annie?"

"In the bathroom!"

She came in, looking like Charlotte Olsen on a good day. I averted my eyes from the bathroom mirror—I didn't even want to know what I looked like. Nosferatu, I presumed, after a late night with the boys.

"Have you been crying?" she said.

I wiped my eyes with my sleeve. "I went a little heavy on the bleach."

She laughed. "Come here, there's something I want to show you."

In the living room, she'd laid a half-dozen swimsuits on my couch, from a skimpy and shimmering bikini in champagne to a turquoise one-piece.

"What do you think?" she asked, with a spokesmodel gesture.

"They're from the organic shoot?"

"No, Annie, they're mine. The designs I've been working on. I'm sick of licensing my name. I want to get involved in the creative side, do the designing myself. Do you like them? They're kinda frumpy—do you think they're frumpy? David says they're beautiful, so I worry—you know *his* taste."

I picked up the bikini. "I think Mr. Fashion Disaster is right, Charlotte. These are great. You made them? I can't believe you made them. They look so professional. When did you learn to sew like this?"

"Plenty of down-time during photo shoots, and there was always someone willing to show me the tricks. Plus, I've been practicing." She pointed to a two-piece with a tiny top and boy-shorts bottoms. "I thought I'd make you one like this, but maybe in red."

"Why the boy shorts? Is my ass getting bigger? I swear, if my ass is getting bigger that's the last straw. I'm hefty, aren't I?"

Charlotte stepped away from the swimsuit. "Okay," she said, softly. "What's wrong?"

I gulped a few tears and was off. No career, no job. Big failure with Monty, big failure with everything. "…and I live in your guest house. I'm like your Kato Kaelin! I'm just—I love you, and I love your family and everything, but I don't want to be your Kato. I want to be Anne. But I don't know how. I mean, I don't know *who*. I mean, I just don't know!"

She hugged me and made hot cocoa. I bet OJ never did that when Kato got the weepies.

Monday afternoon, I called Monty. Easier to make contact once you knew his name. I got a sultry female voice which must have been the Salma Hayek wannabe. I asked if she knew where I might find Monty, and amazingly, she told me.

Half an hour later, I exited the freeway at Los Positas Road. I'd spent Sunday in David's study—he had a color printer, quality paper, the works—putting together a presentation of the many lucrative ways in which Monty could donate the Cypress property to the county. I'd already presented the same ideas orally, but thought glossy paper might persuade him.

I parked in a guest spot at his new condos and took a few calming breaths. This would work. I'd save the Cypress property, and somehow my own life would fall into place. I knew it was magical thinking, but it felt true—this was the scent I was following. I tried to remember a positive thinking mantra but came up blank, so I just pawed the ground a couple times and charged.

The units were white stucco with tea-green trim. They were staggered and of different heights, giving a sort of village-y feel, but they'd been built along an asphalt driveway, with zero room for landscaping. As if someone had plopped a condo complex on top of a parking lot.

I wandered the treeless sidewalk, looking for Monty's car, and the front door of one of the units swung open. Monty backed out of the door looking dapper in a snappy suit—but soaking wet.

"I told you, call the plumber," he was saying to someone inside. "I gave you the number—"

"I don't trust them," a quavery female voice said from inside. "*Tradesmen*. If you're lucky, all they do is steal the furniture."

"I'm sorry, but you can't keep calling me for—"

"Oh!" she said. "Oh! It's starting again! Mr. Montague!"

He removed his hat and wiped his face, clearly trying to summon the courage to enter again.

"Hey, Monty," I said—maybe a bit more amused than I should've been.

He turned, surprised. "Anne?"

"Plumbing problems?" I asked.

From inside the woman warbled, "Mr. Montague, what if it soaks through the floorboards?"

"I have something for you." I showed him the presentation folder. "Think you might find it interesting."

"About the land on Cypress?"

"You're sitting on a gold mine there," I said. "Worst thing you could do is sell it."

"Right," he said. "What kind of person sells gold?"

"Just read it," I said sharply.

"Mr. Montague! It's overflowing!"

"I'll read it," he said, "if you play plumber."

I glanced into the shadowy depths beyond the door of the condo. No telling what I might find inside. But anything for the cause. I squared my shoulders and entered.

The unit was nicer than I'd expected. A tiled entryway, peach walls, light-colored carpet, and sliding glass doors that opened to the back deck. The kitchen was the source of the woman's voice—and the now-audible sound of water running.

The woman at the sink was in her eighties, wearing light blue polyester pants and a matching sweater. She was staring in dismay at the water seeping slowly from the base of the cold-water handle.

"Oh!" she said. "I was expecting Mr. Montague."

"I'm Anne," I said, thanking the Lord that this was a sink problem and not a toilet problem. "I'll be your plumber today."

"It's gushing. It started this morning. I'm afraid it'll get into the floorboards."

The amount of water was about enough to fill a teacup in ten minutes—hardly a threat to the floorboards—but I suppose purists preferred their water coming out the tap, not from around the cold-water knob. I opened the cabinet under the sink and turned the water off. Niagara ceased.

The woman was delighted. "Oh! Thank you! I didn't know *what* I'd do. Mr. Montague said I should call a plumber. He splashed himself something awful. But I don't approve of tradesmen." She lowered her voice. "They can be unscrupulous."

I asked if she had a screwdriver handy. She found one, and I popped the little round thingamabob off the top of the cold-water handle. My ex-boyfriend, Arthur the plumber, may have slept around, but he'd also taught me a few plumbing tricks.

"Oh, don't go to any trouble," the woman said. "I don't really *need* the cold water."

"It's no trouble," I said, and unscrewed the knob from the sink. It came off in my hand, and there were four little pieces inside, including a rubber ring that was broken. "Here's your problem, ma'am," I said. "Got yourself a worn grommet."

I went outside, and Monty was reading the last page of my proposal. I waited until he was done, and said, "What do you think?"

"You fixed the sink?"

"She needs a new one of these," I said, showing him the grommet.

"Don't we all," he said.

"So? What do you think?"

"Well…I'll tell you what I think. Been a few years since I've seen such a well-presented load of hogwash." He tapped the proposal thoughtfully. "But here's what I'll do. You want a job?"

"It's not hogwash!"

"We're past that, Anne. We're on to the job offer, now."

"I'm not past it."

"Yes, you are. You just don't know it. You're unemployed. Someone bright as you, high-energy—that's a pity. Now, I've got a vacant unit here, brand-new. Just waiting for an on-site manager."

"A manager? Of your condos?"

"Property management is the first step. Get yourself a toe-hold in the business. You've got the skills, I can see that. You've got a way with people and plumbing. You're a hot-tie."

"I'm a *what?*"

"You're handy," he repeated.

"Oh. Yeah. Well, a little."

"And God knows you need something to keep you out of trouble."

"Don't mess with the tradesman, Monty," I said. "And it's *not* hogwash."

"So you'll take the job?"

"What does it pay?"

He mentioned a number, embarrassingly low.

"Are you kidding? That wouldn't pay for a single latté."

"Plus you get to live in the manager's unit. Free."

"The unit looks like hers?" I gestured inside. "And it's new?"

"Brand spanking. Nobody's ever lived there. Same layout as you just saw, but with a third floor downstairs. They're lay-ing the carpet as we speak."

Huh. Brand-new unit, never-been-lived-in. No more Kato. And proximity to Monty—I was sure I could change his mind about selling the Cypress property, given a little more time. "What're the job duties?"

"Process association fees, arrange maintenance. Make sure the trash gets picked up, people don't violate the CC&Rs. That sort of thing."

"Brand spanking new," I said. There'd be no questions about where that hair came from, who'd been in the shower, whose food had splattered the stove. And I was twenty-nine years old—it was time to leave the nest. Time to be Anne. Plus, how hard could this be? A little bookkeeping, a few walks around the parking lot perimeter, and I'd be done. I'd have plenty of time to go back to school or whatever. Maybe this was what I'd been on the scent of—the next step toward independence.

"You interested?" he asked.

"Let's talk wages," I said. "'Cause I take my lattés double."

CHAPTER

22

Wren had been avoiding me for weeks—more easily done because sculpture class was finished for the semester—but I finally tracked her to her lair at Element. Her office was empty and her computer turned off, so I worried she'd gone home for the evening until I spotted her behind a rack of Calvin Kleins, chatting with Jenny. They were straightening the clothes, and laughing over something I couldn't hear.

Did *Jenny* know Wren's secret? Maybe I was being paranoid, but something about the way they were laughing spoke of confidences revealed. I was feeling excluded and intimidated, when Wren spotted me. She bounded across the room and kissed me hello.

"I have a secret, too, you know," I said, meaning my potential new job and home. "I have all kinds of interesting news."

"You do? What?"

I laughed scornfully. "As if I'd tell *you!*"

She laughed, non-scornfully. "Oh, Anne—I've missed you. Oh! That reminds me. I put aside some stuff…" And she dragged me around the shop, tossing clothes at me and insisting I try them on. I objected, on the grounds of poverty, but she said everything was discounted today. Manager's Special.

"You're just feeling guilty," I said.

"No, I'm happy to see you."

"Why?" I asked, dubious.

"Because I missed your open and loving personality." She shoved me into the dressing room, a heap of clothing in my arms. "Try the red top first."

"Is this about your secret?" I asked, from inside the dressing room. "This one-day sale?"

"I don't even know if there *is* a secret," she said, but her voice held an edge of exuberance that made it clear there was. "What's your news?"

I slipped on the red top and opened the dressing room door. "You first."

She wrinkled her nose. "Let me get a smaller size."

Ha! Smaller! I wasn't so hefty after all. "And bring one in the blue."

She returned in a minute with two new tops, and I disappeared back into the dressing room. "You first," I said again.

"No, I—there's nothing to tell, really."

"Wren, you've been hiding from me and you're all crazy-headed. There's definitely *something* to tell."

"Yeah, but I—I don't even…" She cracked the dressing room door. "There may be no secret. I'm gonna find out soon. And I want you to be there. You *have* to be there. I don't want to tell you until I know, but—oh, God." Her voice went from exuberant to nervous. "You're gonna yell at me. You're gonna hate me. But it might be nothing. Just tell me your news. You and Rip back together? You and *Ian?*"

"God, no. Me and nobody. Me and me."

I told her about the new job and the brand-new condo—

and that I hadn't agreed to anything until I saw the place with her in tow. Monty told me the carpet guys were done and I could drop by anytime, and Wren agreed to go with me after work. In the meantime, I bought the blue top and a pair of stretch jeans with her discount, neatly saving myself $113.

Wren left Jenny to lock up, and we did a few errands—pet store for me, pharmacy for her—and pulled into the condo complex around six. It was even more barren than I remembered, all asphalt and no grass. I guess it would make my life easier, not having gardeners to supervise, but the place was definitely lacking in curb appeal, though it had more than its share of curb. Monty must've designed it low-maintenance, as part of his bottom-of-the-market strategy.

"Welcome to Monty City," I told Wren. "They paved the parking lot and put up…paradise!"

I pulled into the spot marked *Manager,* feeling important. The key was under the welcome mat and I opened the front door…and was hit with an ambrosial scent. New carpet. New paint. New *everything.*

I inhaled deeply. "Better than roses."

Wren, not entirely entering into the mood, said, "I have to go to the bathroom."

"I don't even live here yet—can't you hold it?"

"I've been holding it for half an hour!" She rushed past, opened the closet door, and cursed. "Where's the damn bathroom?"

"You can't hold it?"

"I'm gonna pee on your carpet," she said, squirming.

"I think the bathroom is…" But then I was in the living room, and forgot Wren's potty problem. The room was small but serene, filled with natural evening light from a wall of windows. French doors led to a deck overlooking a mini-canyon with flowering ice plant and eucalyptus trees. The kitchen was an open concept off the living room, and had stainless steel appliances and white countertops—everything brand new.

"I'll find it," Wren said, bounding upstairs.

Oh, yeah. There were stairs, too, heading both up and down, as this was one of the few three-level units in the complex. All told, it was only about a thousand square feet—but light and airy and the rug was immaculate. The carpet guys had laid plastic strips down, so even *they* hadn't walked on my new berber. I slipped my shoes off and shivered with ecstasy when my bare feet hit virgin rug. Delicious. My toes curled. I was in love. Plus, the light switches were utterly unsullied. Nobody had *ever* used the Venetian blinds, the dishwasher, or the phone jacks. Even the light bulbs were new.

I could flush my fears of Kato Kaelin down the spotless new toilet. This was great. This was beyond anything. This was *me.* Goodbye hand-me-downs, and hello Anne.

I was in the kitchen opening drawers and marveling at the sheer sugary freshness when Wren came back downstairs. She was shaking one of her hands, air-drying it.

"No towel?" I asked. Of course not. No paper towel, even. I'd have to buy a brand-new pack, and break the seal here inside my brand-new apartment. They would be paper towels that had never been exposed to non-Anne air. Pristine and pure.

Hmm. I could really get obsessive about this.

"Mmm," Wren said. "You should see the bathroom—and the bedroom, *oo-la-la*. Nice closet, big windows. How much are these places?"

"I don't know. Monty said affordable housing, but this is so nice."

"Well, affordable housing in Santa Barbara," she said, still air-drying. "What is that?"

"Probably a half million."

We laughed, but sort of sadly, as we'd lived in Santa Barbara back in the days when two people, both working full-time, could afford an entry-level fixer-upper. We headed upstairs, where the walls were a warm cream color, and the rug a soft camel to match. "No one has ever slept here," I said, reverently. I opened the door to the master bath. "Or been in this bathroom." But the toilet was running. Oh. I turned to Wren. "Except you."

"Shower's still cherry," Wren said, waving her hand.

"Would you stop that? Dry it on your pants—that's what they're for."

She opened her hand, and was holding something. Like a thermometer. I wasn't paying much attention, as I was focused on the mirror over the bathroom sink. It was spotless. No water marks, no toothpaste splatter…

"What is that?" I asked absently.

She smiled at me in the mirror. "I'm late."

"For what?"

"I'm *late,* late."

"What? You don't mean—?" But she did. "Ohmigod! What? Shit! When did *this* happen? Why didn't you tell me? What are we gonna do?"

Wren smiled serenely.

"Don't panic!" I screamed. "We'll figure it out. Just don't panic."

"I'm not panicking," she said, giving the pregnancy wand a bit of extra wrist action.

"Would you stop shaking it! Are you supposed to shake it? Oh, my God. You're *pregnant?*"

"I hope so."

"You hope so? What do you mean, you hope so? You don't hope so!"

"I do. I do hope so. I've been trying—"

"Would you stop shaking it!?"

"—to get pregnant. It's what I was afraid to tell you. Anne, I want this baby."

Oh, God. I needed a drink. I needed oxygen. "You don't even know there *is* a baby."

"I *do* know. And you'll know in…" She glanced at the pregnancy stick, then at her watch. "Thirty seconds. Twenty-nine, twenty-eight—"

"Wren, this isn't New Year's Eve."

"You're right. It's better," she said. "Twenty-four, twenty-three…"

I paced, in my calm and tranquil way. "Oh, *God!* We're not ready for this. I can't believe you never *told* me. Do you know what kind of responsibility this is? How's your health insurance? Do you get maternity leave? You've never even been *around* babies—they're like chubby car alarms that spit up on your neck. Oh, God—you are getting married. You and Kevin. You barely know the guy. What do you know about him? He looks good naked? Okay. Don't panic. Oh, God, do you—" I stopped abruptly, as she sat down on the stairs. "What? What? What does it say?"

"I'm going to be a mother." She looked at me and smiled and all the clichés of the beautiful, glowing, pregnant woman were proved true. "I'm having a baby."

"Okay. Okay—but you weren't supposed to shake it. What do you think, it's a can of spray paint?"

"Good thing I bought two tests." She slipped back into the bathroom.

I collapsed onto the stairs. I couldn't handle this. Why hadn't Wren told me? I wasn't ready. I listened to her pee and wondered why *I* wasn't interested in having a family— Rip would've been a great dad. I loved my niece and nephews. I'd helped raise them. Hell, I'd been the person to cut the umbilical cord on Tyler. And it occurred to me: I'd been using my sisters' families to sublimate the need for my own.

I'd co-mothered their kids, I'd borrowed their husbands for errands. I didn't have my own life at all.

Well, one thing was certain. I'd take this job with Monty. I hated the idea of moving away from my family, but clearly I needed to do exactly that. Time to strike out on my own—and living here would be the first step. Ian would approve. Oh, God. Ian was such a sublimation! Hell, even Ny was like a sublimated child. I was stuck in an entirely sublimated life, while Wren was actively living hers. She'd just taken the plunge into the future, and hadn't told me because she didn't want me to rain on her preggy parade. Because I was negative and contrary and a bad friend.

She opened the bathroom door, holding the pregnancy wand and keeping an eye on her watch.

"Well?" I asked.

"Wait for it. Wait for it…"

I held my breath, desperately wishing for something. Wasn't sure what.

"Still pregnant!" she said.

This time, I carefully hugged the life out of her. "Oh, Wren! This is fantastic. I'm so happy for you—I really, really, *really* am! I only wish I was the father, instead of that stinky Kevin!"

Her face crumpled.

"No, I love Kevin!" I said. "I was kidding! I'm so happy for you, for both of you—"

She started weeping, and sunk to the floor. Between hiccups and sobs, she said, "It's not easy for m-me, like it is for you. I can't talk to men. And I want a f-family! And kids. I w-want a family and I don't want to be alone anymore and I-I-I—"

And she started wailing again.

I eventually calmed her. "This was your secret, Wren? You know I'm there for you, no matter what. I was surprised, is all. Of course I'm happy for you."

"The secret wasn't that I'm pregnant. I didn't know until now. Well, I knew. But I didn't *know.* The secret was that I was *trying* to get pregnant. I knew you wouldn't approve."

"I approve of everything you do."

She smiled through her tears. "Yeah?"

"Yeah."

"Okay," she sniffled.

"It was just a surprise. You and Kevin—wow."

She fiddled with the nap of the carpet. "Well, um…Kevin doesn't know."

"Let's call him! No, we have to tell him in person." I was pleased—in a jealous and despicable way—that she'd done the pregnancy test with me instead of him. "He'll be so happy, he'll—"

"Anne—he doesn't know *anything.*"

"What, the birds and the bees?"

"He doesn't know I was trying to get pregnant."

It took a second for me to realize what she'd just said. "He doesn't *what?*"

"I knew you were going to yell at me!"

"I'm not yelling!" Deep breaths. "What do you mean, exactly?"

"I told him I was on the pill."

"But you're not. You're not on the pill."

She didn't say anything.

"Wren—you told him you were on the pill?"

"I want a baby! Everything is easy for you, but it's different for me. You don't know what it's like. I want—I'm twenty-nine, this could be my last chance. You had Rip, and you dumped him, and I—I didn't even have anyone until Kevin came along and…I told him I was on the pill."

"You used him to get pregnant?"

"I don't care. I don't care."

"What is he, a sperm donor?"

"He doesn't have to have anything to do with the baby."

"It's his fucking baby, too, Wren. I can't believe you did this. This is wrong. This is bad."

"It's *my* baby. He put a half hour into this—okay, maybe an hour—and I'm gonna carry it for nine months, and I—"

"You're gonna carry it? If I carry your bags, I own your fucking groceries? This is bad, Wren. Bad, bad, bad!"

So she started crying again, and I comforted her again.

"When are you going to tell him?" I asked.

"*What* am I going to tell him?"

"The truth."

"I thought maybe I'd say I got pregnant, you know, despite the pill."

"The truth, Wren."

"Do I have to?"

I nodded.

"He's going to hate me."

"He has every right to hate you." Before she could start crying again, I said, "But I love you. And I'll be there for you no matter what. And if Kevin's halfway smart, he'll hate you for a while—then he'll forgive you."

"You think?"

"If he's halfway smart," I said.

The day before my big move, Charlotte was sitting on my bed watching me pack, tears in her eyes. "I can't believe you're leaving us," she said.

I shoved my comforter into a laundry bag. "I can't believe your face doesn't blotch when you cry."

"What are we going to do without you?"

"I'll still baby-sit."

"That's not what I meant, and you know it."

I sat next to her. "I know."

"I love having you close."

"I love being close. But we'll still be close. I'll just be…farther away."

Truth told, I was more upset than Charlotte. I'd lived here for eight years. It was home. When I wasn't baby-sitting, I was eating dinner with the family, or we were hanging out in the pool or watching a movie together. Living alone was going to be lonely. As if to highlight my distress, the morning after I'd accepted Monty's offer Hannah had woken me at seven by pounding on my front door and summoning me for scones that she and Mommy had baked. Then the adults had sat on the patio, drinking coffee while the kids skittered through the garden playing Harry Potter. Hannah had been Harry, of course. Kyle and Tyler kept forgetting which one of them was the girl—and had no idea how to pronounce Hermione anyway—and Ny had been Malfoy. God, I'd miss them.

"If it doesn't work out…" Charlotte said.

I wanted to say, *I'll stay! I'll stay!* But knew I couldn't. "You're gonna rent the place to the first person who asks, aren't you?"

"Are you kidding?" she said. "Wait for someone to *ask?*"

We laughed, and I tied the laundry bag air-tight. "Wren's pregnant," I told her.

Instead of expressing shock or dismay, she said, "Really? You know, you should get pregnant."

"I'm hefty enough, thank you."

"You're pushing thirty. You're losing eggs as we speak."

"Yech." I opened the closet. "You mothers are too free with that egg and uterus stuff. It's still just a sex organ to me, thank you very much."

"But for how long?"

"Maybe forever." I grabbed my mother's old white plastic Tourister suitcases from the shelf—one big, one medium, and one oversized cosmetic case—and opened them on the floor next to the bed. "I think I was born to be an aunt."

"I can't believe you still have those," Charlotte said, looking at the suitcases. "I'll get you a set on wheels for your birthday. Brand-new."

"I like these." I smoothed the pink satin on the inside of the large suitcase, and started packing my underwear.

"Oh," Charlotte said.

I stopped packing. "*Oh* what?"

"Nothing." She kicked the medium suitcase with the point of her Paul Green loafer.

"Stop it." I pulled the case out of range.

"The only time you don't complain about hand-me-downs is when it's something from Mom."

"So?"

"So you think you loved her most."

"Oh, that follows. Because I like her suitcases, I loved her most."

"You think you loved her more than Emily or me."

"Jesus, where is *this* coming from?"

"You know you do."

"Charlotte, I don't even know what you're talking about."

"Oh yes, you do."

"Oh no, I don't. Besides," I said, "that's better than thinking *she* loved *me* best."

"Don't you *dare!*" She stalked from the bedroom.

I followed her. "So much for helping me pack."

She flung open the front door. "I can't be with you right now. Unless…"

"Unless what?"

"Unless you admit you think you loved Mom the most."

I stared at her blankly, and she slammed the door on her way out.

Then I said, "You bet I did."

★ ★ ★

Before Mom died, I'd wake early Saturday mornings and crawl into bed with her and Dad. I'd wriggle in on Mom's side, and she'd cuddle me and call me pickle. In a few minutes, Dad would start grumbling, and Mom would lift me over to kiss him on the cheek. He'd smile, eyes closed, and Mom would roll me back to the outside and cradle me in her arms. The two of them would drowse while I'd lie awake, trying not to fall asleep so I wouldn't miss a minute of the love.

For a year after she died, I'd still wake early Saturdays and climb in bed with my Dad. I'd kiss him and he'd smile, but he never cuddled or called me pickle. I'd lie next to him, missing Mom. I guess he was missing her, too. Then one Saturday when I was thirteen, I woke with my first period. I rummaged in the bathroom and found a gigantic repulsive maxi-pad. I crawled into Emily's bed that morning, and told her what happened. She said all the right things—but she still wasn't Mom.

Emily and Charlotte didn't understand that although we all missed Mom, I had actually *missed* her. She was there for their first periods. She was there when Emily hadn't won the national essay contest and Charlotte totaled the car. She was there until Charlotte was eighteen and Emily was seventeen—and I was twelve. They were approaching adulthood, while I was flailing around in childhood. They were normal teenage girls, starting to separate from their mother when she died. But to me, she was still a god. She left at the height of my love for her. I'll always love her best.

Wren met me at Monty City to help me unpack. She was wearing a men's gray T-shirt and black leggings.

"My God!" I said. "Are you okay?"

"What?"

I gestured at her ensemble. "Who are you, and what have you done with Wren?"

"I am pregnant you know."

"You're what, two pounds heavier? I gain more than that walking past a bakery."

"I'm preparing myself. This is what I'll be wearing."

"You wear that and *I'll* get morning sickness."

"I can't afford anything nice. I've gotta save my money for the baby."

"We'll raid Charlotte's closet. She still has all her maternity clothes. I think she's been saving them for me—as if."

"She's six inches taller than me."

"She'll alter them. Believe me, she'll be happy to."

I opened a couple boxes on the kitchen counter and we

started putting away dishes and silverware. We debated the placement of the toaster oven and the wine rack and eventually I asked, "Have you told Kevin yet?"

"Not quite," she said.

"Well, do you know if he wants kids?"

"He wants an Australian Shepherd. That's good, right? It shows paternal feelings. Hey, where's Ny?"

"With the kids. I want his food bowls down before he arrives. Otherwise there'll be trouble." I eyed her. "Speaking of which…"

"I'll tell him. I will."

"What're you waiting for?"

"I just wish we'd been together a little longer."

A bit late to worry about that now. "Whatever happens, remember the most important thing."

"I know, I know. Tell him the truth."

"Not that," I said. "This: You're always welcome here."

Emily and Zach dropped Ny at the condo after Wren left, and they were suitably impressed with my new home. She liked the light and Zach liked the three floors. Ny, however, seemed a little disappointed until I let him romp in the canyon. He returned a half hour later, tongue hanging, tail wagging and covered in burrs. It would do.

I asked Emily and Zach to stay for pizza—then realized I didn't know who to call. My old pizza place was in Montecito. Emily refused the pizza and instead invited me to her house. I was tempted. I didn't want to be left alone, and I *really* didn't want to do any more unpacking. But I was determined not to let the moving-in process drag out all week, so I said no.

Emily called Zach and he trotted downstairs with Ny trailing behind. Ny was wearing the tiara that usually hung on the mirror over my dresser.

"What have you done to my dog?" I said.

"We were playing Little Mermaid."

"Which one of you is the mermaid?"

"Ny," he said. "I'm Sebastian."

"Thank God for that," Emily said.

I clucked my tongue. "Homophobe. If only your colleagues knew."

"Zach knows," she said, "that if he wants to grow up gay, Mommy will always love him."

"And if he wants to grow up gay and *not* dysfunctional," I said, "Aunt Anne will let him live with her."

After they left, Ny pressed his crowned head against my knee. I bent down to remove the tiara, and saw Zach had attached it with duct tape. "Ouch," I said, as a chunk of fur came off with each piece I removed. Ny shook his head in disgust, so I fed him an extra-large serving of dog food and sprinkled Parmesan on top as a treat.

I picked the tape off the tiara and placed it on my head. "I am queen of my domain," I said to Ny. "Ruler of all I survey."

Then I opened the phone book to find the nearest pizza place. Petrini's was pretty close. Best eggplant subs in Santa Barbara, too. Maybe living here wouldn't be so bad.

On the other hand, maybe it would. Someone pounded on my front door at 2:00 a.m. I woke to my unfamiliar room, completely disoriented. My mind was a blur of *wrong:* wrong smells, wrong room, wrong everything. Ny huffed in his sleep, and woke. He hopped onto the bed to peer out the window, and barked as the knocking continued.

I wanted to ignore it. No good news came at 2:00 a.m. But what if it was Wren? What if she'd told Kevin and was here for moral support?

"Just a second," I yelled. I reached for the lamp, but it

wasn't there. So I crawled out of bed and lurched for the light switch—which wasn't there, either. I stumbled in the dark, naked and confused, pawing the wall as Ny barked. I finally found the switch, and the room was bathed in blinding light. My robe wasn't on the hook on the back of the door. In fact, the hook wasn't even on the back of the door. I counted myself lucky that the back of the door was there.

I didn't have my contacts in, so I squinted at the blobs of color on the floor hoping to find something robe-ish. No luck, as the pounding continued. Forget the robe. I grabbed a flannel shirt from the floor, and struggled halfway inside before discovering it was a pillowcase. Fuck it. I wrapped myself in the comforter and stumbled downstairs. It was only Wren anyway.

It wasn't Wren.

I threw open the door, and even partially blind I could tell the knocker wasn't a cute young brunette crying over her imperceptibly ballooning belly. It was a short, chinless guy wearing a mesh T-shirt and cutoffs.

"My toilet's stopped up," he said.

Ny greeted this statement with a volley of barks as I stared in sleepy bewilderment.

"My toilet," the guy said again. "It's plugged."

"Cujo!" I told Ny. "Down!" Then, faux-apologetically, to the chinless guy: "Late for his rabies shots."

The man paled slightly. "It's my grandmother's toilet. It won't flush."

"Wait here," I told him, all neighborly. "I'll call 9-1-1 on you. I mean *for* you. Down, Killer!"

The madman paled further, and his chinlessness became even more pronounced, or recessed, as the case may be. "Um—aren't you the manager?"

"Oh! Oh! The manager. I am. Yes." My comforter started

slipping, and I clasped it more tightly. "Ny, hush! I'm the manager."

"I live here. In number twelve. With my grandmother."

"Oh! You *live* here!"

"You're Anne, right?" He held out his hand to shake. "Anne the manager."

I looked at him. If I shook his hand, the comforter would drop. Chinless perv. "I don't think so," I said.

"But my grandmother said she met a woman named Anne the other day—"

"No, I *am* Anne, but I'm not gonna… Forget it. What's the problem?"

"Her toilet's plugged."

"Have you called a plumber?"

"My grandmother doesn't like plumbers."

Ah. *That* grandmother. Of course. Tradesmen. "Have you tried a plunger?"

"We don't have a plunger."

"She doesn't like plungers, either?"

He shook his head. "Naw, we just don't have one."

"This is my advice—buy a plunger."

"Well, it's like two in the morning…."

I sighed. "One second."

I closed the door on him, found my contacts, got dressed, and dug my plunger from the depths of its still-packed box, and opened the front door again, hoping the crisis was over and I could return to bed. But outside, Chinless hadn't moved.

I thrust the plunger at him. "Here."

He took it. "Thanks! I'll return it tomorrow."

"Oh, no you won't."

"Honest I will. Promise."

"Keep it. Burn it. Bury it. Please. It's yours now."

He eyed the plunger way too happily. "Gee, thanks."

I closed the door. I went upstairs. I undressed. And someone knocked on the front door again. Ny eyed me from the bed. He clearly considered standing and barking, but snuggled deeper into the covers instead. Wonderful. Downstairs, I opened the door—dressed properly this time—and found Chinless again, holding the plunger.

"I *don't* want it back," I said. "I told you."

"My grandmother asked if you'd do it," he said.

"She wants me to plunge her toilet?"

"Uh-huh."

"At two in the morning?"

"Uh-huh."

Well, what was I gonna do? Let the old woman spend the night with a clogged toilet, in the care of her incompetent and chin-impaired grandson? So I went to number twelve to deal with some number two. The short version: there was a clogged toilet. There was a floater. I plunged. Grannie—whose name was Mrs. Wordan—hovered in the doorway, nattering about how she hoped she was no trouble, and she didn't really *need* to use the toilet, she should've waited until tomorrow and gone to a public rest room. And after some aerobic plunger-wrestling, I finally prevailed.

Half hour later, back in bed, I thought, This never would have happened in Montecito.

My good deed did not go unpunished.

Day Two, still only half moved in, there was another knock. A gawky woman was standing on the welcome mat, looking apologetic. She said she was Arlene, and she lived in number four. Ten minutes later, I found myself helping her hang pictures. Actually, I hung the pictures and she said, "It's a little crooked, sorry. Lower the edge a bit. Sorry, no—the other edge. No, the *other* other edge. Sorry."

Day Three, after an early-morning bathtub crisis, I sat down with Mrs. Wordan to try to understand why her plumbing was constantly percolating. She offered me sugar cookies instead of any intelligent explanation. They were tasty, but I wasn't able to drag myself away from her gossip for hours. By which time I was suffering a major sugar-crash. I collapsed in bed and waited for Day Three to become Day Four.

Day Four was relatively uneventful. I went over the condo books with Monty in the morning, the management procedures and the CC&Rs. I hinted gently that he should retain the Cypress property, and he suggested mildly I should soak my head. I spent the afternoon baby-sitting Hannah and her brothers and the evening baby-sitting Wren.

Day Five, I met the cable guy for the young couple in number eighteen, then enjoyed a long afternoon cleaning up after the garbagemen. They'd backed down the driveway early that afternoon, lofted the Dumpster into the air and emptied it into the truck. Well, most of it. At least seventy-five percent. So I bought rubber gloves which extended from fingertip to armpit, and learned more than I wanted to know about my condo-mates. One, judging from the bloody cellophane wrappers, ate kidneys with great regularity. One, judging from the mound of dust and exfoliated skin, had recently installed a new vacuum bag. One, judging from the Kleenex, had TB.

Then I supervised the guys laying the sod. Monty, in all his wisdom, had decreed that the dirt patch between the condos and the canyon would be our one spot of green. Three hundred square feet of rolling parkland. Oddly, the sod guys were not pleased with my input. Still, this was all the grassland we had: the Monty City Town Green. We would meet there for lemonade socials and town meetings and barn raisings and such. Anyway, the guys finally trimmed the edges properly, so that was good.

Then I stared in my closet. It was Thursday. Drinks Night. But I wasn't sure if we'd be going to Red or Durgan's or Café del Sol, each of which required a different outfit. But we were buddies—there was nothing romantic about Drinks Night—so I didn't play coy. I called him.

"Ian," I said. "It's Anne."

"Hey, Anne. How're Green Gables?"

"Getting greener every day. We got new sod today."

"Better the sod you know," he said.

"Sod as in lawn, bonehead." And I told him about Mrs. Wordan's plumbing and sugar cookies, and how great the place was. "How's *All For a Buck?*"

"That's *All For Fifty-Six Bucks* to you," he said. "And pretty good. Sold a stickpin online, and a man I met at an auction last week came in, from Topanga. He collects music stands, and—"

"Oh, he *does* not! You're telling me someone collects used *music stands?*"

"Yeah, he—"

"He needs more than one? How many instruments can he play at once?"

"Well, he—"

"What is he, a one-man band?"

There was silence.

"So he collects music stands," I said, "and…?"

"And I found a Regency duet stand. Gorgeous, a truly beautiful piece. Even you'd think so."

He sounded so pleased that I didn't scoff. "That's great, Ian. What's a duet stand?"

He explained it was a regular music stand, with back-to-back bits for holding sheet music. The one he'd sold was mahogany, with candle sconces and splayed legs with lead ball feet. Sold for thirty-five hundred dollars. "Not in perfect condition, but it's an unusual piece. If it were in good repair, it'd have gone for twice as much. Maybe."

"Seven grand?"

"Some go for twice that."

"Are you kidding? *I'd* go for twice that."

"A bargain."

I couldn't tell if that was a compliment, so I said, "So— Drinks Night? I'm in the mood for margaritas."

"Oh." The playful tone disappeared from his voice. "Drinks Night."

"I mean, if you're interested. If you have time. If you want. Or I could just die of embarrassment for assuming we had a standing date."

"Don't die," he said. "We do. But I can't make it. Helene's back, and she's got an evening planned."

"Oh."

"Next week?"

"Sure."

"Anne?"

"Yeah?"

A pause. "See you then."

"Okay."

We hung up.

I went out back and threw a stick for Ny in the canyon. I actually hurled the stick, but Ny appreciated my enthusiasm. I knew Ian had a fiancée. Was that supposed to be a surprise? She'd been in Chicago, and now she was back. No surprise there, either. Of course she had an evening planned—and it didn't take any imagination to figure how the evening would end. They were engaged to be married, for chrissake. Of *course* he had to spend the evening with the future wife instead of me. C'mon.

But I was lonely.

I tugged the stick from Ny's jaws and tossed it again. I considered calling Wren, but I'd spent five hours with her yesterday, alternately scolding (she still hadn't told Kevin) and supporting, and I was a bit exhausted—until tomorrow, at least. I thought of calling Rip. Odd that I didn't miss him more. But *Polliwog?* He'd already found someone to replace me and was calling her my pet name. It was bizarre. Like he loved me in general, but not me in particular. I considered calling Alex, the screenwriter, then remembered his new girlfriend. Maybe Arthur. He could give me some plumbing tips, too. Or Charlotte or Emily, but they had their own lives. Maybe Mike. Foul-mouthed, sure, but a friend. Or the Sharones.

I hurled the stick again. I didn't really feel like seeing anyone. What was so great about having your own life? I'd been happier as a sublimated Kato.

I spent the next day finishing the move, pausing only to show number nineteen how to operate his mailbox key, tell number thirteen she couldn't paint her front door orange, and fix the sod-tampering which number six reported. During the night, some cretinous lawn vandal had crept into our peaceful village, lifted the edges of the new sod and rolled it back a few feet. What kind of miscreant messes with your sod? Is *nothing* sacred? They couldn't have tossed eggs at the cars or spray-painted the walls?

Then I polished my resume and reread my old copy of *What Color Is Your Parachute?* My favorite part was the list of the Five Worst Ways to Get a Job:

Using the Internet only—4% success rate.
Mailing resumes to random employers—7%.
Answering ads in professional journals—7%.

Answering ads in the local newspaper—5-24%.
Using an employment agency—5-28%.

First, what kind of range was 5-28%? That's like saying they'd either pay you $10,000 a year, or $50,000. Second, who mailed resumes to random employers? Maybe I'd write George Clooney, ask if he was looking for a live-in massage therapist. Third, I really hated the author of *Parachute*. When's the last time *he* looked for a job? Forty years ago?

I read the Help Wanted section in the local newspaper, from Administrative Assistant to Woodworker. There was nothing I wanted. So I was done.

The recycle bins were on the other side of the Dumpster, and as I approached with my stack of newspapers I heard Dale and Tracy—the happy young couple in number three—chatting as they tossed their trash bags inside.

"Did you bring the recycling?" Dale was asking. Or maybe it was Tracy. I wasn't entirely sure which was which. "Yuck! The bag broke."

"What a mess."

"Maybe I should get the broom."

"Nah, leave it. The super'll clean up."

They marched off, as I reeled in shock. The super? I must've misheard. *The super?* No, no. The manager. The property manager. I hadn't left a job as an office manager where I'd been called a secretary to get a job as a condo manager and be called a super. I'd definitely misheard. What they meant was, *Leave it. Anne's super. She'll clean up.*

Not that I was *the* super, just that I was super. That was it. Definitely.

Still, I crept home behind the units, so they wouldn't see me. Halfway there, I froze, aghast.

The sod. My beautiful sod, perfectly trimmed. It was rolled up *again*. And not just the edges. The Lawn Bandit had rolled the grass into loose cylinders, leaving the dirt patch beneath exposed. It was eerie. All that effort, all that stealth, just to roll up our lawn. For a moment, I suspected the people from the Pastel Storage Unit Village next door, but that was ridiculous. If they'd been responsible, there'd be clues. Like footprints in peach, yellow, light blue, and pink.

I fixed the damn sod. It took two hours. Then I went home and watched TV and ate ice cream until I made myself sick. Super.

The next day I took Ny to the Cypress property. We hadn't been back since the Zurich Affair, because I'd been afraid of bad vibes. But when we got there, the vibes were entirely good. Especially after I knocked the No Trespassing sign over again.

Another beautiful day in paradise. It was Southern California delicious. The light was bright and buttery, the breeze smelled of chaparral, the dog's tail curled in pleasure, his eyes bright and his shiny black nostrils flaring. He glanced at me and smiled—don't tell me dogs don't smile—and I laughed and we climbed the trail.

So what if Dale and Tracy called me the super? So what if Ian preferred a night of sexual dissipation with Helene to a couple beers with me? So what if someone was vandalizing my sod and if I was alone and lonely? I still had this.

A warm wind came off the ocean, bringing the cries of seagulls. There were a couple sailboats in the channel, and low waves rolled in messy lines onto the beaches. The yucca was in bloom, and tiny white butterflies flitted about. Almost to the top of the hill, the yellow lab named Tag raced down the trail at us, and Ny greeted him with a gentlemanly lunge at the jugular. Tag dodged, and they were off: wrestling, rolling, and growling with mock ferocity.

Tag's owner followed his dog, a trifle more sedately. We

talked about the day, and the sale of the land—neither mentioning that we were now officially outlaws—as we followed the dogs into the lower meadow. They trotted over for a drink of water from the bottle I carried, tongues lolling like a couple of canine Salvador Dalis. Tag and his owner left, and Ny and I continued up the trail. All was serenity and peace. I was tranquil. I was whole. I was the warm sun and the blue sky.

I really needed to get a life.

Wren called Tuesday morning, while I was flattening the sod for the third time. Every couple days, the Lawn Bandit struck again. I'd check each night around ten, when I let Ny out for his evening ablutions, and the sod would be fine. Come morning, it would be a big grass cannoli. To make matters more pleasant, Ny enjoyed pissing on the sod while I unrolled. And the cherry on top? The dawn unrolling had become a social event for the older generation in the condos. They'd stand in a cluster and watch me lawn wrestle. Better than *The Today Show,* I guess.

I was about to do my patented smack-down when I overheard Old Man Rivers—well, his last name was Rivers and he was old—from number fifteen talking with Mrs. Wardon. He couldn't figure how to program his VCR to record *CSI: Miami,* and Mrs. Wardon suggested he ask me to help.

Old Man Rivers said, "Who?"

"You know," Mrs. Wardon said. "Anne."

"Anne?"

"The janitor."

"Don't call her that," he said. "They prefer 'custodian.'"

They laughed in a manner I can only describe as ghoulish.

Interesting thing about sod: you could bury a couple desiccated geezers beneath it without hardly making a lump. I

Lee Nichols

was back in my apartment, mentally smoothing the shallow graves, when the phone rang. I was expecting Wren—she'd promised to tell Kevin about the nonexistent birth control this week.

I answered. "Olsen Janitorial."

"I've been to the gynecologist," Wren said.

"And?"

"Everything's fine."

"And?"

"Come to dinner with us tonight?"

"You told him?"

"Well, we talked about getting pregnant."

"What, theoretically?"

"Sort of."

"So you didn't tell him."

"He's not totally opposed. If I can convince him we should try, I mean before too much time passes, I might be able to fudge the dates and—"

"Wren. No. No fudging dates. Tell him."

"I will. I just thought, you know—if we can first establish that he actually wants kids, *then* I can tell him. So you have to come tonight. Broach the subject."

She was clearly insane, but she was also my best friend. So after ten minutes of pleading, I said, "All right. Where?"

"The Indian restaurant."

"Which one?"

"On upper State."

"That's only a couple miles away," I said. Every time a landmark was mentioned, I was compelled to calculate how far it was from my new condo. I hadn't yet resorted to logging distances on my odometer, but I was close. I've never been good with change, and this was my way of dealing.

"Not as close as Petrini's," Wren said, knowing about my new pastime.

"Depends how you go."

"Sure," Wren said. "Oh, and dress cute."

"Why?"

"Because Kevin's bringing a friend."

She hung up before I could bellow in outrage. I called her back at home. No answer. Then at work. She wasn't accepting calls. I hated when she did this. She loved to give bad news by phone, then hang up and not answer. When she told me Tom Cruise had been cast as Lestat in *Interview With the Vampire,* she refused to take my calls for three days.

I grumbled to Ny as I tried to decide what I'd wear. Something heinous—that would show Wren.

I wore a blue TSE sweater Wren had sold me and the new stretch jeans with my half-thrashed Blumarines. Yeah. That showed her all right.

Kevin's friend was named Melvin, but he went by "Cash." He was okay. He was polite. I was polite. He joked about his car. I joked about my dog. He told me about his job—as a lawyer. I lied about mine—as a real estate professional. He mentioned he voted for Bush. I coughed up a hairball.

We ordered, and I polished off half a Taj Mahal before saying, "Chicken Tikka. My nephews love that. My niece, too. You have any nieces or nephews, Kevin? Kids. Wow. Nothing's more rewarding, you love them so much. The thing about love is trust. Trust and love, love and trust. And forgiveness. That's the biggie. Forgiveness. You ever had a girlfriend do something you couldn't forgive? Something so awful you couldn't get past it? See, love is unconditional. Take Barbara Bush. Her son's a smirking chimp and still got appointed President, fair and square. Why? Because of her unconditional love. The drugs, the drunk driving, the shady deals, and yet still she loves him. If you don't have that kind of love, you've got nothing."

Oddly, after that Melvin and I didn't really hit it off. Men. Who can figure?

By the time the meal was over, I'd had two large Taj Mahals and bruised shins from where Wren kept kicking me. Still, I was sober enough to drive home—six minutes—and let Ny do his dirty sinful business in the canyon. But still buzzed enough to call Ian.

His machine answered, and told me he wasn't home.

I told his machine: "Ian, it's Anne. Olsen. Charlotte's sister. Who made you pretend you were German. Or Swiss. Whatever. You're probably out with Helene. Hi, Helene. This is Anne. We met at dinner. You had the fettuccine Alfredo. How do you stay so skinny when you eat fettuccine Alfredo? Just saying the word *Alfredo* makes my ass grow a size. How was Chicago? I've never been there. I...um—I forgot why I was calling." Actually, I hadn't forgotten. But somehow didn't want to mention Drinks Night on his machine, in case Helene heard it. "Um. Oh, yeah. Did you vote for Bush? Not that it matters. I'd forgive you if you did—no wait, I don't mean that. I totally wouldn't forgive—"

"I voted Independent," Ian said.

"Hey! You're there!"

He laughed. "You sound tipsy."

"Only a little. Not enough to see pink elephants or vote Independent. I bet you voted for Schwarzenegger, too."

"I didn't vote Independent, Anne."

"So you *did* vote for Schwarzenegger!"

"I voted for—" he paused. "What are we talking about?"

"Nothing. Say hi to Helene."

"She's not here."

"Oh. That sucks."

"Yeah, back in Chicago." Somehow he didn't sound despondent. "We still on for tomorrow?"

"Drinks Night? Is that tomorrow? No, I can't. I'm busy."

"Oh."

Now *that* sounded despondent! Woo-hoo! "Ha!" I said, maturely. "Ha-ha!"

"What?"

"I'm toying with your tiny antiquated mind. How about we go to one of the pretentious wine bars?"

"So we're on?"

"Yeah, and it's on you, Mr. Music-stand. Hey, maybe we should do karaoke night, in honor of the duet stand?"

"I'd rather go to a wine bar. I do pretension better than I do 'Like a Virgin.'"

I sang a few bars.

"No, no." he said. "Stop. Have mercy. Wine bar! Wine bar!"

I hit the high notes, then said, "You want to meet at your shop? It's only nine minutes from my condo."

"No, I want to see your new place."

"I really can make it in nine minutes, you know. You don't think I can, do you? Because you're cynical and crusty-minded. But Anacapa's a straight shot. I hit the timed lights, I can do it in eight. I haven't even tried the freeway, because Carrillo is so slow."

There was a pause. Then Ian said, "There's a term in the antiques trade. *Plique-à-jour.* Reminds me of you."

"Yeah? What's it mean?"

"It refers to pottery. It means slightly cracked."

"Really?" I said, unable to think of a better reply.

"No, not really," he said. "But I don't have the slightest idea what you're talking about, timing the trip to my shop."

"Not just your shop, Mr. Egotistical. It's sixteen minutes to the Bacara. Five minutes to Petrini's. Four to the Chaucer. Eight to Paseo Nuevo—and *your* old, moldering, historic paseo, too."

"Right," Ian said. "So we'll meet at your place?"

"Zero minutes," I said.

"We can drive around timing distances after, if you want."

"No, that's okay."

"Around six, then?"

"Six-oh-nine," I said, and gave him directions.

I sprawled in my Z Gallerie armchair, painting my toes pewter, and caught myself humming "Like a Virgin." Granted, I was half-drunk, but still: utterly disgusting, how eager I was to see Ian tomorrow. This was bad. He was engaged—if he was meant for Helene, there was nothing I could do about it. And he was Charlotte's ex, which freaked me out. Partly it was the incest taboo and partly the fear of competing with Charlotte. And partly the old-fashioned revulsion at used goods. I didn't expect my boyfriends to be unsullied, but with Ian, the sully was too close to home.

If only he weren't so perfect for me. We just…fit.

Well, it would have to stop. He was Charlotte's ex. He wasn't interested in me anyway; at least not in a sweaty, jack-hammer fashion. So that was that. He was funny, he was smart, he was willing to pretend to be Swiss. But there was nothing between us. Nothing but friendship.

Fine with me. I was satisfied. I would put all romantic notions of Ian firmly out of my mind. I was finished with that insanity. And if I happened to Google *plique-à-jour* later that night, it was only because I was interested in expanding my knowledge. One should never stop learning.

Plique-à-jour, which means "windows of light," is one of the most stunning and difficult enameling techniques. The process creates a brilliant translucent effect by suspending enamel in a delicate precious-metal framework. The results are commonly compared to bright sunlight streaming through stained glass windows—luminous, intense, and unique.

Oh, God. Help me.

CHAPTER 24

I woke with a gasp from a dream of beauty and wrestled with my comforter. Ny rolled onto his back next to me, paws in the air, and made a soft grunt of complaint—I was awake too early.

But not because of knocking at the door or the neighbors or the Lawn Bandit. Because of the dream.

I'd been standing in a majestic medieval cathedral, made entirely of stained glass. The air was pure color, but I could breathe. The patterns on the windows were familiar: trees and paths and oceans. There were flowers, birds, fields and a brilliant yellow sun. Suddenly, I realized. It was the Cypress property. The cathedral was on the Cypress property.

And it all made sense.

I poured myself into contacts, clothes, and coffee and sat down to make a list: Monty. Rip. Architects. Engineers. The EIR. The Architectural Review Board. Zoning. Grading and paving. Fire service and proposed density and local schools and—God help me—the Coastal Commission. Why the Coastal Commission, when the Cypress property was miles from the Bluffs? Because this was Santa Barbara County, that's why.

I went to the library. I got online. I spent hours at the court-house, shuttling from office to office, glowing with a stained-glass aura that none could defy. Or perhaps it was merely my manic energy bulling through all obstacles. Either way, come five o'clock I was ravenous, overwhelmed, and thrilled. I could do this. It was scary as hell when you considered every-thing together, but if you approached each thing individu-ally, it was simple. Like running a marathon—just keep going till you hit the finish line. Simple? Yes. Easy? No.

I got home at five-eleven (traffic), aching to tell Ian about The Deal. Sure, there were some question marks: primarily Monty, money, and me. But it was possible. It could happen. I could *make* it happen. The starting gun had fired, and I'd never stop running.

I opened my closet and absently considered the possibili-ties. The comfy black top, or row zoning? Did the denim mini go better with five or seven parcels? The boots, to match the winding drive which would preserve the live oaks? I finally focused, deciding on a low-cut cranberry knit top with ruching at the bodice and a low-slung corduroy miniskirt. I gave my Blumarines the night off and instead wore the brown mid-calf boots I splurged on last year after seeing them in *Vogue*. Just because we were only friends didn't mean I couldn't look sexy.

We real estate developers were hot stuff.

"Boujour, mon petite chou," Ian said, standing outside my front door with a sack of cloth over his shoulder.

"You're three and a half minutes early," I said. And, an-gling for a compliment in a language I actually understood, "What's *petite chou?* Little shoe?"

"Little cabbage," he said, as Ny sniffed him in greeting.

Great. I'm a leafy green that gives people gas. But I couldn't think of any vegetable with which to insult Ian—cauliflower? rutabaga?—so I merely invited him in. He was wearing a coffee-colored shirt, silk tie, and dark dress pants. I'd never much liked ties until I saw one on Ian.

He propped his sack of cloth against the wall—and it wasn't a sack. It was a rolled-up carpet. From his shop. An antique. Which was touching my floor and wall, and polluting the fresh clean air with invisible spores of decayed antiquity.

"*What* is *that?*" I gasped, in horror.

Before I could stop him, he'd unrolled it in my living room. On the pristine berber, which emitted a faint plea for mercy. It was a Persian rug like the one I'd wiped my muddy sneakers on in his shop, but smaller. It was a light bronzey color, burnished and mellow, with a subtle pattern. It would've been beautiful if it hadn't been seeping death germs into my condo.

"It's a Zeigler," Ian said, smoothing it lovingly. "This size is called a *zaroneem*—a Persian measurement meaning a zar and a half. Zeigler and Co. was a carpet company based in Manchester which had carpets made in Persia to appeal to the Western eye. They're a little coarse, not the highest quality, but aesthetically they—what?"

I couldn't answer, because I was engaged in a full-body shudder of revulsion. Fingernails on the chalkboard of my soul.

"Anne," he said. "It's a housewarming gift."

"I love it," I choked out, through my *grand mal* seizure.

"It's new, Anne."

"It doesn't look new."

"Because it's been washed—that is, bleached—to look older, to get that patina. Except it's only a true patina if it's made with vegetable dyes. Then exposure to light and foot traffic polishes the pile and—

I must've made a noise: *foot traffic.*

"But this one wasn't exposed to anything, Anne. All the dyes are chemical—it's new."

"Promise?"

"I promise," he said earnestly. "It's not a day over thirty years."

"The closet!" I shrieked and pointed. "In the closet!"

Ny chose that moment to curl up on the horrible thing.

"Ny likes it," Ian said.

"Ny rolls in dead seal carcasses. Ny, go! Go on!" I opened the coat closet as Ny grudgingly stood. "I do like it, Ian. I'll get used to it. I will. But—roll it up for now. Please. I'll figure out where to put it later."

"You hate it."

"I don't! I want to find somewhere special for it."

"Yeah, like your parking space."

"I'm not *that* bad. It's just you can't spring Aladdin's Ancient Antique on me like this. I have to get used to the idea."

Ian half-bemusedly and half-begrudgingly rolled the carpet, and I realized what a monster I'd been. So I thanked him and told him how much I appreciated the gift. He said something sarcastic, and I said, "You know, I've been doing some rolling myself."

"I'm not surprised," he said, stowing the carpet in the closet. "You seem a bit drug-addled."

"Not joints, Ian. Sod." Before he could take offence, I told him the tale of the Lawn Bandit, finishing with, "I think it might be someone from Pastel Planet next door. Or the guy in number ten. He's got this eyebrow hair that sticks out like three inches."

"Proof of his criminal nature."

"An eyebrow hair that long *is* a crime. Almost as bad as

making me spend five hours a week wrestling sod. And when Old Man River said that the super should provide security to—"

"Wait, wait. The super?"

"Yeah. Want some sugar cookies?"

"Who's the super?" he asked, following me into the kitchen.

"Apparently," I said, grabbing a tin of Mrs. Wordan's cookies, "me." I told him about the abuse I'd been getting from the residents. "And now they gather in the mornings, to attend the Daily Unrolling."

"The *super?*" he said, laughing.

"We're past that, Ian."

"Sure, I don't mean to be *super*cilious."

"Hey, do I call you a used furniture salesman?"

"No, you call me a 'junk-man.'"

"Don't be so sensitive. Anyway, I thought we'd go to Wine and Figs." A wine bar downtown, where I'd tell him about my new career as a developer of gorgeous properties. "Seven minutes."

He shook his head. "No way."

"What's wrong with Wine and Figs?"

"Nothing. I just don't think you can make it there in seven minutes."

I smiled. "Hope you have your stopwatch ready."

I opened the door—and there was Wren.

"He hates me," she said, her voice dull as her eyes. "He said I make him sick."

"You told Kevin," I said.

"He hates me."

She started to cry so I hugged her and made comforting sounds. Over her shoulder, Ian gestured toward the door. He mouthed "rain check," and I nodded as I stroked Wren's back. He slipped outside and closed the door silently behind.

He was perfect.

★ ★ ★

Next morning, I started the coffee and walked Ny around the complex, checking the sod and ensuring the CC&Rs were not being violated. *Eternal Vigilance* was this super's motto. All quiet, and the sod was laying flat. Ask not what your condos can do for you…

Back home, I poured two cups of coffee and took them downstairs to the guest bedroom. Wren was huddled under the comforter, staring at the ceiling.

"You look cheerful," I told her.

She grunted.

I gave her a coffee and we rehashed last night's pep talk. Poor Wren—Kevin had been furious and scathing. Not that she didn't deserve every scathe, but I'd still have to stick a corkscrew in his fontanel if the opportunity arose. That's what friendship means.

She finally allowed me to bully her back home, where she promised she'd shower and dress and go to work—the only sure cure for a broken heart. Of course, she also said she'd cheer herself up with a shopping trip to This Little Piggy, the children's store, so maybe she wasn't quite as demolished as she pretended.

I attended to the morning beauty regime and drove to Parsons Realty. My old desk was empty—it wasn't yet nine o'clock—but showed signs of a new occupant. I rifled through the drawers and found the new person's time slips. Good news, as she wouldn't be in early, but I still didn't have much time.

A voice spoke behind me, "You're a sight for sore fucking eyes."

"Hey, Mike!" I gave him a kiss on the cheek. "Rip around?"

"He's out all morning." He headed to the fax machine, and stared in bafflement, as always. "Don't tell me you've come crawling back? How the hell you use this thing?"

"I'm not crawling back," I said, elbowing him aside and sending his fax. "I'm here on business."

"What's your new business, pink-collar burglary?"

"Rip's gone, huh? Maybe I'll just use his office."

"His office?" Mike fingered the fax transmission sheet nervously. "Tell me you're not going to trash the place."

"I want his computer, is all."

"I sense an incoming shit-storm," he said.

"I can use your office instead, if you'd rather."

I never saw Mike move that fast before. He opened the door to Rip's office for me, like the gentleman he wasn't, and waved me inside.

A while later, I'd learned everything I could from the database. But I still had a few questions that needed the human touch. I checked the clock on Rip's desk and eyed the buzzer. I couldn't. Could I? Aw, what the hell. I swiveled in my chair and touched the evil thing. A moment later, as if by magic, the door opened and the new guy appeared. Yeah, he was a guy. I hadn't noticed his time slips said "John." He seemed surprised to find someone in Rip's office—particularly someone who wasn't Rip.

I didn't give him time to ask awkward questions. "Be a doll," I said, "and tell Mike to get his lazy ass in here, would you? And bring two coffees, black."

He hesitated a moment, then ran to do my bidding.

I suddenly wanted a cigarette.

Next stop, Monty's office. Monty was sitting at a shoddy desk, too miserly to buy mahogany. I put my hands on the rickety top and leaned close. "Okay, Monty—step away from the finger foods, it's time for the main course. Let's talk construction. We need houses. Gorgeous houses."

"And how are you this morning, Anne?"

"Inspired."

"You're giving me a crick in my neck."

"Better than a pain in your ass," I said, but I sat down. "I'm thinking five or seven houses. Cluster zoned, to keep—"

"On Las Positas? You couldn't build a treehouse."

"On the Cypress property, Monty. Stay with me. We keep most of the land free. Put in a walking path that—this is the genius part—is open to the public. See? See? It works coming and going—money from the buyers *and* money from the city. Plus you've addressed issues of public service and environmental impact in advance." I told him about the market analyses and comps I dug up at Parsons Realty, and about what I'd learned at the courthouse and from Mike. And mostly about my vision.

He was silent a moment. "You ran the numbers?"

"Ballpark. But this is what I did for Rip every day."

"You built in your profit?"

I told him what I stood to earn. A healthy, though unpretentious, sum.

He scoffed. "You'd make that much flipping burgers."

"No. I'd make burgers, flipping burgers. Doing this, I'll make five or seven houses surrounded by parkland and I preserve the Cypress property, too."

"Five to seven houses? Unless you double that, you're gonna take a long cold bath on this. It's not easy, Anne. I know a guy converting a four-unit building into million-dollar condos and adding a few units out back. Had the project approved, spent three hundred seventy-five thousand dollars on planning and permit costs. Then the city council backtracked. Cut the number of units, the bank dropped the loan, and he's flat broke."

"That's why we start with fewer units—and public land attached. Keep the city happy."

"But it kills your profit, so few houses. Your figures are

bad. They have to be. You're a talented amateur, Anne—not a pro."

"Not yet." I slid him a sheet of paper. "But numbers don't lie."

He read my ballpark figures, and his eyes popped with interest—then narrowed as he stabbed at a figure on the bottom of the page.

"Ah," I said. "You came to the price." That I'd pay him for the Cypress property.

"Did Melissa tell you this is all I'm asking?"

"That's all I can afford."

"It's fifty percent under asking price."

"Forty-four, actually."

"Forty-four percent less than what I want…" he said, in a strangled, awestruck voice.

"But is it less than what you *need?*"

He hesitated. "Anne, listen closely—"

"No, Monty," I said. "It's all I can afford. Look at the numbers. Where else can I cut?"

Monty ranted and fumed, but there was no denying the logic. It was nothing personal. The numbers dictated that this was my top price. You couldn't fight arithmetic. Plus, I wheedled until Monty told me what he'd paid for the land, twenty years ago. He'd bought it for a song. Not even a whole album. A single track. An illegal MP3 download.

He was stubborn, but doomed. Because my mantra was: *It's a marathon, it's a marathon, it's a marathon.* And sure enough, twenty-six miles later, Monty was wheezing for breath while I sprinted past the finish line. Well, sort of. Actually he told me he wouldn't sell me the land, *but* if I raised the money and dealt with all the hassles, I could develop it myself. He insisted on seven houses, as he said five was a recipe for disaster. And all he asked was that he be given none of the work, and most of the profit.

"Monty," I said, "you're a prince among men."

"You'll pay to have the building lots cleared," he said. "You'll pay for the roads, for the architect, the builders, and the endless permits. Each one of those costs a small fortune, Anne."

"Not a problem. I'll get investors."

The key to investors was simple: the prospectus. The word alone was so solid and respectable it made you want to smash piggy banks and sign on dotted lines.

What I needed was sales literature so glossy, so beautiful and compelling that nobody noticed that the person behind The Deal was me. So I spent all day—when I wasn't helping number six un-jam a window or explaining the concept of reserved parking to eleven—working on the perfect brochure. Pouring my love, my hunger and desire and passion into this one exquisite arty-businessy effort. In fact, I had so much love, hunger, etcetera, that it actually took two days. Well, plus I had to baby-sit for Charlotte and go out with the Sharones and flatten the damn sod for the seventeenth time. Still, when I finally finished the prospectus, it was flawless.

Except for one problem: It was ugly and amateurish.

I was weeping into a pint of coffee ice cream when Ian called. Helene was due back tomorrow, but if I was free we could have our rain check tonight. I looked at my ice-cream-stained T-shirt and ran my fingers through my stringy hair. "Give me half an hour," I said.

We went to Wine and Figs. It catered to a largely middle-aged crowd, and I was probably the youngest person there, which made me love the place. The room was decorated in generic metro, with polished concrete floors, metal tables, and overstuffed velvet chairs. Everything was in pale green, dull ruby, and burnt umber. Picture Starbucks with wine racks.

We sat at the bar, just two friends out on the town. A couple of mates sniffing the cork. Despite having lived in Montecito for the last seven years, I wasn't really a snob. I didn't care if a man was well-off or well-connected or well-dressed (though I'd work on that last one). And being uncomfortable in a wine bar was definitely better than being too comfortable in a wine bar. Ian, however, was just right. A little awkward, a little amused, and a lot of fun. The thing about Ian, he belonged everywhere. He was equally at home at an ex-girlfriend's birthday party as he was among the historical detritus in his shop. Even pretending to be a Swiss businessman hadn't thrown him. He was comfortable with himself. And I was comfortable with him.

We talked about my budding career as a real estate developer. Well, I talked—my career had only been budding for three days, so I needed someone to listen. Needed to get everything straight in my own mind.

Ian made supportive noises and paid for the wine. When I finally wound down, he asked, "You know who you sound like?"

"Ming the Merciless?"

"Me. When I talk about antiques."

It was true. The passion and the drive—to learn more, to know everything, to cling fiercely to the coattails of beauty. "Well, it's better than being a secretary, I guess. Better than being the *super.*"

"Don't do that. Don't downplay how excited you are. This isn't just better than nothing. This is something."

"It *is* something," I said. "And I'm gonna fuck it up."

"That'd be terrible—you screw this up and you might get stuck in some job you didn't care about. Like managing condos." He turned his wineglass on the bar. "Thing is, Anne, you've got to fail to succeed."

"Don't worry, I will."

"No, I don't mean you have to fail to succeed—I mean you have to *fail,* to *succeed.*"

"Thank you, Yoda. Any of the other Jedis looking for an investment opportunity?" Hmm. That sparked a thought. "Hey—on a totally different subject, have you got any extra money lying around?"

He sighed. "How much do you need?"

"A lot."

"A hundred bucks a lot or a thousand bucks a lot?"

"A million bucks a lot."

He opened his wallet and counted. "Seventy-two dollars. You accept coinage?"

"That won't buy a doorknob. I can't even have a professional prospectus designed for less than a few thousand." I'd made some depressing phone calls yesterday afternoon, when the limits of my arty-businessy abilities had become clear. "Plus, they require all kinds of information and disclosures and legal compliance."

"Maybe you should start smaller."

"That's not a bad idea…."

"Yeah. Seven houses in Montecito, with simultaneous public and private sales seems—"

"No, no. That's still on. Don't be silly." But there was another way to start small. I grabbed the cash from his wallet. "My first investor."

"Oh, be my guest," he said. "It's only money."

"Good. I'll put you down for another thousand," I joked before handing him back his cash. Mr. Fifty-six dollars a day could hardly afford to invest.

Luckily he wasn't the only person I knew because the key to investors was simple: personal contacts.

Ian dropped me at home a couple hours later. I wanted to invite him in for a nightcap and sex. I said, "Night, Ian."

He said, "Night."

And he drove away.

CHAPTER

25

Rip and I met for lunch at the Japanese restaurant. We sat in a room with rice paper screens and pale satin pillows for seats and smiled awkwardly. Maybe I should have asked him to dinner—*sake* would've lightened the mood. But no, this was professional, not romantic.

"So you came by the office the other day," he said, after we ordered sushi and tempura.

"Did Mike tell you? That fucker!"

He smiled. "Nobody told me. You changed the colors on my computer."

"Oh. Red on a teal background, Rip? Have I taught you nothing?"

He laughed. "I've missed you, Anne."

"Me, too." We'd had fun together. We were pals. And given that he was already calling some other woman by my pet name, pals was all we'd ever be. "Oh, hey, I've moved out of Charlotte's place."

"I heard," Rip said. "I got a call, asking what kind of employee you'd been."

"From Monty? I hope you didn't tell the truth."

"I said you were the best office manager I'd ever had."

"You *liar*," I said.

"It's the truth," he said. "Everyone else was just a receptionist."

We laughed a bit more than that deserved, and I said, "Monty is the reason I called. He owns the Cypress property."

"Yeah, I heard that, too."

Had he finally badgered the information out of the skeletal Melissa Kent? Was it possible to badger anything out of Melissa without a whip and a chair? Before I had a chance to ask, the waitress came with our food—and I realized I wasn't sure I wanted to know. Didn't want to remind Rip I was already in his debt.

"I'm developing it," I told him, around a mouthful of ahi. "Five or seven houses surrounded by public land we're gonna deed to the county."

"The Cypress property?"

I nodded.

"No way, Anne. Developing? Houses? Bad idea. You can't."

"Why not?"

"Because you have no idea what you're doing."

"First, that is totally false. And second, when has it ever stopped me?"

I told him everything I'd learned about the property, the parcels, the zoning, the planning and building. Told him about my deal with Monty and my grandiose plans. Then I started on what I didn't know—and by the time I finished, our tempura was soggy and cold.

We ate it anyway, in silence. Then I asked, "Can I do it?"

"I have no idea," he said. "You realize Monty's given you all the risk, and taken most of the reward for himself?"

"Well, I can't afford to *buy* the land."

"No. And actually, it's not a bad deal…if you pull it off. But the streets of Santa Barbara are littered with bankrupt developers."

"Uh-huh." I pulled out a notebook. "So you'll help?"

"I'm going to regret this."

"Probably."

He shook his head and started talking. I filled six pages with notes before getting to the true *raison d'Rip.* "Just one more thing," I said. "Investors?"

"Yeah. You'll need some. Preferably risk junkies with trust funds."

"Remember those people who bought the Knox Tower? The ones who do green construction—the elves, the Keebler people? You mentioned they're looking for properties to—"

"No," he said. "No, I don't remember. No. No way. Uh-uh. No."

So I was forced to apply emotional blackmail, greasing the wheels of commerce with barbed comments about a failed relationship. Good thing he'd dumped me—it meant I could appeal to his guilt. We finally compromised. He'd act as an intermediary, and present Keebler with the details of The Deal, if I promised not to hunt them down and demand tribute.

I paid the bill and walked Rip to his car. "I really appreciate this, Rip."

"Just don't…pretend to be someone else, okay?"

"This is totally me," I told him. "This is who I really am. I've never been this sure of anything in my life."

"I mean don't pretend to be a Russian princess, or a third Hilton girl or—"

"Rip, I would *never!*"

"Oh, sorry." He opened his car door. "I must be thinking of a different Ms. Leon."

"Who?" I said, and immediately remembered: Senna Leon. I felt myself flush. "Okay, I'm going to kill Monty."

"He didn't tell me. Melissa did."

"That sea hag!"

"Anne," he said gently. "I'm dating her."

"That *stick?*"

"She's lithe."

"She's a Slim Jim."

"Anne, be nice."

"Be nice? You started dating her seven minutes after you dumped me! She's see-through! She's the invisible woman. Turn her sideways and she could slice cheese. And you call her Polliwog! You called *me* Polliwog. How many women have you called Polliwog? Huh?" I poked him in the chest for emphasis. "That's wrong. The same nickname for every girlfriend? You have some kind of amphibian kink? It's disgusting. Insulting." I paused, to crack my neck. "Okay, here's what we'll do. You still have that monster commission from the Knox Tower sale, right? You've gotta be looking to invest that…"

The days passed in a blur. Things were going perfectly—and getting better every day. It was a trend that would continue until the moment everything fell apart. The light at the end of the tunnel would get brighter and brighter until the bullet train hit me directly over my left eyebrow.

But I didn't know that then. I read and reread my six pages of notes until I'd inhaled them. I haunted Monty's office, pestering him with questions and doubts and demands for food. I spoke for hours with Mike, who was holding my hand through the preliminary process. I had tentative discussions with people about planning and zoning and compliance and permits, and I interviewed architects and contractors and various—as Mrs. Wordan would say—tradesmen.

Of course, I didn't shirk my condo duties…but my patience began wearing thin. I snarled at number three's inability to adjust the volume control on his TV, and glowered at fifteen's proclivity for taking nine's cat to the animal shelter, claiming it was a stray. But overall, I stayed calm. One cannot run a marathon and indulge in temper tantrums.

Speaking of which, there was no word from Rip on the Keebler front. Mike counseled patience, suggesting that I not pounce on Rip like a jungle cat and shake an update from him by the scruff of his scrawny neck. So I didn't. I stopped by Charlotte's house instead. She'd been hounding me for a week, demanding I come for a swimsuit fitting…and now I had some demands of my own.

We met at the guest house, and it was like being reunited with a lover after a long and tragic absence. I swooned at the sight of the beautiful little cottage…until I opened the door. Inside, it was a shambles. There were rolls of fabric and pattern books and lights and a Frankenstein sewing machine and all sorts of scary seamstress paraphernalia, like the garment district in *Blade Runner*.

"Oh, my house," I moaned.

"Anne!" Charlotte said, bustling in from the bedroom. "Just in time. Come in the bedroom and strip."

"Are you pregnant again?" I asked.

She stopped bustling. "Do I look pregnant?"

"You're acting pregnant. Plus, you're wearing a smock."

"It's my sewing outfit. It helps me concentrate."

She prodded me toward the bedroom. "Now strip."

The bedroom was even worse than the living room. I

couldn't see the floor beneath the fabric samples and sketches. "Where did all this stuff come from?"

Charlotte switched on a horrible brilliant overhead light. "I made a few trips to L.A."

"A few?"

"Eight or nine. I got to spend the day at Michaela Walker's shop, and—" she started tugging at my shirt, and I batted her away "—and Sydney Cobb, the woman who designed the— Would you stop wiggling?"

"I'm not wiggling."

"You've been a wiggler since you were three," she said. But she stopped trying to forcibly undress me, and whipped a scrap of eggplant nylon from a pile. "Here, put this on."

I inspected the scrap. "What is this, a headband?"

"It's your swimsuit—put it on."

"I don't even know *how.*"

"Just try it on!" she snapped.

"Okay, okay," I said, removing my clothes. "What is wrong with you?"

"I'm nervous, Anne. This is the first time I've done anything really creative. I know it's cliché, the swimsuit model making swimsuits, but…" She shrugged. "I'm loving it. I just don't know if I'm any good."

"You actually like the sewing?" I asked, slithering into the suit.

"It's the hands-on stuff I love. With my line of swimwear for Super 9, I didn't actually do anything but cash the checks."

"Poor thing," I said, adjusting myself into the suit.

Charlotte eyed me critically.

"I'm no Charlotte Olsen," I said, defensive.

"Honey, these days—neither am I." She fussed with the straps, then made me turn around. "What do you think?"

I cautiously peeked in the mirror and the suit was, in a

word, fantastic. The color set off my skin perfectly—I was pretty fair, but the suit made me look almost tan. It was a one-piece pretending to be two. The bottom was a fairly full bikini, cut high on the legs, and the top crisscrossed my breasts, giving me big cleavage and a small waist.

"Look at me!" I said. "I've got a wasp waist." And my butt looked okay, too. There was enough fabric for modesty, not enough for matronly. "This is amazing, Charlotte. It looks so professional. You know how homemade clothes usually look all home-madey? You could sell these."

She blushed. "You think?"

"Definitely."

"I just—I'd love to. But I don't want some assembly-line business. I want to do the stuff I like. You start selling things, and pretty soon you're just the spokesmodel."

I laughed. "That's never really been a problem in my life, Charlotte."

"You know what I mean…."

"So start small. Do custom suits, one-of-a-kinds. How long does it take to sew one?"

"Well, the first few took forever but it doesn't really matter. I mean, I have all the time in the world…." She suddenly looked glum. "That's the thing. It's just a hobby. It's nothing, really."

"Don't do that—don't downplay your dream. It's not about money. Women will love these suits. Look at this, it's not even riding up my butt. This doesn't have to be something where you have no control."

"You think?"

"I know. You have to talk to Wren about these. They'd be perfect for Element."

"Really?"

"Definitely. Make as few as you want. Do what you

love. If you want hands-on, be hands-on. The fact you don't need the money is a blessing. And, um, actually— I know exactly what you can do with all that extra cash...."

I sped through Montecito, belting "We Are the Champions" at the top of my lungs. Ny chuffed his displeasure at my singing, but I didn't care. It had been a good day for figures—both of the swimsuit and the investment variety. Charlotte had pledged a substantial chunk of money, and now I could pay for the architect and the first round of permits. It was officially at the starting line.

After a celebratory walk at the Cypress property, I got home to find three notes taped to my door. The first was from number seven, who was having a new stove delivered, and wanted me to supervise installation. "Wolf," her note said, in case I didn't notice. The second was from the happy couple, Dale and Tracy, whose front door was sticking. "Please fix before five o'clock." The third was from Mrs. Wordan. "Toilet. Again."

I could've added a note of my own: unroll sod. But I didn't have time for this. Not anymore. I was a champion, my friend, and I'd keep on fighting till the end. I had to be strong. I had to be decisive and unyielding. I had to figure out a solution to this Super problem before I was buried beneath a mountain of work-order forms on Post-it notes.

A half hour later, the answer came to me. I knew exactly how to deal with the condo-dwellers. It was obvious.

I looked up from Mrs. Wordan's toilet, plunger in hand, and smiled.

"Yes, dear?" she said.

"Nothing," I told her. For it wasn't time, yet, to reveal my plan. "Just happy to help."

Then I went home and wrote some notes of my own.

★ ★ ★

It was Thursday night. Drinks Night. Helene was in town, so I didn't expect a call from Ian. Not like I cared. I just curled up with my phone and watched TV.

The phone didn't ring. TV didn't amuse. I went to bed.

Ny's bark woke me at dawn. Somebody knocking at the front door. My first thought was that the condo dwellers were massed outside, waving torches and pitchforks. My second was Wren. My third, and most convincing, was Mrs. Wordan. So I tossed on a sweatshirt and jeans and stumbled downstairs. I reflexively grabbed my plunger, flung open the door and said, "Okay, okay—I'm ready."

"For anything?"

Man's voice. Blurry shape. I blinked a few times. The shape became Ian. He was smiling. I slid the plunger behind my back. "It's the middle of the night," I said, trying to sound cross while my heart did loop-de-loops.

"I can still see the plunger, Anne. It's not hidden."

"I'm not hiding it."

"Scratching your back?"

"Oh, shut up." I went inside to stuff the plunger back under the sink. I splashed cold water on my face and tugged hopefully at my hair.

Back in the living room, Ian was inspecting the floor. "Where's the rug? Upstairs?"

I gestured vaguely. "Bedroom."

"Oh yeah? Let me see." He made for the stairs, but I blocked them.

"What are you *doing* here, Ian?"

He turned suddenly shy. "Well, the thing is, I know it's a little early but…the thing is…" He looked at me with an irresistible combination of boyish hope and wry humor. "I was thinking we could go to the beach?"

"The beach? Now?"

He nodded.

"It's dawn," I said.

"Well, Drinks Night—"

"—was last night."

"Sorry I'm late?"

"Ian."

"Well, it's too early to drink, but the perfect time to surf."

I was so sleepy that that almost made sense. Almost. "I don't surf."

"Sure you do. You used to tag along with me and Charlotte."

"I tag," I said, ignoring the reminder that he used to be Charlotte's boyfriend. "I don't surf."

"But you've been on a surfboard."

"Once."

"Please," he said. "Come. We'll…we'll float."

Maybe it was my imagination, but it seemed like Ian meant a lot more with "come, we'll float" than *get in the car, we're going to the beach.* It sounded like he meant come with him to float on an amazing journey, on an incredible adventure, on a life-partnership.

Or maybe it was my imagination. "We have to stop for coffee," I said.

He smiled. "There's a mocha for you in the car."

I ran upstairs and strapped myself into the swimsuit Charlotte made me, like a fighter pilot doing his preflight check. Cleavage, check. Wasp waist, check. Butt, check. I actually looked better than usual, because I was lacking the bloatage I normally accumulated over the course of a day. I covered up with sweater and jeans and slid into a pair of flip-flops. I pulled my hair into a ponytail and added just enough makeup to look as if I hadn't bothered.

Hendry's Beach was almost empty. There were a few

surfers and a couple workers getting the Brown Pelican restaurant ready for breakfast. Ny hopped out of the Jeep while Ian and I dragged the two boards and wet suits he'd brought out of the back. We walked until we were the only people in sight. Found a stretch of beach with no tar and dropped the boards and wet suits.

"I love when there's no one here," I said.

"Me, too," Ian said, grabbing the larger of the wet suits. "I pretend I own it."

I smiled, surprised I wasn't the only one who played those games. "Where does the money come from?"

"Dead aunt."

"Doesn't work for me—I have an actual aunt, I'm afraid of jinxing her. Usually I'm a movie star."

"Can you act?"

"Not an actor," I said. "A movie star."

Ian laughed, and slipped out of his jeans and T-shirt. He was wearing forest green trunks and had good arms and good legs and good shoulders. Just the right amount of blond body hair and a slight belly. I liked the belly. Men with perfect bodies couldn't be trusted.

He zipped himself into his wet suit and said, "Gear up, dude," and pointed to the other suit.

"Have we met?" I asked. "Do I look even remotely familiar? If you think I'm wearing that suit, you're crazy. I don't know where it's been."

"I bought it for Helene."

Great. The fiancée. "I don't know where she's been, either."

"She never wore it."

I lifted it gingerly between thumb and index finger. "Never?"

"Never."

I squinted at him. "You're lying."

"Well, she didn't. But I bought it used."

I dropped the death-suit and backed away.

"Anne."

"No."

"You'll freeze without it."

"I won't go in. Tagalong Anne, remember?"

"What about mine?" he said.

"Your suit?"

"Yeah. I bought it last year, brand new. I'm the only one who's ever touched it."

"What'll you wear?"

"I'll squeeze into that one."

Well, on the one hand, his suit had already been in the salty and decay-inducing sea. So yuck. On the other hand, I was eager to watch him try to wiggle into a woman's wet suit. And on the third hand—it was Ian.

So he unzipped himself from his wet suit as I shucked my clothes. We sort of accidentally seemed to be watching each other as we undressed. Then he handed me his wet suit and I stepped into the legs and pulled them up. "It's warm," I said.

From his body heat. It was soft and smooth, from my ankles to my thighs to my hips. I zipped myself into the suit and it touched me everywhere at once. I folded the cuffs of the legs and arms and found myself breathing rapidly, hyper-aware that Ian had been here a moment ago, that his skin had touched what mine was touching. By all rights I should be revolted—this was a used wet suit. But it was like a caress. It wasn't toxic germs infecting the suit—it was Ian's warmth and Ian's scent and Ian's skin.

As I swooned, Ian struggled. He wasn't having such a sensual time. Helene's wet suit had turquoise trim on the chest and hips, like a bikini embedded in the black neoprene, and was clearly intended for someone about six inches shorter than Ian. He finally squeezed himself inside, and struck a pose for me. The sleeves and legs only extended as far as his forearms and calves.

I laughed and ran into the waves, board in my arms. The water was bitter cold and I found myself breathless—again. I gasped as Ian splashed down beside me and then I was all the way in. Paddling hard, not so much for distance as for warmth. The sea was flat—not a good morning for surfing— and once we were away from the beach, and the chill was gone, we floated side by side.

The day was calm, and the quiet broken only by the splashing as we paddled to stay close. Gentle waves rocked us and we watched the sun rise higher over the horizon. It was nice. It was beyond nice. The Pacific Ocean was my waterbed, and Ian was by my side. If only—

If only.

I let the thought drain away. A tiny white sailboat drifted past, like a toy between us and the Channel Islands. Ny herded the surf on the beach, occasionally barking at a particularly disobedient wave. I lay there empty as the water swayed and swelled beneath me.

"When I was in high school," Ian said, into the long silence, "we'd drive down to Rincon to surf. I must've been fifteen, the first time I saw dolphins…" His voice trailed off, and I waited for him to continue, drawing patterns with my fingers in the water. "You see dolphins from the distance and they're not so big. But up close? You're sitting on your board, nothing on your mind, and a dorsal fin explodes out of the water five feet away. Your first thought is, it's a shark. I'm dead. Then the blowhole spurts and you realize no, it's a dolphin—and it's huge. These are big animals, and all of a sudden you're very small. You're tiny and you're out of your element. But not afraid. There's a whole pod of them, jumping in every direction, and they're faster and stronger and— and more awesome—than you can believe. And you realize you're surrounded by something bigger than yourself. Something better. The fear turns to awe—it's a privilege to be there." He'd been paddling gently as he spoke, and now we were face to face. "Sometimes," he said, "all you can do is watch for the things that are bigger than you. The things that are scary…but awesome."

We floated, inches apart. I was afraid to speak.

He said, "Helene and I broke up last night. They want her in Chicago full-time. She's moving."

"And you?"

"I'm staying where I belong."

A wave lifted us up and moved us together. We kissed. He was salty and warm and strong. I put my palm on his face and felt his hand reaching underwater to hold my other hand. The wave rolled past, and we moved apart.

I said, "Finally."

The water shifted beneath us and we were together again, and kissing. Then the water parted us, and we were looking at each other like love-struck teenagers. His lip quirked. I giggled. We laughed. Then a wave rolled beneath us, and we were kissing and laughing and touching and I fell off my board.

I kicked up to the surface, still laughing, and scrambled onto the board and paddled to the beach, with Ian following. It was high tide, so we were only a few yards from the cliffs. I stripped off my wet suit as we pressed into a rocky alcove protected from the wind and prying eyes. We kissed and touched and I was unzipping his wet suit and he ran a finger along the strap of my eggplant-colored swimsuit. I froze.

Charlotte. Charlotte's swimsuit. Charlotte's ex. Charlotte's surfer. They'd spent hours at the beach together. She'd tasted him salty and wet from the ocean. She'd probably pulled him into a cliff alcove by the beach.

"Charlotte," I said.

"That was almost twenty years ago, Anne," he murmured into my neck. "We were kids."

"I'm second-best." I pushed him away. "You can't have Charlotte, so you're stuck with me."

"I hope so," he said.

I shook my head.

"Anne." He brushed a strand of wet hair from my face. "I never loved Charlotte."

"So—" I swallowed. "So, I mean…"

"So I love you. Shall I count the ways? I love the way you walk into a room—I love the way you flop into a chair like you've never flopped into a chair before. I love the way you eat. I love when your eyes widen like they just did. I love when you do that thing with your mouth. I love the way you daydream when you think nobody's looking. I love when you're demanding and I love when you're generous, and I love that you're both, all the time. I love the way you flirt and I—"

"I don't flirt," I said, dizzy.

"Skinny-dipping in the reservoir?"

"That was *you!*"

"I love the way you deny the obvious. I love the way you look at me out of the corner of your eye."

I glanced at him under my lashes. "I don't know what you mean."

"I love the way you lie. I love your fits and your starts and I love your smarts and your jokes and your courage."

I liked this game. "What else?"

"You have a really fine ass." He cupped it and pulled me close and kissed me for about three weeks.

"I love that you made me wear the small wet suit," he said. "And that you were willing to wear mine."

"Less talk," I breathed. "More action."

★ ★ ★

After a blissful age, Ny barked down the beach. I roused myself to peek around the edge of the concealing rock. "People," I said, annoyed.

"Probably wondering what seabird was making all that noise."

I blushed, sliding into my jeans and sweater.

"Home?" he asked.

I nodded.

"Yours or mine?"

"Mine's closer," I said.

I was getting a drink of water in the kitchen. As I ran the glass under the tap, Ian came behind me and pressed his body into mine.

"I thought you were showering," I said. We were still salty and sandy and damp.

He kissed my neck and undid the towel around my waist. "There's room for two in that shower."

"It's tiny," I said.

"We'll squeeze in." He reached around me, stroking my stomach with one hand and cupping my breast with the other. He touched my nipple and did something gentle and insistent that made me moan. He nipped my neck and I arched against him.

The glass overflowed in the sink and water splashed my hand.

I shivered. I started to turn around, to face him, but he held me in place. "Not yet," he said, his breath hot in my ear. He stroked me until I sighed, his hands moving inside my swimsuit. My head was back and my eyes were closed, and I dropped the overflowing glass into the sink and the cold water splashed my fingers and wrists and Ian turned me around. He lifted me onto the counter and knelt and kissed me through the fabric of my suit, and kissed me harder and I put one hand in his hair and he edged the cloth out of the way and kissed me again.

I lifted one of his hands to my mouth. I licked his fingers and bit them—my eyes still closed, only wanting *more*. Finally, I pulled him upright and said, "Now."

"Now?" he said, teasing me.

"Now!"

"You sure?"

I growled.

He slammed into me. I screamed. It was perfect.

Afterwards, we cuddled and drowsed on the couch. We said all the stupid, earnest, heartfelt things people say. I loved it. I'd been wanting to sleep in his arms since that day I walked into his shop. Since the day, eight years ago, we met at Emily's book party. Probably, in a chaste and juvenile way, since the day I asked him to my school dance.

There was only one thing missing, but I couldn't figure what it was. Then I realized: "Ny!"

Ian startled awake. "Huh?"

"Ohmigod. We left Ny at the beach!"

"He's upstairs, muffin-ear."

"He can't be." He never disappeared when I had sex. He always stood and watched, like an old man at a construction site. I started to get up. "Ny? Ny!"

Ian snuggled against me, trapping me on the couch—and before I could scold him, the bed creaked upstairs. Dog paws trotted down the stairs. Ny greeted us, wagging and yawning.

"Oh, good boy," I said, relieved. "Who's my fatboy? Who's my best fatboy?"

"Wait a minute," Ian said. "I'm only your second-best fatboy?"

"If that."

"How does one move up in the rankings?" He rolled on top of me, ready to compete again in his favorite event.

"Let's go upstairs," I said.

"Good." He kissed me. "I can visit the carpet."

"It's just berber."

"The Zeigler."

"Oh! Oh." Thank God I hadn't tossed it in the Dumpster. Of course, it was still in the closet, hidden behind the jackets. "That's in the downstairs bedroom."

"We'll go down, then."

I didn't make the obvious, lewd comment. "There's no bed downstairs," I lied.

"Floor's fine. We'll have a magic carpet ride."

I shuddered—and not because of his caresses. No way on this living earth was I having sex on that decrepitated carpet. "How about we stay on the couch?"

He laughed. "You're so transparent."

"Me and Melissa Kent."

"Not skinny," he said. "Transparent."

I bit his shoulder and we went upstairs to bed, like civilized people, and it didn't strike me for another hour that he knew full well the carpet was still in the closet.

Ian left at nine to go to work, and the condo was suddenly emptier than it ever had been. But I wasn't lonely— I was wrapped in a bubble of warmth, like nestling under the covers on a cold morning. I was dippy with love, my girly senses tingling: remembering his voice, his smile, his eyes, replaying every kiss and conversation, every caress.

Yikes. I needed an emergency summit with Wren. But it was way too early for a heavy-duty romantic analysis. What kind of man made his big move at dawn? Now I was stuck at nine-fifteen craving bonbons and scented oils when I should want a bagel and caffeine.

At length, I roused and immersed myself in my development research. Well, mostly I mooned over my development notebook, where I'd been keeping track of the money. Daydreaming about love and money and sex—though not necessarily in that order.

Charlotte's check outshone the rest and David had not been pleased, as apparently some of that money had been earmarked for luxury items such as college tuition for the kids. He'd come around, though, once the profits started. Emily had chipped in with a healthy figure, too, though she'd kvetched about being married to a small publisher. Rip and Mike came through, too, and even the Sharones had chipped in. Well, they'd offered to "interview" any construction workers who'd be working on the houses. Aunt Regina had ponied up a check, and I had calls out to various other relatives. I was speaking to the bank about construction loans, had taken the maximum cash advance on all my cards, and left messages with Doug, the dot-com ex-boyfriend, and Nick, the portrait artist with the trust fund. Alex, the screenwriter, returned my call immediately—he and his girlfriend were having troubles—but I'd told him I wanted money, not sex. He got the two confused sometimes, living in Hollywood.

If Rip came through with the Keebler people, I was set. Even if he didn't, I had enough—barely—to take The Deal to checkpoint one. It was a stretch, but I could swing the planning and permit costs and the architect. I'd bootstrap those into more money—and a bank loan—and jog to checkpoints two through nine. Good thing Monty had insisted on seven houses. Five would've killed me. No margin for error, and—

The doorbell rang. I threw on a bathrobe and I opened the door, expecting Ian, though I didn't know why he bothered ringing—

And found a mob on my doorstep.

Muttering angrily and pawing the asphalt. Numbers three through five were there, clutching sheets of paper, and numbers seven, eleven, and fourteen as well. They were the ones in front, at least. I couldn't see past their bloodshot eyes and sharpened kitchen knives to the great unwashed at the rear of the riot.

"What seems to be the problem?" I asked.

The mob roared a bloodthirsty answer.

"Oh. You got the bills," I said.

Another clamor of stunned disbelief, and the rabble resolved into individuals.

"Forty-five dollars to fix the dishwasher?" Old Man Rivers howled, prodding his bill with a fingernail that needed clipping.

"Noodles in the drain," I reminded him. "If you rinse your dishes—"

"You didn't say anything about billing me," he sputtered.

"Oh, my goodness, you didn't think I was doing it for *free?*" I asked, in mock surprise.

"You *charged* us for cat-sitting!" the happy couple yelled. "Fifteen dollars a day?"

"That's right, Dale—and, um, Tracy. Four days. Sixty dollars."

"But we asked you as a favor to—"

"—thirty bucks for jumper cables—" the guy from four said.

"—cleaning the lawn chairs shouldn't cost a hundred dollars—" whined number two.

"—fifty an hour to install Windows—"

"—wasn't noodles, anyway—it was orzo."

The rumble of antipathy grew until Ny started barking and I considered barricading the door and releasing the boiling oil. "I call it highway robbery!" someone yelled, as the other voices combined in an awful crescendo: "You're the *super!* It's your *job!* Ungrateful janitor…"

Then Mrs. Wordan's voice entered the fray. "This is quite unfair," she said, calmly but sternly. "We've taken dreadful advantage of Anne, and she's been very accommodating."

"Not thirty bucks worth of accommodating!"

"Thirty? You're lucky—try *sixty.*"

"I spit on your sixty! Look at this. A hundred and ten dollars."

In a moment they were fully riled again, and baying for blood. But I simply waited—calmly untouchable in my cocoon of newfound love—until some of the fury was spent.

"I have a compromise," I finally said, into a relative lull.

"That's not all you have," muttered a voice in back. "Greedy little—"

"As a favor to you all," I said, "we'll ignore these first bills. But this is it. Next month, I'll charge the full amount for my services."

There was a collective sigh of relief, and I was pleased to hear a few voices saying, "If I've got to pay, I'll get a regular plumber" and "She didn't clean as well as Molly Maid, anyway."

They dispersed, replete with their victory, and I was left at my door with Mrs. Wordan. "I appreciate you speaking up for me like that," I said. "If there's anything I can do…"

"Oh, you can, dear," she said.

"What's that?"

"Keep your plunger handy."

CHAPTER

26

There are five types of men, post-sex. Six, actually. The first disappears, and you're sad. The second disappears, and you're happy. The third remains, and you're sad. The fourth remains, and you're happy. The fifth, and most common, does all the above.

The sixth is Ian. He came back at two o'clock, having closed early to see me, and we weren't just happy. We were *right*. We fit. He opened the door without knocking—passing the first test—and I stood from the table and we looked at each other and smiled. Just stood there, smiling like idiots, like we'd gotten away with something. Pulled the wool over the eyes of the world. Finally, we kissed and clung, and he asked what I was doing.

"Writing checks." I handed one to him.

He shook his head when he saw the number. "Wow."

"Surveyor, soil tests, and lot prep."

"You could buy a couple nice music stands for that."

"Yeah, and the building permits don't come cheap. Architects, either."

"You're really doing this, aren't you?" he said.

"I am," I said, wanting him to be proud of me.

"Good for you." He kissed me again, emphatically. "How's the funding going?"

I told him about the Keebler people and getting a construction loan from the bank—he already knew about the personal-contact investors—and he nodded and asked some intelligent questions, most of which I could answer.

Then he said, "And your short-term plans? For the weekend?"

Great. Here was the part where he said he was busy, he'd see me next week for Drinks Night. "Well, I—I don't have much planned. I mean, I dunno..."

"How about we spend every waking moment together?"

"Yes!"

He laughed. "Sleeping moments, too."

Then I remembered. "Oh, except I have one thing tomorrow. Lamaze."

"Lamaze?"

"Just an introductory spiel, for pregnant women and their partners." He started to say something, and I held up a hand. "I know what you're going to say. It's way too soon for this. But you can't be too prepared. Lamaze or Hypnobirthing or The Bradley Method. It's a preggy marketplace out there— worse than buying a car."

He ran a hand over my stomach. "You're hardly showing."

"I'm *not* showing!"

"Someone's got a little potbelly...."

"It's Wren! Wren's pregnant. Didn't I tell you?"

"You and Wren both?" he asked, his hand moving a little higher.

"I do *not* have a potbelly," I said.

"A little pooch. An honest handful…"

"*You* have the potbelly." I pulled his shirt from his pants. "Look at this. It's a beer gut. It's a kegger. My second-best fatboy…"

I ran my hand over his stomach to his belt—I unbuckled and unzipped him, and pushed him against the wall.

We faded demurely back in about forty-five minutes later. We untangled and stood, and by silent gluttonous accord checked the fridge and cabinets. There was a bag of tortilla chips and a half-eaten jar of salsa. Normally I was better stocked with new items, but the move, the Super, and The Deal had thrown off my routine. I unscrewed the salsa lid and sniffed.

"Gone off?" Ian asked.

"It's okay," I said bravely. "Just let me—" I was going to surgically remove the top layer with a spoon, but Ian dug a chip in before I could sterilize.

"Eew," I said.

He popped the chip in his mouth. "What?"

"That's been in the fridge a while."

He looked slightly concerned as he swallowed. "How long?"

"Almost a week."

"A week?"

"Almost." I wanted to reassure him, but there was no avoiding the truth. He'd eaten stale nasty food, without allowing me to complete the purifying preemptive scrape. "Since Monday." I tried to break it to him gently. "Five days."

"So?" he asked, dipping again.

"Ian!"

"Was the cap off?"

"No."

"Then what's the problem?"

Well, I could see he was intent on being difficult, so I said, "Nothing."

I took a handful of chips and ate them dry. Ian watched me, and dipped. I ate another dry chip. He ate another with salsa. I crunched. He chewed.

Finally, able to bear it no longer, he theatrically plunged a fresh chip deep into the untainted territory of the jar and offered it to me. "Just try one."

"No thanks."

"For me?"

I could deny him nothing. So I put a Joan of Arc expression on my face—no sacrifice too great for the holy cause—and bit into the chip. Good salsa. Spicy, with plenty of cilantro and a complete absence of fridge-lichen odors.

"Okay," I said. And I dug in.

We walked Ny and we went grocery shopping. We held hands. We discovered a mutual affinity for avocados, dolmas, Limonata sodas, and each other. We went home and it took us two hours to put everything away. When we finished, we were starving. Well, and we were upstairs in my bedroom. These things happen.

I put on jeans and opened the drawer for a T-shirt when Ian pulled the cranberry top from the closet.

"Wear this?" he asked.

"You like it?"

He made a hungry-bear sound.

"Happy to oblige." I slipped the top over my head.

"And the little animal shoes."

I slipped into my leopard mules. "These?"

He sat on the edge of the bed and watched me, like Ny watches kibble.

"Stop it," I said. "I'm hungry."

"Me, too."

"I'm *hungry* hungry."

"Well, I'm hungry hungry *hungry*."

"What're you, fifteen? Act your age. Shouldn't you be watching the game or something? I'm the one who's wanted you since junior high, I should—" Something occurred to me. "Hey. Maybe that's why I never committed. In the back of my mind, there was always you."

"You mean you've been saving yourself for me all this time?"

"Well—not actively."

"You should have saved your virginity for me." There was a far-off expression in his eyes. "That would've been awesome."

"Shut up." I laughed. "If you have virgin fantasies, I'll wear a white nightgown."

I said we should cook dinner together, but Ian insisted we go out. We only got as far as the Jeep. He popped the back and said, "There's something I've been wanting to do with you for weeks."

"Something *else?*" We'd already run through my basic repertoire, and while I was always willing to learn new tricks, one never knew what depraved kink a new boyfriend would casually introduce. "How many weeks?"

He hefted a big black plastic *thing,* with straps and ropes and spikes, from the back of the Jeep. "More than I should admit, given I was engaged. Here, grab the other end."

I grabbed and lifted, a bit unsure.

"Never saw a tent before?" he asked.

"Oh, a tent!"

"What did you think it was?"

"Well, you know. I thought it was a tent."

He looked at me a moment.

"So," I said, "a tent…"

"Yeah, we're going camping."

"Tonight?"

"On your deck. We're gonna catch the Lawn Bandit. Wait, let me get the basket."

He grabbed a woven basket—antique, but I managed not to stiffen in disgust—and we carried everything to the deck. Ian was like a little boy, playing Arctic Explorer in the backyard. His enthusiasm was infectious as he described the benefits of camping within sight of indoor plumbing and a fridge, and I found myself smiling. And who could resist a little Nanookie of the North?

He set up the tent, with pillows and a flickering lantern and an air mattress he assured me he'd scrubbed with bleach. Then he packed the basket in the kitchen, and "surprised" me with it in our cozy hideaway. It was overflowing with things from our shopping trip: the Carina Cellars Syrah, the French cheese wrapped in grape leaves, apples, a baguette, olives, and jars of gourmet relish and pickle. And two lemon tarts.

There was also a small rifle. It had a polished wooden handle and an old metal barrel. I lifted it gingerly. "What is this?"

"My gun."

"Does it shoot?"

"Nah. It's a vintage Red Ryder carbine, a BB gun, but the cocking level is broken. It's cast iron, which means it was manufactured in the early '40s, and—"

I groaned. "I don't know if the Lawn Bandit actually deserves to die, Ian."

"I told you, it can't shoot."

"It doesn't need a bullet—it'll kill him with sheer ancientness." I replaced the gun and grabbed the wine. It was old, too, but at least had never been used. I poured two glasses and raised mine in a toast and said, "Oh! Where's Ny?"

"In the woods, chasing something."

"I hope it's the guy in four, and he catches him."

We looked toward the eucalyptus trees for a moment. The moon was big and round and the night was perfectly clear. It was good to be here, and good to be me, and good to be with Ian. There was scuffling in the underbrush, and the single excited bark which meant Ny was after a ground squirrel.

"To Ny," Ian said, and clinked my glass. "What kind of name is that, anyway? Ny."

"It's foreign. Guess what it means."

"Dog?"

"No."

"Cat?"

"No."

"Okay. What language is it?"

"Norwegian or Finnish, I can't remember. Somewhere up there. Maybe Swedish."

"Animal?"

"No."

"Vegetable?"

"No. And it's not mineral. Want a hint?"

"Not yet," he said. "Where did you get him?"

"I got him *used*. At the pound. Can you believe it?"

"Ah! So Ny means used."

"No."

Ian smiled. "Then it means new."

"Bingo." I kissed him. "Mmm, tasty. Red wine."

"You're kind of a lush, aren't you?"

"Only with you. I was scared if we didn't have Drinks Night, I wouldn't see you again."

"That wouldn't have stopped me from seeing you. Nothing would."

The Lawn Bandit didn't come that night. He was the only one.

★ ★ ★

The next week, I made a concerted effort to scuff my feet on the sidewalk every now and again, because it got a bit embarrassing, floating five or ten yards in the air every time I took a step. A gentle breeze could waft me across the street if I wasn't careful, like a dandelion spore on a summer day. And it wasn't just Ian. It was _everything_.

The woman from the city called and told me the permits looked good. Everything was a go. Green light. Clear sailing. Final word was on Thursday, but barring catastrophe I could build on seven lots. Seven _brand-new_ glorious houses, surrounded by my favorite land in the world. I only wished I could afford one.

Meanwhile, the Environmental Impact Report was done and—given my willingness to protect all God's creatures, great and small—there were no problems. The builder was reassuring. The Architectural Review Board loved my architect—a guy named Louis Merrick, who Monty had recommended. The bank officer expressed some incredulity regarding the cash advances on my credit card, but was overall supportive.

And her support was a good thing, because of the single dark cloud—those back-stabbing Keebler people. You wouldn't think a gaggle of elves who lived in an oak tree would be so cutthroat.

I came home from a trip through the planning permit labyrinth at the county offices, and there were three messages on my machine from Rip at his most conciliatory—the tone he used with clients when deals were falling apart. I couldn't imagine what the bad news was. It's not like I'd be surprised if the Keebler people didn't want to invest. Sure their money would give me some breathing room, but it wasn't absolutely necessary. Rip knew I'd make a fuss if they weren't interested, but only a small fuss, for show. So what was the problem?

It was with an anxious hand that I reached for the phone to return his call. It rang before I touched it: Monty.

"Good news," he said.

"If this is another prostate story, I don't want to hear it."

"Good *business* news, Anne. You sitting down?"

I stood and paced. "I'm sitting."

"We have a buyer."

"A buyer? We don't even have a house yet! That's great. What're we asking? They know the permits aren't finalized? They want to buy one of my houses?"

"Not a house—the land."

"The what?"

"The property."

"Someone wants to buy the land *I'm* developing? They want to buy me out?"

"Exactly. I just got off the phone with Rip Parsons. He had a client up from L.A., a big contractor down there. Somehow they got that prospectus you scribbled up, and they went for a drive out to the—"

"Dirty elves," I snarled. "I sent them that prospectus. It's for investors, not competitors. They made an offer on the *land?*"

"Got it right here on my desk."

"How much?"

He mentioned a fairly huge sum. "Fifteen percent of that is yours. Enough to pay your debts and investors. All you have to do is—"

"Forget it, Monty. We have a contract, you and me—I own the option to buy, to build. Nobody develops that land but me. The Keeblers are supposed to be giving me money, not making deals behind my back."

"It's a strong offer, Anne."

"They want to buy me out. The operative words being *me* and *out*. And this is one time I want in."

"Look at the numbers. You make a quick—"

"This is my project, Monty. This is my development. That's my land and I'm not letting some pointy-hatted munchkins steal it. This project's coming together. I'm making it happen. Who found the land? I did. Who put The Deal together? I did. Who dealt with the county and the city and the salamanders and the sewage? Me, me, me, and me."

"They'll guarantee low-impact construction. Your cut's high enough to pay yourself and get your investors a few pennies, too."

"Okay." He was right. A good deal was a good deal. "And the hiking trail? They'll preserve it? Donate it to the county?"

A short pause. "No. But this is a once-in-a-lifetime deal. You walk away now, take it straight to the bank."

"It's not about the bank, Monty."

"Twenty percent."

"It's not about the percentage."

"Twenty-five, and you're killing me. You're killing me. Can you hear that? I'm dying. Only thing is, we have to sign before they change their minds. You free tomorrow morning?"

"Keep waving that red flag, Monty, maybe it'll convince me."

He was silent a second. "You're being a damn fool, Anne."

I didn't say anything.

"Ah, what the hell," he said. "I'll tell them we don't want their filthy money."

We hung up and I leaned against the kitchen counter, my heart pounding. Maybe I was being a damn fool. But this was mine. I didn't want to build equity, I wanted to build houses. I didn't want to save a few bucks, I wanted to save that land.

When I caught my breath, I called Rip. He repeated Monty's advice. He said it was a generous offer, I should accept. Any idiot would accept. It was a no-brainer. It was connect-the-dots. It was dumb luck.

"Yeah, I get your point," I told him. "And they'll donate the hiking trail to the county?"

He paused. "No."

"Then no deal."

"Anne—as a friend, I have to tell you, *take* this deal."

"The permits are coming through Thursday. The houses are going up. I'll make more money doing it myself, and I'll save that land for public use."

"Or you'll fall on your ass."

"What's that supposed to mean?"

"It means this is a complex, difficult, frustrating process for people who've done it a hundred times. You're in over your head, Anne."

"Maybe I'm learning to swim."

"Maybe you're drowning. You can't do this. Someone's offered you an easy out. Take it."

"You think I can't do this?"

"Remodel a house first. Put up a three-bedroom in Santa Maria. Don't start with a hillside fucking million-dollar neighborhood in Montecito."

I sent Rip his investment back a half hour later. Plus interest.

I spent the rest of the day at the site with my Project Manager. Well, he was just a guy from the construction company, but that's what he called himself: Project Manager on the Olsen Development. I had to stifle a giggle every time he said that. Until you have a Project Manager, you don't know what living is.

My P.M. was an old friend of Monty's, a stout middle-aged guy who knew everything about his subject and loved to answer questions. Conveniently, I had a few. And even more conveniently, there were so many lessons and details and urgent looming tasks that there was no time for a nervous breakdown.

What was I thinking, rejecting the Keebler offer? I definitely should've let them buy me out.

No, I shouldn't—this was my project, and this was my future, and I wasn't selling out.

Oh, God, of course I should've accepted! What if I lost everyone's money? What if I was in over my head? What if I was drowning?

No, I was swimming. I was floating…at the very least I was dog-paddling.

Then how come I couldn't breathe?

My P.M. and I ironed out a few thousand details and I headed home, exhausted. All I wanted was a big meal and hot bath.

Inside, the condo smelled delicious. Ian was in the kitchen, making homemade pizzas. One with Greek olives and garlic, the other with portobello mushrooms. He laid a final mushroom on a pizza and saw me. He smiled, and I exhaled a breath I'd been holding for four hours. My big meal was ready, and Ian was my hot bath.

I collapsed into the overstuffed chair and kicked off my shoes and moaned. "Ask me about ordinance violations and underground piping. I dare you."

"You look exhausted."

I told him about my Project Manager and the people at the county offices. And, with heart in throat, about the Keebler Double-cross.

What if he said I should have taken their offer? What if I should have? If he said I should've, I definitely should've.

"—so I told them no," I finished. "I don't want an easy way out. I want to build these homes and preserve this land."

"I can't believe you did that," he said.

"Oh," I said, in a small voice.

"I mean—I really can't believe it."

"Why not?" I asked, my voice even smaller.

"It takes real courage to say no, Anne. I'm impressed. You had this dream, and you're following through. Someone offers a shortcut, but you don't take it—because the dream isn't about shortcuts to someone else's destination. It's about getting where *you* want to go."

So I started crying.

"It's gonna work out, Annie." He stroked my hair. "It's gonna be all right."

"What if it isn't? What if I can't do it?"

"You can."

"What if I can't? What if I fail?"

"If you fail," he said, "then I'll love you. And your family will love you. And your friends will love you. And you'll try again."

That's when I knew I'd really come home.

CHAPTER

27

The next day, Charlotte and I met Wren at Element for lunch. Charlotte was carrying a sleek case to display her swimsuits, and wearing a large pair of sunglasses to disguise her identity. They learn this in Celebrity 101, like Clark Kent with his glasses—no mortal senses could penetrate the opaque mystery of eyewear.

I, on the other hand, was hefting a massive cardboard box of used maternity clothes and wearing a pair of sunglasses to prevent further wrinkles. Was probably about as successful as Charlotte, too.

Wren was in the middle of a sale, so I plopped the box outside her office and we flipped through racks of frilly skirts and lingerie tops. Charlotte looked nervous—afraid Wren would hate her swimsuits. I distracted her with chatter about the kids. Hannah was in an uproar about Zach. He wasn't as mindlessly obedient as her brothers, and had stubbornly refused to play a hobbit, insisting upon being an elf instead. Hannah was having sibling rivalry with her cousin.

"Oh, that reminds me," Charlotte said. "Has Emily told you about her new book?"

"The one everyone hates?"

"No. The new new book."

I shook my head. "I've been sort of caught up in my own stuff lately."

"Have you?" she asked, wide-eyed. "So *that* explains the flip charts at dinner last week."

"Okay, those weren't flip charts."

"They were charts, Anne. At dinner. About pouring foundations and paying for fire service."

"But did they flip? No."

Charlotte smiled. "Anyway. Emily's got a new topic." She dug in her bag for a picture of the three of us as kids. We were standing in a row in front of some palm trees, with Emily in the middle. "You know she decided her book wasn't—"

"Let me know if I can I help you," a salesgirl interrupted. "Oh, hi, Anne."

It was Jenny, blond and pert. I swear she hadn't aged at all since Banana. It was eerie. I pitied her. Poor thing, doomed to look twenty-three forever. "Hey, Jenny. How are—?"

Before I could finish, she'd spotted Charlotte. "Ohmigod! You're Charlotte Olsen. I am such a fan!"

Charlotte blushed becomingly and murmured something polite.

"So much for the sunglasses," I murmured.

"It's sunny outside," Charlotte said, exasperated. "Everyone's wearing sunglasses."

I introduced Jenny to Charlotte as my former manager at Banana Republic. "She taught me how to fold."

"Wait a minute," Charlotte said to Jenny. "You weren't there when she did the display window thing, were you?"

"The mannequins? Ohmigod! That got written up in company policy reports. That's like, legendary."

And they were off, examining my humiliation from every angle before Wren finished ringing up her sale. I tore Charlotte away from Jenny, and we trooped into Wren's office where we presented her with the box of used maternity clothes. When she was done oohing and ahhing, she turned to Charlotte. "Now tell me about your swimsuits."

"Okay," Charlotte said, taking a deep breath. "I want an honest opinion. I know they're rough, but I'd like your ideas about what direction I should go—I mean, if I want people to like them. These aren't very good, but I could make different ones. These are just—"

I elbowed her aside and opened the case and started showing Wren the swimsuits. Wren went silent, suddenly looking like a professional buyer. Of course any one-of-a-kind suit made by Charlotte Olsen would sell, but Charlotte didn't want her name on these. She wanted them to succeed—or fail—on their own merits. And Wren had agreed to be brutally honest.

She examined all six suits as Charlotte squirmed in the chair. Finally, she asked, "How attached are you to this fabric?"

I could see Charlotte vacillating. She lovingly ran a thumb along the strap of one of the suits and said, "You can't separate the fabric from the cut. You design with the fabric in mind—for the support, and the sheen, and the silhouette."

"You used molded cups instead of underwires or push-up pads."

Charlotte explained why.

"And the design?" Wren asked.

"It's an interpretation of the…" And she blathered on about nothing I understood. She was the Emily of swimwear. "And with the sarong—" she wound down "—the diagonal folds of the drape will really hide figure flaws." She glanced around, as if looking for a visual aid, and saw me. "Here, Anne, put this on."

"Figure flaws?" I said. "Charlotte, if you think—"

Wren interrupted. "No, no—not necessary. Hmm." She nibbled her lower lip. "How can I put this, Charlotte…"

Charlotte paled. She looked beautiful, pale.

"These," Wren said, "are fabulous."

Charlotte glowed, and was even more beautiful.

"See what happens when you follow your bliss?" I said.

"I learned it from you," Charlotte said. "With your flip charts and short-term air-quality mitigation. We're both finally doing what we really want."

Wren put a hand on her stomach. "All three of us."

Thursday evening, Ian called hello at the front door and I caromed toward him from the living room. "The permits are coming! The permits are coming!"

"One if by air," he said, "Two if by—"

"The building permits!" I was about to launch myself into his arms when I saw they were already occupied—by a rolled Persian rug. Better than a deflector shield. I rebounded off the invisible wall of antiquity, but even this did nothing to blunt my enthusiasm. "I got the permits! Oh, God, I can't believe it!"

He laughed and put the rug aside and kissed me. "Congratulations! When did you hear? The planning board called?"

"An hour ago." I filled him in on the good news, while part of me focused nervously on the rug. We hadn't had our big antiques fight yet, and were days overdue. Ian had started gently suggesting we spend the night at his place instead of mine. Sadly, his place was knee-deep in the decayed bones of a previous age. Still, I was too excited to worry much. "The woman at the board says I'm all set. Seven houses on the land left over after I sell the hiking trail to the county."

"That's amazing," he said. "You're amazing."

"Now there's no stopping me. It's official. I had to ask Dad for a final chunk of cash, but it's actually going to happen. I think I'm in shock."

"You know what we should do to celebrate?" He showed me his boyish smile. "Drinks Night."

"Perfect! Our first Drinks Night as a couple."

He patted the rug. "And I got you a present, too."

I frowned. "Another rug."

"It's not another rug."

"Another carpet."

"It's not another carpet, either."

I looked at it. It was a long rectangular hand-woven floor covering. "Well, it's not a dozen roses, Ian."

"It's the *same* carpet."

I involuntarily glanced at the closet door.

"I smuggled it out when you were in the shower." The mischief quotient in his smile doubled. "To have it cleaned. Not just cleaned—the poor thing's been steamed, swirled, pounded, and decontaminated. The guy did everything short of immersing it in a bleach bath. You could use this thing in a surgical theatre."

I sniffed the edge of the rug. It did have that New Carpet smell.

"Anne, you're gonna love it." He unrolled it in the living room and placed the coffee table on top. Ny sniffed it curiously—exactly as I had—then lay down and rolled onto his back, paws in the air. Ian sat next to him and scratched his belly. They smiled up at me, waiting for my approval.

"It's clean?" I asked. "You promise?"

"Sterile. Like—" he thought for a second "—like when you rip open a Band-Aid."

He knew I loved ripping open Band-Aids, releasing that tiny packet of perfectly hygienic air into the atmosphere. "Really?"

Ian and Ny nodded.

I sat tentatively between them, attempting to hover a millimeter over the rug's surface.

"No moldering death germs?" Ian asked.

I twitched my nostrils, attempting to detect any putrefaction spores in the air. "No," I said, surprised. "The bleach bath must've killed them all."

"And you're sure it's better to have toxic chemical fumes deadly to all organic life than a bit of old dirt?"

I looked at him.

"Right," he said. "Silly question."

An hour later, we were walking Ny at a park on the Mesa. It was like walking into a Kodak commercial. The happy bounding dog and the happy blue ocean, the happy loving couple holding hands.

So I panicked.

We'd spent every day together since Surf Dawn, and still I hated when Ian went to work in the morning. I had separation anxiety from a guy I'd been dating a week? Was that normal? Was it natural? No: it was ab- and un-. I'd become a needy, clingy limpet-girl. Anne Olsen, the Human Barnacle. Ian was probably dying to spend the day alone, eating pretzels in his underwear and throwing empty beer cans on the floor. God, he definitely was. He had a sort of caged, pretzel-hungry look in his eyes. Well, actually his eyes were on the tennis ball he was tossing for Ny, but still.

Maybe I was dying to spend the night alone, too. Had Ian ever thought of that? Noooo. He's dying to get away from me, but does he even consider that I might feel the same? Mr. Self-Centered. Mr. Caught-Up-in-His-Own-Drama.

"I'm thinking of going to my dad's for dinner," I said.

He wrestled the soggy ball from Ny's jaws and tossed it again. "Tonight?"

I nodded.

"Instead of Drinks Night?"

"I try to get over there once a week. It's sort of a ritual."

"Okay. Do you bring food? Your dad's a meat and potatoes guy, isn't he?"

I said he loved pork chops. Ian said he wasn't really in the mood for pork but how about chicken? And I said, "So you're telling me you don't want to come."

He stopped walking.

"If you don't want to come, don't come," I said. "I'm not forcing you."

"Um." He cocked his head, like he was rewinding the conversation in his mind. "Am I invited?"

"Of course you're invited."

"It's okay if you don't want me along, Anne."

"I do. I do want. I just thought—" I swallowed. "Maybe we need a break? We've seen each other every day."

He was silent a moment. "I can't tell if *you* want a break, or you think *I* do."

I knelt down to hug Ny and avoid eye contact.

"Anne," he said. "I don't want a break."

I leapt up and clung to him. "Neither does the Human Barnacle."

Two o'clock in the morning, I nudged Ian. He said mmmph and snuggled closer.

I nudged harder.

"Mmm?" he said, half-awake.

"Tell me you're happy."

He nuzzled my hair. "I'm happy."

I stayed awake, snug in his arms, not wanting to fall back asleep and miss any of the love.

Five minutes later, Ian sat up and said, "Let's go."

"What? Where? There's pasta in the fridge."

"Not pasta." He gestured across the room. "The Lawn Bandit."

Ny was standing with his front paws on the windowsill, staring intently into the darkness, his hackles raised.

We dressed and crept downstairs. Ian grabbed the flashlight. I grabbed the plunger. We silently opened the door to the lawn and I put a hand on Ny's collar to keep him from racing ahead. We stole through the moonlight, like members of the Scooby Doo Reenactment Brigade.

We closed noiselessly on the sodding villains. The night air was clean and cold, the traffic sounds from the freeway sounded like surf. The sod was moving as if by its own accord—a slow undulation of grass and dirt, the culprit hidden by the lawn he'd already rolled.

Ian flicked the flashlight and said, "Hey!"

A pair of dark eyes flashed at us, and a small body froze, caught red-handed in midroll. For a moment, I couldn't make sense of what I was seeing in the shadow of the sod. The culprit was a little person. Two feet tall. Wearing a black harlequin mask and a fur coat.

Ny tore from my grip and shot forward, hackles raised, legs pumping. He leapt at the little person and they rolled across the lawn in a cloud of dust like a tussle in Looney Tunes. The dust parted and I saw it was a raccoon, clinging to Ny's undercarriage with sharp claws. I roared like a tigress concerned for her little tiglet and entered the fray, my plunger swinging with deadly intent.

The raccoon dashed for the canyon as Ny trotted after,

his hackles high and his tail crazily puffed. I stood before Ian victoriously, my plunger a sword of righteousness. The flashlight beam wobbled wildly, and a strange sound issued from behind the light. Choked laughter.

"I just got even happier," Ian said.

On Sunday, we caught the raccoon in a humane trap from Animal Control. Apparently the little bugger had been foraging for grubs underneath the new sod.

And it struck me: everything was perfect. The Deal was mine. Ian was mine. Even the Lawn Bandit was mine.

Then, on Monday, the planning commission called. They'd changed my permits, and were only allowing two parcels.

Not seven. Not five.

Two.

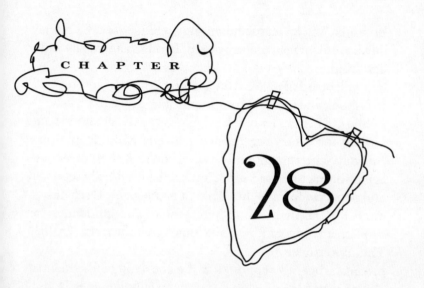

CHAPTER

28

The Director of the Planning Commission was a beefy middle-aged woman with dark eyes and a tired blond perm.

"There's been a tiny mistake on my building permit," I said, approaching her desk.

She looked at me with all the warmth of a cinder block. Calling it a blank stare would be an exaggeration. "Anne Olsen," she finally said. "Cypress Road Residential Project."

I laughed gaily. "That's me. There's been a mix-up, I guess I filed the wrong form or checked the wrong box. But my permit, which was for seven houses? Now it's only for two. Which makes the whole thing impossible. It's all just a silly mix-up, I'm sure, but—"

"You have two parcels," she said.

"Exactly! But there should be seven. So if you could just change it back, I'll get out of your hair."

She frowned. Maybe I shouldn't have mentioned hair. She said, "No."

"Ha-ha! But seriously, two lots is impossible. All I can

do with two lots is lose my money, and my family's money, and my financing, and my credit. But I can't actually build anything."

"The board met. We reduced the number of lots to two."

I shook my head. "That's impossible. You can't have."

She did her cinder block impression again, then stood and crossed the room. She opened a drawer and fiddled interminably with its contents. I wasn't sure if I should encourage or distract her, so I stayed quiet. She eventually returned and slapped a form on her desk. "The Negative Declaration, Article III Zoned 5-E-2, pursuant to the guidelines for implementation of the California Environmental Quality Act. Two parcels."

"Yeah, but it's supposed to be the Design Residential Zone District, to develop seven single family homes," I said, not even pausing to be amazed that I knew what I was talking about. "And to approve the Tiered Mitigated Negative Declaration."

"That was last week. After this morning's meeting you're now approved for—" she glanced down at the form, as if she'd forgotten "—two parcels."

"But I paid for the permitting on seven. I did my financials based on seven. With two, I have nothing. With three, I have nothing. With four through six, I go bankrupt. Do you follow me? I'm selling twenty percent of the land to the county, as public open space, and getting seven lots. As agreed. I need this form to say seven. Not two."

"The commission will only allow two. Maximum. But we will re-zone the 5-E-2 for nonmanufacturing commercial—"

"I'm not building a fucking factory! I'm building houses. And two lots isn't gonna do it. That's the same as zero lots, or negative two lots. Two lots is no lots."

She stared at me, froglike.

"You can't do this," I said. "We had an agreement. I spent—we had an agreement."

"The Planning Commission reconsidered its decision. Two parcels."

"Are you telling me," I said, suddenly having difficulty breathing. "Are you saying I spent hu-hu-hundreds of thousands—on nothing? I borrowed from everyone I've ever met, from my father and—and I—I, for nothing? I lost all their money down the drain? Is that what you're telling me?"

"Would you like to appeal the decision?"

"Yes! Yes." A wave of relief left me weak-kneed. "That's exactly what I want."

"Then get a lawyer," she said. "And prepare to lose."

I stumbled into Ian's shop, weeping. He was with a customer, extolling the dubious virtues of some nasty old vase. I fell into his arms. "I'm fucked," I moaned. "It's all fucked. Everything's fucked."

He murmured and patted me and told me to wait for him upstairs.

I ran up to his loft. Unearthed his whiskey. Filled his coffee cup to the brim, sat in the comfy yellow chintz-upholstered chair, and drank deeply, listening to the customer buy the vase. When she'd gone, Ian came upstairs. "What happened?"

"I hate antiques!"

"I know you do, but what—"

"They're disgusting, and I hate them. They're old and gross and old. And gross. And used."

"Anne, look at yourself."

"You mean I'm gross, too? Old and gross and a big fat failure?"

"Well, that, too. But what I meant was, you're drinking

out of my old coffee cup and sitting in an antique chair. Whatever's happened, it can't be worse than that."

I grudgingly half-laughed.

"Come here," he said.

I went there.

"What's wrong?"

I told him.

He held me and asked what he could do.

"Nothing," I said. "There's nothing left to do."

"At least see a lawyer before you say that."

So I saw a lawyer. Kevin's friend Cash, in fact. I presented him with my predicament and watched as he nodded thoughtfully. "In legal terminology?" he said. "The designation for someone in your situation is, Terminally Fucked."

I spent three days stalking the people on the planning commission, speaking to other lawyers, and pleading with the Board of Supervisors. But County Code Chapter 21 was clear: the Planning and Development Department could do whatever they damn well pleased. I could divide the land into two parcels. Not seven.

The next day, I called Charlotte. She answered brightly, still bubbling with enthusiasm over her swimsuits. I asked for David. I told him I'd lost all their money.

I called Emily and told her the same.

I called Mike and the Sharones and the ex-boyfriends and Monty and Aunt Regina. I called Dad.

They told me what I already knew: I'd fucked up. They'd given me more than money—they'd given me trust—and I'd let them down. I swallowed the tattered remnants of my pride and called the Keebler people and begged them to buy me out. They weren't interested in two lots. Thanks, but no thanks.

Well, I'd have to leave Monty City and get a real job. It would take twenty or thirty years to pay everyone back, but so what? I had no plans for the next few decades.

When I'd finished my calls, I climbed into bed with Ian. He kissed my forehead. "I'm proud of you."

When I stopped crying I said, "I hate myself."

I spent the next three days in bed, leaving only for food and bathroom. The phone rang. I didn't answer. The sun rose. I didn't care. Ny whined for a walk. I shoved him outside. Ian was supportive. I snapped at him. I needed to make more money than I'd earned total, in all my previous jobs combined, just to pay back what I owed—forget about my own expenses. I'd bankrupted the people I loved most. They'd trusted me, and I'd betrayed them.

Day four. The bedroom was ripe with failure. The curtains were closed and the lights were off. I guess it was after six, because Ian opened the front door and called my name. I didn't respond.

He came upstairs and stood in the doorway. I rolled toward the wall. He opened the curtains and pulled the covers off me and said, "Enough."

"I'm not through with those," I said.

He tossed the covers across the room. "Yes, you are."

So I launched into my litany of woe. I'd failed everyone and everything and they all hated me. I couldn't even stay here, not only because Monty was mad but because he wasn't paying the $50/hour I'd need to earn, working 80-hour weeks for the next seventeen years, to pay back what I owed. "—and I can't even move back with Charlotte, her stupid swimsuits are in the guest house. Plus, you know, even *I* might be slightly mortified to live there after losing the kids' college tuition. I'm a stickler that way. A big fat stickler of failure. A big fat—"

"Move in with me," Ian said.

"—jug of lard with no future and—" I lifted the pillow from my head. "What?"

"Move in with me."

"You mean…?"

"I mean I want to live with you."

"With me? With *this?* Are you crazy? Are you sure?"

"I'm both."

"Like, living together?"

"Exactly like living together."

"You want to live with the Typhoid Mary of money? Two days after I move in, you'll go bankrupt. I'm the financial Bermuda Triangle."

"You're mine." He sat on the bed and kissed me. "Move in with me."

I said, against his lips, "Okay."

"Then it's settled."

"Except…"

"We can sleep in your bed, Anne. I'll put mine in storage."

"And—"

"And I'll bring some stuff to the shop, so there's room for furniture you're willing to sit on."

"Thank you."

"What about the carpet?" he asked.

"The Zeigler?"

"Mmm-hmm."

"A house isn't a home without my Zeigler," I said. And, oddly, I meant it.

He smiled and said, "You stink." And he meant it, too.

He chased me into the shower. Scrubbed me vigorously. Dressed me in non-sleepwear. Took me for a walk with a very relieved Ny. Fed me dinner. Washed the bedding and ravished me in the crisp, clean, fresh bed.

★ ★ ★

He should've quit while he was ahead. But the next morning, when Emily called, hoping to take me to lunch, Ian coerced me into agreeing. Emily and I hadn't spoken since I'd confessed that I'd taken Jamie's retirement money and thrown it into the bonfire of my vanities. But Ian said she'd understand—the first version of her latest book had been such an abysmal failure, she knew just how I felt. Plus, she'd been calling twice a day, worried about me.

I met Emily outside the Sojourner, and she offered a brusque greeting which I found somehow comforting. Inside, she got into an argument with the waitress while ordering, which I found even more heartening. At least *she* was in a good mood. After the waitress went in back to spit on our food, Emily said she'd taken my advice.

"But I told you to have the stew," I said.

"I mean about my book. I tossed everything and started over. Something totally new."

"I advised that?"

"You got me thinking. It's your whole follow your bliss thing. I don't much care about theory, and I really don't care about porn. God, I think back to those blissful days of innocence when I thought a 'pearl necklace' was jewelry, a 'facial' was skin care, and a 'money shot' was—"

"Wait," I said. "Aren't we going to talk about how I stole all your money?"

"That's for dessert."

"I'm serious. Don't you want to yell at me? I lost half of Jamie's retirement fund."

"I already yelled at you," she said. "You're still an irresponsible, spoiled little brat. But we're talking about me now, Anne."

"But, but—"

"Anne, it's done. You fucked up. Are you going to fix it?"

"I don't know if I can." I fiddled with my fork. "I pretty much can't."

"Are you going to try?"

"Yes."

"Okay, then," she said. "Anyway, I was thinking about the foundations of feminist theory, like the personal is political. That was my entrée into the motherhood and film book, but... well, I got to thinking." She handed me an old photograph. "Look."

It was the same photo Charlotte had shown me at Element. The three of us as kids, with Charlotte, at thirteen or fourteen, already budding into her unearthly beauty. Me, at seven or eight, adorable and exuberant. And Emily, between us, dark and solemn and Emily.

"I don't get it," I said.

"It's the cover of my new book."

"I'm gonna be on the cover? This better not be a porn thing."

She laughed. "It's about family and sisterhood and the development of political consciousness."

I looked more closely at the photo. Maybe the political consciousness was hidden behind the palm trees.

"The title is *Between Youth and Beauty,*" she said. "It's about growing up the middle child, stuck between Charlotte on one side and you on the other."

"You didn't grow up the middle child," I said, a little sharply. "You grew up the *smart* child."

"Overcompensation. The new book's about being constricted by the two values considered most important for women in our society. Beauty and youth. Not just in society, but in family. In our family. Between beautiful Charlotte and wonderful you. About constructing a self in a narrative environment which devalues—"

"Wait a minute. *You're* the middle child? Maybe techni-

cally, but I'm the one who should be writing a book. Call it
After Beauty and Brains. Two older sisters, one's the most
beautiful girl in the world, the other the smartest. I'm like
the leftovers. The afterthought. I was the third Brontë sister. Charlotte and Emily Brontë and…who's the third one,
again? I'm the nobody."

"Anne," she said. "You're the baby. You're the favorite. We
all love you best. Don't you know anything?"

An hour later, my world had improved immeasurably.
Not only had I actually left my bedroom, but I'd had a
yummy lunch of crispy tofu and onions—tastes better than
it sounds—and Emily didn't hate me. Partly, perhaps, because
she was afraid I'd object to having my picture on her book
cover. But considering she and Jamie would be spending
their golden years in a cardboard box because of me, it was
the least I could do.

Emily glanced at me as she paid at the register. "You look
a little less awful."

"I feel less awful. I dunno. I'll pay everyone back. Eventually. Somehow." I grabbed a mint. "Maybe I should marry
money. Oh! Ian asked me to move in with him."

Emily stopped counting her change. "He's great, isn't he?
Not rich, though."

"Maybe he'll find some old bedpan worth a million
bucks. Anyway—" I smiled a secret smile "—he has other
talents."

"Yeah," she said.

I stopped smiling, secret or otherwise. "What do you
mean, yeah?"

"I mean yeah, I'm sure he does. You're happy with him?"

"Totally, completely, and entirely happy. With him, at least.
If I wasn't such a loser in every other way, I'd— But what
did you mean, yeah?"

"I meant yeah." She pushed open the door and we stepped onto the sidewalk. "I'm not surprised he has talents."

Ah. Emily must've been talking to Charlotte, who was no doubt reliving the adolescent fumblings of the proto-Ian. "I'm not talking about teenage talents, Emily. He's all grown up now."

"I'm sure he is," she said. "What does he think about the Cypress property?"

"He's been great. Deluded, but great. He's totally confident in me. He says I'll figure something out."

"Like what?"

"No idea. But if not for him, I'd still be locked in my bedroom, cringing from the sunlight. He…I don't know, he makes me feel safe. Like he's always on my side. Sort of protected and secure. I know you don't think women should say that about men, but—"

"I feel the same way about Jamie." She pressed the crosswalk button as we waited on the corner. "But I never felt that way with Ian. I always thought he was teasing me."

"What? Ian? When?"

"You know, back when—"

"When he was with Charlotte?"

"—he and I were lovers. That summer right before my first book came out, and I started dating Jamie."

I grabbed the traffic pole as the street lurched beneath me. "Lovers? You and— *No*. You were dating the porn star that summer."

She lifted her hand to her mouth. "You didn't know."

"You and Ian?" Something cold expanded in my stomach. "You weren't—you never dated Ian, Emily."

"We—no."

"Ian was the *porn star?*"

"Annie, I'm sorry. We kept it quiet because of him being Charlotte's ex. I thought you knew."

"You thought I knew."

"Anne, I—"

"Of course I didn't fucking know! Jesus! Charlotte was bad enough—now *you?* I can't believe he didn't tell me. That bastard. How could you, Emily?"

"Annie, please."

"No!" I yelled. "No!"

Ian had gone to the gym while I had lunch with Emily. His Jeep was in the lot, so I knew he was still inside, but I resisted slamming repeatedly into his bumper, because I didn't want to scratch my truck. Instead, I calmly parked and checked the lobby, the weight rooms, the aerobics and yoga rooms. I checked the pool and the basketball court. The snack and lounge area. The racquetball courts.

He was nowhere. I checked the courts again, and the weight rooms. Then I had a brainstorm. I shoved open the door to the men's locker room and a bearded guy with a gym bag said, "Um, this is the men's—"

"Fucking *men!*" I snarled, and stomped past him through a fog of rage and musky, chlorinated air. I looked in the showers and the steam room and finally found Ian sitting on a wooden bench in front of his locker, his hair wet and a towel wrapped around his waist.

He smiled when he saw me. "Annie, what are—" He saw my expression. "What's wrong?"

I slammed my hand against a locker. "You slept with Emily!"

"Anne, this isn't—"

"This isn't what? This isn't true? She just fucking told me. I can't believe you! You two-faced, two-timing, two—"

"It was a long time ago. It didn't mean—"

"How could you not tell me?"

His jaw clenched. "Because I knew how you'd react."

I slammed the locker. "Of course—" Bang! "This is how—" Bang! "I'd fucking react!" Bang-bang! "You slept with my sister. You slept with *both* my sisters."

A man's voice from the next row said, "Way to go, dude."

Bang! Bang! Bang-bang-bang! "You—!" I lobbed Ian's can of shaving cream over the lockers. "Shut up!"

"Anne," Ian said, "I was—"

I threw his shoe at him. "How am I suppose to respond? You run around behind my—"

A naked, chubby man appeared at the end of the row.

"What do *you* want?" I hissed.

"Well, um," he said, "my locker is—"

I shrieked and banged. The chubby man scurried away—and behind him, there was an exodus of half-dressed men. No right-thinking man wants to deal with a woman scorned, especially if he didn't have the fun of the scorning.

"It was eight years ago," Ian said, insufferably calm. "It doesn't mean anything."

"It means you lied to me."

"Because you're neurotic about your sisters. It's ancient hi—"

"I'm neurotic? You're the one who's sick—you needed a third helping of the Olsen sisters? You want to sleep with all of us at once? Maybe I should call them, see if they're busy tonight."

"Dude!" the voice from the next row said. "You rock."

Bang-bang-bang! "Go away!"

"This isn't about a lie," Ian said, pulling on his pants. "It's that you think I'm used goods and—"

"I don't believe you." My rage overflowed into tears. "I t-trusted you, Ian. I l-lo-lo—" I threw his other shoe at him and shoved blindly through the door. The wrong door. Instead of the lobby, I ended up in the pool. There was a water aerobics class in progress, but they stopped splashing as I stood in the open door and yelled back at Ian. "You slept with both of them! I hate you!"

Ian followed me into the pool area. "It's not about that," he said, his voice echoing off the tile. "You don't care who I slept with eight years ago. It's about your sisters. Everything's your sisters. You wore their old shirts for a couple years, and now you're fucking phobic about hand-me-downs. What are you afraid of, Anne? When are you gonna stop feeling inferior and—"

"Inferior? Why would I feel inferior? Because I'm not even your *second* choice? Because I'm the last in line? I'm sloppy thirds!"

"Anne," he said, stepping forward.

"Shut up!" I yelled, and shoved him as hard as I could.

"No horseplay," the lifeguard said, as we fell into the pool.

I drove directly to my father's house and collapsed soggily onto the twin bed in my childhood bedroom. I toyed with One-Armed Barbie, then ripped her remaining arm off, as I considered the situation:

Charlotte, beautiful and famous, had her burgeoning swimsuit business. She had her loving husband and her three adorable children. Oh, and she was rich. And beautiful. Have I mentioned that she's beautiful? Emily, brilliant and famous, had her burgeoning bestseller. She only had one adorable child to go with the loving husband, but had bounced back from her failed book with an inspiring story of personal triumph…over me. And I, the bankrupt nobody, didn't have The Deal. Didn't have a man. Didn't have a job. Didn't have a hope in hell.

When I was a kid, I'd been utterly sure my life would follow the Olsen Girl script. I'd explode onto the scene in a spectacular supernova of success. I hadn't known precisely which scene or which success, but that hadn't mattered. I'd watched, as first one sister and then the other had been wrapped in the glory of her girlhood dreams come true. We were three fairy-tale princesses, and we'd be showered in turn with all the gifts dreamt of by our fairy godmothers.

My turn would come, and my life would transform into a feel-good Hollywood film. Hell, I wasn't greedy—I'd be satisfied with an upbeat Movie of the Week. Sure, maybe I'd have to overcome a few obstacles, learn a couple lessons or whatever, but Act III was clear: happiness, love, and success. Why not? I'd watched this movie twice before. I knew how it ended. Charlotte, Emily, then Anne. I only had to wait.

So I waited. And waited. And…nothing.

Nothing tragic, nothing triumphant. Just plain old nothing.

Eventually, I understood. I wasn't playing the lead role. I was a bit part, a little local color. I wasn't Charlotte and I wasn't Emily. I was the nameless GIRL IN BAR, or SECRETARY #2. Actually, I was SISTER #3.

I guess that's called "growing up." My sisters had been touched by the gods, but not me. I was destined for mediocrity, for a life of quiet desperation. So I adjusted. I lowered my expectations. I wasn't gonna be a pop star or an actor or a famous artist. I was just gonna lead a boring little life, nothing special…and I was okay with that. I'd taken a slow, deep breath, and settled.

Then it turned out that Charlotte was unhappy, and Emily's second book was awful. And I thought, well, if they could fail, maybe I could succeed! I could grab my own handful of success. Nothing grandiose. Make a little money, preserve a little land. I hadn't asked for much. Just The Deal. Just Ian. Not fame, not fortune or talent.

Just happiness.

And what happened? Charlotte bounced back. Emily

bounced back. And I lost everything and was lying in dripping clothing on a narrow bed with Kirk Cameron posters looming over me.

I hid at Dad's house until I figured it was safe to return to the condo. Ian would've gone there, to explain or argue or persuade. But I was past arguments and explanations. This wasn't about him—it was about me. I'd hoped for too much. I'd tried to be someone else, someone better. Now I had to admit the truth. I had to lower my expectations. In my life. In my self. In my dreams.

Ian's Jeep wasn't parked outside the condos, so I pulled into my spot. Manager, ha. I couldn't manage my way through an open door. I locked the truck, and Wren stood from the next car, with a bottle of wine for me and Perrier for her, and double-chocolate cake for both of us. "Emily called me," she said.

"I hate her." I twitched nervously when a car turned into the drive.

"He's gone," Wren said.

"He came?"

"Dripping wet."

"He fell in the pool at the gym."

"He told me," she said, as I unlocked the front door. "Serves him right."

"Yeah!" I said, only it came out: "Yeah?"

We devoured the cake and I polished off the wine and became drunkenly belligerent. Fuck Ian, anyway. Who needed him, with his stupid old antiques and his sexy eyes? It was all his fault. If he hadn't given me a false sense of security, if I hadn't been living in a completely deluded bubble of happiness, I'd have known not to stick my neck out. Well, screw Ian. I didn't need him. I had Wren. I'd help raise the baby, and we'd be like asexual life partners, and I'd go to PTA and soccer practice and lead a full and fulfilling life.

Then Wren said, "Kevin called yesterday. He wants to talk."

"Oh, God, no!" I wailed. "He's going to forgive you. Then you'll be happy, too. I can't stand it."

She promised not to be happy.

"Never?" I slurred. "You have to promise never to be happy."

"I promise," she said.

"You better not. How can he forgive you for the spermjacking when I can't even forgive—when Ian can't forgive—" I couldn't remember who needed to forgive whom, or for what. "When my whole life is shit!?"

I slid onto the floor and curled next to Ny, who was sprawled on the Zeigler, and wiped my tears with the thirty-year-old fibers.

I woke at seven-thirty the next morning, still on the rug. My brain hurt and my mouth tasted like soggy peanut shells. I groaned and rolled over.

I woke again at twenty after eight. I heard Wren fussing in the kitchen, and moaned. She came into the living room with a cup of coffee and said she had to work. She kissed me on my carpet-imprinted cheek and left.

At noon, I showered and dressed and pulled myself together. I had to scale down my expectations. Get another secretarial job or two, and pay off my debts over the next few decades. My life's calling was now to provide an annuity to the deluded souls who'd believed in me. The idiots.

And Ian? I missed him already. Why hadn't he called? Because he hated me. He was probably on the phone with Helene already.

It didn't matter. I hated him. Evil Ian, who'd slept with Emily. Sure, it was eight years ago, but still—he should've told me.

He was probably moving to Chicago, to be with Helene. Good. Let him move.

God, I missed him.

I tried to drown my sorrows in busywork. I sent a resume to fifteen random employers. With a seven percent chance of success, I'd have a new job by next week. I sat down and thought about all the money I owed. I listened to my messages: The woman from the bank, the architect, and a credit card company. *Great.*

I cleaned the house. I mopped and scrubbed and bleached. I tidied. I collected all of Ian's stuff in a box, then redistributed it around the house again. I realized I was starving—and stone broke. I could try mooching dinner at Charlotte's, but was afraid David would be nice to me. I could try Emily's, but…yuck. Horrible mental images of her and Ian. So Dad's house.

He was watching golf on TV when Ny and I arrived. I rummaged in the pantry and found two bags of Ruffles, one new, one opened. I took the open bag into the other room.

Dad glanced at me. "There's a new bag."

"I saw."

"You don't want the new chips?" he asked.

"I don't deserve the new chips."

He clicked off the TV.

"My life is crap," I told him. "I've screwed up everything. The Deal's dead, everyone's money is gone, and my credit is ruined. I owe more money than I've made in my entire life. Wren's ecstatically pregnant, Emily fixed her book, and Charlotte is Charlotte. And to top it off, I had a hand-me-down boyfriend, and now even he's gone."

"Anything else?"

"Gimme a second, I'll think of something." I tilted the bag and tapped the crumbs into my mouth. "Oh yeah—I'm a totally mediocre human being. And I was fine with that, until I started getting my hopes up. Did you know about Ian and Emily?"

He sighed. "I suspected."

"You! Even you knew? Why didn't you say anything?"

"Seemed best to let them work it out themselves."

"Is that what you want me to do?" I asked. "Work this out myself?"

He picked up the clicker.

"I don't want to work it out myself," I said.

"For a totally mediocre human being," he said, shaking his head, "you demand a lot of attention."

I refused to smile, and we were quiet a moment. Then he said, "Times like these, I miss your mother."

"Me, too."

"She'd have been proud of you."

"Sure, look at all I've achieved. I cast poor Charlotte and Emily in the shade."

"They're jealous of you, you know."

I snorted.

"They both got very successful, very young," he said. "Too successful, too young. They worry that they're frauds. That they don't deserve this. They worry that they've peaked, that nobody sees beyond what they've done to who they are. Charlotte can't leave the house without an hour on her makeup and Emily spends half the day reading journals she hates, because she's afraid her ignorance will show. It's not so wonderful, being your sisters."

My eyes felt hot and full. "But what if I never achieve anything?"

"You already have, Anne."

"What? Name one thing."

"Achievement isn't only what you do—it's who you are."

"I am a living monument to my own failure."

He shook his head. "You know how important I think

history is—and how powerful. But history doesn't dictate the future, it informs the future. It's not a force reaching out from the dead past to keep you down—it's a force to lift you up. Not like a basement, Anne, but a springboard. Charlotte and Emily are taking their pasts and using them. You can do the same."

I stared at him for a long moment. "Do lectures like that actually work with your students?"

"Never."

"That's what I thought," I said, and got the new bag of Ruffles.

29

The next morning, I took Ny to the Cypress property to say goodbye to the land. I parked on the side of the road, stepped out of the truck, and felt my body unclench. The scent was aromatherapy to the soul, the Mexican sage and the little yellow blossoms on the low shrubs. The breeze was warm and golden light bathed the hillside chaparral. There were clouds in the sky, high and white with dark underbellies, cruising quickly past.

I faced the woods and said, "Sorry. I tried."

I'd tried. I'd risked everything. And I'd lost.

But this land had been worth fighting for. Worth losing for.

I blinked back tears, thinking of Dad saying that Mom would be proud of me. Thinking of Ian saying how proud *he* was. This is what he'd meant: I'd finally found something worth losing for.

It felt like years ago that I'd tracked down Monty and Little Lamb. I smiled tearily, thinking about Senna Leon and Herr Daunen. Hell, even Melissa Kent and Monty made me smile. And Rip. Wasn't his fault we hadn't been right for each other.

I uprooted the No Trespassing sign, tossed it in the back of my truck, and followed Ny up the trail.

The houses would've been brilliant. The drive would've curved around that stand of live oaks, the deck of the first house would've faced the ocean right over there. To my left, the picture windows and to my right, the rose gardens. But as I continued to walk, my images of the houses faded. The trail was just the trail, the trees were just the trees. The meadow was just breathtaking.

I sat on a big flat rock. The wind was stronger, and carried the tang of desert air. The long brown grass swayed and the clouds gathered. After a long silent time, I stood and said, "Goodbye."

But I couldn't bring myself to leave. There was nothing to return to. No job, no home. And the walks at the beach and the Bacara resort were only second-best. All I wanted was to pitch a tent and stay here forever.

The wind whipped over the meadow and a raindrop hit my cheek. A spray of drops splashed my face and the back of my neck. I spread my arms. I loved Santa Barbara in the rain. Everything became fresh and clean, shedding the dust and—

A tent? Pitch a tent?

A distant thought twitched and raised its sleepy head. A tent?

Yes! Yes, and maybe a cistern and solar energy, too. Green construction. And, and…the Bacara resort—only better, like Esalen. And something else, a faint echo: *Article III Zoned 5-E-2, pursuant to the guidelines…5-E-2 zoning.*

Rain poured over me. It should've been thunder and lightning. Because I finally knew what I had to do.

★ ★ ★

I worked all day and into the evening on my plan. I got into bed, thrilled and eager—and suddenly alone. There was nobody to share my excitement with. Nobody to plot with, to worry and plan and exult with.

Nobody? There was only one person I wanted.

I got out of bed and dressed, and was halfway downstairs when the doorbell rang. I opened the door and it was Ian.

There was nothing I'd rather see, when I opened a door, than him. He saw something in my expression, and he smiled. A slow, relieved smile that spread across his face until he was beaming. I guess I smiled back. It was like we'd never been apart. We fit. Maybe Dad's lecture about springboards and history had taken root. Our past together was what made us *us*. It wasn't just the story of what we did, it was the story of who we were. The reason we matched so perfectly.

"I'm sorry," he said.

"I love you," I said. And finally, I knew exactly what that meant.

It was a Saturday morning in midsummer when we met for the ceremony at the base of the Cypress property.

Ian and I set the tables with fruit, cheese, and wine as Ny snuffled in the underbrush. Dad arrived first, with a familiar-looking woman who turned out to be the freckled caterer from Charlotte's birthday. Then an oversized SUV disgorged Emily, Charlotte, their husbands and broods. Soon, the base of the trail was packed. Wren was hugely present, arm in arm with Naked Kevin, who was wearing an expression of bemused resignation, like a man who'd tried not to fall in love but failed. Shannon and Shayla forgave me for missing all their recent outings after I introduced them to Mike and my ex-boyfriend, Nick of the trust fund.

Mike took one look at Shannon and said, "Anne, I'm fucking in love."

Monty was there. Rip came, escorting the Keebler people and Her Stickitude, Melissa Kent. She wasn't as twiggy as I remembered. Maybe Rip was feeding her, in the hopes of turning his newest polliwog into a frog. The Keeblers weren't elfin, either. They were a middle-aged couple with impeccable taste, who'd immediately grasped the brilliance of my second prospectus.

It had been simple. Two weeks of frantic activity, doing research. Then a week of frantic activity, making the prospectus. Then, for a change, two weeks of frantic activity, dealing with the Planning Commission. Then a week of frantic salesmanship. Then a frantic couple months, keeping the deal together with desperate applications of blood and sweat. And love.

For my labors, I was rewarded with the most beautiful words in the English language:

A Conditional Use Permit to allow the establishment of a retreat center offering a broad range of artistic, educational, and psychological programs and single and multi-day events under provisions of Article III Zoned 5-E-2; and the approved Negative Declaration, pursuant to the State Guidelines for Implementation of the California Environmental Quality Act...

The bottom line was this: The Keebler people did low-impact green construction; my zoning had been restricted to two parcels, but broadened into limited commercial use; and I'd always known Montecito needed a little gem of a retreat center, a la Esalen.

Anyway, the elves loved the idea, and seeing as I'd cut my profit to zero they got the land for a steal. There was plenty of room for guest cottages, energetic healing seminars, and hollow tree bakeries. For them, at least, the deal was uncommonly good.

The investors did okay, too. I sold the second parcel—the hiking trail—to the county, which agreed to maintain it as public land. The sale paid my debts, plus a two percent profit. Not bad, for an investment of mere months.

As for me, I'd have made more money working as a temp. But it wasn't about the money. It was about the land. Well, that and the adoration of the cheering crowd.

"Thank you all," I said, after Monty called for attention. "Thank you for everything. I'd like to welcome you to the future home of the Cypress Center, open for classes, workshops and retreats—and, constructed with reclaimed lumber and salvaged material, thanks to the people at Keebler Construction." I politely indicated the elves. "Now for the real reason we're here. This is for all of you. This is for my family and my friends, and everyone who's both. I give you—" I took a breath, and gestured to the hiking trail. "The Amelia Olsen Hiking Trail."

Later, after most of the wine and cheese had vanished, I detached Emily from a conversation with the Sharones and liberated Charlotte from her children's tyrannical clutches.

"Strap on your hiking boots, girls," I told them. "We're going for a stroll."

"Now?" Emily asked.

"Now," I said.

"But, um," Charlotte said. "All the way to the top?"

"All the way to the top."

"I dunno, Anne...."

They didn't have the right shoes, they said. They had to watch the kids. They were feeling bloated. They had to get home to clean the tub.

But hell, I was the baby in this family. Charlotte called me Hannah, and Emily called me Hannibal, but I got my way in the end. They followed me up the trail, complaining for the first stretch, then growing quieter as we continued. By the time we reached the meadow, we'd been silent for five minutes. We walked together toward the rise, and looked over the foothills. I don't know how long we stood there, quiet, together. Sisters.

Charlotte finally broke the silence. "Mom would be proud of you, Anne."

"She'd be proud of *us,*" I said.

On the way back down, Emily said, "So what's next?"

"Cleanup," I said. "The kids threw cheese cubes everywhere."

"You're the Queen of Clean," Emily said. "You don't need us. But I meant, what's next with you? You're done with this property, right?"

"Except for walking Ny here."

"So what's next?"

"Well, Ian wants me to work in his shop. Which I would," I said, "except for one thing."

"Your antique-ophobia?" Charlotte asked.

"Toxic schlock syndrome?" Emily said.

"Actually," I said, ignoring their giggles, "there's this vineyard for sale in Santa Maria. They want to build a big box store there. I think it'd make a great art colony…."

By the time we emerged at the base of the trail, I'd fully explained this excellent investment opportunity. And now I'd proven I could make a profit—and had conquered the learning curve—they had absolutely no reason not to invest.

"There's one thing that worries me," Emily said, "about the Cypress Center here."

"What's that?" I asked.

"Reclaimed lumber? Salvaged material? You're gonna use old floorboards?"

"And used fixtures?" Charlotte said. "From old buildings?"

"You'll never come within a hundred miles of the place," Emily finished, shaking her head. "You hate hand-me-downs."

"That's true," I said, glancing toward Ian. "But I love heirlooms."

That night, Ian and I snuck into the reservoir. The air was cool, and we stripped by the light of the three-quarter moon.

"Bottoms up," I said.

"Top down for me."

"Mmm-mmm." I eyed him lecherously. "Boxer briefs."

"Panties," he said, relieving me of them.

We were quiet for a while, then I said, "Fukui-san!"

The water was freezing, but Ian kept me warm.

In her new novel, Jody Gehrman,
author of *Summer in the Land of Skin,*
explores what it means to live a *tart* life.

Claudia Bloom aims to lead a tart life. Meaning she wants
everything she does to have that sharpness, that edge of
almost-too-out-there to be tasty, but not quite.

After stealing her ex's VW bus, which promptly explodes
on the drive from Austin to Santa Cruz, Claudia meets and
falls hard for Clay, whose never-mentioned estranged
wife is her colleague and whose mother is her boss.
Looks like she is on her way....

**Available wherever
trade paperbacks
are sold.**

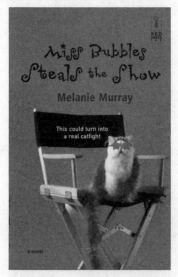

From Lauren Baratz-Logsted, author of
The Thin Pink Line and *Crossing the Line,*
comes the most unusual make-under story.

A Little Change of Face

Scarlett Jane Stein has it all—great body, pretty face
and incredible breasts. So when her best friend makes
a comment that Scarlett has gotten everything because
of her good looks Scarlett undergoes a make-under to
become the dowdier, schlumpier Lettie Shaw. But will she
find someone who loves her for who she is inside?
Or will it turn out to be one big mistake?